About the Author

Sandy Barker is an Australian writer, traveller and hopeful romantic with a lengthy bucket list and a cheeky sense of humour.

Many of Sandy's travel adventures have found homes in her writing, including her debut novel, a contemporary romance set in Greece, which was inspired by her true-life love story.

Follow her on Twitter @sandybarker

ONE SUMMER IN SANTORINI

Sandy Barker

avon.

A division of HarperCollins*Publishers*
www.harpercollins.co.uk

Published by AVON
A division of HarperCollins*Publishers* Ltd
1 London Bridge Street
London SE1 9GF

www.harpercollins.co.uk

A Paperback Original 2019

Copyright © Sandy Barker 2019

Sandy Barker asserts the moral right to be identified as the author of this work.

A catalogue copy of this book is available from the British Library.

ISBN: 978-0-00-835434-3

Typeset in Birka by Palimpsest Book Production Limited, Falkirk, Stirlingshire
Printed and bound in UK by CPI Group (UK) Ltd, Croydon CR0 4YY

MIX
Paper from
responsible sources
FSC
www.fsc.org
FSC™ C007454

Chapter One

I woke suddenly, and even though I was forty thousand feet in the air, I already felt jet-lagged. You know that unique mix of queasiness and exhaustion? That.

I hate long-haul flying. Wait, let me correct that, I hate long-haul flying in *economy*. Flying across the world when I've been upgraded to business class is awesome – I highly recommend it. But this wasn't one of those times.

I checked my watch. I had slept for five hours – if we're calling it 'sleeping' – more like 'dozing upright'. Either way, I felt achy and groggy. I yawned a big, ugly yawn, the kind I usually reserved for solitary moments – one of the few benefits of sitting in a cabin full of people I'd never see again.

I stretched my neck from side to side and pushed my palms into my eye sockets. My eyes wanted to be anywhere else, and I didn't blame them. I dug around in the seat pocket for my eye drops, tipped my head back, and irrigated my eyes with soothing coolness. Resting my head against the seat, I longed for a bed – *any* bed. I just wanted to lie flat so I could stretch out my stiff muscles. I certainly didn't want to be cooped up with all those strangers, sitting in a ridiculously uncomfortable seat, breathing that stale, nasty air.

Yup, I'd definitely woken up on the wrong side of the plane.

Still, irritable was better than anxious. For weeks, I'd been fighting mini panic attacks about the trip, and that wasn't like me. I'd travelled quite a lot and was more than capable of handling whatever catastrophe came my way. In fact, catastrophes had become such a regular part of my travels, I was starting to wonder what I'd done in a past life to piss off the travel gods.

One flight to Melbourne was cancelled outright. A flight out of Chile was delayed for so long I had to sleep on the airport floor. There was a hotel reservation in Florence that disappeared, and while I was arguing with the manager, my iPad was stolen from my bag. Not forgetting the time my whole suitcase somehow vanished between Sydney and Auckland. On the next trip, my new suitcase emerged a mangled mess on the baggage carousel – hello LA and, yes, fellow passengers, those are my knickers, thank you very much. And I *barely* recovered from a raging case of malaria in Peru. Okay, so it wasn't actually malaria. It was salmonella, but it still knocked me on my bum for five days when I was supposed to be hiking the Inca Trail.

I looked out the window at the passing clouds. Maybe all the panic was because I hadn't travelled in more than a year; I'd lost my mojo. Still, I should have been excited. After one night in London, I was flying to Santorini. Yes, *the* Santorini – of Greek Island fame.

Even though it was only for a night, I was really looking forward to London, as I was seeing my little sis and I'd missed her like crazy. Catherine – Cat – had moved to England years before. Actually, we'd moved there together, but she stayed and I moved back to Australia. We only saw each other in the flesh every couple of years when she came to Sydney or I went to

London. I knew she'd ease my worries – real or imagined – with a firm dose of tough love. It was one of the many, *many* reasons she was my best friend.

The rest of the flight was pretty uneventful. I had a breakfast of rubbery eggs and something that resembled a sausage, washed my face with a moist towelette, and watched three episodes of *FRIENDS* back to back. Finally back on *terra firma*, I disembarked and shuffled along the hallways of Heathrow, cleared immigration, and before long, I was waiting at baggage claim for my backpack. I was normally a suitcase kind of a girl, but the brochure had said to pack light. Apparently, there wasn't much space inside the yacht.

Oh, did I forget to mention that? My trip started in Santorini and then I'd be sailing around the Greek Islands for ten days. Not by myself – I don't know how to sail. The skipper would be doing the sailing, and there'd be some other people with us, but most importantly there would be *me* – on a *yacht*!

As I watched bag after bag pop out of the baggage chute and tumble down onto the carousel, I finally started to feel it, the excitement. *There you are, you elusive little minx!* It bubbled up inside me, and I had a sort of 'baggage claim epiphany'. I was going to Santorini! In Greece! And then to a bunch of other Greek Islands!

I could picture myself on the bow of the yacht wearing my new tangerine bikini and duty-free Prada sunglasses, which both looked fantastic on me by the way, the wind whipping through my hair like Kate Winslet in *Titanic*. Only before the iceberg. And about a hundred years later. Oh, and sans Leo.

Finally, after what felt like a millennium, my bag appeared. Good thing too, as my yacht fantasy was degenerating into an 80s music video. I grabbed for the handle, fumbled with it a bit, then lugged it off the carousel. It wasn't big, but it was filled to the brim with the perfect Greek Island trousseau: the obligatory summer dresses, bikinis, shorts, flowing skirts, cute tops, and a sunhat. I was a travelling cliché and I didn't care. Did I mention I was going to Greece?

I dragged the backpack over to one of the airport trolleys, swung it aboard, plopped my beautiful new leather handbag on top, and headed for the 'Nothing to Declare' exit. The only thing I had to declare was that I was going sailing on the Aegean, and I didn't think the Customs agents gave a crap about that.

Cat was waiting behind the silver railing on the other side of the security door. We look almost identical, except I am five-foot-six and she's five-foot-nothing. She says she's five-foot-one-and-three-quarters, but she's not. She did get the good hair, though – cow. It's the only thing I hate about her. While I'm stuck with masses of curls – the really curly ones that do whatever the hell they like – she has thick cascading, chestnut waves. Like I said, cow.

'You're here!' she declared, ducking under the railing and throwing her little arms around my neck. I stopped pushing the trolley and returned the hug. We stepped back and regarded each other.

'You look fab!' I squeaked, tears in my eyes.

'You too!' she lied.

'I just got off a twenty-eight-hour flight. I look like crap.'

'You're right, but it's nothing a shower and a good night's sleep won't cure. Come on.' She took over pushing my trolley, and I followed obediently as she parted the crowd with a series of slightly rude 'excuse mes'.

Back in her Docklands flat, my hair wet from the best shower I'd ever had, I sat on her couch, a cup of tea in one hand and a chocolate biscuit in the other. We emailed and FaceTimed regularly – we weren't estranged or anything – but nothing was the same as actually being together, and we chatted non-stop, catching up on all the things that sisters chat about.

'So, tomorrow you fly to Athens and then what?'

'I pretty much fly straight to Santorini. The stopover in Athens is only four hours. I thought about sightseeing but knowing me, I'd get caught in a traffic jam on the way back to the airport and miss my island-hopper.'

'You probably would.'

'Thank you. No *really*, I mean it,' I replied, my voice thick with sisterly sarcasm.

'What? You *do* tend to have shitty luck when you travel.' See? But impending bad luck aside, I happily realised that excitement was thrashing anxiety's ass.

'Cat, I'm going to Santorini tomorrow!'

'So, *that's* where you're going,' she said, giving me crap. Jealous. I ignored her.

'It's just … It feels like I booked this trip *ages* ago. And, yeah, I was excited at the time, but it's been *months*. After a while it stopped feeling real.' I grinned at her. 'Until now. I can't believe I'm really going!' Then I stopped grinning. 'I'm not being too obnoxious, am I?'

She smiled. 'No, I'm happy for you. *Really*, I am.' So not jealous, then.

'I wish you could come.'

'So do I, but there's no way I could.' Cat was a teacher like me, but while I was on holidays, her school year had just started.

'Probably for the best. It could be a huge disaster of a trip.' My inner pessimist was back, the lurker.

'Don't say that. It won't be a disaster.'

'You don't know that. You *just* said I have shitty luck. And I do! Every time I travel somewhere, things go wrong. Look at last time in Peru! Plus, I won't know anyone, and ...'

'Sarah, it's not *every* time. I was only teasing. And Peru was ages ago. It's a little bad luck now and then ...' She trailed off, shrugging. 'Besides, you used to run tours for weeks at a time – for fifty people! You're an *experienced traveller*.'

'I know, but ...'

'But nothing. Random bad luck aside, you're *you*. You know how to make friends with strangers. *And* you've been around.' I threw her a stern look. 'You know what I mean. I mean you've *literally been around*. You'll be fine.'

See? Tough love. Everything she said made sense, but ...

'But what if it's completely horrible?' She laughed at me. I probably deserved it. No, I definitely did.

'It's not going to be horrible. It's going to be amazing, and you'll probably meet some really cool people.' Then she hit me with the one thing I didn't want to hear. 'You know, you might meet someone.' And then she gave me that look – you know the one.

And in an instant, my sister, my best friend in the entire world, joined the 'poor Sarah' pity party.

'Did you *really* say that?' I asked, shooting fiery daggers from my eyes.

'What?' She feigned innocence, her eyes widening.

'You know exactly *what*!' I didn't think it was possible, but her eyes got even bigger. 'Do you know how many people have said that to me since I booked this bloody trip?'

She shook her head, giant eyes fixed to mine.

'A bazillion!' Okay, so sometimes I tend towards the hyperbole. It was probably more like twelve, but in my world, that's a lot of people.

'Fine!' she retaliated. 'I'm sorry. I didn't realise it was such a sore point.'

'Well, it is. I've been single for, what, a few months? Right now, I just want to be on my own.'

'Great!'

'I mean, can't I go on this trip, and have it be about me? Seeing somewhere new and hanging out and sailing and shit?' I was whipping myself into quite the little frenzy.

'All right. *Yes.* I'm sorry. I hope you *don't* meet anyone.'

'Thank you.' It came out angry.

'And, especially *not* someone cute, who makes you laugh, and is an all-round great guy. Actually, I hope all the men you meet are old and mean and ugly. No! Better yet, I hope there are no men. I hope you sail around the Greek Islands with a bunch of lesbians! I hope you go to Lesbos and are surrounded by lesbians!' She pinned me down with a 'so there' stare, and after a beat, we both fell about laughing. My laughter quickly turned into a yawn. 'How are you doing over there?' she asked.

'Good!' I replied with more enthusiasm than I felt. She looked dubious. 'Okay, I'm shattered, but I need to stay up and get on European time. I'll be fine. The tea's kicking in.'

'How about a top-up then?'

'Yes! Definitely more tea.' I drained the last of my mug and handed it to her. She took it into the kitchen and put the kettle on.

With her back to me, she asked, 'So, as long as you're staying up for a while, do you want to talk about it?'

'It?' She turned to face me, looking mildly uncomfortable, like she was holding in a fart or something. 'What?' I asked, knowing exactly what she meant.

'*Neil.*' My break-up with Neil was literally the last thing I wanted to talk about. I would have put a lively conversation about Trump's presidency, or the Syrian crisis, or even Brexit ahead of talking about the pile of shit I'd called my boyfriend for almost a year.

'Not really.' I feigned what I hoped looked like indifference.

'Oh. All right.' I could see the disappointment on her face. I could also see her mind working. 'It's just ... well, we never really talked about it. Properly, I mean.'

She was right. I hadn't wanted to talk to anybody about what happened with Neil – not my girlfriends, not my Sydney bestie, Lindsey – not even Cat. It was too humiliating.

'True, but ...' I hesitated. *Please don't make me relive it all now when I am so exhausted. I'd rather stick a fork in my eye.* I thought that, but what I said was: 'Okay, you're right.'

She brought fresh cups of tea back to the couch and pushed the chocolate biscuits towards me. She knew me so well. 'So, what happened?' She folded her legs under her and looked at me expectantly.

'Well, Neil was a dickhead, and it took me far too long to get rid of him.' I took a bite of a chocolate biscuit.

'But I don't get it. If he was so bad, why did you stay with him for so long?' It was a question I'd asked myself a thousand times. I swallowed the hard lump of biscuit.

'I really don't know. I mean, almost immediately there were all these alarm bells going off. And I kept dismissing them –

time and again. I told myself it wasn't weird that he wouldn't meet my friends, or that he never wanted to go anywhere or do anything. You know, I realised after we broke up that I stopped travelling when I met him. He wouldn't even go away for the weekend with me. That's why this trip ... well, it's not just the chance to return to Greece. It's more. I knew as soon as we broke up, I had to go *somewhere* – anywhere.'

I looked over at my sister, and she was nodding sympathetically like she got it. It felt great to be 'got'.

'Oh, and he hated it when something good happened to me.' Cat's brow furrowed, questioning me. 'You know when I got promoted to head of department?' She nodded. 'Well, I told him, and he said – and I quote – "Well, thanks for rubbing it in. Right after I got passed over for that promotion. Now I feel like shit. Nice one, Sarah."'

'He did not!'

'He bloody did. And even *then*, I didn't end it.'

'Jesus. So, who was this slapper he cheated with?'

'A friend.'

'Hardly,' she scoffed. 'Do I know her?'

'No, she was a new friend – from yoga – or at least, I thought she was my friend.'

'But, how did they meet?'

'At my place, would you believe it? I'd invited her over for a barbecue and I didn't think anything of them talking for most of the night. I was just happy he was finally meeting my friends. Apparently, it started right after that.'

'How did you find out?'

'Well, he started acting way weirder than usual, so I figured something was up. Then I did something I never thought I would do – something truly awful.'

'What?' I could see the suspense was killing her, but I had never revealed this detail to anyone before. I sucked in my breath through my teeth.

'I still can't believe I did this. I hacked into his email account.'

'Oh my god! That's brilliant. *How?*' I laughed with relief, loving her for saying it was 'brilliant', rather than 'stupid and illegal'.

'Well, it wasn't exactly hacking. I guessed his password, and I got in.'

'Seriously?'

'Yep. Second try. It was his footy team.'

'What an idiot.'

'Yep. And there was an email trail of the whole thing. *Months* it had been going on – and get this, the whole time she was telling me *to my face* about this great new guy she was seeing.'

'Utter bitch!'

'I know!' I bit into the biscuit and chewed furiously. Cat was perched on the edge of her seat. 'So, I confronted him about it, and he lied *to my face* and told me not to be ridiculous. I looked at him – straight in the eye – and said, "I know for a *fact* you've been fucking her, you lying cheat. That cow can't keep her legs *or* her mouth shut. So, we're *done*. Never contact me again. Oh, and I hope you catch her chlamydia." Then I left his place, and that was it.' I shoved the rest of the biscuit in my mouth.

'That's like a scene from a movie.'

I nodded and swallowed. 'Well, I did practise it a few times before I went over there. I knew he would deny it. In the emails, they were always saying how dumb I was for not knowing what was going on.'

'Oh, Sez.'

I started to tear up. When I glanced up at Cat, she was looking at me as though I was a wounded puppy. I looked away and blinked the tears from my eyes. I wasn't shedding any more tears for fucking Neil.

'He's a stupid bastard!' she declared.

'Yes, he is. But I haven't told you the best part. After I broke up with him, I kept logging into his email so I could watch the aftermath.' Cat peeped with glee. '*Boy* did it get ugly. He accused her of telling me, and she denied it. He asked if she had chlamydia, and she was outraged. He called her names, she called him names back, and eventually, she told him to fuck right off. So, in the end, he lost both of us.'

'And you were with him for what, a year?'

'Nearly – a few weeks shy. God, a *year* of my life, Cat. At least I didn't have to buy him an anniversary present.' I spat out a bitter laugh. Cat was quiet, and sadness took over. 'I can't believe I stayed as long as I did.' The words came out as a whisper, and the tears threatened to return.

'You thought he loved you.' I nodded. 'But, fuck him. His loss!'

I love my sister. She doesn't mince her words. 'You know, I booked this trip the day after I broke up with him. It was my 'escape real life' plan.'

'Well, I'm glad you booked this trip – no matter why you did it. It's going to be amazing.' She paused. 'And, Sez, you deserve *way* better than that fuckhead. You know that, right?'

I did know that, yes. I knew I deserved more than to be cheated on by every man I'd ever called my boyfriend, starting with my high school sweetheart and ending with Neil the fuckhead.

'Anyway, I just want to be on my own for a while. I'm not sure how long 'a while' is, but for right now, I think it's best.'

'Oh.' She looked surprised, which after everything I'd told her, surprised *me*.

'I'm happily single.' I wasn't sure if I was trying to convince her or me.

'In that case, I'm sorry about what I said before – about you meeting someone on the trip.'

'It's cool. I know you're just looking out for me.'

'And your lady parts.'

'Well, that's disturbing.'

'Why?'

'I don't need my sister worrying about my 'lady parts'. I may have sworn off men, but they're just fine – thank you very much.'

'So, you've totally sworn off men?'

'Well, not forever, but until ...' *Until what, Sarah?*

'Until what?' Even Cat wanted to know.

The thing was, I didn't know myself what I was waiting for. I only knew I wasn't interested in meeting anyone. Actually, the thought of meeting someone new was utterly unappealing – exhausting even. I couldn't imagine throwing all my energy into getting to know someone new. I had no idea when I'd be ready for that – or if I ever would.

A wave of fatigue hit me, sucking up my last ounce of energy. 'Hey, would you hate me if I went and lay down for a bit? I can barely keep my eyes open.' I could see Cat mentally noting that I'd dodged her question.

'Of course not,' she said, letting me off the hook for the second time in as many minutes. 'I changed the sheets in

Alex's room, so you're all set. What time's your flight in the morning?'

'Pft. Stupid o'clock. Six, I think.'

'Well, I'm a *hundred* per cent sure I'll still be asleep when you take off, so it's highly unlikely I'll be up when you have to leave for the airport. Want me to book you a taxi to Heathrow?'

'Sure. If I leave here at four, will that give me enough time?'

'Should do. I'll book it. Fuck, I'm so glad it's not me.'

'You know, I'm only going to lie down for an hour or so. I still want to meet Jane and have dinner with you guys.'

She looked at me with a knowing smile. 'Sure, Sez.'

The next thing I remembered was the hideous bleat of my travel alarm intruding on my coma-like sleep at 3:30am. I'd set it – just in case – when I went for my nap the evening before. I lay there for a moment and tried to figure out how long I had slept, but it didn't matter. I felt even worse than when I'd woken up on the plane the morning before. I needed a hot shower and a bucket of tea, and I only had thirty – make that twenty-nine – minutes until my taxi arrived. *Crap.*

The minutes flew by, but I only made the taxi driver wait for five minutes, which I thought was pretty good considering how disoriented and horrendous I felt. We made it to Heathrow in record time – sometimes London *does* sleep and it's at 4:15am.

The sun was lightening the sky as I handed over a small fortune to the driver. Then it was just me and my backpack and the behemoth of Heathrow's Terminal Five. The nerves were back. I don't know why on earth people refer to them as butterflies. They felt more like baby elephants to me.

Chapter Two

On the flight to Athens, I was stuck in the middle seat between a husband and wife, one who wanted to sit by the window, the other by the aisle. They spent the entire flight talking across me in their thick Birmingham accents, as though I was some sort of aeronautical soft furnishing. When I politely asked if they wanted to sit together, they scoffed. 'Oh no, love, we're perfectly fine sitting apart.' *I* wasn't perfectly fine. I was developing a tension headache, but they didn't seem to care about that.

I figured if I was going to survive the flight without having some sort of mid-air meltdown, I was going to need more tea. Tea calms me, tea revitalises me, tea is a miracle drink – tea drinkers will understand what I mean. Thank goodness it was a British Airways flight, because I knew they'd have the good stuff – *proper English tea*. I rang my call button three times during a four-hour flight and every time was to ask for more tea. This, of course, meant I had to pee twice, but I considered those few moments of silence a reprieve from Douglas and Sharon's non-stop and not-so-sparkling repartee.

I made a point of losing them as soon as we were inside the terminal. I leapfrogged around other English tourists, striding purposefully towards immigration where I discovered two things: a massive queue and a slew of ridiculously handsome Greek men in uniforms. Apparently, the Greek government had hired a flock of Adonises – or is it Adoni? – to staff the immigration booths. This discovery made the first one much less annoying, and I waited patiently in line while appreciating some of Greece's natural wonders. When it was my turn, I handed over my passport and endured the handsome man's scrutiny as he weighed up the Sarah in my photograph – slicked-back hair, no makeup and glasses – with the Sarah in front of him.

As I met his gaze, I was glad I'd kept the London taxi driver waiting a few minutes so I could tame my wayward curls into some semblance of a style and put on some blush and mascara. It's not like I thought the immigration guy and I were going to run away together, but at least I didn't look like a complete hag. My heart jumped a little at the sound of the Greek entry stamp being added to my passport. Then it jumped again when the Adonis smiled and welcomed me to his country. Moments in and I was back in love with Greece.

After being so warmly welcomed, I headed off to find the gate for my next flight. Right as I started wondering if it would be quicker to swim to Santorini, I finally found it at the far end of the airport and on the other side of a security check. As I was collecting my things from the tray on the conveyor belt, a giant man who smelled like he'd been steeped in nicotine hacked a wet cough down the back of my neck. *Really?* I turned and gave him a hard stare, but he was oblivious.

My stuff gathered, I looked around for somewhere in the small transit lounge to wait for the connecting flight. Spying an empty seat in a far corner, I made a beeline to stake my claim, but I was too late. A different middle-aged British couple sat their duty-free bags down on what should have been my seat, then stood next to it complaining about the long walk to the gate.

Clearly, this couple was as clueless as Douglas and Sharon, so I found the nearest empty patch of floor and plonked myself down. I was beyond exhausted, and I still had a couple of hours to kill. I spent the first eight minutes calculating what time it was in Sydney, how many hours it was since I'd left there, and how much sleep I'd had. I came up with such a depressingly low number, I promised myself never to think of it again. I could sleep as soon as I got to my hotel in Santorini.

Instead, I opted to read. I'd preloaded my Kindle with such a broad variety of reading materials, I could match any reading mood I found myself in. And right then, my mood dictated a gloomy crime drama where lots of people got stabbed. I reached inside my handbag to retrieve the Kindle. Unlike the borrowed monstrosity that held all my clothes – and was hopefully being moved from plane to plane at that very moment – the handbag had been a splurge right before I left for my trip, along with my Prada sunglasses.

It was a compact leather backpack – stylish enough to be my handbag, and practical enough to be my daypack. It really was a thing of beauty. And, importantly, a handbag wouldn't cheat on me with a slut from yoga class.

Three and a half hours later – why did I think a Greek island-hopper would depart on time? – I was seated in a very small plane next to a very large man who was turning greener than Kermit the Frog before my eyes.

'Sorry, ma'am,' he said. *Texan*, I thought, identifying his origin right away – I'm talented like that. 'I don't usually fly on such small planes. I'm afraid I may need to get up to use the restroom.' Even in the throes of air sickness, he was using his manners. Texans are so polite.

'Of course!' I unbuckled my seatbelt and stood up in the tiny aisle. 'How about I sit near the window – in case you need to get up again?'

He nodded and rushed up the aisle to the only bathroom on board. Poor man – at least it was a short flight. As I strapped myself into the window seat, I heard a chorus of 'Ooohs' from the other passengers. I looked out my window as the plane banked and there it was, Santorini, a crescent of rusty land in a sea of deep blue. It was stunning.

'Sorry 'bout that, ma'am,' I heard over my shoulder as the Texan sat down.

'Look,' I said, leaning back so he could see past me.

'That's mighty pretty.'

I nodded in reply.

As we approached the tiny airport, I could barely wrap my mind around how beautiful the island was. The rugged red land contrasted with the brilliant blue of the sky and the stark white and creamy pastels of the buildings. It was so striking, it took my breath away. By the time we landed, I was practically hyperventilating.

Santorini's airport terminal was kind of kitschy, looking more like a Las Vegas hotel from the 70s than an airport. We disembarked via a rickety metal staircase and as we walked across the tarmac, a warm breeze tickled my face. Divine.

Inside the terminal, I noticed that everyone moved at a more leisurely pace than they did in the constant chaos of

Sydney, as though someone had slowed a video playback ever so slightly. I liked it.

My bag arrived on the baggage carousel after only a short wait, but it seemed to have gained weight in transit. I hefted it from the carousel and said goodbye to the nice Texan. Stepping back into the sunshine, I crossed the road, almost dragging my backpack, and stood in line for a taxi. And I didn't mind – the waiting, that is. The island was already having a calming effect on me. While I waited, I breathed in deep breaths of Santorini's clean, briny air. It was the exact opposite of Athens' air – or London's, for that matter.

Before I knew it, the taxi pulled up, the taxi driver got out and took my bag, stashing it in the boot, and I gave him the name of my hotel as I climbed into the back seat – all very normal. But *then*, two strangers climbed into the taxi, one in the front seat and one next to me.

'What's happening?' I asked as several bags were shoved towards me. I soon found myself squashed against my door, while two voices apologised.

'Apparently we have to share. I'm so sorry,' said a young woman from the front seat. *What?* I've been in taxis in so many places in the world I've lost count; I've never had to *share* one. The driver got in.

'Excuse me. I would rather not share my taxi – no offence,' I added to the young couple. They didn't seem offended. They probably didn't want to share either.

'If you want a private taxi you need to arrange it,' said the taxi driver. What the fuck was he talking about?

'Where in the world is a taxi *not* private?' I asked incredulously. 'What are you even talking about?'

'Look this is Santorini. We have thirty-six taxis on the

whole island.' He seemed undaunted by the rising tension in the car. Then we took off.

I fumed from the back seat and mumbled under my breath, 'Welcome to fucking Santorini.' Really, it wasn't that bad. The young couple were nice enough – she was English, and he was a Kiwi – and we chatted through the awkward tension. We also seemed to be collectively trying to ignore that the drive itself was a harrowing exploration of Santorini's narrow, winding roads, which our driver tackled by driving very fast with one hand riding the horn.

We pulled up at my hotel, and I offered thanks to Zeus that I'd arrived in one piece. I begrudgingly paid the driver what was obviously the same fare I would have paid if I was travelling by myself in a *private* taxi, and climbed out of the car. He retrieved my bag from the boot, dropped it on the ground, and before I knew it, he was speeding off to the couple's hotel, likely to gouge them for another thirty euros. A cloud of dust followed in his wake. I stood for a moment, taking in my surroundings and catching my breath.

I was standing in the heart of Fira, Santorini's main town. With the amount of whitewash and brilliant blue I could see, there was no mistaking I was in Greece. Despite the shared taxi and the fact that my backpack was sitting in the dirt, joy bubbled up inside me. Around me people ambled along the road, stopping to have leisurely and lively conversations with their neighbours. Scooters, trucks and cars whizzed past, stirring up dust. The air was hot and dry and smelled of petrol fumes mixed with something herbaceous.

Across the road from my hotel were congregations of people – mostly locals – at a handful of tavernas, each indistinguishable from the next to my uneducated eye. They sat at tables playing chess or cards – many of them smoking. Some drank coffee, some sipped clear liquid from tiny glasses. Ouzo, most likely. Laughter and chatter filled the air around me.

It occurred to me that it was a Thursday afternoon, which took some realising given my jet lag. Didn't these people have jobs? Maybe the whole town was on holiday. Like I was. I was on holiday! The realisation hit me again in a wave of wonderfulness. Greece!

I picked up my backpack from the dusty kerb and walked up the path of my hotel. Inside, the small lobby was cool, and the scent of bougainvillaea wafted in from an open window. A lovely woman, who spoke little English and had a warm smile, greeted me at the front desk. After a simple check-in – I showed her my passport, and she gave me a room key – she led me to my small, neat room. It was basic, but I didn't need anything more. I was only staying for one night.

It did smell slightly, but I'd travelled to Greece enough times to expect it. The Greeks don't flush toilet paper; it goes into the little bin next to the toilet. I know what you're thinking – I'm thinking it too – the Greeks invented civilisation, but they haven't worked out how to make a sewerage system that can handle toilet paper. It meant that many hotel rooms smelled just like mine did. It was a minor blip. I'd survive.

I wouldn't, however, survive much longer if I didn't eat; two packets of airline biscuits, a muesli bar I'd discovered at the bottom of my handbag, and a gallon of tea did not a balanced diet make. And especially not when there was Greek food all around me waiting to be eaten. I decided that sleep could wait.

I stashed some valuables in my room safe and packed my handbag for an early dinner followed by an evening of exploring. Leaving the hotel, I eyed the tavernas I'd seen across the road on arrival. The crowds in two of them were thinning out, as though the jobless folks suddenly had somewhere to be. At the third one, chess sets and ashtrays were being replaced with platters of food, and it looked like it was filling up with local diners. I consider this a good sign whenever I travel, because locals tend not to go out for crappy food.

I crossed the road and took a seat in the taverna at a table for two near the kitchen, where the aromas were unbelievable. My stomach grumbled with appreciation. A waiter appeared and stood patiently while I tortured him with my terrible Greek. I started with, 'Kalimera' – good morning – before correcting myself. 'No, sorry, kalispera.' He smiled and spoke to me in English.

'Good evening. I am Demetri.'

'Hello, Demetri. I need horiatiki,' I said, not even looking at the menu. I knew it would be on there, because it's what we non-Greeks call a Greek salad. 'And lamb, do you have lamb?' He gave me a funny look. Of course they had lamb. 'And giant beans.' I love giant beans. It's a dish, by the way. I mean, the beans are big, but it's essentially a stew made with beans. It's the second-best thing in the world after horiatiki.

Demetri gave me a smile and a nod, and then he offered me some retsina to go with my dinner. It's Greek wine, of sorts. I declined. I am what you might call a wine lover and as a wine lover, I can't really abide retsina. 'I'll have a Mythos, parakalo.' Greek beer – much more drinkable.

The salad came to the table within minutes and it was a thing of beauty. It looked like it belonged on the cover of a foodie magazine and it smelled incredible. I piled up my fork with the optimal first bite. As soon as it hit my mouth I groaned with pleasure, half-expecting to hear, 'I'll have what she's having,' from the next table.

I need to explain something important.

The Greeks grow the best tomatoes in the world. And I know I exaggerate sometimes, but I mean IN THE WORLD. Add to the best tomatoes in the world some freshly made feta, Greek-grown and pressed extra virgin olive oil, fresh fragrant oregano, Kalamata olives grown in luscious Greek sunshine, and all the other bits of goodness that go into a *horiatiki*, and you have the one thing I could eat every day for the rest of eternity.

The lamb and beans arrived next, and the lamb was so tender I could have cut it just by staring at it. The giant beans were particularly huge and the sauce was rich and tangy. I glanced around me as I finished off all three plates. The taverna was now full – I spotted a few travellers like me, but it was mostly locals who obviously knew where the good stuff was.

When the bill arrived, I thought it was wrong, but Demetri assured me that eighteen euros was correct – for three plates of food and a beer. I wished I was staying on Santorini longer; I'd have happily eaten at that taverna every night for weeks.

When I'd planned the trip, everything I read about Santorini mentioned the sunset to end all sunsets at Oia, which is a tiny town perched on the northern point of Santorini's crescent. With only twenty-four hours on the island, I'd added the Oia sunset to my list, and when I mentioned it to Demetri, he kindly wrote down directions – in Greek *and* English. Smart.

Armed with my mud map and a full belly, I set off from the taverna to find the local bus station and the bus to Oia. It wasn't difficult – Demetri's instructions were spot-on – but to call it a bus station would have been generous. It was basically a square filled with dusty buses.

I bought a ticket – by holding up one finger and saying 'Oia' – from a man who sat inside a grubby booth. He had a cigarette dangling precariously from his mouth, which he managed to inhale from without using his hands. Talented. I picked my bus out of the line-up – using Demetri's directions again – and climbed aboard.

As I waited for the bus to leave, I watched the stream of people passing through the square. I noticed a tall guy in a baseball cap hefting a large duffel bag and trying to get directions from the passing locals. American. I could pick an American out at a hundred paces. He was a pretty cute American too.

He was tall – over six foot, I guessed – and dressed in long shorts and a T-shirt. The T-shirt was fitted just enough that I could see he had a lean, muscular body. Dark brown curls peeked out from the cap, and although he was wearing sunglasses and I couldn't see his eyes, he had a general 'good-looking' thing going on. I would have stepped off the bus to help him, but I'd already bought a bus ticket to take in the sunset to end all sunsets. Not that I knew my way around any better than he seemed to, but he looked like he could use a friendly face. No one was stopping, and he seemed to be getting increasingly frustrated.

As I was contemplating my next move, the bus lurched forward – I hadn't even noticed the driver get on – and my last glimpse of the tall, cute American was him throwing his duffel on the ground and sitting on it dejectedly. Poor guy. I promised myself that if he was still there when I got back, I'd go talk to him.

The bus stopped in the centre of Oia, where the smooth, curved walls of whitewashed houses contrasted with the rugged stone walls of others. Walkways and steps separated the homes, and the yards were marked with either rock walls or white picket fences. In the warm milky light, whitewash took on the colour of cream. It was a quaint and quintessentially Greek town.

I found a little spot to sit on one of the steps and gazed westward, taking it all in. The cooling evening air was deliciously fragrant, floral notes mixed with the sea. I took a slow, deep breath. Around me were hundreds of people, and the atmosphere was abuzz with chatter while we waited for the sun to set. Then in a single unspoken moment, the crowd quietened – it was time. The spectacle changed second by second, gold slipping into amber, then crimson, then inky purples and blues.

I could almost feel my heartbeat slowing down.

When the sun disappeared completely, and the last rays of light retreated, the crowd applauded as though we were at the symphony and the concerto had just ended. I clapped along with those around me. When in Santorini ...

I wonder if Neil would have liked that, I thought.

Where the hell did that come from? All of the serenity I had felt as I watched the sun seep below the horizon vanished instantly. Bloody Neil. I got up, dusted myself off and followed the others up the steps and onto the road back to Santorini.

Thankfully, a bus was waiting at the same place we'd been dropped off, and I climbed aboard along with about eighty other people. No seat for me this time – it was standing room only – but the tightly packed group was in good spirits. As we jostled along the bumpy road back into Fira, I held on tightly to a handrail and tried to shake residual thoughts of Neil from my mind. To distract myself, I trained my ears to the conversations around me, listening to the various languages and accents.

I was glad when the bus depot appeared in the glow from the headlights. Exhaustion had set in – both physical and emotional – and I desperately wanted sleep. I stepped off the bus, oriented myself and set off for my hotel. And yes, I forgot all about the cute American.

Back in my room, I locked the door behind me, slipped off my already travel-worn clothes and put on my pyjamas. To shake off the lingering thoughts of Neil, I focused instead on the next day, the day I'd start the sailing trip, and damn it if those wretched nerves didn't come flooding back.

What if I don't like anyone on the trip? What if they don't like me? What if this whole thing is a complete disaster?

'Shut up, Sarah,' I said aloud. I was annoyed with myself. I'd had a good dinner, seen a nice sunset, and suddenly random thoughts of doom and gloom were sending me into a spiral. I had to change tack.

'You need to get organised,' I told myself. I knew if I put things in order, I'd exorcise the demon nerves. It was my tried and tested method of crisis management, particularly if the crisis was all in my head.

Except that when I emptied my handbag out onto my bed, I made a sickening discovery. My wallet was gone. I frantically ran my hand around the inside of the bag, but it was definitely empty. I sifted through all the things on the bed – hat, note-book, pen, camera, lip balm. No wallet. It was gone.

I took myself back through the previous couple of hours. I had it at the taverna, because I paid for dinner. Maybe I left it there? No, because I also paid for the bus ticket and that was *after* dinner. Did I remember putting my wallet back in my bag? Yes. Did I have it when I took my camera out of my bag in Oia? I *think* I remember seeing it then.

That meant I'd lost it on the bus ride back. But I hadn't taken it out of my bag. I hadn't even opened my bag. Oh my god! Someone stole my wallet from my handbag. While it was on my back! The panic kicked in, and I burst into tears. 'Fuck!'

Realising I was wringing my hands, I stopped and shook them out. 'Okay, think, Sarah. What was in the wallet? What do you need to do?' I willed myself to breathe, slowly, consciously, in and out. I stood in the middle of my room and closed my eyes. The safe! Of course, I had put valuables in the safe before I went out. I rushed to open it.

I took out a credit card, a wad of cash and – thank god – my passport. So, I'd lost my other credit card, about twenty euros and my driver's licence. 'Shit.' I was going to need my driver's licence to rent scooters on the islands. Well, maybe they would let me rent one with my passport. It was Greece after all, and they weren't exactly sticklers for that sort of thing. At least the thief hadn't got my passport.

I tried to remember who was around me on the bus, but I hadn't registered any faces. We'd been packed in there so tightly, and I'd watched out the front window most of the trip. I sighed and sat on the bed. I needed to call my bank in Australia and cancel the credit card. Even though my room smelled like a toilet, at least it had a phone.

After two aborted attempts to get the international operator to put through a collect call to my bank, I finally spoke to a person who could cancel the card and send me a replacement – to London, where I wouldn't be until most of my travelling was over. At least that was something, I supposed. I did have my back-up credit card, the one with the ridiculously exorbitant fees for taking out cash and spending in foreign currencies, but at least I wasn't completely stranded.

I hung up the phone and stretched out on my bed. Exhaustion had devolved into full-blown fatigue. I flicked off the lamp, but my mind was on high alert. I wanted to sleep, but instead I lay there for a long time wondering what else could go wrong. The travel curse had struck again.

*

I woke with a start, not knowing where I was, and smacked the crap out of my travel alarm to shut it up. I looked around the room and recognition seeped into my fuzzy mind – I was in Santorini. I smiled. Then I remembered I had been robbed the night before. The smile vanished.

It had been a restless night. Falling asleep had taken forever. And then there was the nightmare. I was lying in my bed in Sydney in the middle of the night and backpackers were robbing my flat while I pretended to be asleep. No prizes for guessing why I dreamed that.

Dread washed over me as I recalled the moment I'd emptied my bag onto my bed the night before. 'Oh, Sarah!' I admonished myself, again out loud. 'Put your big-girl knickers on and get over it. Everything is going to be fine!'

Surprisingly, giving myself a good talking-to was actually effective. Ignoring the fact that I was now talking to myself on a regular basis, I threw back the covers, showered in my smelly bathroom, and got dressed in a flowery blue and white skirt and a white cotton top with spaghetti straps. I had a big day ahead of me and some bad luck to turn around, and I wanted to look good. And, the better I looked, the better I felt. What is it they say? Fake it 'til you make it?

I tried to make some sense of the mass of curls on my head, but they refused to behave. Sometimes my curls want their own way, and sometimes I have to let them have it. I opted for what I hoped was a sexy-messy ponytail, then looked in the mirror and told myself everything was going to be fine. I'd spend the morning sightseeing, have something to eat, and then meet up with the people from the sailing trip in the afternoon.

An hour later, I was deep in the heart of Fira's labyrinth of walkways, exploring. Okay truth be told, I was shopping. Not that I'm one of those women who lives to shop or anything, but there was something comforting about buying myself a new wallet. I also found a beautiful beaded bracelet for Cat. Wanting to see a bit more of Fira than the insides of shops, I stowed my purchases in my handbag and escaped the rabbit warren of stores.

There is a walkway running along the ridge of Fira like a spine, and I followed it south. A whitewashed *campanile e cupola* soon stood out high above the tops of other buildings, and I headed towards it. In a few minutes, I was standing in front of an enormous church. Its imposing façade comprised a dozen archways either side of a long, covered walkway.

From my days as a tour manager, I knew not to enter a church in Greece with bare arms, as it's considered disrespectful. I didn't have anything with me, so I had to settle for admiring it from the outside. It *was* impressive, but given that I was in Greece, I was bound to see another hundred churches before I left the country. Time to move on.

Even more spectacular than Fira's architecture was the view of the *caldera*. I walked over and cautiously perched on a low, whitewashed stone wall. As I peered out over the town, I marvelled at how it clung fearlessly to the cliff face. It was an exquisite sight.

The town below was dotted with several bright blue pools, each surrounded by beach umbrellas. White-clad waiters were attending to holiday makers on sun-loungers, delivering cocktails. *Rich people*, I thought.

At the bottom of the cliff, I could make out the old port. From there, a stream of donkeys ferried people back up to the top of the zigzag staircase. For a moment, I considered a donkey ride, but then I looked down at my outfit and decided against it.

'Where are you from?' I heard from behind me.

I turned and saw an extremely handsome man in his late forties, sitting on a bench about five metres away. He was wearing beige linen pants and a white linen collared shirt, open to the third button, and he was smoking a slim cigar. His whole look, including his salt and pepper hair and deep tan, was a throwback to a more elegant era. He regarded me while he drew from the cigar, smiling, and for some reason, I felt compelled to answer him. Maybe it was because of his eyes, which crinkled at the corners as he smiled. I like crinkling eyes.

'Australia – Sydney.'

'Of Greek ancestry?' I couldn't place his accent, and I could *always* place an accent, but I guessed it was somewhere in

Western Europe. His head tilted slightly and I felt a twinge in my stomach – the good kind – as he watched me.

'No.' It wasn't the first time I had been asked that. Greek, Spanish, Italian, Maltese, Lebanese. I took it as a compliment whenever someone asked. I couldn't imagine anyone asking about my family background to insult me, but rather to pinpoint the origin of my looks. And even though I'm not, I look Mediterranean.

He smiled and the crinkles intensified. So did the twinge.

'Sorry,' he said, seeming to laugh at himself, 'I don't mean to intrude on your day.'

Intrude away, handsome man. I shrugged as though I was used to good-looking strangers engaging me in conversation. 'It's an exquisite view,' he added, gazing past me.

'I don't think I've ever seen anything like it,' I replied.

'So, not of Greek descent? Do you mind me asking what your heritage is? You've piqued my curiosity.'

'Actually, my dad's English and I look like him. He says he's proof that the Romans were in England for hundreds of years.'

He smiled at that. 'Well, you're very beautiful,' he said matter-of-factly.

I tossed my ponytail and allowed a smile to dance across my lips. 'Thank you,' I replied, not flinching under his fixed stare. I silently congratulated myself on such advanced flirting skills.

'Have lunch with me.' It was a statement, not a question. Smooth.

'Maybe,' I said, as though I was actually considering it.

'I know a very nice place around the corner. Excellent seafood. Ellis, it's called. We'll eat, have some wine. And you'll tell me what brings you to Santorini.'

My mind had a quick-fire discussion with itself. Stay? Go? Skip lunch altogether and spend the afternoon making love with this beautiful stranger? I was flattered – of course I was – I'm a human woman with a pulse and he was gorgeous. Reason won out, however. It would be time to meet my tour group soon. Or maybe I was hiding behind reason, my confidence merely bravado.

I started to walk away, but called over my shoulder, 'Perhaps.' I wanted to leave it open in case I got around the corner and changed my mind. He *was* super sexy.

'Two o'clock. See you there.'

And then I did something incredibly cool. I faced him and as I walked slowly backwards, I blew him a kiss. Then I turned and walked away. How awesome was that? I'd never done anything like that – well, not for a long time, not since my touring days, but *that* was a whole different Sarah. It was fun to bust out the sassy girl who once got up to no good. I hoped he had watched me go. There was a little pep in my step as I continued my meandering exploration of the town.

When two o'clock came, I was not having a leisurely seafood lunch with a silver fox dressed in linen – and I wasn't off somewhere making love with him either. Instead, I was back at Fira's not-so-charming bus depot. This time, however, I had my backpack as well as my handbag, and no instructions written in Greek. All I knew was that I needed to get to Vlychada Marina within the next couple of hours to meet my sailing group.

After a false start – I got on the wrong bus and only realised when I heard all the tourists around me talking about Red Beach – I sat on what I hoped was the right bus, awaiting a departure that would be sometime in the next forty-five minutes. Apparently, in Fira, bus timetables are merely a loose approximation of a schedule, a suggestion. 'Greek time', it was called.

While I waited, I thought back over my day. It had already made up for the previous night's theft. After my encounter with the silver fox, I had walked down the wide zigzag stairs to the old port. It was a tricky exercise, because of the donkeys. When they're not taking people to the top of the island, they are lined up along the stairs, with their asses out. I don't trust any equine creatures I don't know, especially when I have to navigate around their behinds. Fortunately, I made it to the bottom without getting kicked in the ass by an ass with its ass out.

The old port was bustling with activity, and I spent some time watching people arriving on little wave-jumpers from the cruise ships. Right before 1:00pm, I took the funicular to the top of the island and set off for my little taverna. I had a quick lunch, then collected my backpack from the hotel and lugged it to the bus depot.

My attention was drawn back to the bus when a skinny older man wearing a tweed cap climbed into the driver's seat and started the engine. I heard a cry of 'Wait!' and as the bus started pulling away, on jumped the tall, cute American in the baseball cap – out of breath and looking just as frazzled as he'd been the day before.

Chapter Three

As the bus lurched along the dusty, winding roads of Santorini, I watched the cute American with considerable interest from behind my Prada sunglasses. He seemed anxious, as though he might be on the wrong bus or something.

For all I knew, *I* was on the wrong bus. I realised my usual MO would be to panic all the way to Vlychada – or wherever we were going – but there was something about handling the stolen wallet ordeal that put the whole 'wrong bus' thing into a more realistic perspective. And if the bus didn't go to the marina, I'd ride it back to Fira and start again.

I focused my attention back on the American, who was even better-looking up close than he'd seemed from across the square the day before. He was also far younger than he'd initially seemed – like, *maybe* twenty-two. Twenty-two was way too young for anyone I would get involved with, or even have a fleeting holiday flirtation with. And besides, I wasn't looking.

I wondered if the cute American would be joining my sailing trip. We were the only two non-Greek people on the bus, and it didn't seem as though Vlychada was somewhere frequented by tourists, so it was looking possible, if not likely.

If he *was* going to be on the trip, that led to an important question. Would we become friends? I decided that if we were sailing together for the next ten days, then yes, there was a good chance we *would* become friends – unless he was a dickhead. He didn't look like a dickhead, but you can never be too sure until you actually meet a person. And even if you did meet someone and decided they weren't a dickhead, they still might be, and it might take you eleven and a half months to figure it out. I knew this from experience. By the way, Neil is the dickhead in this scenario.

I dismissed the thoughts of Neil the fuckhead – I was getting much better at that. Instead, I let it wander to happier places as I imagined a lifetime of friendship with the cute American. After the trip, we would become pen pals writing actual letters back and forth for years. Then we would go to each other's weddings and, over the next few decades, share all our major life events via letters and phone calls. During our widowed twilight years, we would live in the same city, in side-by-side houses, all the while denying we were more than 'just friends'.

The bus groaned to a stop at a marina. I stopped daydreaming and looked out the dirty bus window, seeing a sign that made me smile: 'Vlychada'. I was in the right place. See? No need to worry.

I gathered up my stuff and got off the bus via the back door, and the cute American got off via the front door, swinging his duffel bag over his shoulder. The bus pulled away, and we were the only two people standing on the pier. We looked at each other for a moment, then I walked towards him – awkwardly, because my wretched backpack was swinging heavily against my legs.

'Hello,' I said.

34

'Hi,' he replied. So far it was an excellent conversation.

It seemed my witty repartee from a few hours before had completely dried up, so I figured I'd get straight to the point. 'Are you on the sailing trip?'

'Oh, thank god, I'm in the right place,' he blurted. Then he seemed to chastise himself. He walked over to meet me with his hand outstretched. 'Hi, sorry – I was a little worried I was on the wrong bus.' I shook his hand. Firm handshake. Nice.

'No worries. I was too, to be honest,' I lied. 'I'm Sarah.'

'Josh.' I was right, by the way – American. I picked his accent as mid-western, but I didn't ask. We had ten days to learn about each other. I was sure we'd get there eventually.

'Shall we try to find the boat?' he suggested.

'Good plan.' My backpack was getting heavier the longer we stood there.

We walked towards the rows of moored boats, discussing how we would know which one was ours, when Josh spotted a flag fluttering from one of the masts and pointed to it. 'That must be us.' It had the tour company's logo on it, so we headed in that direction.

'Hang on,' I said, stopping short. 'There's two. Look.' He followed the line of my arm to another of the company's flags waving at us from a mast.

'Huh. Well, let's go to one and if it's not right, then we'll go to the other.'

'Okay.' By this stage I didn't care what boat I was on, I wanted to put my cumbersome backpack down – stupid bloody thing.

We came to the first of the two yachts, which was docked parallel to the pier. It was about fifteen metres long and, like most boats, the bulk of it was white. It struck me how little I knew about sailing and boats, as I couldn't really point out any distinguishing features – it looked like a sailboat.

We both dropped our bags onto the pier, and Josh called out, 'Hello!'

A head popped out of the hatch, followed by some shoulders, then a torso and the rest of a man's body. 'Hello,' he said back. He was handsome in the way that Harrison Ford was handsome when he played Indiana Jones – the first couple of times. I couldn't help making a note of how many good-looking men I was running into on Santorini.

'Hi, I'm Gary.'

'Hi, Gary. Sarah. And this is Josh.'

Gary turned around and called down into the boat, 'Duncan. The last two are here!' To us, he said, 'I'm not the skipper. I'm on the tour like you – although I do know quite a bit about sailing.'

'Good to know that if the skipper falls overboard, we can keep on going,' quipped Josh. Funny.

Gary offered an unsure smile in response and joined us on deck as another head popped up out of the hatch. 'Josh and Sarah?' said the head.

'Yes,' we said in unison.

'Great.' The second man, who I presumed was Duncan, leapt into action. He climbed out of the hatch, jumped off the boat and onto the pier, and grabbed both of our bags as though they weighed nothing. He climbed back onto the boat and said, 'Come aboard! Oh, and shoes off please.' Then he disappeared back below deck with our bags.

He was spry, I'd give him that. In fact, the whole exchange happened so quickly I caught myself standing and staring at the black hole where he had disappeared. 'Well, I guess we found the right boat,' Josh said to me quietly.

'Absolutely,' I replied. I slipped off my sandals and climbed over the railing onto the boat. It was a little trickier than I would have liked because I was wearing a short skirt. I hoped I wasn't flashing my knickers to all and sundry. I noticed an amused smile on Josh's face as he reached out to help. Was it smugness or chivalry? I took his hand, regardless. I didn't want to fall into the water on my first day – or ever, for that matter.

Gary spoke up. 'There's actually two boats leaving from here tomorrow morning. That's the other one, there.' He pointed to the second boat Josh and I had seen from the end of the pier.

'Oh, will we be sailing with them?' I asked.

'No, not really, but we'll likely run into them from time to time. All women apparently.' He laughed to himself. 'I think our mix of people will be far better, hey Josh?' He gave Josh what looked like a knowing grin.

What was this? The menfolk conspiring already? And how were Josh and I to know what the mix was? We had only met Gary and Duncan. *Oh god, I hope I'm not the only woman!* Josh, to his credit, answered Gary with a non-committal shrug.

I went below deck, and Josh followed. It was so dark I couldn't see anything, and then I remembered I was wearing my sunglasses, so I flipped them on top of my head. I could see better, but only marginally. It was pretty dark below deck.

Duncan emerged from one of the cabins and soon after, two women appeared from two other cabins – I was not the only woman, then. Gary had also climbed down below, so there were six of us standing in the cramped dining nook, looking at each other.

'Oh!' said the man, breaking the awkward silence. 'I didn't introduce myself. Sorry. I'm Duncan. I'm your skipper.' Australian – Queenslander.

I waved at him from two metres away. 'And this is Hannah and Marie. And you've met Gary, Marie's husband.' So, the Harrison Ford guy was married. I wasn't particularly disappointed, as he wasn't really my type – a bit too blokeish – and besides, I wasn't looking.

I smiled at the strangers I would be living with for the next ten days.

'And these two are Josh and Sarah,' added Duncan to finish the round of introductions.

'I'm Sarah, he's Josh,' I added, in an attempt to break the ice, and thankfully everyone laughed.

Then the tiny space erupted into activity. Hannah came forward and said hello. 'You're sharing with me,' she said. 'In there,' and she pointed to the left rear cabin. 'Come on, I'll show you.' She sounded Canadian – Vancouver, I guessed.

I followed her the extremely short distance to our cabin, and she showed me the highlights. It was a tight space, but at least we had our own bathroom. There were two bunks, one very narrow and about a metre from the ceiling and the lower one, which took up the width of the cabin. Whoever slept on the top bunk would have to climb onto it from the bottom bunk. Some of Hannah's things were on that bunk, so I guessed the lower one was mine.

We also had a hatch in the ceiling and a porthole for fresh air. The cabin was tiny but clean and it would be fine. I doubted I would be spending much time in there, anyway. It was really just for sleeping and showering, so who cared if it was compact?

'Sarah, can I ask you a question?'

'Sure,' I said as I unzipped my backpack and started pulling stuff out.

'How come you're not sleeping with your boyfriend?'

'What?' I looked at her in surprise. What on earth was she talking about?

'Josh. How come you two aren't sharing a cabin?'

'Oooh!' I said, probably too loudly for the confined space of a boat. I'd seen Josh disappear into the cabin next door and realised he could be listening. I lowered my voice. 'He's not my boyfriend. I just met him, like, five minutes ago on the pier. We were on the same bus to the marina, that's all. So, yeah ...' I finished, feebly.

'Oh. I thought you guys were a couple.'

'Nope. And believe me, if he *was* my boyfriend, I *would* want to sleep with him.' Great. I sounded desperate, or sex-starved. Or both.

She gave me a funny look, confirming it was both. 'I'm going to head up top. Duncan's making another round of cocktails, and then he's going over the trip information with us. I'll see you up there.'

What the hell was the thing I'd said about wanting to sleep with Josh? I didn't want to sleep with him. He was a baby. No, an *infant*. And I wasn't going anywhere near him, even if he was cute. I wasn't going near *any* men. At most, I might admire them – and only from afar. I had to get it together. I didn't want Hannah thinking she was sharing a cabin with a nymphomaniac weirdo.

I spent the next few minutes nesting. Whenever I arrive

somewhere new, I like to unpack the essentials and stash my luggage. Both tasks were a little awkward in the tiny cabin, but at least I found a nook in the bathroom for my toiletries. Out of necessity, I stuffed my backpack, still full of clothes, at the end of the lower bunk. It would have to do.

'Hey,' said a voice behind me as I gave my backpack a final shove. I looked over my shoulder. Wonderful. Josh was standing in the doorway and had an excellent view of my bum sticking up in the air.

I flipped over and scooched off the end of the bed, trying to keep my skirt from riding up my thighs. I was going to need to rethink my wardrobe for this trip. Of course, with the super tight quarters, as soon as I stood up, I was practically on top of the poor guy. He backed up a little. That was when I got a proper look at his eyes without the sunglasses.

They were incredible. Large, almond-shaped dark grey eyes with thick lashes – lashes *any* woman would kill to have. I wanted him to put his sunglasses back on. Those eyes were far too much power for one man to wield. He was talking, so I told myself to pay attention.

'So, apparently I'm sharing with a woman called Patricia. She *was* here, but she went back into town to do something. Duncan says she'll be back later.'

'Oh. Are you okay with that, sharing with a woman?'

He shrugged. 'Sure. It'll be fine. Want to go up on deck?'

'Okay.' I put on my sunglasses and followed him up the ladder. *Cute bum*. Yeah, I was really going to have to stop that. Nowhere on the boat could be mistaken for 'afar'.

Josh sat on one side of the boat, and I sat on the other, perhaps more than anything to show Hannah that he and I were definitely *not* a couple. It was only after I sat down that

I realised there was another woman in the group – an incredibly beautiful woman. This must have been the elusive Patricia who Josh was sharing a cabin with.

'Sarah, Josh, this is Geraldine – Gerry – my girlfriend.' *Wait. What?* Our skipper had brought his girlfriend on the trip? Was he even allowed to do that? Before I could list all the reasons why it was a terrible idea, she turned to me with the biggest smile and said, 'Sarah, so nice to meet you. Your hair is *beautiful*! I love it!' There was no sarcasm or cattiness in her voice. In a whisper of a moment, she had disarmed me, my reticence at her very existence on the boat vanishing in the glow of her compliment.

'That is so sweet, Gerry. Thank you. It's lovely to meet you too.' She went on to greet Josh in an equally enthusiastic and authentic way. Had he not already put his sunglasses back on, I am sure I would have seen his gorgeous eyes light up. At least she wasn't Patricia, and he would not be sharing a cabin with the beautiful buxom woman. Not that I actually cared who he shared a cabin with.

Her accent stumped me – the second time that day. Was I losing my gift? Gerry's was from *somewhere* in South America, but where? 'Sarah, you need a drink!' Duncan declared. Truer words had never been spoken, and I was grateful when Duncan poured me a generous serving from a pitcher. He passed the plastic cup across the circle and then poured one for Josh. I sniffed it. Definitely rum, but I couldn't make out what else.

'So, now we've all met – first names, at least – I'd like to propose a toast.' I was really starting to like this Duncan chap. 'To new adventures with new friends.' Good toast. Yep, I liked Duncan.

We all tapped our plastic cups against each other's and took sips of his concoction. Holy crap. My throat was on fire. 'Uh, Duncan, what's in this?' I asked, my voice straining.

'What's *not* in it is more to the point,' replied Gary. I looked at Duncan, who was smiling mysteriously and then back to Gary. 'We got here about two hours ago. This is our third. You'll get used to it.' I nodded and took another cautious sip. And then another.

As I moved closer and closer to inebriation, Duncan pulled out a large nautical map and pointed to a crescent-shaped blob somewhere in the middle. 'We're here,' he said. 'Santorini.' He pointed to a cornflake-shaped blob north of Santorini. 'We're going here – Mykonos – and it takes about twelve hours to sail there.' He paused, probably for effect. Duncan seemed like a pro. 'We're going to take *ten days* to sail there.'

I found myself breathing out a deep sigh of pure pleasure.

'So, I'll pick the islands we'll go to, 'cause I know this part of the world really well. I'll also keep an eye on the sea and the weather, that sort of thing. When we get somewhere, if we all like it and want to stay another night, we'll decide together. Sound good?' Five of us nodded our responses, and I noticed mine wasn't the only peaceful smile in the group. I also saw Gerry grinning proudly at Duncan. Cute couple.

That was the moment Patricia decided to make her entrance.

'Welll, helllooo, everyone. Isn't this cosy?' We all looked up at the woman standing on the pier next to our boat. She had close-cropped red hair and wore layers and layers of flowing batik cloth. She also wore big Jackie O-style sunglasses.

Duncan, possibly the most gracious host ever, leapt up and offered her a hand so she could climb aboard. She seemed drunk. I caught myself frowning at her and consciously set my expression to a more welcoming one. 'Everyone, this is Patricia.' The hellos from the group were far less effusive than the ones Josh and I had received.

Duncan did a whip-around of everyone's names and we lifted our hands unenthusiastically in response. She didn't seem to absorb them anyway. She pushed in next to Josh and turned to Duncan. 'What does a woman have to do to get a drink around here?' she said. Perhaps it was an attempt to be funny. It wasn't.

'Right, yes,' said Duncan as he looked around for a clean cup. Gerry handed one over, and he poured a drink and handed it to Patricia. She grabbed it and took a loud gulp. I tried to catch Josh's eye, but as we were both still wearing sunglasses, that was a little tricky.

'Anyway, Patricia, I was just going through a few things about our trip.'

'Don't mind me.' She waved her hand as though she didn't want to be a bother. Yeah, right. As quickly as I had decided I liked Duncan, I decided I did not care for Patricia.

Duncan moved on to formal introductions. He asked us to go around the circle and tell each other a little bit about ourselves. I always hate this part; I've never liked giving a dust-cover blurb about myself. I worry too much about how I'll come across. As a result, I get all self-conscious, and then I end up sounding like an idiot.

Hannah put her hand up. 'I'll start.' Hannah was one of those well-put-together women – basically the opposite of me. Her hair was in an actual style, her nails were done – hands *and* feet – and even sitting on a boat in the middle of the Aegean, she looked polished to perfection.

'I'm Hannah, and I'm from Vancouver.' So, I had nailed at least one accent that day. 'I'm in financial management, and I work crazy long hours – this is actually my first vacation in three years.' *Three years? Geez.* 'I'm thirty-three. And recently single.' She flashed a slightly sad smile around the circle. 'I've never been to Greece before, and I'm really excited to be here.'

I figured we'd probably bond over the whole 'break-up' thing. Yes, it had been months since Neil and I had parted ways, but the humiliation of his cheating still rose its head on occasion.

Marie went next. She told us that she Gary were in Greece celebrating their tenth wedding anniversary, and the sailing trip was the end of a one-month stay. They'd rented a place on Crete for two weeks, before spending a few days in Santorini ahead of the trip. It sounded incredible, and I was starting to realise I should have arrived earlier and spent more time on the island. I'd barely scratched the surface, but I had to fit the entire trip – including a week in London with Cat after the sailing trip – into three weeks. I was already taking an extra week's leave, and I'd had to do some pretty serious begging to get my principal to agree to it.

I'll have to come back, I decided.

I turned my attention back to Marie and Gary. They both worked in tourism, which is how they met, and were from California wine country. Travel *and* wine? We were going to get along great. We'd drink crappy Greek wine and commiserate while we longed for a delicious Californian pinot. They were a super sweet couple too, holding hands and sneaking cute little glances at each other. Ten years. That was certainly something to be proud of.

Josh went next, taking his sunglasses off and revealing those eyes again. 'Hi, I'm Josh. I'm from Chicago. This is my first time leaving the US.' Whoa. Really? I held my breath as I waited for any snippet that would reveal how old he was. 'Uh, I work in software development, and I'm twenty-eight.' Did he say he was twenty-eight? So *not* an infant. Not way off limits. Crap. No, double crap.

'Oh,' he said, as though remembering something, 'and I came here because I was watching a Rick Steves episode on Santorini, and I suddenly thought, I have to go there. So, I researched trips for a couple of days and booked this one.' He smiled, and I could see the excitement in his eyes. So, he'd booked an international trip – his *first* international trip – practically on a whim. It was as good a reason as any. I'd pretty much done the same thing, only my whim took hold after a sad and lonely night that included a bottle and a half of expensive wine and an entire box of tissues.

No one said anything after Josh finished, so I put my hand up to go next. 'Hi, I'm Sarah from Sydney – easy enough to remember, I guess – I teach high school English, which I love – mostly. Sometimes the kids are ratbags, and sometimes there's too much pointless paperwork, but I like the actual teaching part. I have been to Greece before, but not this part, and not for a really long time. I'm mostly looking forward to the food.' And then for some reason, I added, 'And I'm thirty-six.' I glanced over at Josh. Did he bite his lip when I said that?

Duncan looked at Patricia, who had fallen asleep, and he artfully skipped over the drunk lady. 'I'll be quick. I'm Duncan, and I'm from Townsville in Queensland. I've sailed my whole life, and I've been working at this job for the past five seasons – which works out well for you lot, 'cause I know my way around the islands, and I know the locals – we're gonna have an awesome trip.'

'Gerry and I met online last year.' She waved at us all, and I found myself waving back. 'She's studying in the UK, and we meet up whenever we can and go travelling together. This trip lined up with the end of her summer break, so I invited her to come along.' Wow. They were dating long-distance? 'And, I promise that this –' he signalled to himself and Gerry '– won't get in the way of this.' He then signalled to the boat and to us. So apparently my concerns were expected, but I felt like Duncan addressing it head-on was a good thing. Not only a pro, but a proactive pro.

Then he went on to tell us all the stuff about the boat we needed to know – like what to do if we fell overboard, which was good to know even though I planned not to do that. He saved the toilet talk for last. 'You can flush the toilet paper down these toilets – it just goes into the water.' Gross. 'But, uh, if we're moored and you need to use the toilet, and it's heavy and technical, then I'd recommend going ashore and finding a café who'll let you use theirs. Otherwise, it's gonna float next to the boat until we leave.'

The rest of us were stunned into silence. Heavy and technical? So, if I needed to poop while we were docked, I had to go ashore? Great. 'See you in a few minutes, everyone. Just going for my morning poop!' Duncan seemed to sense the embarrassed tension – I'm sure it wasn't the first time he'd experienced it – and broke it with, 'More cocktails?'

There was a resounding chorus of 'Yes, please,' as the group laughed nervously. Patricia started at the noise. 'Wait!' she cried. 'I didn't get to do my introduction.'

'How about I make another pitcher of drinks and then we

do your intro?' asked Duncan. That seemed to satisfy her and she sat back regarding the rest of us, almost aggressively. I wondered how much of our introductions she'd heard.

When we all had fresh drinks in hand, she stood up, albeit a little shakily. 'I am Patricia,' she said with more dramatic flourish than the intimate setting called for. 'I am originally from New York, but now I am a citizen of the world.' And then she sat down. The rest of us looked at each other, while she sipped her drink and squinted out at the marina. I'd taken my sunglasses off, as the sun was going down, and so had the others. We conveyed a lot to each other without speaking, and I knew we were all onside *against* Patricia. I even saw Duncan frowning at her.

I glanced at Josh and he winked at me. I wondered if he was still happy to share a cabin with her. Poor guy. I would have offered to swap with him, but I *really* didn't want to.

'I thought we'd head up to the restaurant there for dinner,' said Duncan, pointing to a café at the top of a giant set of stairs. 'How does that sound? Early dinner, come back, maybe have some more drinks, then your first night's sleep on the boat.'

We all showed our agreement by leaping into action – all of us except Patricia. She stayed put while the rest of us went below for jumpers and jackets and to get money for dinner. Less than ten minutes later, seven of us stood on the pier as Duncan tried one more time to get her to join us. 'I'm going to stay here and soak it all in,' she said, dismissing us with a wave of her hand. Soak it all up was probably more like it.

Gary led the way, and we all followed without a glance back to the boat. The climb left all of us breathing heavily, except Duncan who looked like he ran steep flights of stairs for fun, and we stood at the top catching our respective breaths while he went to get us a table. Without much fuss from the waiter, we were soon seated outside with an incredible view of the sun setting over the marina. There was a lively discussion about what to order, but we left most of it up to Duncan.

The food came and then kept coming – plates and plates of fresh seafood, *horiatiki* and tzatziki. We drank watery retsina – actually, I stuck to Mythos, the Greek beer. As we ate, we talked, learning more than the snippets we'd shared a couple of hours before. And we laughed – a lot.

After I piled another helping of fried calamari onto my plate, I settled back in my chair and looked around the group. All those fears, all those concerns about who they would be and how I would get along with them, had gone. This little group was going to be my floating family for the next week and a half and I already liked them. It felt good being part of this group. It was going to be a great trip.

And then I remembered Patricia.

Chapter Four

Around three the following morning, the snoring from the cabin next door woke me from a restless sleep for the thousandth time. I guessed it was Patricia, because I could hear the melodic undertones of drunkenness. I whispered to Hannah to see if she was awake too.

'Oh my god,' she whispered back. 'I've been lying here wondering if I could climb down and get into the bathroom without waking you. I've got sleeping pills.'

Sleeping pills? I never thought I would be so excited to hear those two words.

'You sharing?'

'Sure.'

'Then I'll get 'em. Where are they?'

'In my toiletry bag.'

I climbed out of my bunk and rooted around in the bathroom in the dark, finally finding both the toiletry bag and the Ambien. Ahh, Ambien. You can't buy a Kinder Surprise egg in America – choking hazard, apparently – but you *can* buy a blissful little over-the-counter sleep aid called Ambien.

It kicked in fast, and when I eventually emerged from a hazy, drug-induced sleep the next morning, it was after nine.

I was now properly exhausted; it had been my fourth night in a row of bad sleep and I made a mental note to nap sometime that afternoon – maybe for all of it.

Hannah was still very much out of it, her face buried in her tiny boat pillow, so I showered as quietly and as quickly as I could, then got dressed in the tiny bathroom. It was quite the feat, as water covered every surface, including the floor. I'd tucked my clean clothes inside a cubby to keep them dry during my shower, but I couldn't outsmart the bathroom design completely.

It required some rather impressive yoga-like moves to get my clothes onto my body without them getting soaked. And it was a little too early in the trip for a wet T-shirt competition.

Between the lack of sleep and the rudimentary ablution situation, the whole 'I'm on holiday' feeling was quickly becoming a distant memory. Finally dressed, I stepped back into our tiny cabin. I thought about putting my pyjamas and dirty knickers away, but I couldn't see how to without waking Hannah. I was going to have to get used to being messy – along with tired and a little bit damp.

When I climbed up on deck, it turned out that Hannah wasn't the only one still asleep. Gerry was too. Marie was up, but still getting dressed. And Patricia was still sleeping it off. That left me alone with the three men, and it took me about two seconds to realise that no one was eating yet – no one was even having a cup of tea!

Maybe they thought getting breakfast was women's work and were waiting for the women to emerge and serve it to them. Perhaps they weren't sexist at all, just lazy. Either way, I was starving, so I did what anyone who knew her way around a kitchen would do. I offered to make breakfast for everyone.

'Uh, yeah, I bought some basics for brekkie before we left Santorini,' said Duncan, 'but we'll need to stock the pantry when we get to Ios.' Duncan had told us during our orientation talk that we would all put money into a kitty to share food for breakfast and lunches, and we could buy stuff for ourselves if we wanted anything different.

Below deck – that's boat lingo by the way – I hunted through the kitchen, or rather the galley – also boat lingo – and soon realised Duncan had understated 'some basics'. All I found was two loaves of bread, butter, milk, sugar and teabags – not even instant coffee.

I had been hankering for Greek yoghurt – would it just be called 'yoghurt' in Greece? I made a mental note to add it to the list. I also hoped the shop on our next island stop of Ios sold muesli. I know I was travelling, and I probably should have been thinking about adopting some of the local customs, but I also knew what the Greeks had for breakfast. I wasn't too keen about starting each day with Nescafé and a cigarette.

Toast and tea would have to do. I put the kettle on and put two slices of bread into the toaster. While I waited, I looked through all the cubbies for plates, mugs, spoons – the usual kitchen stuff. It wasn't a large galley, so it didn't take long to learn my way around.

'Need some help?' said a sexy American voice from behind me. Josh. I smiled over my shoulder and nodded. Not sexist and not lazy.

He took over toasting duties while I set about making mugs of tea. I hadn't bothered asking if everyone wanted toast and tea for breakfast, because that's all there was. Fifteen minutes later, we carefully climbed the ladder to the deck, him carrying a mountainous plate of buttered toast and me balancing a tray with mugs of tea, milk, and sugar. I was going to get nimble moving around this boat.

Marie had joined our breakfast club, emerging from her cabin a few minutes after Josh had come down. Everyone gratefully took a mug of tea and a piece of toast. It was quiet in the marina, and I could hear the gentle lapping of the water against boat hulls as we ate and drank in companionable silence. After we decimated the mountain of toast, the conversation turned to the day's journey to Ios.

Duncan said it would take about four hours and then we'd have the rest of the day to chillax – his word, not mine – but I was all about some 'chillaxing' after that crappy night's sleep. I was also looking forward to a nap, which I guessed fell under the whole chillaxing umbrella.

We wouldn't see Gerry or Hannah until much later that morning, and Patricia wouldn't emerge from her alcohol-induced coma until the afternoon.

*

'Wanna steer?' I looked up from my Kindle, which is sealed in a Ziploc bag for waterproofing, to see that Duncan was talking to me.

'Really?' I hadn't known I'd get to steer the boat.

'For sure.' I looked over at Gary who nodded at me encouragingly.

'Okay, yeah!'

'Stand here.' I put my Kindle down and stood in front of

Duncan. 'Hold the wheel here and here.' I held my hands at ten and two like he showed me. 'It's not like a car; it takes subtle adjustments. We want to head to the right of that island in the middle of the *caldera*. You got it?' I nodded. 'If we start to go too far in one direction, correct our course, but gently. Okay? And I'll be here if you need help, or if you get sick of it.'

'Me too,' added Gary.

'I got it.' A grin spread across my face. I was sailing! In truth, I was only steering, but it was one of those cool things I could check off my endless bucket list. Some people have a finite bucket list, but I keep adding to mine. I figure it's the best way to make sure I keep going out and doing things. Imagine saying, 'I'm done,' and then staying home for the rest of your life. That would do my head in. So, sailing (okay, steering) a boat through Santorini's *caldera* – check!

It was incredible to feel the responsiveness of the yacht as it sliced through the water. We were sailing under power, as the winds were not cooperating that morning, but it wasn't like I knew the difference between steering with wind power and engine power. Did I mention I was sailing?

As we passed to the right of the small island, I could see the town of Fira far above us. It was just as spectacular from the water as it was from within. The contrast between the stark white of the buildings and the craggy, reddish cliffs was incredible. I was definitely regretting not spending more time on Santorini. I promised myself I would return someday, adding to the bucket list again.

The sun was already hot, even at ten in the morning, and I tipped my heavily sun-screened face towards it. I

53

inhaled deeply and felt the warm, salty air in my lungs. I'd abandoned my hat as soon as we left the marina, because it kept blowing off, and my unfettered hair whipped around my face. I must have looked quite alluring, because it wasn't long before Josh came and sat close by, anchoring his feet against the boat and gripping the railing with one hand. 'Having fun?'

'Yes!' I grinned at him. 'Did you want to have a go?' I asked, hopeful he'd say no and I could keep my sailing gig a little longer. He may have picked up on that because he waved off my offer.

'Plenty of time for that. You're doing a good job.'

'So, how *did* you sleep?' I asked.

'Yeah, not that well. That's some pretty loud snoring. I ended up putting in earplugs. They helped a bit.'

'I thought about you last night.' *Oh crap, not like that.* 'I mean, because of the snoring. Hannah and I were up for most of the night – we took Ambien at around three. I was out after that. She's probably got more – you should ask her for some.' *Quit rambling, Sarah.*

He shrugged. 'I guess I can always go sleep in the dining nook if it gets too much.'

'And how is Patricia otherwise? Did you talk to her much?'

'A little when we got back from dinner. She seems pretty interesting. She's travelled a lot.' I felt like I'd been rebuked.

'Oh, I didn't mean anything by that.'

'It's cool. I didn't think you did.'

I hoped not. I didn't want him thinking I was bitchy. I wasn't – well, not really. I decided I would talk to Patricia when she eventually woke up – she couldn't be that bad.

Several hours later, Patricia emerged wearing a voluminous

kaftan and a sour expression. She squinted at us, then sashayed over and plonked down next to Josh. I got a waft of sweat and stale alcohol and tried unsuccessfully to stop my nose from scrunching.

She can't be that bad, I reminded myself, but it didn't take long to regret my decision to engage her in conversation.

'Well, there's your problem right there,' she said. I hate when people say that, as though it's *soooo* obvious why you're *soooo* stupid.

'Sorry? What do you mean?'

'You went all the way to Lake Titicaca, but you didn't cross the border into Bolivia? Rookie mistake. You missed the best part!'

We were talking about my trip to Peru. Her being a citizen of the world, I'd decided that travel would be a safe topic on which we'd find some common ground. I was wrong. Apparently having world citizen status gives you carte blanche to be a superior twat about everywhere you've been that other people haven't.

'Well, I couldn't really cross the border considering we were on an organised trip.' She scoffed at this with what sounded like a 'huff'. I thought it was somewhat hypocritical considering she was currently on an *organised trip*. 'Well, anyway, I really enjoyed Peru.'

I'd given Patricia nearly half-an-hour of my time, and most of it was spent defending myself. I figured that was enough of an effort and decided I was done with her for the duration of the trip.

And poor Josh was sleeping with her, so to speak.

'Hey, guys, check this out,' Gary called from the bow of the boat. Grateful for a reason to extricate myself from

Patricia's snarly glare, I climbed up onto the side of the boat and made my way up to join Gary. This may sound easier than it was, because the boat was moving and there wasn't a lot to hold on to. I had to be very careful I didn't get pitched over the side into the raging sea. Well, gently rolling sea. Hannah and Marie followed closely behind me, also carefully.

The boat was rounding the tip of an inlet on Ios and at its mouth was a stunning white church, an island sentry of sorts. Unlike most churches I'd seen on Santorini, it didn't have blue or gold embellishments – it was stark white, gleaming against the green scrub and red earth of the surrounding hills. Its spire rose from the curve of the roof like three tiers of a wedding cake.

'Whoa,' said Hannah behind me. 'Whoa' was right.

Gary turned to grin at us. 'Yeah, pretty nice, huh?'

As we sailed into the inlet, the port of Ios sat directly ahead of us. While Gary and Josh darted about the boat following Duncan's orders, I searched for signs of life along the waterfront. The grocery store was open, so that was good. And it looked like there was at least one café open – we wouldn't starve. I got called away to buoy duty and joined the others to secure the large rubber bumpers along the length of the boat on both sides. I was going to have to get better at tying knots.

As we neared the dock, Duncan turned the boat around and manoeuvred it into a slip next to a slightly longer yacht bearing an Italian flag. As we approached, an older man wearing a straw porkpie hat ran up his gangplank to the dock and signalled to Gary to throw him our tow rope.

There was some reverse throttling of the engine and some

more quick footwork by Gary – he really *did* know his way around a boat – and with the Italian skipper's help, we were soon secured to the dock. We called our thanks to our new neighbour, and he waved it off modestly and tipped his hat at us. I adore Italians.

A flash of red hair and swish of flowing fabric pushed past me. 'Don't wait up!'

'As if we would,' I muttered as Patricia swayed her way along our gangplank and staggered off into the town. Hannah, who was now in the land of the semi-living and was standing next to me, smirked in solidarity.

'Off to find the nearest bar, is my guess,' said Gary. I heard murmured agreement from the others. I obviously wasn't the only one who'd decided to steer a wide berth from our citizen of the world.

After Duncan secured the boat cabin, the seven of us headed to the only open café for a late lunch.

'Hey, I'm going over to the supermarket after we eat,' I said to Josh who sat next to me. 'Wanna come? Stock up on some essentials – like *food*?' He was up for it, and we agreed to leave as soon as we'd finished eating.

We were sitting outside on plastic garden furniture so tired, it should have been sent to the dump years before. We did have a gorgeous view of the port and its neighbouring beach, and it was a much prettier port than Vlychada, but we were the only patrons at the only open café. Where was everyone?

I asked Duncan. 'Gone,' he replied. Okay, Captain Obvious. 'Where? Why?'

'This is actually one of the most touristy islands – lots of kids – but they're usually gone by mid-August – back to uni, most of them.' It was the tail-end of August, so that explained why the town was deserted. I hoped when we got to other ports, they'd be a little livelier. I was all for relaxation, but I also wanted to get amongst the Greeks and experience some local flavour.

Speaking of which, a Greek woman appeared like an apparition and threw laminated menus onto the table. Starving after our pauper's breakfast, I practically snatched one up. It was sticky to the touch, but at least it matched the table, which was dotted with unidentifiable splotches of goop. I flicked through it, reading the bastardised English, and the others did the same. The woman hovered impatiently while we turned its many pages.

I was craving something, but couldn't find it on the menu. I caught her eye by waving at her, 'Kalispera – hello – do you have dolmades, efharisto?' A look of utter puzzlement crossed her face. I said it more slowly, 'Dol-ma-deez?' The puzzlement remained, and she turned to the others to signal they should order something – as in, she didn't understand me and the best way to deal with me, was to ignore me altogether.

Duncan stepped in and ordered enough food for all of us, plus seven beers. He was so charming in the way he spoke to her that I even saw the corner of her mouth twitch into the semblance of a smile. But what about the dolmades? I love dolmades, and I was in Greece. Could I not get some dolmades? PLEASE!

She came back out a few minutes later with our beers and Marie, the goddess that she was, tried to support my dolmadic efforts. 'Excuse me, we'd really like an order of dolmades if you have them,' she said in her most-enunciated North American accent.

The frown returned to the woman's face, and she left without saying or doing anything to indicate that *dolmades* were on their way. But it turns out they were! A few minutes later again, she pretty much tossed a plate of them onto the table. *Dolmades*!

But I was wrong.

'Doll-mah-dezzz,' she said at me slowly. Then she turned on her heels and huffed away. Right then, I guess I'd been told.

The doll-mah-dezzz were delicious, by the way.

After we finished eating, Josh and I told the others we were heading to the supermarket. We asked if anyone wanted to come, but the others seemed happy to linger and have more beer. Duncan had everyone put twenty euros each into a pile on the table – our kitty for the shared food. By default, I was now in charge of said kitty for breakfasts, snacks and lunches on the boat. I was also under strict instructions to get beer, but that was just for Duncan. He slipped me an extra twenty.

'Any other requests?' I asked, getting a small notebook out of my bag.

'Water,' said Duncan. 'Bottled water and lots of it.' I wrote down 'water – LOTS'. Then I wondered how we would carry lots of water back to the boat.

'Tzatziki,' said Marie. 'Oh, and something to eat it on – bread, I guess? Oh, and tomatoes.'

'Oh god yes,' I replied. I underlined tomatoes three times.

'Snacks,' replied Hannah, unhelpfully.

'What snacks?'

'I don't know. Whatever they have. Just snacks.' Great. So far, being on kitty duty sucked.

'I'll help figure it out,' said the cute guy next to me. I looked up at him – gosh, he was tall – and he was smiling down at me, damn him.

'Right,' I said, tidying up the pile of cash and putting it into my bag. 'We will see you back at the boat.'

I cringed a little as Hannah called out after us, 'Have fun, you two. Don't do anything I wouldn't do.' Wonderful – she was still running with the whole 'you look like a couple' thing.

The grocery store was a couple of blocks away from the café, and Josh grabbed a trolley when we got inside. Walking the aisles side by side, we stocked up on breakfast foods – muesli, cereal, jam, bread, peanut butter, milk, yoghurt – they do just call it 'yoghurt', by the way, rather than 'Greek yoghurt'. As we tried to guess what the others might enjoy, we discovered we liked a lot of the same things.

Snacks were a little trickier than breakfast, but we found crackers, cookies, nuts, chocolate, and fresh fruit. I hoped Hannah would approve – I didn't want to get on the wrong side of my roomie. For lunches, we went with the stuff for Greek salad, pita, tzatziki, cured meats and extra tomatoes. So far, the shopping experience was exactly like shopping back home in Sydney, which I admit was a little disappointing. I had been looking forward to a more authentic experience – local markets, having the grocer select the best tomatoes for me – but this shop was obviously catering to the tourist crowd.

Then we got to the liquor aisle. 'Oh my god. Look at how cheap it all is!' I exclaimed, immediately realising how I must have sounded. But the prices *were* ridiculous – about half of what we would pay in Australia. And right in the middle of the middle shelf was a familiar, pretty blue bottle. As I reached for the Bombay Sapphire gin, so did Josh. I looked at him. 'Hey! That's my fave.'

'That's my favourite too,' he replied.

'No way.'

'Way.'

'That's brilliant – we can share. And it's only seventeen euros. That's like ...' I tried to do the conversion to dollars and came up short '... cheap.'

'For sure.'

Then I had a real brainwave. 'We should get two.'

'Will we drink two?' he asked.

'Even if we don't, the others will. I don't know if you've noticed, but we're sailing with a bunch of drinkers – and that's not even including Patricia.'

'I have noticed that, yes.'

'And thank god!' He laughed at my effusiveness. 'Can you imagine the alternative? Being on a boat with a bunch of teetotallers? I mean, kill me now!'

'Torture.' I think he may have been making fun of me, but I didn't care.

'Exactly.'

We got two. And beer for Duncan.

I looked down at our nearly full trolley. Did we have enough food? I hated the thought of running out while we were in the middle of the ocean. Yes, I do know the Aegean Sea is not an ocean, but I figured that running out of food on any body of water would be a bad thing.

'Is this enough?' I asked my kitty buddy.

He responded by laughing at me.

'Uh, yes, probably for the rest of the trip and I am pretty

sure there will be other grocery stores in our future if we run out of anything.'

'How are we getting this back to the boat? We can't carry all this.'

'I figure we'll just steal the cart.' He smiled cheekily. I frowned at him, 'Or, we could *use* the cart, and I can bring it back when we've unloaded it.'

'That'll work.' We paid, we bagged, and we pushed the wonky-wheeled trolley three blocks to the boat where we were greeted with great enthusiasm by our boatmates, who then insisted they put the stuff away.

I was totally cool with handing over the reins; I'd hit a wall of exhaustion. So much so that, when the shopping was put away, and Duncan announced an expedition to explore more of the island, I declined. My plans included my bunk and a nana nap. I probably should have gone with them – who knew when I'd be back on Ios again – but I desperately needed to sleep.

I had only been asleep for about an hour when I woke to a loud voice in the cabin next door. 'You know, you're a smart guy. I like you.' Patricia. She was back from her drinking spree, and I could only guess she was talking to Josh – and what was he doing back so soon?

Patricia continued her diatribe. 'You're not like the others on this boat. They have no idea what real life is all about; they have no *soul*. You take those two next door – Princess and Queenie. That blonde one, moping about 'cause she's lost the *supposed* love of her life – well, guess what, sweetheart? Get over it. Find a new man – they're everywhere! And the other one! The Queen of fucking Sheba. She thinks she's all that. She thinks she *knows*. She doesn't *know*! She's misguided, see?'

Finally, I heard Josh's voice, but he spoke so softly I could only make out a few words – 'smart', 'sweet', and 'friends'.

Then she laughed one of those taunting I-know-better-than-you laughs. 'That's a joke. That girl's not your friend. She's collecting people like they're trinkets for her charm bracelet. I'd watch that one if I was you.'

'Yeah, we're going to have to agree to disagree there, because I like her. And we *are* becoming friends.' Well, I heard that! He *was* sticking up for me.

'Listen, kiddo,' she said, interrupting my thoughts about what great friends Josh and I were becoming. 'You do your thing. But don't say I didn't warn you. Look, I'm going to head back out. I'll catch you later.'

'Later.' And then I heard her leave the boat. I got up and opened the door of my cabin to make sure she was gone. Josh must have heard me, because he popped his head around the corner from his cabin.

'Hi.'

'Hi,' I replied. I really had to concentrate on not staring at his torso, because he was only wearing a pair of shorts. And it was a nice torso.

'Did you hear any of that?'

'Most of it. Boy, she really hates me, huh?'

'I wouldn't take it personally. She kind of hates everyone.'

'Except you.'

'Yeah, except me for some reason.'

'Hey, I thought you were going out with the others.'

'I was going to, but then I realised how tired I was – especially as I didn't really sleep last night. When they left, I took the cart back and then came back to sleep. As soon as I drifted off, Patricia came in and woke me up.'

'Oh. Bummer.'

'Yeah.' I was still avoiding looking at his half-naked body, so of course, I ended up staring at his lips. He must have just licked them. They were shiny and looked very kissable.

'Well, I'm going to try to get some more sleep,' I said, as though the two of us lying on our respective beds with only a paper-thin wall between us was a perfectly platonic way to spend an afternoon.

I mean it was, but I knew I wouldn't be able to sleep. Instead I'd end up lying there thinking about Josh lying on his bunk half-naked and of course, I'd be wondering if he was thinking about me. The whole thing was far too sexually charged for my liking, and even though I was still ridiculously tired, I found myself saying, 'Actually, scratch that. I'm going for a walk instead.'

'I'll come with you.' Josh coming with me wasn't part of my revised plan. A walk was my version of a cold shower. Didn't he know that?

'Sure. Sounds good,' I lied.

'Just let me get a shirt on.' *Yes, for god's sake please put on a shirt! In fact, please never forget your shirt around me again.* Damn him, he was causing a real stir. As I picked up my sandals, I reminded myself in no uncertain terms that I was *not* on this trip to have a holiday romance, especially with someone too young for me who lived on the other side of the world.

I was relieved when we departed the confines of the boat and I could breathe nonsexually charged air. As we walked along the pier away from the boat, I took in huge gulps of it, hoping to clear my head of extremely impure thoughts. *Just friends, just friends, just friends*, I chanted in my head.

We walked past waterfront cafés and bars, and there were a few more boats docked than when we'd arrived. The sun, still warm on our faces, was hanging low in the sky. It was magic hour, the time in the late afternoon when everything was bathed in golden light.

The water in the bay was an incredible blue, deep and inky, with patches of aqua near the surface where the light caught hold. It was a beautiful place, even if there was hardly anyone there – or maybe it was because of that.

Without talking about where we were going, we made our way up to the church we'd seen from the boat as we sailed in. It was just as breathtaking as it had seemed from far off – and much bigger than I'd thought. There was a low wall on the seaward side. I climbed up and swung my legs over so we could sit and look at the water. Josh did the same, coming to rest a few inches from me, our fingers nearly touching. *Just friends, Sarah.*

Away from the boat and fully clothed, the conversation flowed easily with Josh. Sometimes you meet someone, and even though on the surface they seem really different from you, you soon realise that you see the world through a similar lens. I'm not really one to talk about kindred spirits or anything hokey like that, but I found it refreshing talking to someone without having to edit everything I was thinking. As much as I loved my friends back home, too often I'd say something, and they'd tilt their heads to the side a little and look confused.

For some time, I'd felt that maybe I was just really weird. Talking to Josh made me feel understood – normal even.

Our conversation eventually turned to siblings, and we discovered we were both the eldest of two. 'There's this unspoken expectation that you'll be the one to lead the way, to always get it right,' he said matter-of-factly. 'No matter what "it" is.'

'At least in your family, it was unspoken. I was *always* being told to set a good example, to be responsible, to be good. So, I did – I was. Maybe that's why I wasn't exactly what you would call a happy child.' I paused a moment, absorbing what I'd said. I was onto something, and I let the thought continue. 'Even as a little girl, I was hyper-conscious of doing the right thing. I was so afraid to make a mistake.' My heart twinged a little for that girl – for me. 'Meanwhile my sister spent most of her childhood having a ball. She was so cute and charming, and *so* funny. People adored her. Even today she's the freer spirit.'

'So, do you think it's in there somewhere?'

'What?'

'Your free spirit,' he replied.

I looked at him for a moment and then back out at the water. 'I hope so. I'm kind of exhausted by being good all the time. But you know, I put more pressure on myself to be perfect, to get it right, than anyone else does. I'm my own harshest critic. It's tiring.' I hadn't ever expressed it in those terms before – not even to Cat. *Especially* not to Cat.

'I've been thinking a lot about this sort of stuff lately,' Josh said, breaking through my thoughts.

'Oh yeah?'

'What I've realised – and only recently – is that I want my life to be bigger.'

It was such an elegant thought. So simple. Succinct, yet all-encompassing. He didn't need to explain it beyond those few words, because I completely understood. Bigger than routine. Bigger than normal. Bigger than the constraints of expectation.

'Well, this trip is a good start, I'd say.' We shared a smile.

'Yes.'

I remembered the moment on the bus when I'd wondered if we would become friends. It was hard to conceive how, in such a short time, we'd got to the point where he could share something like that with me. Or that I was comfortable enough to say what I'd said, something no one knew about me, not even my closest friends.

Josh and I *were* becoming friends.

When we got back to the marina, the others had returned to the boat – except Patricia, of course – and the all-women boat was docked beside us. Their skipper, Stuart – a guy who in any other circumstance would probably *not* be surrounded by women – looked like the cat who'd got the cream. I knew that look. I'd seen it on the faces of coach drivers I'd worked with in Europe during my tour managing days. That look said, 'I'm going to shag every one of them if I can.' Not that I blamed him – they were a very attractive group of women.

Duncan and Stuart had arranged for all of us to have dinner together that night – except Patricia (again). Duncan had chosen a restaurant he'd been to many times before, and when we arrived, he was greeted with lots of fanfare by an effusive Greek woman with very dark curly hair and warm brown eyes. She regarded the large group and waved her hands dramatically at the waiters, indicating for them to move tables together so we could sit at one long table – family style.

We stood out of the way as tables were lifted above heads, chairs moved two at a time, and place settings reset. When everything was in place, the woman smiled and told us to 'Sit, sit, sit,' as she bustled about giving us menus.

I sat with Josh to the left of me, Marie to my right with Gary next to her. Hannah was across from Marie, with Gerry next to her and Duncan on her right. On the other side of Josh was one of the women from the other boat, a petite, redheaded American named Kiersten.

Kiersten was the only one from her boat who wasn't vying for the attention of her skipper during dinner. Instead, all her energies were directed at Josh, and it was quite entertaining watching it all unfold. She was behaving as though she'd been at sea for months with nary a male in sight, rather than on a boat for one whole night and one whole day. And she was ploughing through the white wine like it was water.

The flirtations began as giggles – everything Josh said was hilarious, even when he wasn't saying it to her – and then she ratcheted it up a few notches by adding hair twisting and licking her lips a lot. All the while, she was getting drunker.

When she put her hand on Josh's thigh, he jumped in his chair, then scooched it so close to mine, our elbows bumped while we ate. Marie, Hannah, Gerry and I watched this spectacle while swapping amused looks.

'So, Hannah, how do you like the calamari?' I asked, as though nothing weird was happening to my left.

'Hmm. I can do the whole Greek salad thing, but I can't say I'm particularly into the rest of Greek food so far.' Her face scrunched up as she looked up and down the table at the array of dishes.

I shook my head at her. 'You're gonna be pretty hungry for the rest of the trip if we don't find you *something* you like.'

Marie tried to help. 'Goat?' she asked, passing Hannah a

plate piled high with roasted goat meat. Hannah's face went from scrunched to contorted, and Marie put the goat back where it had come from. She looked at me with a smile. 'I guess not.'

Just then Kiersten laughed loudly and Josh practically climbed onto my lap. 'You alright there?' I asked him quietly.

'Not really,' he said, pointedly. '*Please help me*,' he added in an urgent whisper.

I made eye contact with him. 'Seriously?'

'Yes.'

'Like, how much help do you want?'

'*A large amount of help.*'

'Like, "pretend to be your girlfriend" level of help?'

'*Yes. Please.*'

I looked over at Marie, who was listening in. 'Can you please hand me the goat?'

She passed it over, and I made a huge show of putting some on Josh's plate. 'Here you go, babe,' I said loudly enough for almost everyone at the table to hear. 'You wanted to try the goat, right?'

Josh caught on. 'Sure, honey. Thanks.' I took a piece of tomato from his plate with my fingers, and put it in my mouth, licking my fingers seductively.

We smiled at each other, and I added a cute little nose wrinkle to really seal the deal. Kiersten watched me agog. I winked at her and kept eating. She didn't miss a beat, suddenly turning her attention to her left and laughing at Stuart's last comment, something she couldn't possibly have heard. She was a professional-level flirter, I had to give her that.

'How's that?' I asked.

'I think it did the trick. Thanks.'

'Any time, *compadre*.'

Later that night, Hannah, Josh and I were sitting on the front deck of the boat, sipping some of Hannah's Scotch – straight up, no ice – from plastic cups. After we told her about the liquor prices at the store, she'd rushed over to buy some.

'I kept thinking, "What's going to happen here? Do you want to have sex with me? Where would we even do that? We're both living on boats – *and* sharing cabins!" I mean, seriously, what the hell was she thinking?' Josh was obviously still reeling from Kiersten's overt sexual pursuit.

'Well, maybe she thought we all wanted dinner *and* a show,' replied Hannah. She and I both laughed while Josh glared at us.

'Oh, come on,' I teased, 'it was funny.' When he didn't respond, I added, 'What? Too soon?'

'Okay, I'm going to bed.' He got up to leave.

'Nooo. Sit. We're only teasing you,' I said, tugging on his hand.

'It's all good. I'm just tired. Thanks for helping me out, Sarah. And thanks for the Scotch, Hannah.'

We waved him off with, 'You're welcome,' and 'Goodnight.'

When he was below deck, Hannah topped up my drink and said quietly, 'He likes you, you know?'

'Josh? No. We're friends – that's all.'

'He does. I've seen him watching you when you're not looking.' I shook my head. It wasn't what I wanted to hear. Even if I was attracted to him – which since the bare torso incident, I realised I was – I didn't want it to be reciprocated. Because it would mean that something could happen. And I didn't want anything to happen. I'd sworn off men for a good reason, and I wasn't going to get my heart tangled up in a stupid holiday romance, especially with someone who was becoming a friend.

No way. Hannah was wrong.

Chapter Five

Hannah was right.

After she mentioned it the night before, my senses went on high alert for any sign of attraction from Josh. We made it all the way through breakfast the following morning without so much of a whisper of it, and I nearly convinced myself Hannah had imagined it, but then he did something that changed my mind.

We were about to set sail for Naxos. Josh was seated in the dining nook fiddling with his camera, and I had just finished cleaning up after breakfast with Marie. As I walked past, he grabbed my hand and said, 'Hey.' Tingles shot up my arm. 'Come 'ere.' He pulled me gently towards him, and I obeyed. 'Let me see.' He turned me slightly and looked at my hip.

Part of my tattoo was peeking out from my waistband, and I realised he was asking to see the rest. Without a word, I pulled the waistband down a couple of centimetres, revealing the tiny spray of cherry blossoms.

'I like it,' he said, looking up at me with those steel grey eyes. I felt a twinge in my stomach and another one further below.

I righted my shorts and replied, 'Thanks,' as nonchalantly

as I could. Then I went up on deck before he gave me any more twinges. Twinges were not good when you were trying to stay 'just friends' with someone.

Marie, who had seen the whole thing from the kitchen, joined me on deck shortly after. She raised her eyebrows at me – not like she was being judgemental, but more like, 'what's going on with you two?' I shrugged my shoulders at her. I had no bloody idea.

'You know,' she said in a low voice, 'Gary is a younger man.' She emphasised 'younger'.

'Oh?' She certainly didn't look older than Gary. It also didn't take a rocket scientist to work out where she was going with all of this.

'Yes, and he pursued me for a long time before I gave in.'

'Gave in?'

'Uh huh. I resisted because I'm ten years older than him.'

'Wow. You don't look older than Gary.' I figured I should pay the woman a compliment; whatever she was doing to look after herself was working. 'So, can I ask how old you are?'

'I'm forty-eight.'

'Marie, you seriously don't look forty-eight. I would have said you were only a little bit older than me.'

'Thanks.' She smiled. 'I think it's being with a younger man that keeps me young. They have a lot of *energy*.' She raised her eyebrows at me again, and this time I laughed. 'Look, this really isn't any of my business. I'll butt out,' she added.

But I was quickly learning that when eight people live on a fifteen-metre boat, everything becomes everybody's business and, besides, I didn't want her to butt out. I wanted advice. 'No, you don't need to. I mean, I don't know what to do here.

I'm not looking for anything – casual or otherwise – and it's not like we can spend any *real time* together if you know what I mean.' I paused. 'Though I *do* like him ...'

'And he's *so* handsome,' she interrupted.

It was my turn to raise my eyebrows at her. 'Really?'

'A blind woman could see that Josh is a good-looking man.'

'A good-looking *younger* man,' I said, bringing us full circle.

'Look, you don't need to decide anything right now. Enjoy the flirtation. If something happens, let it.'

'But—'

'No buts. You can't control everything, Sarah, especially feelings.'

I considered what she'd said. I did like to control things. Maybe that's why the whole thing with Josh was messing with my head – and other parts of me. I didn't want any kind of romantic entanglement with him – or with anyone – and I did *not* want anything happening in such close proximity to six other people.

*

The sail to Naxos was incredible. Unlike our trip to Ios, we could sail the whole distance without power, and for most of it the boat was at a forty-five-degree angle. I had to wedge myself into the galley to make a ploughman's lunch of tzatziki, bread, tomatoes, olives and feta. Josh helped to ferry the dishes to everyone who was up on deck, which was everyone except Patricia. She was still sleeping. Shocker, I know.

After sending Josh up with six plates – one at a time – I negotiated the ladder myself and popped out into a mist of briny sea spray. It was one of those moments you read about in travel magazines, with the sun bright in the sky, and the sounds of the mainsail snapping against the wind and the hull smacking into the waves.

With a little difficulty, I settled onto a bench next to Marie and held on to the railing with one hand while I ate with my plate balanced on my lap. She smiled at me as she finished a bite. 'This lunch is delicious. Thank you so much!'

'Of course! It's my pleasure.'

'Gary and I'll do the grocery shopping next time, and we'll do the lunch prep. That way we all get a chance to help out.'

'Sounds perfect, Marie.' I shoved a huge blob of tzatziki into my mouth with a piece of bread. It was delicious, and I moaned with pleasure at the taste.

'I told you it was good!'

I had literally bitten off more than I could chew, so it was a while before I could reply. 'I could happily drown in a vat of this stuff.' She laughed, and I took another bite of bread piled up with tzatziki. I was blissfully in love with life.

'You know,' she said, leaning closer, 'I'm worried I may have been a little too nosy this morning.'

I immediately looked up to see who might be listening to us. Even though Marie was right next to me, it was a small space and not really the best place to have a private chat. Josh was deep in conversation with Gary and Gerry, something about studying abroad. Hannah appeared to be reading a fashion magazine, which was an incredible feat considering the angle of the boat and the whipping wind. And Duncan was, of course, skippering the boat. Still, I lowered my voice.

'You don't need to apologise. You're just looking out for me, and I enjoy talking to you. It's one of the reasons I booked this trip – to meet new people. And I think we have a great group here.'

'I agree. We do. Even if one of us is a little, um, *challenging*.' I didn't need to ask who she was referring to.

'I mean, can you imagine being on the other boat with all of those flirty women?' I asked.

She laughed. 'God no! I wouldn't want them anywhere near Gary, either. That one from last night, the redhead, she seemed hell-bent on getting together with Josh.'

'Yeah, poor guy.'

'Well, as long as I didn't overstep earlier ...'

'You didn't. We're good.'

She took the last bite of her lunch and signalled she was taking the dish below deck. She navigated the short distance carefully, stopping to take Gerry's and Gary's plates, then disappeared below. I went back to my own lunch, and right as I took another big bite, Josh caught my eye.

He'd pushed his sunglasses down onto the bridge of his nose and was looking over them. He smiled at me and then slid them back into place. Damn those twinges. I promised myself to rein it all in – all of it. The attraction, the flirting, everything.

*

After docking at the marina in Naxos, Duncan took us to a scooter rental place. I did my absolute best to convince the man with the scooters that a passport was as good as a driver's licence, but he wasn't having any of it – not even when I offered a large deposit. I was going to have ride on the back of someone else's – and that person was going to have to rent a bigger scooter. With the two couples sharing and Patricia off at the nearest bar, it came down to Hannah and Josh.

And when Hannah said, 'I don't know how confident I would be riding a 70CC. I've only ridden a 50CC scooter before,' I did nothing to assure her that she'd be fine and that there was barely a difference between the two.

Nope. I kept quiet and looked at Josh, who didn't miss a beat. 'You can ride with me,' he said.

And envisioning sitting behind him on a scooter, my legs straddling him, my arms wrapped around his waist, I said, 'Okay,' and then followed it up with a slightly too enthusiastic 'Thanks!' A niggling thought about keeping things platonic raised its head. I shushed it.

The 'who's riding with who' thing settled, we donned our helmets, climbed onto our respective scooters, and followed Duncan and Gerry out of the town and up into the hills. It was getting late in the day, but Duncan wanted to take us to a vantage point where we could look out over the town and the marina.

We pulled off the road and took in the view. Like Santorini and Ios, Naxos was magnificent, especially with the sun low in the sky, streaking the rugged landscape with broad strokes of pink and orange. Unlike the previous islands, however, Naxos tugged at my heartstrings a little. It felt almost like a homecoming.

'Tomorrow we'll head out after brekkie and explore the whole island. There are lots of ruins, and nice little towns to see. We'll get lunch in one of 'em – I know a great place. You'll love it.'

We got back on our scooters – I placed my hands as chastely as possible on Josh's waist – and headed back to the marina.

As we were keeping the scooters overnight, we lined them up next to our boat. Duncan grabbed a heavy chain from the boat, ran it around all the scooters, and padlocked them together; he'd clearly done this before.

I suddenly realised how hungry I was. 'Duncan! What're we doing for dinner tonight?' Duncan hadn't led us astray yet when it came to food. We were welcomed everywhere we went – he seemed to know everyone on the islands – and the food was always excellent. Fresh, tasty, authentic and delicious. I was in foodie heaven. He proved himself again that night when we settled in at a waterfront café for pizzas, sans Patricia of course.

Although it was a departure from the traditional Greek fare we'd been enjoying, the café didn't disappoint. I devoured a whole pizza to myself – without any self-consciousness and without any remorse. I thought about it briefly afterwards, realising how freeing it was not to berate myself over some-thing I ate, or to calculate it in terms of how much cardio I would have to do to negate it. I hadn't thought about calories or working out in days. It felt good.

After dinner, there was some discussion about what to do next. Most of the others wanted to go to a bar Duncan had mentioned, but I was keen to get back to the boat. I'd slept better the night before than I had for days, thanks to Hannah's sleeping pills, but I was still catching up, and I wanted a chilled-out evening. 'I'm going to head back,' I said to the group.

'I'll come with you,' replied Josh. My stomach flip-flopped, and I looked at the others. The guys didn't seem to care what was going on with Josh and me, but Marie and Gerry exchanged a look, and Hannah's expression soured. I didn't know what else to say, so I turned on my heels and started walking away. 'Have a great night,' I called over my shoulder. It didn't take long for Josh to catch up.

'Hey, wait up.' He fell into step beside me.

'Good pizza, huh?' I was really going to have to work on my conversation skills.

'Yeah. Seriously good pizza.' So was he.

We both fell silent, and I became overly aware of the lack of conversation. Since we'd met, we'd done nothing but talk – books, movies, travel, family, life, the universe, everything – and suddenly I was struggling to find anything to say. Apparently, my hormones had rendered my brain useless.

Then I realised it was the first time we'd been alone since he'd done the flirty thing with my tattoo. My senses went on high alert. Was he going to make a move? And if he did, would I let him? When we arrived at the boat, Josh offered to make us a drink. Was that a good idea, or the worst idea ever?

'Sounds good,' I said, even though I was leaning towards it being the worst idea ever. 'I'll wait up here,' I heard myself say, trying to do what I'd promised myself – rein it in. Because all I could think of was being naked with him on his bunk, and I knew that was far less likely to happen if we didn't go anywhere near his cabin.

I carefully climbed onto the top deck of the boat, directly over the dining nook and the galley, and got settled on the inflatable dinghy. I'd found the spot a couple of days before when I was looking for a comfy place to read. A few minutes later a cup appeared over my shoulder, and I gratefully took it. I had a sip while he sat beside me. 'You make a hell of a G&T, you know.'

'I do know. I even have it on my résumé.'

'You do not.' I smiled at him over the rim of my cup, grateful he'd broken the awkwardness between us. I took another sip. I missed drinking out of a proper glass, but otherwise, it was a good drink.

'No, you're right. But I did tend bar in college so I could put it on there if I wanted to.'

'Ever thought about coming out of retirement?'

'No, this software thing seems to be taking off, so I think I'll stick with that for now.' He winked at me, which was kind of flirty, but not enough to scare me away. There were a lot of stars out, and I stared up at the sky, sipping my drink. It started to warm me through.

'Hey, Sarah?'

'Yeah.'

'I hope you don't mind, but you know, it's a small boat, and I couldn't help hearing when you were talking to Hannah about your ex earlier.'

'Oh. I thought you were reading.'

'I was. It's just ... I got pulled out of the story once in a while by some of the things you said.'

'Oh.'

'He's an asshole, you know.'

'Yeah, I know.'

'Not all guys are like that.'

'I know that too,' I replied far too defensively.

'Sorry. I shouldn't have said anything.'

I sighed. 'It's okay. It's just ... I have the *worst* taste in men.'

He didn't respond and when I looked at him, he had an odd expression on his face. Did he think I meant him? *Oh crap.* I mean, it wasn't as if we had anything going – not really – but maybe he thought I was lumping him in with all the others. *Double crap.*

I gracelessly changed the subject to him. It was either that, or go into some ridiculously long explanation of what I'd meant, which would mean admitting I was attracted to him.

'What about you?' I asked, trying to keep my voice light.

'Me?' He looked surprised.

'Yes. You leave anyone special at home?' He shook his head and took a sip. 'How about any exes you want to whinge about?'

'No. There's no one.'

'No exes?'

'Nope.'

'Ever?' I was intrigued. Meeting a man of twenty-eight with no exes was like sighting a unicorn.

'Well, sure, yes. A long time ago, but I don't want to whinge about it, as you say.'

'Okay.' Not a unicorn then.

'I'm celibate.' I *really* didn't see that coming – a unicorn after all.

'Celibate?'

'Yes. I haven't been with anyone for several years.'

'By choice?' I tried to wrap my mind around a cute, smart, funny guy who could probably get any girl he wanted, but chose to forgo sex.

'Yep.' And then, as if convincing himself more so than me, he added, 'Definitely by choice. And it's good. I don't actually want anyone in my life – to be part of a couple, or in a relationship, or anything.'

So, what's with all the flirting then, huh? 'Were you hurt? Badly? Is that why?' I could address the flirting thing later.

81

'Yes and no. I mean, I had a girlfriend – in college. It ended.'

'How long were you together?'

'Two years – just over two years.' *This is like pulling teeth.*

'That's quite a while. How did it end?'

'She met someone else – she didn't cheat or anything. She ended it because she realised that if she had feelings for someone else, then she probably wasn't in love with me anymore.'

'Oh.' I couldn't help but feel for him. It had clearly affected him. I wondered if people felt the same way towards me when I told them about Neil. I needed to stop talking about Neil – I didn't want anyone's pity.

Josh was frowning. I promised myself to drop the subject – as soon as I asked one more thing. 'So, you've not dated, or had sex, or *anything* since then?'

'No.'

'Wow!' I couldn't help it – it just came out. Fortunately, Josh seemed undeterred by my amazement.

'I realised after we broke up that loving her was like an addiction – I had become addicted to feeling like that, being part of a couple, I mean. And it wasn't so much that I missed *her* – I mean, I did – but it was more that I missed the feeling of being part of something, the relationship itself. And it *sucked*. I felt like shit. And I couldn't understand why anyone would risk feeling like that. I never wanted to feel like that again. So, I've stayed away. I'm free and clear of it.'

I couldn't think of anything to say, so I stayed silent.

He continued, 'And ...' he laughed wryly '... *so* many people tell me I just haven't met the right woman yet – as if that's going to change my whole way of thinking.' I couldn't help but think that maybe they were right, but I didn't say it. I didn't want to add fuel to the fire. And I certainly didn't want him thinking that I thought *I* was the right woman.

I mean, I was just someone he met on holiday. We would probably never even see each other again after the trip, so I was hardly the one to convert him back to love.

We didn't speak for a while. My heart ached a little for him. He seemed so raw, even though this had happened years before. It was as though he carried this around with him right below the surface, which I'd somehow scratched, and there it was in all its fresh, gory glory.

And then my mind went where it absolutely shouldn't have.

I'd sworn off men – and wished that one, in particular, would die a heinous death – and I was spending time with a guy who I could talk to easily, who was becoming a good friend, and who I increasingly found attractive. And he was clearly attracted to me too. And even though he said all that stuff about love and sex and not getting close to anyone, wasn't that what we were doing? Getting close? And what if we lived in the same city? Would we abandon these self-protecting philosophies? Would we be together?

'I should go to bed,' I said suddenly. Seeing as I'd asked myself some fairly profound questions, I thought it was the best thing to do. I got up, nearly falling on top of him in the process. He helped me right myself with a steady hand.

'Sarah ...' He looked as if he wanted to say something. I couldn't read his expression, but I felt like shit. I'd made him dredge up all the stuff he'd locked away so intently, and now I was battling with my own edicts about love and sex.

He didn't finish his thought, so I said goodnight and went below deck. Shortly after, I heard him come below and close the door to his cabin. I quickly got ready for bed and was about to climb into my bunk when I heard his door open. I stood still, listening. There was a faint knock on my door.

I opened it a few centimetres, and we locked eyes. 'I'm sorry ...' we both said at the same time. We laughed – nervous laughter.

'You go first,' he said.

'I'm sorry I dragged all of that up. I didn't mean to pry or to make you feel bad.'

'I know. It's fine, *really*. The weird thing is, I've never been able to express it like that before. It's the first time I've said a lot of that stuff, but it's all good. I promise I'm not upset.'

I sighed, relieved. 'So, what are you sorry about?'

He paused, as though he was considering his words carefully. 'After you came down here, I realised I must be confusing the hell out of you. I went on this whole big rant about never being with anyone ever again, and yet it must be really obvious that I like you. I mean, *like* like you.'

I nodded. So, I didn't imagine it.

'I can pontificate for hours about the merits of celibacy and give you all the reasons in the world why I'll never have a girlfriend again, but at the same time, I feel like I can tell you anything. And I feel like we're becoming friends – close friends. Not to mention you're sexy as hell. And ...' he took a deep breath '... I think if we lived in the same city, I'd ask you out.' My resolve was weakening with every word, and the twinges came back with full force.

'I didn't want you to think I'm not attracted to you, because I am. And ever since I first saw you standing on the pier, I've wanted to do this.' Then he leaned down and touched his lips to mine in the most gentle, sweet kiss – ever.

84

When he pulled away, all I could say was a breathless, 'Oh. Okay.'

Resolve. Completely. Gone.

He smiled. 'Goodnight, Sarah.'

'Goodnight, Josh.' His eyes stayed on mine as I closed the door. I sat down on my bunk as shivers worked their way up and down my spine. The only thing I knew for sure – right then – was that the guy could kiss.

Oh, and that I was in serious trouble.

*

I woke to the rumbling of the boat's engine. 'Hannah,' I whispered, but there was no answer. My eyes adjusted to the darkness and I saw she wasn't in her bunk. I checked my watch – 2:00am. We were moving, which wasn't in Duncan's original plan for the trip, so I threw on some shorts and opened the cabin door.

The lights in the main cabin were on, and I could hear voices up on deck, so I climbed the ladder to join the others. There was a flurry of activity, as Josh and Gary coiled the tow lines and Duncan steered the boat away from the dock. Gerry, Marie and Hannah were huddled together on one of the bench seats, sharing a blanket. I wondered how Hannah had got out of her bunk without waking me; I must have been in a deep sleep.

'Hey, guys, what's going on?' I asked no one in particular.

Gary, who was closest to me, responded. 'We've kicked Patricia off the boat.'

'Thank god!' said Hannah from behind him.

'Why? What happened?'

85

Duncan answered me. 'She came back to the boat about an hour ago with a group of people, and they were really loud, and when I came up and asked her to send them away, she refused.'

'Didn't you hear any of that, Sarah?' Hannah scolded. She was annoyed with me for some reason.

'No, sorry. I guess I slept through it all.'

'Anyway,' Gary continued, 'there was a bit of a kerfuffle, and I came out, then Josh did, and we sent them on their way. Then Patricia said she was leaving the trip.'

Duncan finished the story. 'So, we let her pack, and she left. And now I'm moving the boat to the middle of the marina, so she can't change her drunken mind.' It was the first time Duncan acknowledged that Patricia was a drunkard.

A lot had happened since I'd said goodnight to Josh. 'Okay. So that's it? She doesn't get to come back?'

'Nope. She's gone for good,' said Duncan.

'I didn't care for her,' added Gerry. 'She was rude.' That was putting it mildly.

'I'm glad she's gone,' said Hannah. 'Did you know she called me *princess*? To my *face*? And she didn't mean it as a compliment.'

I commiserated with Hannah. 'Yeah, I wasn't too fond of her either. I overheard her saying nasty stuff about us when she thought she was alone on the boat with Josh.'

'Bitch!'

'I thought she was okay,' said Josh. All eyes turned to him.

'Well, you shared a room with her, Josh, *and* spent the most time with her, so you probably have a better understanding of what she was really like ...' Marie was so diplomatic, even after everything that had happened. Meanwhile, I'd started singing 'Ding-Dong! The Witch is Dead' in my head.

Josh spoke up. 'Well, I guess. I mean, she was an interesting person. For some reason, she didn't seem to have a problem with me, but she was really bitter and angry about – well, pretty much everything else.' Josh was also more gracious than I would have been.

'You'll have a room to yourself now,' said Hannah. And then she looked right at me. What the hell was that supposed to mean? Did she want me out of our cabin?

'I guess so, yeah. No more snoring, so that's good,' said Josh, tactfully.

Duncan shut off the boat engine. 'This is good enough. We'll drop anchor here, and in the morning, we'll head back in to get our scooters. Even if she comes back tomorrow, I'll have the boat all locked up, and she won't be able to go below.'

'I doubt she'll come back,' said Gary. 'She was pretty clear about her disdain for us. And if she does, we can do the whole thing all over again.'

Marie stood up and hugged her husband. 'You're a good bouncer, honey.' They really were cute together.

'I'm going back to bed!' declared Hannah. We all said our goodnights and made our way below deck. When I climbed into my bunk, Hannah rolled over to face me. 'I would have thought you'd be sleeping next door tonight.' Snarky.

'No. Why?'

'Well, you said that if Josh was your boyfriend, you'd definitely want to sleep with him, *and* ...' She didn't finish the thought to its obvious conclusion.

'Josh is not my boyfriend,' I whispered, pointedly.

'Mm-hmm,' she replied, smugly, and rolled over. Now she

was all pissed off with me, and for nothing, I might add. I let it go; it was the middle of the night, and I figured I would talk it out with her the next day. We'd just got rid of one person who didn't like me – I didn't want Hannah to hate me too.

Chapter Six

As I roused myself from sleep, my mind leapt to the incredible kiss Josh had sprung on me the night before. My stomach did a little flip-flop. Then I remembered it couldn't – well, shouldn't – happen. My mind started screaming at me: *he's practically a teenager! He lives on the other side of a giant ocean! He's a commitment-phobe!!* My flip-flopping stomach just flopped.

Men who tell you they don't want to be in a relationship generally mean they don't want to be in a relationship. Full stop. I liked Josh, but there was no denying that getting tangled up with him was a bad idea. *BAD.*

But less than two hours later, as we rode around Naxos on our scooters, my resolve had dissolved. Having tasked myself with keeping things platonic, I was doing a superbly crappy job. For one thing, my hands were in his pockets, *and* I may have been leaning into him more than was necessary to stay on the back of his scooter.

The pocket thing was legitimate, or so I kept telling myself, because my hands got cold while we were riding. But I had no good reason for the rest of it – the leaning, touching his stomach through the fabric of his jacket, squeezing my thighs around him. All of it was inexcusable considering how much it was going to suck when this whole thing blew up in my face. I was ridiculous.

But my body seemed to have a mind of its own. The thing was, Josh wasn't the only one who'd been celibate for an epoch. My drought wasn't quite as long as his, but once I got a whiff of how good the back of his neck smelled, my mind turned to mush and the rest of me turned into a raging ball of oestrogen. And, Josh was flirting back – running his hand along my thigh, squeezing my hands through his jacket, flexing his abs whenever I touched his stomach.

So, it wasn't all my fault.

As we explored the island, we formed a convoy of four scooters, with Duncan and Gerry in the lead and the rest of us following like baby ducks – Josh and me, Gary and Marie, and then Hannah. From time to time, we pulled off the road so Duncan could show us something cool – or so he said. The stops varied in levels of coolness and Duncan's commentary was, well, *interesting*.

At the first stop, he regaled us with his version of the local history. 'There was this big head honcho guy, and he totally loved being all-powerful and stuff, and he was totally up himself, so he decided that the people should build a monument to him. And then the people decided they didn't like being ruled by him, so they revolted and told him to finish building it himself, which he didn't, 'cause he didn't know how to do any of that stuff, so the project was abandoned. This arch is all they built before they revolted.'

Duncan motioned to a giant rectangular arch and nodded his head as he regarded it solemnly. Perhaps he was imagining all the Greek slaves telling the big head honcho guy to take his job and shove it. The arch was remarkably intact, but I had seen a *lot* of ruins when I was touring, and I guess they ruined me – pun intended – from getting excited about an ancient erection. I was more interested in Duncan's take on history, which got even more entertaining as the day progressed.

'The people of Naxos built these pigeon houses to house their pigeons.' Halfway up a giant hill, we had stopped by the side of the road and were looking at a sloping field filled with large clay structures – pigeon houses, apparently.

'But why did the people of Naxos build houses for their pigeons?' asked Hannah. It was a reasonable question. Were they carrier pigeons? Were they domesticated? Were they *food*?

'Because they thought they were nice,' replied Duncan. *Okay, thanks, Duncan – that clears everything up.* The rest of us looked at each other while Duncan, oblivious to the fact that we were all baffled, put his helmet on and climbed onto his scooter. As Gerry climbed on the back, he called out over the sound of the engine, 'Next stop is for morning tea!' I liked the sound of that. Maybe we could get Duncan to tell us more about the pigeons.

We rode further into the undulating hills of Naxos and right as we crested another, we pulled off into a dusty make-shift car park next to a cliff-side bar. The view was incredible, and our small group made a lot of noise with all our oohing and aahing. We could see down through the peaks and valleys of red earth to the jagged bays of aquamarine water. It seemed like we were the only souls for miles. Perhaps we were.

We were greeted effusively by an attractive Greek man of about forty-something, so not the only ones there, but the only patrons. He signalled that we should take seats at a table outside where we could continue to take in the view. We gathered around a long table as he took our orders for soft drinks and iced coffee, or 'Nes' as the locals call it. I knew Nes was just Nescafé coffee granules, sugar, water and a bit of condensed milk frothed up and served to tourists for four euros a pop. It was a total rip-off, so I ordered a Coke No Sugar instead. Before the drinks arrived, Josh excused himself to take photos, and I caught myself watching him go.

'Having a fun day?' asked Hannah from the seat next to mine. Was I imagining the pointedness of her question, or was she was just being friendly? I looked down the table to where the two couples were talking about Paris. Gary and Marie were going there on their next trip. They seemed pretty caught up in their discussion, so I figured it was a safe enough time to talk things through with Hannah.

'Oh, for sure.' Our drinks arrived, and our host arranged them around the table, remembering precisely who ordered what. 'You?'

'What's not to love?' she replied, as she fiddled with her straw and took a sip of her iced coffee.

'Right? I mean the sun's out, the views are epic.' I looked out at the one we were enjoying. Then I lowered my voice. 'Duncan's history lessons are quite, uh ...'

She smiled back at me conspiratorially. 'Creative? That the word you're looking for?'

I was winning her back. 'Exactly. I can't imagine how badly I would have been crucified on my tours had I spouted such *creative* histories.' I looked over at Duncan, who was oblivious to our conversation. I was glad considering I was pretty much using him to get back in Hannah's good graces. 'How's your scooter?'

'It seems fine. I'm loving riding on these roads; you really get to lean into the curves, you know?'

'Totally. Although truth be told, Josh is not the best rider.'
Great. Now I'm throwing Josh under the bus to score points.
'Oh?'

'Yeah, I mean it's mostly okay, but there have been a few times when I was worried that we'd slide off the road into the gravel.'

'Why?'

'Well, he's not very experienced – this is his first time riding a scooter – so he sometimes takes the corners a little too sharply. More than once today I've thought that shorts were a bad option.' She looked at me quizzically. 'Because if I come off the scooter, I'm going to have serious gravel rash.'

'I'm really sorry, Sarah. I should have got a bigger scooter. I mean, I'm not like a really experienced rider or anything, but I've at least done it a few times before – in Mexico.'

I needed to curb my embellishment of Josh's riding, or Hannah was going to insist that she and Josh swap and *she* ride me around. 'Oh, no. You don't need to apologise. It's all good – he's getting better as the day goes on. It's fine really. I didn't mean to make you feel bad about it or anything.' I'd gone from having a friendly chat to grovelling.

'You know,' said Hannah, interrupting my self-rebuke, 'I've worked out who Josh reminds me of.'

'Oh yeah?'

'Yeah. He reminds me of my ex.' *Oh dear.* 'Maybe that's why I haven't really warmed to him.' *Yes, Hannah, that would explain it.* I thought it best to get her mind away from Josh and onto something else.

'So, what happened there? You haven't really talked about it much,' I inquired. She bit her lip. *Oops. Retreat. Retreat.* 'You don't have to if you don't want to.'

'No, it's okay. I don't mind talking about it. I guess the best way to explain it, is that he didn't love me, and he was just using me for sex.'

'Hannah, that's awful!'

'Yeah. He kept telling me he loved me and I would get all caught up in it, but it transpired that he didn't. It never went anywhere. Actually, *we* never went anywhere. Literally.'

'Like out?' She nodded. 'He never took you out?' She shook her head. 'Not even to the movies?'

'Especially not to the movies. Not to dinner. Not anywhere.' I was genuinely appalled. I also empathised. Her ex sounded a lot like mine.

'What a prick,' I replied, eloquently. Marie's head popped up. I was talking too loudly. I lowered my voice. 'Hannah, you know you didn't deserve that, right?'

'Thanks,' she said weakly.

'No, I mean it!' I leaned closer. 'You are a gorgeous, accomplished, smart woman. You deserve to be with someone who is proud of you and treats you well.' In truth, I barely knew Hannah, and I was only making educated guesses about how wonderful she was, but I also knew that if I was on the other side of this conversation – and I had been too many times – *I* would want a pep talk.

'Thanks, Sarah.' She seemed to mean it. I'd done something right.

'You know, even though he reminds you of your crappy ex, Josh is a good guy.'

She stared out at the view. 'He probably is.' She paused, and I waited. 'I guess, I'm feeling a little left out with all the couples on board.'

'Hannah, we're not a couple,' I said, as convincingly as I

could. She looked at me, but I couldn't tell if she believed me or not.

'Well, you seem really cosy. I just ...'

'What?'

'When you told me you and Josh weren't together – you know on the first day – I was so glad we were roommates. I thought we'd be two single gals together in the Greek Islands – you know?'

'I guess.'

'But we haven't really got to do that. You're off with Josh a lot.' She sipped her Nes. I liked Hannah, but it seemed she and I had different ideas about the trip. I was open to making friends but not to the exclusion of others. I didn't *think* I was doing that with Josh. Maybe I was.

Regardless, it was Hannah's holiday too, and I didn't want her feeling left out. 'I'm glad you told me about feeling left out. I'm sorry about that. I'll be more conscious of it, I promise.'

She smiled and thanked me, and I got the feeling it mattered a lot to her that I'd said that. I wondered how Josh would take being told we were too cliquey. Speak of the devil, he chose that exact moment to come back to the table. I watched Hannah watch Josh. Was she comparing him to her ex again and, if she was, would she land on the side of Josh being a good guy?

I hoped so. My roommate and the boy next door were the closest people to me in our little group, and I needed there to be peace. I was relieved when Josh asked Hannah about her drink, forcing her to engage with him rather than just glaring at him.

When we'd all finished our drinks, Duncan gave us the

not-so-subtle signal we were leaving by waving his arm around in the air and yelling, 'We're moving out!' like we were a bikie gang or something. We settled the bill and filed out to the parking lot, thanking our host as we waved goodbye. I wondered when his next group would come or if he'd be on his own for the rest of the day. There wasn't a lot of traffic where we were.

Josh climbed onto our scooter and rocked it back off the kickstand. I climbed on behind him and happen to glance over at Hannah as she got onto hers. 'You okay?' she mouthed. I nodded as though I wasn't really, but that I was being brave by riding with Josh. Poor Josh. I was going to have to find a way to assure her that Josh's riding skills had vastly improved since the start of the day.

'Next stop, the beach!' shouted Duncan over the screeching buzz of our scooters.

'Awesome!' exclaimed Josh, steering the scooter away from the café. We'd talked about the beach over breakfast. Josh was excited because the only beaches he had ever been to *in his life* were on the shores of Lake Michigan. This would be his first time swimming in an actual sea. Yes, really. *I* was excited about the beach because I am Australian and therefore it is part of my biological makeup.

We descended to the coast along winding roads, a little caravan of travellers. What a glorious day it was in the Greek Islands. Out of habit, I looked at my watch to check the time. Or rather I looked at where my watch would normally have been, but I hadn't put it on that morning – deliberately.

Even though this may not seem like a big deal, it was to me. At home, I lived by my watch. I am one of those people who is never late – well almost never. I plan my activities, my workouts, my chores, and my classes down to the minute. I'm a bit of a freak, actually – a totally organised freak.

But as I was holding my watch, ready to put it on like I did every morning of my life, I took a moment to think through the previous days on the boat. I realised I had barely even looked at my watch the whole time – and when I did it was usually out of habit more than anything else.

I'd eaten when I was hungry, and I'd slept when I was tired. For the first time since I could remember, I didn't need to know what time it was. So, I left it off.

Only days before, I had been a giant ball of stress, but with the warm air rushing past me, the sun on my upturned face, I recognised that sometime since I got on the boat, the tension had eased, then seeped away entirely. I was on holiday, and it felt amazing.

We pulled up at the beach and parked in a small, but busy car park. It was not the most beautiful beach I'd ever seen. Australia does beaches pretty well and this beach, with its grey sand and murky water, would not rate highly back home. But as I'd *just* said to myself, I was on holiday. I was also somewhere new – a new place to experience, to soak in – and when I thought about it in those terms, the beach was fine.

There were several buildings close by, including a rudimentary bathroom, where Gerry, Hannah and I went to change into our swimsuits. Marie declined to join us, and I would soon find out she'd made the smartest decision.

Despite the heat of the sun beating down on us, despite the anticipation of cooling off in the murky Naxos water, it was way too cold. I'm talking shockingly, if-I-had-testicles-they-would-have-leapt-up-into-my-throat cold. I bravely waded in up to my crotch, then completely wussed out. No number of taunts from Josh or Hannah or any of the others was going to convince me that swimming in that water would be fun.

I trudged awkwardly out of the small breakers and dried myself as best I could with my super-absorbent travel towel. Travel? Yes. It was compact – well, *tiny*. Super-absorbent? Not so much. Still, I made do and then went back into the crumbling bathroom to revert to my shorts and top. By the time I joined Marie on the beach, two little boys – obviously brothers – were playing with the others in the water while their mother watched from the shore.

Josh was loving it. He was picking the kids up and tossing them up in the air so they could dive into the water. They resurfaced and asked for another go, time after time. '*Pali, pali*,' they called out – or something like that. It must have been Greek for 'again'. Eventually, their mother called to them from the beach, and they reluctantly swam back in. Marie and I looked at each other and smiled.

'Cute kids, huh?' I asked.

'Adorable. Josh seemed like a natural with them,' she replied.

She was right. He did. I wondered how kids factored into his abstinence philosophy. Did he want them? If he did, how was he going to wangle that without getting involved with a woman? I wasn't sure I wanted to get into a discussion about children with him, mostly because then I'd have to explain that I didn't want them. It had proven to be a contentious topic on more than one occasion over the years. I wasn't sure why, but almost every time the topic had come up in all manner of situations, I'd had to defend my position.

'Do you want kids?' Was Marie reading my mind?

'No.' I kept my tone light, but I didn't offer any further explanation. She didn't press, and remarkably she didn't seem to be conveying any sort of judgement either.

'We do – or rather, we did.' I hadn't expected that. I turned towards her to let her know I was listening. She watched Gary as he showed Josh how to body surf. 'When we met, we talked of having one, maybe two, but we discovered quite early on that we can't have them. It's me.' She offered no further explanation, and I didn't ask. 'We tried pretty much everything you can try – and I don't mean to be crass, but it's a good thing we earn decent money because that stuff is expensive. I can't even imagine how hopeless some couples must feel without even the opportunity to try.'

I looked back out to the water. I'd never heard a woman talk about infertility like this. Most of my friends had children, and a couple were pregnant. I had assumed the others either didn't want them or weren't ready to start trying. I considered my handful of childless friends. Had I been super callous not to discuss it with them, or even worse, to argue with them about why I didn't want kids? What if I had friends who were suffering like Marie obviously was? I was suddenly hit with how self-centred I was.

Mental note: be a better friend to my childless friends.

Marie continued. 'I felt quite useless for a long time, and all the while my beautiful husband was right there with me, telling me how much he loves me, no matter what.' I looked at Gary out in the barely there surf, showing Josh the ropes of proper beach swimming, and I had a newfound appreciation for him. Marie sighed. I figured I should say something, but I wasn't sure what the appropriate something was. Still, the silence hung heavy in the air.

'Marie, I am so sorry to hear that. Thank you for telling me.' I hoped it was adequate.

'Well, I feel like we're becoming friends, Sarah. It's also good to talk about it. So, thank *you* for listening. And you know what? I think we may even have a happy ending to this whole thing.'

'Really?'

'Well, at the start of the year we signed up with an adoption agency, and because we're happy to take an older child, not just a baby, they said we could have a placement as soon as December.' She grinned.

'Oh my god, Marie! That is incredible news.' I pulled her into a sideways hug, and she tipped her head to touch mine.

'Right? I mean, nothing is set in stone yet, but the thought of actually becoming parents sometime soon – it's ...' She had tears in her eyes, and I tightened my grip on her shoulder. She smiled through the tears and left the rest of her thought unsaid.

It felt so good to share her news, and even though I had only known her a few days, I agreed with her. She was becoming a good friend.

Eventually, the seafarers dragged themselves onto dry land. Josh was smiling as he towelled himself off, and I tried to keep my eyes on his face and not his lean, muscular body. 'How was that?' I asked, looking up at him and shielding my eyes from the sun with my hand.

'Awesome!' he replied. 'Did you see us body surfing? Gary taught me – it's so cool!'

'Well, if you liked that, wait 'til you come out to California and we take you to a real beach! You're gonna love body surfing in Santa Barbara!' said Gary.

'Is that a serious invitation?' asked Josh.

'Sure! It's an open invitation to all of you. You get yourselves to Cali, and we'll gladly put you up.' I immediately started thinking about when I could go. I love California, and I always like to have travel plans in the pipeline, especially when I'm on a trip. Why not have the next one to look forward to? Wasn't that the best way to avoid the post-travel blues?

'I'm there!' replied Josh. He looked euphoric.

Maybe Josh and I could go to California together. Or maybe I had lost my frigging mind.

As I gathered up my things, I saw Marie and Gary exchange a kiss and look at each other lovingly. I supposed it would be nice to have what they had, but I had done more damage to myself than good in search of it. I was better off staying clear of the whole love thing – *and* the whole lust thing. When I climbed back onto the scooter, I left my hands out of Josh's pockets and instead held on to the handles on the sides of the scooter. I needed to keep my distance from the sexy American boy.

Chapter Seven

Only minutes after we left the beach and ascended again into the hills of Naxos, the heavens opened. It didn't take long for the plummeting rain to seep into every nook and cranny of my clothes, especially the crannies. I couldn't have been wetter if I'd stood under a shower fully dressed. It was a good thing I wasn't wearing my watch that day, because it would have been ruined.

Duncan didn't stop riding, though, so we kept following. I hoped for a bus shelter or something to appear ahead of us on the side of the road, but there was nothing. Miles and miles of road, but no shelter. Despite my vow to stop flirting with the cute American, my hands were planted firmly in his pockets to stay warm. The rain was not only hard and fast, in complete contrast to the hot sun we'd enjoyed up until then, it was also freezing. I could feel my lips turning blue.

After a million years, Duncan pulled his scooter over to the side of the road and parked up. We all did the same. 'This is the town where we'll eat lunch,' he called out over the driving rain. But there was no town. There was just road and at the side of the road, seven very wet people. He must have seen the confusion on our faces, because he pointed behind him. 'It's down there!'

We walked away from the edge of the road and looked down into a steep valley. Sure enough, there was a town down there, clinging to the side of the hill, all quaint and whitewashed and boxy, just like in the Greek postcards. Duncan signalled for us to follow him as he descended a set of stairs. We followed single file, water gushing around our feet as it flowed from the top of the hill down the town's walkways and stairs. The rain relentlessly pounded us from above as we navigated steep steps and a reasonably sized flood.

And then I started laughing, at first a giggle and then a belly laugh. I couldn't remember ever being wetter while fully clothed, and the whole situation was ridiculous. The laugh caught on, and the others joined in – even Duncan. So, there we were, seven laughing maniacs tromping into a flooded Greek village to have lunch – as you do! At the bottom of the valley, the town levelled out, and we entered a small courtyard. Its white walls were covered in thick ropey vines of bougainvillaea and hundreds of colourful flowers reached out to us in bright clumps. It was pretty, but I was *so* wet and cold, I could hardly care.

A woman appeared in a doorway, a smiling woman who looked like someone's grandma – or *YaYa* as they say in Greece. She signalled vigorously for us to come in and we happily obeyed. Right inside the doorway, we gathered close to each other, dripping water onto the tiled floor of her little café. There were four tables, two long and two small, and at one of the small tables sat a man in a pair of trousers and a singlet, smoking. He read the paper and grunted at its content, ignoring the bedraggled septet in the doorway.

The woman didn't ignore us, though. She fussed about,

tutting at the state of us and eventually signalled for us to take a seat at one of the long tables. We filed around it, and I was delighted to see a heater affixed to the wall next to one of the chairs. I claimed that seat and slipped off my saturated sandals under the table in the hopes of warming up my poor toes.

Duncan explained how he always went there – every trip – because the food was so incredible and Martika – the smiling woman – was so nice. Martika had disappeared, and I hoped it was to get menus. I was starving. She returned, not with menus but with something better. A large stack of towels and clean, dry T-shirts. She motioned for us to dry off and get changed. Modesty was abandoned as we each did what was necessary to get into the dry shirts. I reminded myself that a bra was pretty much the same as a bikini top and that everyone had already seen me in one of those.

Drier – we were all still wearing our wet shorts – and warmer, we sipped the soft drinks Martika had brought to the table. It turned out there were no menus. She would bring food to the table – whatever she had prepared that day – until we were full. While she bustled around her tiny kitchen, we nibbled on her home-made bread, which we dipped in her home-pressed olive oil, and both were so good I nearly cried with joy.

Three large bowls of *horiatiki* appeared next. She pointed to the thick slabs of feta sitting atop the salads, each one drizzled in olive oil and sprinkled with fresh oregano. Then she pointed to her chest. Even though I knew she didn't speak any English, I blurted out, 'You made the feta?' She seemed to understand and nodded. She smiled as she watched us take big helpings and then went back to the kitchen. 'Holy crap, can you believe she makes her own feta?' I asked my table-mates.

There were no replies; everyone was already stuffing their mouths. I did the same. Remember how I said that the Greeks grow the best tomatoes in the world? Well, as soon as I took a bite of that salad, I knew Martika grew the best tomatoes in Greece, which made hers the best of the best.

As we drew near to the bottom of the three bowls, she came back to the table with a vat of tzatziki, a pile of steaming hot pita bread, and an enormous platter of roasted meat. After a series of *Old McDonald's Farm*-style noises and actions, and quite a bit of laughter, we arrived at the conclusion it was goat. It looked delicious and it tasted even better. I glanced over at Hannah who was on my left. 'Gonna try the goat?' She had screwed up her nose the last time we'd ordered it.

'Hell yeah,' she said, heaping a pile onto her plate. I must have looked a little shocked, because she added, 'Starving!' and then tucked in. She moaned shortly after, so I guessed she'd been converted.

'So,' I said to Marie and Gary between bites. 'You guys are going to Paris next?'

'Yes!' exclaimed Marie. 'We're having our do-over trip.'

'Oh, why's that?' asked Hannah, coming up for air between bites of meat.

'Last time we were there, it was a disaster,' said Gary.

'To start, I had the flu,' said Marie. 'I'd felt it coming on before we left London on the Eurostar, so I'd stocked up on cold and flu tablets and lots of the other good drugs. But it was *bad*. By the time we got to the hotel, it was coming out both ends, with snot everywhere. Sorry to say that while we're eating, but not only did I feel like hell, I also looked horrendous – not exactly how you want to spend a Parisian holiday with your handsome husband.'

'You didn't look bad; you just looked sick.'

'Thank you, honey, but as gracious as you're being, you're a total liar.'

'In any case, just as Marie is starting to get well enough to actually see some of Paris—'

'More than the hotel room—'

'Yes, more than the room – *I* come down with food poisoning!'

'The poor man! We're pretty sure it was the crepes, right, honey?'

'I think so, yes. We had stopped at this little café near Musée d'Orsay for crepes in the middle of the afternoon – and you know, I nearly told the woman "no cream"—'

'*I* told her no cream—'

'That's right you did. Anyway, I didn't, and I'm pretty sure it was the culprit.'

I was fascinated by how they told the story together, each of them performing their part as though the whole thing was scripted. Marie continued.

'But of course, food poisoning doesn't typically come on right away, so there we are at dinner that night up in Montmartre. And I'd pulled myself together for this dinner, because it was our last night and I was so desperate to have at least one romantic evening out with my husband, even if I still didn't feel the best—'

'You did look beautiful.'

'Thanks, honey.'

'Anyway, right after they cleared our dinner plates, it hits. I mean, full force. I had to excuse myself from the table.'

'And the poor man is gone for ages, and I'm not quite sure what's happening—'

'But as soon as I get back to the table, I'm like, "Honey, we need to leave. *Now!*"'

'I practically threw money at our waiter – didn't I, hon?'

'She really did. The waiter had to pick it up off the floor. So, we run out of the restaurant and hail a cab—'

'Thank god there was one right on the street outside—'

'And we get back to the hotel just in time, and then all hell lets loose.'

'And he spent the rest of the night sitting on the toilet and vomiting into the sink. The poor man.'

'And the next morning, we're packing, because we're taking the train back to London that day, and I am really struggling.'

'And of course, we didn't have any more of the good drugs, which keep things in check, so to speak, because I'd finished those off the day before,' said Marie.

'So, we finish packing, grab a cab from the hotel, and we have the cab driver stop off at a pharmacy on the way to the station.'

'And there I am using my best high school French. "*Mon mari est très malade*" – my husband is sick – but beyond that, I haven't got the vocab. So the pharmacist pretends to cough and we're shaking our heads.'

'And then Marie pretends to throw up, and the pharmacist seems to understand, and then she asks if I also have diar-rhoea – but she does it with hand gestures next to her butt and farting noises.'

Even though it really wasn't suitable mealtime conversation, the rest of us were laughing so hard it didn't matter.

'Anyway, we establish that, yes, he is vomiting and, yes, he has diarrhoea, and we get the drugs to stop both on the train ride back to London.'

'So that was our tragically *crappy* first trip to Paris together.' Gary emphasised the word 'crappy', and we all groaned. Marie laughed and looked at her husband adoringly.

My mind flicked to Neil the fuckhead. I searched my memory for any instance where we'd shared a story like that with our friends. There were none. For one thing, Neil and I didn't share any friends, which was entirely his fault. Throughout our relationship, he baulked at any suggestion to get together with my friends, or even his. And he would never have taken me to Paris – or anywhere like it – because he couldn't be adventurous or romantic to save his life. Also, Neil wasn't remotely interesting enough to tell a good story.

I stifled a derisive snort, disguising it as a cough. No one seemed to notice, except Josh. He glanced in my direction, and I cleared my throat while tapping my chest. Sure that I'd sold my fake cough, I nestled into thinking about how much energy I had expended mourning my relationship with Neil. I had wasted a lot of time crying about a man who didn't really love me, if I was completely honest with myself, and who didn't deserve my love – a man who was, in fact, a dick. For months, my friends and my sister had been telling me that exact thing, but it was the first time I realised it for myself.

I swung my attention back to the table. They were flogging the dead horse with puns about defecation. 'That is certainly the shittiest story I have ever heard,' said Duncan. I joined in on a collective groan.

'Okay! Enough!' Marie cried out through her laughter.

'But seriously, though, it's the best reason I've ever heard for going back somewhere,' Duncan added. The rest of us agreed – even Hannah who seemed way more messed up about love and romance than me.

An hour later, my stomach hurt and it was my own doing. I had eaten the bodyweight of a small child in delicious, home-grown, home-made Greek food. I sat back from the table and rubbed a hand over my food baby. Martika returned to the table carrying what I could only guess was more food. I would have shooed her away, but I could no longer lift my arms.

She placed a worn wooden cutting board on the table, and on it were several apples cut into eighths. Next to the pile of apple pieces was a block of hard, salted cheese. By this stage we didn't need to ask – she grew the apples and she made the cheese. Despite my engorged state, I reached for a few slices of apple and a piece of cheese. They were both delicious, especially together. I told my groaning stomach to shush as I took another bite.

Even though the meal was winding down, the chatter continued in a lively manner, and I found myself watching the group, slightly detached. I knew I was stone-cold sober, because all I'd had to drink was Coke – albeit the diet version, which in larger-than-normal quantities can make me go a little loopy lala – but I felt all warm inside like you do after a couple of glasses of wine. And then I realised why. I was happy. Not only that, I loved these people – these irreverent, hilarious, caring, fun people – people who were strangers to me less than a week before. At that moment, those people became my family.

When we emerged from our three-hour-long lunch – yes, three hours is how long it takes to eat the best meal you've ever had – the clouds were gone, the sun was out, and all the flood waters had receded. It was like a completely different day. Martika saw us off, and I hugged her as a thank you for the lovely food. Of course, we paid her – a ridiculously small amount considering the feast she had served us – but she had shown us great kindness and had been a gracious hostess, so hugs were in order too.

The others then crowded around to give her hugs and she waved as we began the slow ascent back to our scooters. It took a little longer than you might expect for reasonably fit and relatively young people, but in our defence, we were all suffering from chronic overeating. I just wanted to take a nap. We finally made it to the top of the town and assembled around our scooters. Josh got his travel towel out of our scooter's small storage compartment and dried the seat, the helmets and the handlebars.

'Hey, Duncan?' asked Gary.

'Yeah, mate?'

'So, are we heading back to the marina now?' I could have kissed him right then for saying what I was thinking. Six pairs of eyes looked expectantly at Duncan, including Gerry's. Thank goodness I wasn't the only one who wanted to crawl onto my bunk and have an afternoon snooze.

'You don't want to go to Halki, to the distillery?' Duncan asked, directing the question to the whole group.

A chorus of mumbled responses ensued. 'Heading back would be okay.' 'Only if you wanted to.' 'The distillery's okay if it's just for a little while.'

'It's on the way back,' he added as if to sway our decision.

'You know what?' said Gary. 'If it's on the way, we might as well.' *NOOO! Gary! You were doing so well, but then you betrayed us, brother.* Needless to say, I no longer wanted to kiss him. I couldn't place all the blame on Gary, though – the rest of us hadn't exactly backed him up with a decisive, 'Take us back to the boat now!'

'What did you want to do?' I asked Josh as he put his helmet on.

'Truthfully?'

'No, lie to me. I love it when men do that.'

He looked right into my eyes and whispered. 'I want to go back to the boat – just us – and spend the rest of the afternoon making out with you.'

I gulped – actually gulped, like they do in cartoons – and I am sure my eyes were the size of saucers. He grinned and got on the scooter. It was a cool move, I'd give him that. 'Making out' – it so American, so high school – and for some reason, super sexy.

I climbed on the scooter and grabbed hold of his waist as he zipped off in pursuit of Duncan, mindful that no matter how many times I promised myself I would steer clear of the cute American, I literally couldn't keep my hands off him. I concluded that I was truly pathetic and had the willpower of, well, someone who has no willpower.

Or maybe there was more to it?

As I pressed myself against Josh, I remembered what he'd told me the day that Patricia had said all those nasty things – that he wanted a bigger life. It had really struck a chord with me, and I'd thought about it a lot ever since. And every time I did, I wondered what it would mean for Josh. I also wondered what it would mean for me. I wanted my life to be bigger too; I'd been stuck in a rut for too long. Maybe those two bigger lives would be connected somehow.

We resumed our four-scooter formation and headed for

our final stop of the day – at least I really hoped it was. I thought longingly about the foam mattress on my bunk. I thought even more longingly about how a sexy American boy would look on that foam mattress. Quite good, I decided as I tightened my grip on his stomach. He flexed his abs in response. Nice.

The distillery turned out to be rather fun. We were shown around by an older Greek gentleman who had limited English and an eye for the ladies; he grinned and winked at us the whole time. I was also fairly certain he poured us larger samples than he poured for the guys. *Kitron*, the drink they made, was tasty, but even the weakest variety was potent; they were not messing around with that stuff. To be polite, I bought a little bottle of the weakest one, which was bright green. At least the colour was nice.

'You okay to ride?' I asked Josh as we geared up to ride for the final time that day.

'Yeah, I only had a few sips. I'll be fine. Do you trust me?'

'I trust you.'

I knew, with a pang in my stomach, I was commenting on more than his scooter-piloting skills. Sure, we were friends, but trusting him the way you trust a guy you're romantically involved with – that was different.

Was I seriously reconsidering the whole 'holiday romance' thing?

No matter what I did to distract myself on the ride back to the marina – *oh look, a Greek farmer on a donkey!!* – I couldn't stop myself from returning to this one thought. It was like when you get a sore in your mouth, and you keep touching it with your tongue. It kinda hurts, but it also kinda feels good?

Thinking about hooking up with Josh – for absolute real – was like tonguing a mouth ulcer.

*

Believe it or not, some of us actually wanted dinner that night, but only some of us. It was me of course – I have the appetite of a lumberjack – and Josh and Gary and Marie. Hannah was off with the people from the other boat – traitor – and when we invited them to dinner, Gerry and Duncan opted to stay on the boat. Alone time must be hard to come by when you're sailing with five other people. I was more than happy to give them some privacy.

Sometime after nine, the four of us set off into the town with no clear idea where we were going. We eventually found somewhere off the main thoroughfare, which had more locals than tourists. We took a small table out front on the footpath – four chairs crowded around a table that would typically fit two. Cosy. Gary and Josh spent the first few minutes engineering a solution to the table's rocking issue – we *were* on cobblestones – and by the time the waiter came, the table was stable. He placed a basket filled with bread in the middle.

'English?' he asked in a curt tone.

'*Ne*,' I replied, using one of my five Greek words. His face crumpled into what looked like a judgemental frown. He then rattled off a series of specials in thickly accented English, tossed a stack of laminated menus on the table, and disappeared.

'How much of that did you get?' asked Gary.

'None,' admitted Josh.

'Me neither,' added Marie.

I picked up one of the menus. It was sticky. Yuk. What was with all the sticky laminated menus in Greece? This one was written in what I guessed was meant to be English. I held it up to the others. 'It's in English – sort of. I say we skip the specials and order from here.'

'Good idea,' said Marie. 'It's not like this is going to be anywhere *near* as good as what Martika served us today.'

'That was the best meal I've ever had,' said Josh. 'And I'm from Chicago. *And* I travel all the time for work, and I get to eat in some high-end places, but *that* – that was ... Actually, I don't think I have the words for it.'

'I agree,' said Marie. 'I don't think I will ever be able to eat another tomato after today and not think of how it pales in comparison to hers.'

'Or bread,' said Gary.

'Or cheese,' I added.

'Oh my god, the cheese,' groaned Marie.

'Okay, we need to stop reminiscing and order.' I looked down at the menu and tried to concentrate. It wasn't so much the memory of lunch that was making it difficult, but the feel of Josh's thigh against mine – especially as we were both wearing shorts.

On the ride back to the marina earlier, I'd convinced myself that if I didn't go straight to my cabin, Josh would make some kind of move on me. When we arrived, I went to my cabin under the pretence of taking a nap. I did eventually fall asleep, but not before I had imagined in great detail what making out with Josh would be like, and of course those thoughts had evolved into making love with him. Thank goodness Hannah was hanging out with some girls from the other boat. At least I could fret in private.

I'd emerged from my nap in a sleepy haze around six, knowing that only a shower would help shake it off. And, looking in the bathroom mirror, I'd discovered I looked more like a drowned rat than a woman. Why hadn't anyone told me I had mascara smudges down to my chin, or that so much of my hair had escaped my ponytail it had formed a brown halo of fuzz around my face? I definitely needed to freshen up before I faced the world – well, Josh – especially if I wanted to feel remotely attractive.

The waiter placed, or rather slammed, our plates of food down on the table and when he left we had to do a bit of rearranging to make everything fit. Gary was in the middle of telling us a story, and I could see where it was heading.

'So, there we are, we've just finished this great meal – turns out Jack is an awesome cook. And then Janine grabs my hand and then Marie's, and she says, "So, there's something we've wanted to talk to you about for a while now, but we wanted to wait until the time was right."'

I groaned and put my head in my hands. 'Nooo. I don't think I want to know any more.'

'You can see where this is going, right?' asked Gary.

I nodded, then lifted my hands and looked over at Josh. He seemed interested, but not quite sure where Gary was heading with the story. 'Just finish, Gary,' I said, laughing, and took a bite of my fish.

'So, *then* she says, "Jack and I find you both very attractive—"'

Josh gasped; he finally got it. '"And we'd like to invite you into our bed."' Gary punctuated his punch line by putting a bite into his mouth and chewing. I shook my head and laughed along with Marie.

'That whole time we're getting to know them, Gary and I are saying to each other how much we liked them, how fun they were, how glad we were to have met new friends that live so close to us.'

Josh was still flabbergasted. 'So, what did you say? How do you get out of something like that?'

'Awkwardly,' replied Gary with a mouthful of food and I laughed again.

'No, really. How?' Josh asked, his food forgotten.

'Gary said – and, honey, I think it was pretty much as gracious as you could have been – "Well, that's very flattering, thank you, but that's not really for us. And I think we should go now."'

Josh nodded his head as though it was precisely what he would say in that situation.

'That's very diplomatic,' I said. 'So, I'm guessing you got the hell out of there and never saw them again?'

'Oh, we see them,' answered Gary. 'They live right by us, and we seem to run into them *all the time*.'

'Seriously, *all* the time,' said Marie. 'And of course, it's uncomfortable. I mean, what are you supposed to say? "Hello, people who used to be our friends until you tried to sleep with us. Have you tried the new coffee house on Lincoln?"'

By this stage we were all in fits of laughter. It got louder when Gary said, 'So, Sarah, Josh, there's something Marie and I have been wanting to tell you ...'

Without missing a beat, Josh added, 'Well, I finally have something to write about for my "Dear *Penthouse*" letter,' and then I laughed so hard I wasn't making any sound, except for the occasional squeak.

I glanced around, suddenly aware of how loud we were.

Some of the other diners in the packed taverna looked annoyed with us, but our table was quickly forgotten when a ruckus erupted two tables over, and all the attention turned there, including ours.

A group of six middle-aged Aussies – three couples – had finished their dinner and were quibbling over the bill. A look passed between the four of us as we openly eavesdropped. One of the men, who was sitting at the head of the table, had a brash Ocker accent. He was simultaneously making a dick of himself and upsetting the waiter.

'Listen, mate, I don't know where you get off charging us a service fee – a *service fee* – for what? A paper tablecloth? That's bloody ridiculous – and how can it come to that?' He stabbed a fat, red finger at the bill. 'You've written it all in Greek, and you've obviously added it up wrong. No way does it come to that much – that's sixty Aussie dollars!' The other five added their agreement that they had been ripped off.

I looked at the table, filled with empty plates and two empty carafes of wine; it looked like they'd had a feast. How could they be so horrendous? I couldn't stand it any longer.

'Excuse me,' I said loudly enough to shut down the barrage of insults directed at the waiter. 'What's the problem?' The man was too stupid to detect from my tone that it was a rhetorical question. I continued to talk over him as he attempted to get me on his side. 'I noticed your table when we sat down. It was filled with plates of food, which you ate, and those plates were replaced with more plates of food. You've had at least two carafes of wine. And you're quibbling over *this* meal –' I gestured to the table '– costing you fifteen Aussie dollars each – wine *and* dinner?

'You couldn't get wine and dinner for fifteen dollars at the local RSL in Australia, and you know it. And furthermore, this is Greece, *mate*, and you're going to be charged a service fee of a euro each for the bread, the olive oil – and yes, the paper tablecloth – no matter where you eat. So, why don't you pay your bill and leave.'

I turned back to my dining partners, who looked both shocked and impressed, and took a bite of my food. Replies of 'Well, I never,' and 'Come on, let's get out of here,' emitted from the other table. As he passed me the man said, 'You're a rude girl, you know that?'

I replied with, '*You're* the one making Australia look bad,' and then turned away from him and took a sip of the crappy wine. My heart was beating very fast, but I was glad I'd said something. People like that should not travel. They should stay the fuck home. At least they paid their bill.

'Impressive,' said Gary, looking at me as though seeing me in a new light.

Marie was laughing. 'That was brilliant. I don't know if I could have done that.'

'I thought I might have to fight the guy,' said Josh, winking at me.

'You could have taken that middle-aged guy,' I replied.

'Hey now – no derogatory talk about the middle-aged. Especially as I am well within that demographic,' added Marie.

'You're not *middle-aged*,' I retorted.

'Well, depends how you define it. If I live 'til I'm eighty, then I'm more than halfway. Doesn't that make me middle-aged?'

Uh oh. I back-pedalled – vigorously. 'Middle age is less about actual age in my mind – I think of it as a term to describe a mentality – like the word 'youthful'. I mean, my parents are in their sixties, but I don't even think of *them* as middle-aged – they're youthful people. They're vibrant and adventurous. Like you, Marie.' I *really* hoped I hadn't insulted her. I looked at her with a hopeful smile.

She laughed – probably more *at* me than *with* me. 'I get what you're saying. I like the concept – I might steal it to describe myself from now on. I am forty-eight years young!'

At hearing her age, Josh looked a little shocked and caught my eye. I nodded slightly as if to say, 'Doesn't she seem much younger?' He surreptitiously checked Marie out while she and Gary shared a moment and with his own slight nod, Josh agreed with me.

The waiter – the same officious one who had served us earlier – appeared at our side with a smile on his face and a carafe of wine. 'Hello, this is for you and your friends. That man was very rude, and I am thankful for you, for your help.'

Well, I hadn't expected that. 'Oh, you're welcome.'

He signalled to the wine, said, 'Enjoy,' and then went back inside.

'How thoughtful of him,' said Marie as she poured the wine into glasses.

I was about to say I'd had enough crappy wine when Gary took a sip and said, 'Oh, wow. This isn't half bad. I think he broke out the good stuff!'

The three of us took sips and agreed. 'To the good stuff,' I toasted, holding my glass aloft. There were clinks all around, and we finished our meal on an even better note than we'd begun it.

We walked back to the boat in our pairs. It had been a fun dinner, even though the meal itself paled in comparison with lunch.

'Tired?' asked Josh.

'Not really. I had a nana nap, remember?'

'I remember. I also remember telling you what *I* wanted to do this afternoon.' Swoon.

'You said you wanted to do that if we were alone on the boat. We were hardly alone.'

'I am well aware of that, believe me. So, do you want to have a nightcap when we get back to the boat? We could sit up top,' he asked.

'Sure.' Ahead of us, Marie and Gary held hands, and I can't tell you how much I wished Josh would reach down and hold my hand. But he didn't.

At the boat, we said goodnight to Gary and Marie, which included hugs from Marie. I wanted to get a jacket from my cabin, and I was super quiet opening the door so I didn't wake Hannah. I needn't have worried; she wasn't back yet. Josh made us gin and tonics – sans lime or lemon, because we'd run out – and we climbed up onto the deck and moved to the bow where we could talk without disturbing the others.

'Nice night,' I said, when the pressure of the silence became too much. I wondered why, when we could usually talk about anything, there were still times when it felt awkward between us. And then I wondered if it was just me, because Josh seemed to be studying the stars contentedly. He turned and smiled at me. Yup. It was just me. I really needed to chill out.

'You know how you said you want your life to be bigger?' I asked. It was a non sequitur, but he fell easily into step.

'Sure.'

'Well, I do too.' I took a sip of my drink.

'How do you mean?'

I paused for a moment, not quite sure how to phrase it. 'Well, right now I feel completely stuck.'

'In what way?'

I laughed a wry laugh. 'In every way. Even in the way I think about things. We're sitting here, not saying anything, and I'm all tied up in knots because I think it's awkward. You're probably not thinking that at all.'

I was relieved when he didn't mock me. 'No. I just like being with you.'

'Me too. But why can't I be like you, and just *be*? Why do I fret so much?'

'You're very hard on yourself.'

'I haven't even got started. The reason I long for something else, something *bigger* is that I feel so dissatisfied – and I have no reason to be, which makes me feel like the most ungrateful person alive.' His brow furrowed, but he didn't say anything, so I continued.

'I mean, I have a good life. I do. I have good friends, and a good job, I get to travel quite a bit – which I love.'

'There's a *but* coming,' he said, encouragingly.

'*But*, so what? So, I have a "good job" ...' I made air quotes – I usually hate them, but they helped make my point. 'But I don't really enjoy it anymore. I mean, I love the kids – mostly – some of them *are* little ratbags ...'

'You said that before once – "ratbags". Can't say I'm familiar, but I can guess what you mean.' He was lightening the mood. I appreciated it.

'Well, they are.' I smiled. 'Anyway, the job itself is so polit-ical now, and a lot of it is unchallenging – it's boring. I'm sick of it, but it's a stable job, and it pays okay. Either I stay in it and continue to work my way up, which means less time in the classroom with the kids – the only part I still enjoy – or I take the leap and do something totally different, which scares the fuck out of me.'

'It *is* scary thinking about changing jobs. I've been with the same company since I left college, and I am totally ready for something else. I mean, I see the guys around me at work – guys my age – and they're getting married, and taking on mortgages and having kids, and I want the exact opposite of that.'

'But you're not actually worried you'll get sucked into all that?'

'No, but they're on the treadmill, you know? Like ...' He made a gesture with his hands to show perpetual movement. 'I want to do something more innovative, something dynamic. Not just nine-to-five with no end in sight.'

'Have any idea what that is?'

'Nope.'

I laughed softly. 'Me neither.'

'And what about your friends?' he asked.

'I love my friends – I do – and I'm not really a person who has a lot of friends – just a few close ones. But at my age, all my friends are either married or married with kids, and as much as I love them, it's not really the same between us anymore.'

'No one to hang out with.'

'Exactly. And how selfish is that? I mean, I want my girl-friends to be happy – and I think most of them are – but what I want for *me* is someone to go to the movies with, or go to dinner with on a Tuesday, or drink a bottle of wine with. I am *so* tired of drinking cask wine, which is the only kind I buy anymore, because it doesn't go off if you drink it one glass at a time.'

'You need new friends,' he said, matter-of-factly. I looked at him to see if he was joking. He was.

'That's what I mean about sounding ungrateful. I don't need new friends. I need to find a way to stop complaining and be grateful that, if I really needed them, I could call any one of them at three in the morning and they would be there for me.

'Instead, I bemoan that I'm in a job that does my head in, I'm single – even though I really do think most men should fuck off and die – present company excluded, of course – and I am pretty much one floral bedspread and another cat away from becoming the quintessential spinster schoolteacher.'

'Wow, you really are messed up.' I could tell he was teasing me, but I was on a roll.

'Right? That's what I've been trying to tell you. On paper, what do I have to complain about? I mean nothing, right? Yet, the truth is, I'm stuck.' I paused, because what I was about to say really hit home, and my voice caught.

'And I am really, really lonely.' *Wow, Sarah. You sure know how to impress a guy.*

Josh didn't say anything for a moment, so of course, I apologised for my big reveal. 'Josh, I'm sorry, I—' And then he touched his hand to my chin and turned it towards him and kissed me, gently at first and then with more fervour. It was a different kind of kiss than the flirty one from the night before. I leaned against him as he wrapped his arms around me, and I realised I was seriously falling for him. Then – damn him – he pulled me closer and kissed me more deeply.

Finally, we pulled apart and when we looked at each other

there was no awkwardness – real or imagined – and there was no pretence, just honesty and affection.

'Sarah, I think you're incredible.'

'I don't feel very incredible.'

'You *are* hard on yourself. Sarah, you are so sexy.' I began to shake my head at the compliment, but he ignored me and continued. 'And smart about so many things – and fun. You're fun to be around – you're always happy.'

'*I'm* happy?' Who was he talking about?

'Yes – well, I mean maybe not right this second, but otherwise, yes. You laugh a lot. You notice the little things, those details most people miss because they have their head up their ass. And you take time with people – you get to know them, you care. You're engaged in life, Sarah – I consider that a mark of a happy person.' He paused, looking at me while I reflected on everything he said.

'You don't see yourself that way?' he asked.

My eyes filled with tears, and I started laughing and crying at the same time. Josh was right. The Sarah he knew *was* happy. So, who on earth was the Sarah *I* knew – the one who hated her job, and felt left out of her friends' lives, the Sarah who was too afraid to fall in love again, because it would lead to heartbreak? What was she doing while happy Sarah was on holiday in the Greek Islands with new friends and a handsome American boy?

I looked at Josh with what must have been both shock and joy in equal measure. 'I am happy – right now, I am. And this feels right, you know? I want to be this person all the time. I've missed being this person.'

He wrapped his arms around me again and held me in a hug.

'I want you to sleep in my cabin tonight.' I pulled back from the hug and looked at him. *God, his eyes are beautiful.* 'We don't have to do anything,' he added, as if trying to reassure me. 'I just want to be close to you, to sleep next to you.'

'Okay.'

'Really?' He seemed surprised.

I laughed. 'Yes really, handsome American boy.' He smiled, but with a look that said, 'Handsome American boy?'

'It's what I call you in my head,' I replied, hoping I didn't sound ridiculous.

'I like it.' With that, he kissed me on top of my head and stood up, pulling me with him. 'C'mon, sexy Australian girl, let's go to bed.'

Chapter Eight

When I woke the next morning, it was to sunlight filtering through the ceiling hatch and dancing across my eyelids. Glorious. I stretched luxuriously. I had slept so well! My bed partner stirred beside me as I rubbed the sleep from my eyes. I reached for my water bottle and took a quick swig. Morning breath can be a bitch.

'Good morning.'

I swallowed, then rolled onto my side and propped my head on my hand. 'Good morning.'

'Sleep well?'

'So well. You?'

'I slept well too.' He was smiling and I smiled back.

You may not believe this, but we didn't do *anything*. I mean, he did kiss me goodnight – rather chastely, I'd like to add – but then we fell asleep. Besides, even if things had got a little hot and heavy, there was no way I was going to have sex on a boat with paper-thin walls and five other people on it! It would have been too embarrassing. I was already wondering how I would explain to Hannah why I hadn't slept in our cabin.

My thoughts turned to the sleeping part of the night. Usually, sleeping next to someone new meant I barely slept at all. Instead, I'd sort of dozed, waking up at the slightest noise or movement, hyper conscious of the other person in the bed. It wasn't like that with Josh. It felt normal.

'I liked sleeping next to you,' I said looking at the sky through the ceiling hatch. 'It was nice.'

'Nice?'

'Yeah. Nice.'

'Okay.'

'What's wrong with *nice?*'

'Nothing. Nice is good.'

I stared hard at the patch of sky. How had we gone from contented to annoyed in three-point-two seconds? And, now what? How was I supposed to get myself out of there graciously? 'Thank you for a lovely night of chastely sleeping side by side. See you at breakfast.' Definitely not that – that was awful.

While I had an internal discussion about the most socially acceptable way to extricate myself from Josh's cabin, he seemed to be on a totally different tack. He reached for my water bottle, took a sip, and said, 'Now I can kiss you good morning.' He followed up with a lovely, gentle kiss. It was a very boyfriend-girlfriend kind of a moment, and even though it felt nice – there was that word again – I couldn't help wondering what else it meant. I didn't want a boyfriend, and he had been particularly clear about not wanting a girlfriend. Now I *really* needed to get out of there.

I reached for my skirt – I had slept in my T-shirt, knickers and bra – while trying to retain some semblance of modesty. It was a little tricky, because the skirt was at the foot of the bed.

Contorting myself to reclaim it, I then shimmied into it

under the covers. All the while, I avoided eye contact with Josh. I had no idea what was going on in his head, but whatever it was, I didn't want to know. I was zipping up when he climbed out of bed and slipped on a pair of shorts. He had slept in his jocks by the way.

'Okay then ...' he said, obtusely. Was he wishing me gone, or wishing I would chill the fuck out? If it was the latter, he was right – I did need to chill the fuck out. I climbed out of bed fully dressed, and then we were standing face to face in the tiny space – actually it was more like face to chest – his *bare* chest, his bare *sexy* chest. Damn him and his chest. Did I mention I really needed to get out of there?

'Okay, well, thanks. That was nice,' I said in a whisper. Was I for real? *Again* with the nice!

'Yep,' he replied, more curtly than necessary. I ignored his tone and gently turned the doorknob. I eased the door open a crack and looked out into the common space. Deserted – thank god. I completed my one-metre walk of shame – even though I had nothing to be ashamed of – and eased open the door of my cabin quietly, so I wouldn't wake Hannah. Again, I had no need for stealth; her bunk was unslept in and the cabin was empty. I thanked god again, even though I don't believe in him – or her – or whatever.

Where is she? I wondered. I concluded almost immediately that no matter where she was, good on her! I dragged my bag from the far end of the bunk and dug through it for something to put on. I chose a clean tank top and a nearly clean pair of shorts. Stepping out of the skirt, I scrutinised its level of filthiness.

I had worn it twice already, but there was no way to wash clothes on the trip and I still needed at least another wear out of it. I rated it as wearable and put it back into my bag. Only clothes that reeked or had been spilt on went into the plastic washing bag. And I'd only open *that* when I got back to London. The skirt was fine. And I knew I had enough clean knickers to get through the whole trip – twice over. I grabbed a fresh pair before tucking my bag out of the way.

Then I stripped off, stepped into the tiny bathroom and turned on the water. The best part about Hannah being out was that I was guaranteed a hot shower, and even though the water flow was little more than a trickle, it felt great.

While I showered, I thought about Josh. Okay – that came out wrong. I thought about our *situation*. I liked our little slumber party, but the moment with the good morning kiss was a little too cosy for comfort. Quite possibly we would become lovers, but even if we did, we needed to steer clear of the coupley stuff. I mean, what could happen, really? I'd probably never see him again after the trip. He *was* cute, though. And even if I did try to keep my distance, for the foreseeable future he was sleeping approximately a metre plus a few millimetres of plywood away. *Crap*.

The day before, the group had decided we'd stay another day and night on Naxos and then leave the following morning. I was fine with that, but they all wanted to go out on the scooters again. Another day riding around dusty roads, waiting to get rained on? I was less than fine with that. And it wasn't just the rain. Scooter riding was a super coupley thing to do.

The five of them – Hannah still hadn't made an appearance – stood on the dock, looking at me expectantly, while I stared back at them from the boat. Marie had her hands on her hips. 'So, you're not coming?'

Why did I feel guilty? Wasn't this my holiday too? Couldn't I do whatever I wanted with my day?

'Uh, no. I'm going to stay here and read, maybe do some journal writing ...' Marie wasn't buying it. 'And, wait for Hannah.' It was a last-ditch effort to convince them – and probably myself – that I preferred staying on the boat to riding on the back of a scooter with my arms wrapped around Josh.

Marie actually tutted when she shook her head at me; I knew I was going to hear about it later. She turned and put on her helmet, and the others did the same. Except Josh. Josh ran back across the gangplank – quite nimbly, I noticed – and planted a big kiss right on my lips. 'See you later, gorgeous,' he said. And before I could reply he was back on dry land, straddling his scooter and putting his helmet on. My mouth had formed a silent O and as soon as I realised, I closed it.

Definitely boyfriend behaviour. And everyone saw it. *Double crap – no, make that triple crap!*

*

I was sipping hot tea out of a plastic mug and half-reading one of the magazines Hannah had brought with her, when – speak of the devil – she sauntered onto the boat and plonked herself down on the bench opposite me. She was still wearing the clothes she'd had on the day before, and her sunglasses looked like they were glued to her face. I doubted they were coming off until she'd had caffeine and a shower, regardless of which came first.

'Good night?' I asked as I took another sip of tea.

'Excellent night,' she said, her usual frown exchanged for a grin.

'So ... don't leave me hanging.'

She nodded towards the lower deck. 'Anyone else here?'

'Just us. The others went out on the scooters for the day.'

'And you didn't want to go?'

'I wanted to read,' I replied, holding up the magazine.

'Uh huh.' I could feel her eyes scrutinising me behind the big lenses of her sunglasses.

'Don't change the subject,' I said, doing my best to change the subject. 'What did you get up to last night?'

'And this morning,' she retorted with a sly grin. She was enjoying herself.

'Okay, *and* this morning.'

'Stu.' One word, but it spoke volumes.

'The skipper of the other boat?'

'Yep.' She seemed particularly pleased with herself and considering that *Stu* was skippering a boat of six single women, I had to give her props for leaping to the head of the queue.

'Wow. So, you've gotta be, like, the most hated woman in the Greek Islands.' I couldn't help but smile at her.

'Yep – well at least the most envied.'

'So, Stuart ... how was it?'

'Great fun. And you know what? I knew those sour cows could hear us, and I didn't care! Not *my* boat, not *my* family on the sea. And, let's be honest, I *really* needed that.' We both erupted into laughter.

'Good for you, Hannah.'

'And?'

'And what?'

'And what about you? You and Josh finally get together?' I bit my lip. How much did I want to tell Hannah? Nothing – I

131

wanted to tell her nothing – as much as I wished there was nothing to tell. I was more convinced than ever that it was not a good idea to hook up with Josh on this trip.

And then I thought, *Fuck it, I'll tell her*.

'Sort of. I mean, we kissed. And I slept in his cabin last night – but we didn't have sex or anything. Actually, I didn't know you weren't in our cabin until this morning, but even so, I am *not* having sex on this boat. This *is* my family on the sea – and you don't shit where you eat and all that.' I was rambling, as I have a tendency to do when I am defending myself. Not that Hannah was judging me – I mean, she didn't appear to be – which was nice, because she'd been a little judgey up until then. And not that it mattered anyway. I was judging myself enough for both of us.

She let my verbal diarrhoea dribble off and appraised me frankly. 'You know what?' she asked.

'What?'

'You're really hard on yourself.' Hannah, who had only known me a few days, had me properly pegged – *and* it was exactly what Josh had said. *And* they were right. I was hard on myself.

I could congratulate Hannah for hooking up with the much-in-demand skipper of the other boat, but my chaste sleepover with Josh was sending me into some sort of meltdown. I mean, I was in Greece on a beautiful island with super cool people, and I was sitting on the boat reading a stupid magazine! And that's when I realised I was paying a ridiculous, self-imposed penance.

'Go get showered. We're going into town,' I declared.

Hannah jumped up at my instruction. 'That a girl,' she said, ducking below deck to get freshened up. I closed the magazine and looked out at the other boats on the marina. I didn't know where the thing with Josh was going – or where it *could* go – but for some reason it felt like he had leapt ahead from being a friend to being a boyfriend, and it was creeping me out. I had to tell him that. We needed to be cool and friendly and not get in too deep. I could do that. I could be honest. I could be cool.

Hannah was back up on deck within twenty minutes, which impressed me, especially because she looked better than she must have felt. 'Coffee,' she said, confirming my assumption.

'It'll be our first stop.'

Coffee, it turned out, was our first stop and our third and our fifth. It wasn't that Greek coffee was particularly good – just that Hannah seemed to need a lot of it. In between hits of caffeine, we shopped – her choice, not mine, but the shopping wasn't bad. Bags, shoes, gauzy cotton tops, ceramics, silver jewellery, tacky souvenirs. I bought some of the latter to hand out to friends back home. Don't disparage the humble fridge magnet; I know people who go crazy for that stuff.

We stopped for a late lunch overlooking the marina at around two o'clock, choosing a little taverna with tables outside, so we could watch the world go by. And by 'world' I mean English tourists we could make fun of.

When that got old, Hannah stabbed a piece of tomato with her fork and addressed the elephant on the island. 'So, besides having a slumber party, what's happening with Josh?' She shoved the tomato into her mouth and chewed vigorously. I pushed a piece of cucumber around my bowl.

'The short answer is, I don't know.' I looked at out the water and watched a fisherman steer his boat towards the shore. 'Last night we went to dinner with Gary and Marie, and we had such a good time – they are so fun – aren't they so fun?' I was stalling. She gave me the hand signal for 'get on with it'. 'And then Josh and I stayed up and talked.' She threw me a look over the top of her sunglasses. 'Yes, *just* talking,' I insisted. Hannah went back to her *horiatiki*.

'I feel like I can tell him anything, you know? I can't think of the last time I was with a guy I could talk to like that, without having to worry about sounding self-absorbed, or boring, or even stupid.'

'You're not boring *or* stupid,' she said, punctuating her point by pointing her fork at me.

'Thank you. I mean, I do know that, but there are those guys, you know, and they can make you feel so small.' My mind flicked to Neil – the prick. He had this incredible way of making me feel insignificant. Hannah nodded, seeming to understand. 'But Josh, he's my friend. An actual friend – like you.' I could tell she liked that. 'Even if that's *all* that happens on this trip – we end up being friends – that's great. But there's this intense attraction. I mean, he's so fucking cute—'

'Puppies are cute,' Hannah interjected.

'Okay, then what? Handsome?' She screwed up her nose and shook her head.

'Sexy?'

'If you say so.'

'In any case, I think he's extremely attractive, but even though he's not as young as I first thought he was, he's still a *lot* younger than me, *and* he lives in the US, *and* the likelihood of me ever seeing him again after this trip is like, zero. So, with all of that, I don't think anything should happen between us.'

'So, just sleep with him.'

'Well, that's the thing, see? I don't want a boyfriend, and Josh made this whole song and dance about not wanting a serious girlfriend, but this morning he got all boyfriend-y on me and it was weird.'

'Wow. You've got a lot going on.' I nodded. 'You going to finish that?' she said, motioning towards my plate of salad. I had barely touched it. I shook my head and she leaned across and helped herself to a hunk of feta. 'I can't get enough of this stuff. I love the feta here.'

'So, what should I do?'

'Look, I am the last person who should give you advice about men. But, this guy seriously likes you.' I started to protest, but she cut me off. 'No matter what he says about not wanting a girlfriend and all that – that's bullshit. He is super into you, and if you only want to be friends, you should tell him and keep your distance. And I'm not just saying that so I can have you to myself.'

I smiled. 'On the other hand, Sarah, if you like this guy – if it feels different from all the crap you've been through before. If he makes you feel good, and you think he's cute or sexy or whatever, then maybe you should stop worrying about it and see what happens.'

'But—'

'There is no but. You asked for my advice. That's what you should do. Stop analysing the situation and enjoy it. We're in the middle of the fucking Greek Islands, and quite frankly it's turning into *Riverdale* around here.' She had a point. 'So, chill the fuck out, okay?'

'Oh-*kay*. You know, Hannah, you really should get laid more often. I kinda like this side of you.'

'Agreed. I'm all for getting laid more often than *never*. Too bad Stu and the girls sailed on this morning.'

'Where to?'

'Syros.'

'I think Duncan said we're going there next.'

'Let's hope so. I could definitely go me some more of the sea captain!'

'Yeah, it's been a while for me too.'

'Maybe not for much longer.' She had a sly look on her face.

I pointed a finger at her. 'Do *not* say a word to anyone about this. No one. Promise?' She was right. I did sound like I was in an episode of *Riverdale*, but I didn't want her playing matchmaker and I needed her to promise she wouldn't. It was bad enough that Marie had intentions along those lines.

Hannah crossed her fingers over her heart, haphazardly. 'Cross my heart, blah, blah, blah.'

'I'm serious, Hannah. I mean it!'

'Anybody want a peanut?' We both burst out laughing. I liked this Hannah. I really did hope she got laid again – if only for selfish motives.

*

'How was it?' I asked as five weary-but-happy-looking travellers crossed the gangplank onto the boat and plonked themselves down. I was sitting exactly where I'd been when they'd left, and I wondered if they wondered if I'd spent the whole day there.

Hannah stuck her head out from below deck as the others took up spots around the deck. 'You're back! Just in time for cocktails. Who's in?' Six hands went up, including mine. 'I'm already making yours,' she said, scolding me playfully. 'The rest of you, give me a couple of minutes.'

'I'll help,' Duncan called as he unfolded himself from his seat. I was impressed by how much energy he put into being hospitable, even at the end of a long day.

'Sooo, how was it?' I asked again to no one in particular. 'What did you get up to?' Gary, never one to shy from telling a story, took me through a blow-by-blow of the day. It sounded like they'd been to some secluded parts of the island. And apparently the weather had held up, so at least there was no repeat of the previous day's drenching. I kept catching Josh looking at me.

He had a goofy grin on his face – I didn't know what to make of it.

Duncan started handing drinks up to those of us on deck, and when we all had one in hand, he and Hannah joined us. 'To Naxos!' he said, holding his plastic cup aloft. 'To Naxos!' we repeated, tapping our cups against each other's. I had a sip. Hannah must have taken her cue from Duncan's bartending practices. The drink was like rocket fuel. 'So,' said Duncan, 'I got a text today from a guy I know – he used to be my boss, actually – and he's here on Naxos and wanted to meet up with us for dinner tonight, if that's okay with you lot?'

There was general agreement from the group. 'He was your boss?' asked Josh.

'Yeah. He has a yacht in the Caribbean, and I used to be the skipper. He only ever used it a few times a year, so for the rest of the time, I lived on the yacht and took care of it. And when he was heading down, I'd have some lead time to hire a crew and stock it with everything we needed – you know.'

'So, essentially, you lived on a rich guy's boat and then a few times a year you had to work?' asked Hannah, incredulous.

'Pretty much, yeah.' The rest of us exchanged looks – the lucky bugger.

'What kind of a yacht are we talking? Like this one?'

Duncan snorted. 'Sorry. I don't mean to come off like a dick, but no, not like this one. It was a forty-metre boat – not a *sail*boat – one of those boats with a living room and a full kitchen and five bedrooms – that kind of boat.'

Six pairs of eyes were glued to Duncan and no one spoke for a moment. Gary broke the silence with: 'Well, what in the hell are you doing here with us, if you could be there skippering *that* boat?' It was a good question.

'Again, I don't want to seem like a dick, but even though it sounds like a good gig—'

'Ya think?' interjected Josh.

Duncan nodded modestly. 'Well, it was, yes, but it was also rather limiting. I mean, I didn't actually get to sail much – little day trips once in a while. When the boss wasn't there with his guests, it was moored. And, yeah, it was in a good spot, but after a couple of years, the gig got old, you know?'

I can't say that I do, Duncan. It sounded brilliant to me, but you don't really know what that kind of job is like until you've lived it. I'd been paid to travel around Europe in my twenties, but it was hard work and it wore me down after only two years. And as much as I loved sailing around the Cyclades Islands, I don't know how much I would love it if I had to do it for a few months at a time.

Duncan seemed embarrassed by the attention – even Gerry was looking at him with newfound awe – so I threw him a lifeline. 'So, you said this guy is meeting us for dinner?'

'Yeah. I know a place here in the main part of town where we can get great spit-roasted meat. He's going to meet us there and then after dinner, we thought we could go to a bar and have some drinks.'

'Sounds good!' I said, and other voices chimed in agreement. 'What time are we meeting him?'

Duncan looked at his watch. 'In about an hour. Enough time for another round!' he declared and then disappeared below deck to make another round of drinks. Josh sidled up and sat next to me. I looked straight ahead, pretending to watch the boat traffic around us as though I was genuinely interested in it.

'Did you stay here all day?' he asked.

'Here in this spot here, or just here on the boat?'

'Either.'

'Neither.'

'Oh.'

'Hannah came back right after you left and we spent the day out. We did some shopping, wandered around town a little, had coffee, had lunch ...'

'Girls' day out?'

'Yeah, something like that. Sounds like you guys had a good day too.'

'It was fun. I missed you, though.' I couldn't help but turn towards him – a reflex.

'You did?' He nodded. He wasn't shying away from eye contact, either. My heart quickened in my chest – traitor. God, his eyes were beautiful. *Relax, dork*, I told myself. I swirled the drink in my cup and pretended aloofness.

'Well, it was kind of nice to have some time with Hannah, but I missed hanging out with you too.' 'Hanging out' – casual, cool, friendly. Right?

His demeanour shifted, almost imperceptibly, but enough for me to know my comment hadn't landed well. He'd definitely taken it the wrong way. Crap, I needed to make it right.

'She's not as much fun as you, though. And I don't want to put my hands in her pockets.' He smiled.

'I'm gonna head down and get cleaned up for dinner.'

When he got up, Hannah filled his spot. 'How did that go?'

'I don't know what I'm doing. I mean, I want to keep Josh at arm's length, but that makes him feel bad, and I don't want him to feel bad, so I end up being flirty, but I don't think I want this to go anywhere. And, I'm starting to agree with you – he is smitten.'

She nodded slowly.

'So, there's no way this could be a "casual sex" thing.'

'*And*, you've said you won't have sex on the boat.'

'And there's that.' How could I be even *more* confused, particularly having talked it out with Hannah over lunch? Because I was pathetic, that's how. And no matter what I told myself, I was falling for the cute American. *Crap, crap, crap*.

Before dinner, I changed into a little summery dress and sandals and pulled my hair up into a loose chignon. I even put on a little makeup – blush, lip gloss and mascara.

'You look beautiful,' Josh whispered as we walked towards the town with the others. Duncan and Gerry led the group, like they usually did, and Josh and I were in the middle of the pack.

'Thanks,' I replied with a smile. 'A little something from the "clean enough" pile.'

He laughed. 'It is a bit like that, isn't it? I've already worn this shirt twice, and I had to scrutinise it thoroughly before putting it on. Looks clean, smells clean – it's clean enough.'

'I like it.'

'Thanks.' And then he did the one thing I hoped – and dreaded – he would do. He took my hand in his.

I was suddenly fourteen again, and the boy I liked was walking me home from school – *and he was holding my hand.* I scoured my foggy brain for something to say – damned hormones. Josh beat me to it. 'I'm looking forward to meeting Duncan's old boss.'

'Oh, really?'

'Yeah. I was talking to Duncan about him, and it turns out he just travels the world, making money, spending money. The guy is seriously loaded.'

'That whole "having a yacht in the Caribbean" thing wasn't a dead giveaway?' I don't think he detected the sarcasm in my voice.

'He's rich, he travels all the time, no ties – the ultimate bachelor lifestyle.'

I could hear the awe in his voice, and before I realised what I was saying, I replied with: 'You'd love that.'

'Doesn't it sound incredible?' Did he really just ask me that? 'I mean I haven't even met the guy yet and he's practically my hero.' *Way to make a gal feel special, Josh.* I couldn't believe he was extolling the virtues of a life spent in bachelorhood, while making a play for me. I wished he wasn't holding my hand. And on that subject, why the hell was he?

By the time we arrived at the restaurant and were shown to a large table in the back, I had worked myself into a bit of a lather. I was really pissed off with Josh.

Duncan's friend had yet to arrive, so we spread out around

the table, leaving a space for him next to Duncan. I didn't want to sit anywhere near Josh, but he wangled in next to me, and it would have been too obvious something was up if I'd moved. I pretended to absorb myself in the menu looking over the vast array of roasted meat. There was the ubiquitous goat. It was fast becoming a favourite.

Then I heard Duncan say, 'Here he is. Everyone, this is James.' And when I looked up from the menu, I could not believe it. Duncan's friend was the silver fox from Santorini. *Holy fuck*.

I must have looked like a stunned mullet – whatever a mullet is. I was vaguely aware that Duncan was introducing everyone in turn. When he got to me, he said, 'This is Sarah.' I didn't even manage a hello, just an odd kind of nod.

The silver fox, however, held out his hand and said, 'Sarah. So lovely to see you again and to finally learn your name.'

I smiled, awkwardly I'm sure, and replied with a weak, 'Yes.' I reminded myself to breathe while pretending not to notice that everyone else at the table was staring at me, mouths open.

Including Josh.

Chapter Nine

Duncan leapt into the midst of the awkward silence and directed James to the seat we'd saved for him. Right across from me. I hadn't taken my eyes off him since he'd arrived, and I'm not big-noting myself or anything, but he hadn't taken his eyes off me either. And he was smiling – a big, fat, self-satisfied smile.

'So,' said Duncan, rousing the group from their stupor. He held up a menu, 'Everything – seriously, *everything* – is good here. So, what do you say we order some platters, add in a couple of Greek salads and some tzatziki and do this family style?'

There were affirmative responses of varying levels of enthusiasm from around the table. Josh was silent. He had stiffened beside me the moment the silver fox had alluded to our interlude.

I broke off my staring competition across the table and read the menu. 'Lamb!' I called out, far louder than I needed to. Nerves. I lowered my voice for the follow-up, 'I think we should definitely get some lamb.' I couldn't remember ever sounding so excited about lamb.

'Good idea – and chicken.' Gary jumped in to help save a drowning woman. *Thank you, Gary. I love you.*

Eventually everyone contributed something to our order and Duncan signalled for the waiter. I risked a sideways glance at Josh. He looked like a thundercloud had taken up residence above his head. I wondered if he still considered James his hero. Probably not. From revered to despised in the blink of an eye.

Meanwhile, it was obvious that the silver fox thought he was in the hen house and had his eye on the prize hen. And for the record, that would be me. He did nothing to hide his interest, and I really wished he would; it was becoming embarrassing.

And yes, okay, I admit I *had* spent some time thinking about James since Santorini. And why not? I wasn't attached – not really – and it gave me something lovely to think about when Josh talked about his career bachelorhood. If there was no future for 'Josh and Sarah' beyond the trip, what harm was a fantasy – or two – or three – about the silver fox?

In the various versions of this fantasy, we were lovers who savoured the relative anonymity of our meeting, not dwelling on who we were in the real world. We sailed the Greek Isles – the kind of sailing that happens in commercials, with windswept hair, white linen clothes, and deck shoes – hopping between locations on a whim. We talked of politics and history, art and philosophy – ours was an intellectual connection as well as physical. And speaking of physical, we made love three times a day – sometimes hard and passionately on the deck of the boat, other times unhurried, taking time to explore each other's bodies. And at the end of each day, we got drunk on Ouzo while we watched the sunset over the Aegean.

As I said, I *may* have spent a little time fantasising about the silver fox.

Seeing him again and up close, I was struck by how handsome he was – even more so than I'd remembered. And I mean *really* handsome, in the way that slightly older guys are when they dress well and look after themselves and were probably supermodels in their younger days. He looked like he'd stepped out of an ad for Ralph Lauren Polo.

James was talking, but I wasn't listening. I tuned back in, trying not to get too distracted by his eyes, which were alight with amusement and especially gorgeous. It was a story about Duncan messing up the dates for James's arrival in Barbados. When James arrived, he found Duncan sunbaking on the deck of his boat – naked – with an equally naked girl beside him. My eyes flicked to Duncan, who I thought was unflappable, and wouldn't you know it? He was completely flapped. Gerry nudged him in the ribs good-naturedly while he turned a fantastic shade of red.

'Why, Duncan, you've been holding out on us!' declared Gary. I glanced over at Josh; even he was smiling.

James continued, 'So I clear my throat to announce my arrival, and of course both of them stand up – on impulse, I suppose – and so there we are, the three of us standing there staring at each other. Eventually I say something like, 'Duncan, aren't you going to introduce us?' and then the poor girl suddenly comes to her senses. She squeals, grabs the nearest towel, throws it around herself and goes below deck. Meanwhile, Duncan is *still* standing there, stark naked and obviously trying to work out what the hell I'm doing there ...'

'I still think you changed the date on me.'

'In any case, it was a simple mix-up – except, I think I scared the girl away. I didn't see her again.'

Duncan, who was a good sport about being the butt of the joke, added, 'No, neither did I – oh, and thanks for that, James.'

'I think you came out ahead on that one,' replied James, smiling at Gerry. 'Gerry, you are a beautiful woman. I have no idea what you're doing with a schlub like Duncan, but I can say that he is a good man. Perhaps not good enough for you, but a pretty decent sort. That said, if he gives you any trouble, call me and I will happily kick his rear end for you.'

Gerry played along. 'It's okay, James. I'm a big girl. If he gets out of line, I'll handle him myself.'

'I'll drink to that,' James said, and they clinked glasses across the table. I noticed the mood of the table had eased significantly since James had started his story about Duncan. Even Josh had joined in on the laughter rippling around the group at Duncan's expense. Maybe he was softening towards James. Maybe he would stop being a grumpy dick and we'd all get along, and when Josh and I looked back on the time when we met, we'd remember the silver fox with fondness.

Maybe I had an overactive imagination.

'So, shall we go and get a drink? I know a great place,' said Duncan, standing and glancing around the group.

'A drink or three,' muttered Josh amid an affirmative chorus. I glanced at him. His jaw was clenched and he was sporting a frown. Still being a dick, apparently. Was he *actually* jealous about some brief encounter with the silver fox – which led to *nothing*? Not that he knew that, but all he needed to do was ask.

He was being ridiculous.

When the group moved outside, I took the opportunity to get away from Josh. I had been pissed off with him before dinner; *after* dinner, I was hovering closer to furious.

Duncan led us to a swanky-looking bar called Cosa Nostra. We followed him out to the balcony and got situated around a large table. I can't say how much of it was by design, but James claimed the seat next to mine, while Josh ended up at the opposite end of the table. Good – he could stay down there and brood for all I cared.

Besides I had other things on my mind. With the silver fox sitting right next to me, I could not avoid talking to him any longer. And of course, he smelled sublime – like sunshine and citrus and gorgeous manly man.

I buried my head in the drinks menu as a stalling tactic. James seemed to think it meant I wanted privacy – with him. He moved closer and pretended to read the cocktail list over my shoulder.

'I waited for you that day – at the restaurant. I was disappointed you didn't show up.'

'Really?' I asked, as nonchalantly as I could. His cologne was ridiculously distracting. I wanted to nuzzle his neck – maybe even lick it. I hoped it would taste as good as it smelled. Crap – I was in serious trouble.

It was my turn to order, and I hadn't even read the menu. I'd been too busy fantasising about licking someone's neck. 'Gin and tonic for me,' I said, defaulting to my favourite. I snapped the menu closed, nearly catching James's nose inside. He ordered some kind of whisky I'd never heard of – neat – and returned to our conversation without missing a beat.

'Yes, really. There's something about you that captivates me,

Sarah. I noticed it that day, and believe me, I am noticing it again tonight. I'd like the chance to figure out what it is.' I pretended I wasn't flustered, picking some non-existent lint from my dress.

I mulled over what he'd said. Did I want him to have that chance? And if so, where did that leave Josh?

I'd done a side-by-side comparison of the two before, but until then, the silver fox was mostly a character comprised of fantastical traits I'd dreamed up. Seeing him again, witnessing his charm, unfailing confidence and blatant sexiness, the comparison took on more meaning.

There was Josh, with his boyish good looks, self-deprecating humour, youthful wonder, and the fact that I felt like *me* when I was with him, and James, who on top of everything else I just said, was more sophisticated, worldlier, more accomplished – and, dare I say it – more of a man, really.

But, I wasn't sure I was ready to risk my friendship with Josh for a fling with the handsome silver fox. I cared about Josh; I liked him as a person. And I was pretty sure that even if he didn't end up wanting me *that* way, he wouldn't want me running off with the silver fox either.

So, you see the dilemma?

James had started a conversation with Marie, who sat on his right, and to my left, Gerry was teasing Duncan about the naked woman on James's boat, so I was mercilessly left to my own convoluted thoughts. When the drinks arrived, I snatched mine up greedily. I would need some Dutch courage if was going to handle James's advances with any sort of maturity or grace, especially as I rarely exhibited those traits in everyday life.

I risked another peek at Josh, and wouldn't you know it?

He was looking right at me. *Crap on a stick!* He raised his eyebrows, and then looked at James, as if to say, 'get a load of this guy'. I frowned and looked away. Definitely jealous. Did I want him to be jealous? Well, yes. And no. I didn't want him to feel bad, but then, if he did have feelings for me and he *was* jealous, then maybe he would drop the whole 'I want to die a bachelor' thing and do something about how he felt.

The annoying voice in my head told me I was being melodramatic, and it was right. I was going to finish the drink I was on, order another one, and get to know this gorgeous man, whose thigh was now pressed against mine, a little better.

I signalled to the waiter to bring another round for the table. Too bad if no one else had finished their drinks; we were there to have fun, right? After ordering, I attached what I hoped was a detached look to my face, and stared hard at the view. The silver fox leaned in close.

'You really like your gin and tonic,' he said, a teasing tone in his voice.

'I do,' I replied, keeping my eyes on the horizon. 'It's the perfect summer drink. And this is a perfect summer's night.' *How am I coming up with this rubbish?*

'Is that so?'

'It is.'

'What makes this night so 'perfect'?' he teased.

Until then, I'd been playing a role, my disinterest an affectation. He may even have known that, but I was done playing. I didn't want James thinking I was a vacuous dolt. I turned to him and gave him my full attention for the first time that night.

149

'Because, I'm somewhere I have always dreamed of being – and it's as beautiful as I'd imagined, maybe even more so. I've eaten a delicious meal ...' As if on cue, my next drink was placed in front of me. 'I'm sipping my favourite drink while looking at *that* view, and most importantly, these people.' I gestured to the assembled group. 'They're my family now, and I adore every one of them – and being with them is what makes this night perfect.' There, that wasn't rubbish; that was the truth. I was pleased I had come up with such a mature and gracious response.

He smiled and whispered, 'Sarah, you take my breath away.'

My, my, the silver fox had a silver tongue.

From anyone else it would have sounded cheesy, but believe me, he pulled it off. Talk about taking someone's breath away! Mine caught in my throat. And was that stirring in my loins? Without thinking, I reached for my earlobe, and gently caressed it. And as soon as I realised I was doing it, I stopped. I've read enough romance novels to know exactly what signal a fondled earlobe sends.

When I regained my composure – and we are only talking microseconds here – I replied the way I had been taught to respond to a compliment. I said, 'Thank you.'

He immediately countered my thank you with, 'But men have told you that many times before.'

Was he asking me or telling me? If he was telling me, he was wrong. And I'm not fishing for compliments, here. I know I am reasonably attractive, but I certainly don't look like a Victoria Secret's model – or any kind of model for that matter. Let's just say that Gisele Bündchen's job is safe from me.

I hadn't responded to his comment – my ability to banter was taking a beating. 'Not really, no.' *Wow! Good retort, Sarah.*

150

He seemed amused, and not in the charming, 'I'm on your side' way — more like in the, 'you're cute, little one' way. I sipped on my drink and chewed my straw a little.

Gary chose that moment to ask James a question. I wondered if he was saving me, or just seeking out interesting conversation. Regardless, I took the opportunity to talk to Gerry. I needed a breather from the silver fox.

'Hey, Ger.'

'Hey, Sar.'

'So, how's this trip going?'

She shook the ice in her drink and smiled at me. 'Really good, don't you think?'

'Yeah, but I meant, *how is it going*?' I looked over her shoulder at Duncan, who was chatting with Marie and Hannah. 'Isn't it hard being in a long-distance relationship?' It was a big question, but I had wanted to ask her since I'd met her and there had never really been a good time. She and Duncan lived in different places and only saw each other occasionally, and they seemed great together, but I wanted to know if it was for real. It mattered to me, because I liked them together. Okay, *and* because I wondered if a long-distance relationship could really work.

'How do you mean?' she replied. Maybe there was a translation issue; I was going to have to spell it out.

'I mean, how does it work with you two living so far apart?'

She looked thoughtful, as though she was phrasing the ideal response in her head. 'It is hard sometimes, but we make it work because we want to be together, and for now, we can't be in the same place — to live.'

I'd been holding my breath waiting for her answer and let it out. 'That's good,' I replied.

She nodded. 'Yes. You know, when I first met him in the person ...' I didn't correct her misuse of the idiom; I knew what she meant '... I knew my search was finished. A person can spend forever looking for someone who makes their heart sing. Maybe that person is not someone close by. Maybe you must look far away for that person. Even across the world. With the phone calls, and Skype, and emails, Duncan he always made my heart sing from the beginning.' I was mesmerised by her, the beautiful expression on her face while she talked about the man she loved. 'And *that* is well worth crossing an ocean for – many times. So, *esto es maravilloso*. I am very happy.'

I grabbed her hand and squeezed it. She leaned over and kissed my cheek. God, I adored this woman – no wonder Duncan did too. She was beautiful and smart and funny and so incredibly loving. 'And when my studies finish, then we find one place to live.'

'When is that?'

'Next year.'

I smiled. I had no doubt they'd make it to the following year.

She whispered conspiratorially, 'And what about you, Miss Sarah?'

'Me?'

'You seem to have two suitors now, yes?'

'No!' I whispered emphatically. Methinks I doth protest too much! Gerry obviously thought so too, and she gave me a knowing smile. She continued our conversation at a discreet volume. 'Yes. Two suitors. Josh is behaving like a baby, watching you with the handsome man.'

'He *is* handsome, isn't he?' I really wanted a second opinion.

There had to be a reason I'd reacted so viscerally to the silver fox.

'Oh, yes, very. And he seems to be taken with you too, Sarah. You have to make a choice, yes?'

'Do I?'

'I think yes, you do. Josh, he would like to be your boyfriend – for the trip, maybe longer. I think James, he would like to be your lover – for tonight, maybe longer.' She raised her eyebrows at me, and the more she spoke, the more panicked I felt. Gerry's take on things made it clear that the whole situation was just as messed up as I thought it was.

So, what did I want? I could turn down the man for the boy, but would the boy want me after all? Maybe I only wanted a holiday fling, a juicy story to dine out on when I got home. I'd sworn off men indefinitely, and now I wanted two at the same time! Well, not at the same time, obviously. I wasn't planning a cross-Atlantic threesome. Gerry was looking at me with an odd expression on her face. Concern? Horror? Pity?

'Crap on toast,' I muttered under my breath.

'I don't think I know this expression.' She was humouring me. I shook my head vigorously, as though clarity was just a little head jiggle away.

'What do you think, Sarah?' I heard from across the table. *Oh bugger*. Gary chose that exact moment to draw me into his conversation with the silver fox. Gerry patted my leg gently and turned back to Duncan. I was on my own. *Wonderful*.

'About what, Gary?' I tried to look interested. Scratch that – I was trying to look interes*ting*.

'We're talking about living the semi-retired life – travelling, meeting new people, only working when you want to – or need to – and only then for yourself. Doesn't that sound ideal?'

'Actually, it sounds incredible.' I turned towards James. 'Is that what you're doing? You work when you want to, travel the rest of the time?' Maybe Josh was right, after all – perhaps it was the perfect lifestyle.

'Yes, of sorts. Sometimes I get to do both – like this trip. It is both business and pleasure.'

'What do you do, James? When you *want* to work, that is.' I could sense the tables turning as I waited for his response. And the gin was finally kicking in! I had a nice warm feeling flowing through my veins, and a little boost of confidence came with it.

'I'm in art,' he said. Okay, that was extremely vague. I looked at him expectantly and waited for him to elaborate. 'I consult on works of art – for Sotheby's, other auction houses, some galleries.' I was impressed so, of course, I tried not to show it.

'Have you always been "in art", as you say?'

'For about twenty years now, but not always, no. I worked in finance through my twenties, and when I made enough to start collecting, I invested in some pieces I liked. Eventually, a few years down the track, I realised I was passionate about the work I was collecting – particularly that of up-and-coming artists. So, when I was in my early thirties I took a leap of faith, quit my job and started apprenticing, I guess you'd call it, with an art dealer in New York. I studied, I travelled, I worked my way up – it's as much about connections as it is about knowing the work and having a good eye – and by the time I was forty, I hung out my own shingle. That's about it.'

154

Dozens of thoughts buzzed around my head. From what he'd said, he was in his early fifties. He looked good – *really* good – and I hadn't pegged him for more than forty-five. At fifty-something, he was at least fifteen years older than me, and I wasn't sure how I felt about the age difference. He hadn't mentioned a wife, or kids, or anyone else connected to him. And I still had no idea what sort of art he was into. Even though I wanted to know about the possibility of a wife – or ex-wife – and if there were some kids out there somewhere, I decided not to lead with that.

'You haven't said what kind of art you collect – or consult on.'

'I focus mostly on contemporary artists – the up-and-comers, as I said. I made some smart investments early on, took a chance or two on artists whose work I liked, and a few of those investments paid off.'

Duncan, who must have been listening, interjected. 'He's being modest. James is considered one of the best in his field.' Everyone at the table was now listening. Looking at James, his face gave nothing away. 'It's true. He consults all over the world. If he discovers a new artist, they're almost guaranteed success on his name alone.' *Wowser*.

James waved off Duncan's words. 'Okay, Duncan. That's enough about that.'

The rest of the table went back to their respective conversations. I turned to Gary. 'So, to answer your question from earlier, yes. I think it does sound like a good way to go through life.' I picked up my drink and held it aloft. 'To doing what you love.'

Gary and James clinked glasses with mine, and we all took a sip. Marie nudged Gary and whispered something in his ear. He laughed aloud and whispered something back.

I had the silver fox to myself again – or did he have me?

'I hope this doesn't come off as completely trite, but your work sounds really interesting.'

'Why would it sound trite?'

'Because you have one of those jobs where you must get told that all the time.'

'I do, but I also like that you think so. And you're so right about doing what you love – it makes life immensely enjoyable.'

'And what about someone to share it with? Does that matter too?' *Geez, maybe hold back a little, Sarah.*

The amused glimmer reappeared in his eyes. Well, what did he expect? He was hitting on me – although, with what intention I couldn't divine. I wanted to know if he was attached, and if he wasn't, how would I fit into his globe-trotting life?

'Are you asking me if there *is* someone?'

'It's more of a general question about how another person fits into – or would fit into – all of this.' I waved my hand around, as though to indicate life, the world – possibly even the universe and everything. I caught the pointedness in my voice too late. I'd already said what I said, and I couldn't take it back. He seemed to be considering his words.

I was certain that I'd blown it.

'Sarah, there is no one. Not now. There was, quite a while ago, but she was not as taken with the lifestyle as I am, so she left. Now it is only me. And I like to think that, yes, I am leaving room for someone to be part of all of this.'

I hadn't blown it.

He took a sip of his drink and looked out at the marina, perhaps intentionally giving me a moment to digest what he'd said. He was talking about more than a holiday romance, and it frightened me a little. A lot, really. The silver fox was a grown-up, and even this short conversation with him made me feel girlish – and not in a good way. He was the real deal. And the real deal was interested in me. For real.

I looked across at Josh; he was talking with Hannah and laughing about something. I immediately felt a twinge of jealousy I had no right – and probably no reason – to feel.

The boy and the man. What to do?

But only *one* of them was alluding to something more than a flirtation – more than a sexual encounter and a good story to dine out on when I got home.

A waft of delicious, masculine scent enveloped me. James's mouth was next to my ear. 'I want you to come with me later. There's something I want to show you.'

'What?' I whispered, both nervous and excited.

'Are you asking me to repeat myself – or are you asking what it is that I want to show you?'

'Well, I heard you, so let's go with the latter.' My banter was fantastic.

'I am meeting up with an old friend, and he's introducing me to this artist I've come to see – I want you to see his work.'

'Oh.'

'You sound disappointed.'

'No, no, not at all.'

'Did you think I meant ...'

'No, of course not.' I was doing a poor job of hiding that I thought he was inviting me back to his place, *and* that I was disappointed he wasn't.

He brushed his lips over my ear – which I felt to my very toes – and said, 'Well, I do want to make love to you. Of course, I do – but first I want to show you some incredible art. Will you come?'

I don't mean to sound crass, but I could have come at the sound of his voice in my ear. Okay, that *was* crass – sorry. But I was absolutely going with him.

Chapter Ten

'Sarah, what are you doing?' Josh. He looked hurt.

'What do you mean?' Playing dumb.

'You're really going off with this guy?'

'We're going to meet up with a friend of his – and a new client – an artist.' I tried to make it sound as innocuous as possible.

'But—' He stopped short, a pained expression in his eyes.

'What, Josh?' I looked at him intensely. '*What?*' I could tell he didn't want me to leave with the silver fox, but would he say it? Would he finally articulate how he felt about me? I realised I was clenching my fists as I waited for his response.

'I just ...' I was willing him to say something – *anything* – that would make me want to stay. I had only known him a few days, but I cared about him. I was attracted to him, and *maybe* I wanted to be with him after the trip. But not if he was going to pout like a little boy, and not if he wouldn't say he wanted me too. I searched his eyes for what I hoped – and sort of feared – was there. *God, he has beautiful eyes.*

'Never mind.' A weak smile pulled at his lips for a heartbeat, then disappeared. 'Have a good night.'

Then he walked straight past the others towards the marina. I waved to the rest of the group, not stopping to wonder what they were thinking, and walked over to James. I was excited about spending more time with him, but a shitty feeling had made itself at home in my heart.

Here I was, thousands of miles from home, not having expected to meet anyone – not *wanting* to meet anyone – and wouldn't you know it? I had two suitors – Gerry was right – and they couldn't have been more different.

I gave my attention to the one I'd chosen to spend the rest of the evening with.

'Everything all right?' He looked genuinely concerned.

I flashed a million-watt smile, even if on the inside I felt about seventy watts. 'Absolutely. Let's go.' He didn't seem wholly convinced, but didn't press me for a further explanation. He started walking and I fell into step beside him.

'So, tell me about this new artist we're meeting.'

'In broad strokes, he pays homage to ancient Cycladic art. You've probably seen it depicted on urns and other objects, but he works on canvas. So, it's a modern take on an ancient art form. It's quite innovative, and at the same time, there's something classical about it.'

'Do you only work with artists whose work you like, or are you able to step back and say, 'This isn't to my taste, but the art world will embrace it'?'

'Great question. It's both, actually. Sometimes I pursue an artist – or I take them on – purely because they're someone I want to collect personally. Other times, I can appreciate the work, even if it doesn't move me.'

'I can see how both perspectives could work for you. You must have an extensive collection by now.'

'I'll say this, it's a carefully curated collection.'

'So, huge and worth a lot of money?' I was being cheeky.

I must have felt more comfortable with him. He smiled. Maybe cheeky was his thing.

'When you put me on the spot like that, what can I say?' I looked at him expectantly. 'Okay, yes, huge and worth a lot of money.'

We both broke into laughter, enjoying the joke between us. 'So where *is* it all?'

'I have quite a few pieces shared amongst my homes, some on the yacht, a few pieces on loan to galleries in New York and in Europe, and the rest is in storage.'

I was stuck on the first part of what he said. 'Homes?'

He nodded, but didn't say more. Was he embarrassed? Humble? I liked that he didn't want to brag about having *homes* – plural – but I'd want to know more at some point. We walked in silence for a while, and I mulled over what I knew about him. It would be an exciting life if I ended up attached to the silver fox.

And if I *did* end up with him, the rest of the evening was a great start to our life together. We went to his friend's house, which was a steep uphill walk from the bar, but well worth the climb. It was one of those homes that only the truly rich have, a modern take on the traditional whitewashed boxes that are ubiquitous in Greece.

The house had sharp edges and clean lines, which contrasted starkly with the craggy rock it clung to. It was long and narrow, with vast windows that overlooked the town and marina below. The living room opened onto a patio with a lone olive tree planted in the middle of it, and a lap pool ran the length of the house. Inside, we sat on low-slung white leather couches, and sipped Metaxa Private Reserve from ornate brandy glasses.

James's friend, Armando, was charming and welcoming, and his good humour and Spanish accent put me at ease immediately. I love Spanish people. Every Spaniard I have ever met – and that is quite a few – dresses well, enjoys the good things in life, and knows how to have a good time. Armando was true to the stereotype. I got the sense he and James had known each other for a lot of years. They had a kind of shorthand between them, and there was genuine affection when Armando teased James about me.

The artist was less charming, but that may have been because his English was limited and he didn't really have anything to say to me. He stuck to Greek most of the time, which Armando translated for James and me. Well, for James. It was his meeting. I tried to be unobtrusive.

The work was incredible, though. As James had said, it was both unique and familiar at the same time. I'm not saying it was something I would want on my walls, but I could see why others might.

Watching James work was the most intriguing part. If I hadn't known why we were there, I don't know how obvious it would have been that some sort of deal was being struck. James directed the conversation so that the artist, Ari, could express how he wanted his work viewed, who his audience was, and what he envisioned for his first major exhibit. Mostly, James listened, only offering a few interjections to confirm a key piece of Ari's vision.

And before I knew it, the whole thing was over, and Ari was packing up his portfolio – he'd brought a handful of smaller pieces and some photos of the rest of the work. Then he left. And I was stuck with two crazy Europeans who seemed to share a constant private joke. I loved it.

'Sarah,' said Armando, smiling wickedly at me, 'what are you doing with Jimmy, here? He is a cad, don't you know?'

'Hey now,' said James. I detected a slight edge to his voice, and he looked sideways at his friend. I wasn't sure what to address first – that Armando had called James 'Jimmy' – he *so* wasn't a 'Jimmy' – that he'd asked what I was doing with James as though we were a couple – which we most certainly were not – or that the silver fox was supposedly a cad.

I went with the nickname; it was the easiest to deal with. 'Jimmy?' I raised my eyebrows at James.

'Very few people in the world call me that and Armando happens to be one of them. Let's just say he earned it.' Another in-joke, apparently. Armando laughed a hearty belly laugh and poured himself more Metaxa. Armando held the bottle of Metaxa aloft as if to ask if I wanted a refill. I shook my head; I'd had more than enough to drink, and I wanted to keep my wits about me.

'So, I don't know how you two met,' I said, trying to redirect the conversation as far away from me as possible.

'No, no, beautiful, you do not get off that easily,' countered Armando. 'How do *you two* know each other? *That's* what I want to know.'

I looked at James, floundering for an appropriate response. He had basically tried to pick me up outside a church.

James, however, was not flustered and answered with, 'Sarah caught my eye on Santorini. I asked her to lunch, and she let me down. But, as fortune often smiles on me, it turns out she is travelling with Duncan, and we met again tonight.' He smiled at me smugly. I frowned and his smile broadened. Why did he always have the upper hand?

'Duncan, the skipper?' Armando obviously knew Duncan too.

'The very one.'

'Wonderful! I *love* how these things work out.'

'What things?' I finally spoke.

'You and Jimmy. He probably thought he would never see you again.' He looked at James who nodded by way of confirmation. 'And then, here you are on Naxos. How wonderful.'

'I think so,' said James.

'And you, Sarah? Do you believe in fate, in kismet?' Armando was putting me on the spot – again.

'Hard to say. I suppose that will depend on what happens next.' I'd said it as a challenge, but who was I challenging? The silver fox? Me? I didn't know what was going to happen in the next few minutes, let alone the rest of the night. What if James did ask me back to his hotel? Would I go? Would I make love with the handsome silver fox, when the American boy was no doubt waiting up for me? Was kismet responsible for this mess? If it was, then kismet deserved a kick in the bum.

'Well, I know what's happening next,' said James, as he made to leave. 'Time to get going, I'm afraid.'

Hang on – we were leaving? I was going to be alone with him, and I wasn't even sure yet what that would mean.

'So soon, my old friend?' Armando replied as he stood to say goodbye.

'Watch who you call old,' retorted James. It was great that they were enjoying friendly banter while I was having a mild panic attack. I stood up and hunted around the roomy couch for my handbag. I found it just as I caught James's eye. 'I must see Sarah back to the yacht. It's getting late,' he added.

Back to the yacht? Not back to his hotel? I wasn't sure if I was relieved or disappointed. I think there was even a smidge of 'insulted' in the mix of emotions churning inside me. Or was that the brandy mixing with the gin?

'Yes,' I said thrusting my hand towards Armando, 'we must be off. It's getting late, and you know how old people are if they have too many late nights.' *Well, that was a tad bitchy, Sarah.* Armando ignored my hand and pulled me close for a series of kisses on my cheeks. There were so many, I lost count after three.

'Sarah,' he gushed, 'you are delightful. It's wonderful to meet a woman who can handle Jimmy so deftly.'

Handle him? Is that what I'm doing? I thought I was behaving like a toddler.

James put a light hand on my shoulder and gently steered me to the door. He gave Armando a hug and two cheek kisses – Europeans! – and then we were outside in the fresh evening air, alone. My chin jutted out at an angle that would have made Reese Witherspoon proud. I tucked it in a little lest I looked too impertinent.

'Shall we?' he said, gesturing towards the pathway leading to the marina.

'We shall,' I replied. We walked in silence for a few minutes. The air was still, and it smelled intoxicatingly of bougainvillaea. I inhaled deeply, knowing I'd forevermore think of the Greek Islands whenever I smelled that sweet aroma. Thousands of stars lit up the sky and lights from homes dotted the hillside down to the marina. The island was stunning.

'It's beautiful, isn't it?' I found myself saying.

'It is.' He touched my hand and pulled me to a stop. '*You* are also beautiful.'

'You make me nervous,' I blurted out, the tranquil moment shattered. To his credit, he responded by laughing – not a mild, smarmy laugh, but a throw-your-head-back-and-laugh-out-loud kind of a laugh. I found myself laughing too – mostly at how silly I was being.

'Why *on earth*,' he said through the laughter, 'do *I* make you nervous?' He shook his head as though he couldn't believe it.

'Because. You're a grown-up. You're an adult in every way, and I feel like a ridiculous schoolgirl around you.'

'Sarah, I hate to be the one to break this to you, but you, my lovely, are all woman – there's not a schoolgirlish thing about you.'

'Really?'

We were walking again. 'Really. And not only that, if I'm completely honest, you make me a little nervous too.'

'I do?'

'Yes. You're so forthright. There's no pretence with you – you say exactly what's on your mind.'

'Not always.'

'Maybe not, but enough. It's refreshing. Look, I meet a lot of people – women –' I frowned at that '– but I rarely meet a beautiful woman who keeps me on my toes like you do.' I felt myself start to relax; I liked hearing nice things about me.

'When I first saw you on Santorini, you really did take my breath away. I asked you to lunch, because I thought we would have an interesting conversation – and if not, it was just lunch. And then you didn't show up, which made me more intrigued about you. You cannot know how pleased I was to see you in the restaurant tonight. I thought our one meeting was all there would ever be – and then, there you were.'

166

'There I was.' I was transfixed by his words.

'Exactly, and over the course of dinner, and drinks and more drinks, I discovered you are witty – mostly at your own expense. You're interested in others, you have an adventurous spirit, and most surprisingly, you don't let me get away with much.'

'Oh.'

'Is that all you have to say?'

'That's a lot to take in. I don't think of myself like that.'

'I understand. I don't mean to overwhelm you. I mean, despite everything I've said, we only just met and I am probably making a lot of assumptions.'

'About?'

'You. Us. What could happen.'

'Oh.'

"Oh' again? Suddenly you're not so articulate. I think I'm making you nervous again.'

'No. I just – I don't know what to say. I—'

'What?'

'Well, you're taking me back – to the boat – and I thought—'

'You thought I would ask you back to my hotel.'

'Yes.'

'And would you have come?'

'I don't know.'

'Ah.'

'But I think I wanted you to ask me.'

'I wanted to, but there are a couple of things stopping me – maybe more than a couple.'

'Oh? Sorry, I mean, what things?'

'Well, for a start, I leave early in the morning for Athens and, presumably, you'll be heading to the next island.'

'I didn't realise you were leaving so soon.'

'Back to Athens, and then straight to London, I'm afraid.'

'So, "early" means?'

'My plane leaves at six.'

'Right – that *is* ridiculously early.'

'Exactly, and believe me, the first time I make love to you, I don't want there to be any reason to rush.' My stomach did a somersault, followed by a backflip. It did *not* stick the landing.

'I see. The first time? So ...' We stopped walking and stood, facing each other.

'That's my next point. If something happens between us, I don't want it to be a one-night thing. Those are horrid. And, frankly, I gave them up in my thirties.'

I nodded as though it made perfect sense – even though *I'd* been willing to have a one-night thing with James up until a few minutes before.

'And there's one last thing.'

Oh god! He was going to tell me he *was* married – or dying – or both!

'The young man on the yacht ...'

'Josh?' I said, a little too loudly.

'Josh, yes. I got the sense something is going on between you, and I don't want to be *that* man.'

'What man?'

'I don't want to insert myself somewhere I'm not welcome.' *Did he really just say that?* I thought. I couldn't let it slide.

'Did you hear what you just said?'

'Yes – actually, I did – as soon as I said it, and it was quite awful, and if you could forget I said it, that would be excellent.'

'Totally forgotten.'

'Good. Now back to Josh ...' But what about Josh? What could I say?

'Josh and I only met a few days ago ...' *Sarah, no matter how tipsy you are, you absolutely must not pretend that nothing is happening with Josh. That isn't fair to him – or James – or you.* Sometimes the voice in my head can be so damned reasonable.

'... but we've become really close in a short time.' That was good – and true. 'Somehow, despite living on opposite sides of the world, and that I didn't even know him a week ago, I feel like he's going to be important to me.'

'Oh.'

'Now *you're* saying "Oh".'

'Yes.'

'But the thing is, I don't know what will happen with him. He doesn't want a relationship. He has been adamant about that – in fact, before he discovered you and I had already met, he wanted to pick your brain about the incredible bachelor life you lead.'

'It's probably not like he thinks it is.'

'I'm sure that parts of it are,' I said, smiling.

'Just not the "bachelor" part. Unlike your friend, I *do* want to be in a relationship.'

'And therein lies my dilemma.'

'I see that now. Look, we don't need to decide the rest of our lives tonight. How about I get in contact with you when I get back to London? Let's keep in touch, then see how it all pans out?'

'You're letting me off the hook.' I started walking again. We were close to the marina.

'Perhaps. Do you remember you said that to me on Santorini when I asked you to lunch, "perhaps"?'

'I do remember. I was trying to be way cooler than I felt. You kind of took my breath away too, you know.'

'So, I can contact you?'

'Of course.' I rummaged around in my handbag for a notepad and pen, wrote out my email address and mobile phone number – neatly, so he would be able to read them – and tore out the page. 'Here. Oh, and I forgot to say that I'm heading to London at the end of this trip – my sister lives there, and I'm staying with her for a week.'

He returned my smile, obvious delight in his eyes. 'That, lovely Sarah, is wonderful news.'

'I think so, too.'

We arrived at the end of the pier, and I stopped and turned to him. 'This is me,' I said.

He took both of my hands in his and lifted them to his lips, kissing them in turn. 'I still cannot believe you were at dinner tonight. It was a lovely surprise.'

'And after I recovered from the shock, it was a lovely surprise for me too. Thank you for taking me to Armando's – I had fun with you crazy Europeans.' He laughed.

And then he stopped laughing and looked at me with those ridiculously sexy eyes. 'I'm going to kiss you now.'

'You'd better,' I replied as I slid my hands around his neck and stood on my tiptoes. The kiss was incredible – slow, sexy, strong. He *really* knew what he was doing. But, then again, so did Josh. Josh was a great kisser – which was wonderful, but not something I wanted to be thinking about while kissing the silver fox. I pushed the unwelcome thought away and sunk back into the kiss I was in.

We pulled apart, and I think I may have purred a little.

'Goodnight, beautiful. I hope to see you in London.'

'Goodnight,' I said dreamily as I turned and walked back to the boat.

Chapter Eleven

I wasn't wearing my watch, so when I arrived back at the boat I had no idea what time it was – late, I guessed. I crossed the gangplank cautiously. I didn't want to fall between the boat and the dock for two reasons – I wanted to avoid drowning, and I didn't want to wake the family. I made it across without doing either, stepping onto the deck of the boat as lightly as I could.

'Hey,' came a soft voice from the top deck of the boat. Josh was silhouetted against the moonlight.

'Hey,' I replied just as softly. Had he been waiting up for me? I remembered thinking earlier in the night that he might, but still, it surprised me.

'Fun night?' he asked.

'Yes.' I didn't know what else to say. Had he seen me at the end of the pier with James? *Oh god! Did he see the kiss?*

A moment went by in silence – a big, fat moment. 'Goodnight,' I said, for want of anything better to say. I was still basking in the euphoria of kissing James.

I wasn't ready to deal with my feelings for Josh. I ducked below deck and heard a quiet, 'Goodnight,' in return.

I tiptoed across the dining nook, knowing that every tiny sound was amplified on the small boat. I didn't want to disturb anyone, especially not Hannah. I slowly turned the knob to our cabin and saw that she was asleep on the bottom bunk – *my* bunk. She seemed completely out of it, which I was glad for, but I was going to have to break out some pretty impressive manoeuvres to get over her and into the top bunk without waking her up.

I slipped into the small bathroom and washed up as quickly and quietly as I could. Moonlight pooled in through the ceiling hatch, and I caught sight of myself in the mirror. I looked – what? Happy, I looked happy. I eased the bathroom door open and stood beside the bunks for a moment, trying to work out my course.

I figured if I put my foot on the edge of the lower bunk and swung up and over Hannah, who was now lying spread-eagle across it, I might make it without disturbing her. I cursed the last glass of brandy and how tipsy I was, but holding on to the edge of the top bunk for leverage, I executed my plan flawlessly. I looked down at Hannah; she hadn't even stirred. Either I was uber stealthy, or she was uber out of it.

I lay back on the bunk and thought back over my night with James. No one was going to believe this story when I told them; it sounded made up.

*

The next morning, the sun was a less than welcome sight. My eyes hurt when I tried to open them, and my head hurt when I tried to lift it off the tiny pillow.

'Good morning, sunshine,' crowed a cheery Hannah, as she stepped out from our bathroom. She was standing in the half-a-square-metre area, which made up our floor space, wiggling her eyebrows at me. I frowned – that hurt too. 'Fun night?' she asked, her voice dripping in insinuation.

'Not *that* fun,' I replied, a little tersely. Great – speaking hurt too. How much had I had to drink?

'Well, you must have come in *late*. I was totally out of it – and that only happens for me in the middle of the night.' She wiggled her eyebrows again. Damn her and her wretched eyebrows.

'I did come in late – yes, but nothing happened – not really.'

'You mean you *didn't* sleep with the billionaire?' She sounded disappointed.

'He's not a billionaire – he's just a millionaire many times over.' *Did I really just say that? Is this who I am now, a person who casually mentions multi-millionaires?*

'Well, whatever he is. You didn't sleep with him?' Yep, she was disappointed.

'No. I didn't. We were at his friend's place most of the night, and then he walked me home. And that's it.' She looked crestfallen. 'Hannah, why do you care?'

'Because. I do. If my friend can find a rich, handsome older guy who's into her, then maybe I can.' Seriously, she was making this about her? Fine. If that was the case, then I could at least give her some hope.

'He did kiss me,' I said, simply.

Her eyes got wide. 'He did? How was it?'

'It was great. He's super sexy. He's interesting—'

'And interes*ted*, by the sounds of it.'

'He is. Yes.'

'*AND*? God, girl, getting any kind of information out of you is like interrogating a secret agent!' She had a point, but

I was only holding back because I wasn't sure what was going on – or what was going to happen – *or* what I wanted.

I groaned under the weight of it all and dropped my head back on the pillow, heavily. *Ouch, that really hurt.* 'I'm sorry, Hannah. I'm hungover. Can we talk about this later?' Chickening out, I blamed the monster hangover, rather than telling her the truth. Of course, I would eventually tell her – but not before a lukewarm trickle of a shower and a hot cup of tea. And maybe some toast.

Hannah harrumphed a little and then made a big show of putting her sunglasses on. 'Fine. I'll see you up on deck when you have dealt with *this*.'

I knew that by 'this' she meant my atrocious state, because when she said it, she waved her hand in front of me to encompass all the grossness that was me. She even slammed the cabin door closed after her. I hoped the others were awake already, but as Hannah was usually the last one up, I figured they probably were. I wondered what time it was. Then I realised two things – it didn't matter, and the boat was moving.

At least that explained why I felt like the cabin was moving – it was. Maybe I wasn't as hungover as I thought I was. I sort of rolled off the top bunk and made it to a standing position. Oh, yeah, I *was* that hungover – it had nothing to do with the boat being on the move.

When I finally showed my face, freshly showered but still feeling off, Marie took pity on me, and plied me with tea and buttered toast. I didn't deserve her kindness for my self-inflicted pain, but I appreciated it – especially because it was a sailing day.

In full sail, we sliced through the indigo waters of the Aegean as we headed north to the island of Syros, the sky a brilliant blue. I braced myself against the rolling of the boat and marvelled at where I was and what I was doing. It was incredible. And despite my queasy stomach and sore head, it was one of those moments when I was in love with my life. It may have also had something to do with the lingering memories of the previous night. Each time I thought of James kissing me, I smiled.

Until ...

'Hey,' said Josh, sitting down next to me.

'Hey yourself,' I said, trying to sound casual. Did I sound casual – or did I sound like I'd spent the last hour thinking about another man?

'I wanted to show you these,' he said, holding up an iPad. I couldn't see what was on it because I could only see the reflection of the sun.

'What, what am I looking at?' *Snippy, Sarah. That was snippy.* 'I'm sorry, I can only see the sun reflected.'

'Sorry.' He angled the screen towards me. 'It's my photos from the trip so far. I've been uploading them as a back-up, and I thought you might want to see them.' Wait, a retrospective of our trip the morning after I spent the evening with James? Was Josh manoeuvring? Was he so savvy he would plan a move like that just to get ahead of the silver fox? If he was, it was well played. After all, who knew when I would see James again. And I could hardly blame Josh if he wanted to cash in on a home ground – make that a home *boat* – advantage.

That said, I wasn't ready to give up basking in the glow of my evening with James. *That* said, how did I politely refuse? 'I'm sorry, Josh, I am a little busy right now reliving another man's kiss.' Definitely not that.

What I *did* say was, 'Uh, sure.'

He scooched closer to me and deftly flicked through the photos, skipping ones which he said hadn't turned out well, and lingering on the shots he seemed proud of. There was one of a house that particularly impressed me. 'This is extraordinary, Josh.' It was a shot of the sharp-edged corner of a bright orange house – a rare find amongst the whitewashed ones – contrasted against a vibrant blue sky.

'Thanks.' He seemed genuinely modest.

'I mean that. People should see this – it's really beautiful. You have a lot of great shots in here, but this is my favourite so far.'

'Well, I'll be uploading some of the best ones to Flickr when I get home.'

'Flickr?'

'Yeah, you don't know about that?'

'Nope.'

'It's a photo-sharing website. I can show you next time we're online.'

'Okay.'

We resumed skimming through the photos, some snapshots – all of us at dinner, or shots of us on the boat – and other more artistic, well-composed shots. There were quite a few of me, including a couple 'Josh and Sarah' selfies.

Then we came to a shot that made me say, 'Wait.' He lifted his finger from the screen, and the image remained. 'That's me.' It was a silly thing to say, really. There were a lot of photos of me; it wasn't like I'd made some sort of surprising discovery.

Only, maybe I had.

In the photo, I was sitting on the top deck of the boat, and we were under full sail. I was holding on with one hand,

177

while the other arm was outstretched. My hair flowed behind me and my face was tipped towards the sun. I knew that exact moment – we had just left Ios and were in full sail for the first time.

I remembered feeling completely unfettered by responsibility, by expectations, by remorse. All I had felt in that moment was joy. He had captured that feeling so perfectly, I was dumbstruck.

A moment later, I found my voice. 'We didn't know each other very well then. It was only the second day.'

'What do you mean?' he asked.

'I'm wondering why you took this. I mean, it's quite an intimate shot.' I looked sideways and caught his profile. His jaw was tense. Crap, I hadn't meant to upset him, but the photo had taken me off-guard.

'You looked so happy. I wanted to capture it.'

'You did. It's beautiful.' I hoped it was enough to make everything okay.

He sighed softly. 'I guess I knew early on you were going to become important to me, even if I wasn't sure at the time why – or how.' It was the same sentiment I'd shared with James the night before, and suddenly, all the breath rushed out of my body and my eyes prickled with tears. I blinked them away. *What* was happening?

'You'll have to send me a copy,' I said, finally. I didn't know what else to say. I didn't know what to feel, to think, or do. I *did* know I couldn't look at photos anymore. 'I need to lie down a bit more. I'm still feeling queasy. Will you please excuse me?'

He looked hurt. He probably was hurt. Dismissing his admission like that was horrible, but I needed some time alone. I got up and moved past him. 'Sure, no problem,' he said, but I sensed he didn't mean it.

I carefully made my way below deck, which was a dumb move because we were sailing and I was queasy, which was exacerbated by the movement of the boat. There was no way I would be able to rest in our cabin, which was in the stern – I'd be tossed around. I made my way over the dining nook holding on to something the whole way, and lay down. It was in the middle of the boat, so if I was going to be below deck – and really, I didn't feel like facing anyone – it was the best place to be.

As my body settled into the rise and fall of the boat on the water, I thought about what had just happened. And then I went back over everything I remembered about Josh and me together – the things he'd said, how sexy he was, how he made me laugh, what it felt like to be kissed by him, and how it stung to hear him talk about his life of bachelorhood. All of it.

And with tears rolling down my cheeks, I made a decision. As much as I was falling for the cute American boy, I could see there was no future with him. He was too young, too naïve about love and relationships, and too much of a boy. And, a grown man was waiting to see me when I got back to London, a man who wanted me – a man who'd been honest about that.

I decided that for the remainder of the trip, I would keep Josh at arm's length. I would be his friend – friendly, but not girl-friendly. No more of that. I'd end up hurt, and he probably would too. We had four more days on the trip. I could keep my distance for four days. Better to hurt a little then, than a lot later on.

Somehow, remarkably, I fell asleep. I woke up when the boat engines roared to life. We must have been nearing port, which meant I had been sleeping for hours. Gingerly, I lifted my head and sat up. The headache and queasiness were gone. In my mind, I said a quiet thank you to the Greek gods.

'Especially you, Dionysus,' I said aloud.

Then I climbed the small ladder to the deck, and watched as the others hurried about hanging buoys off the starboard boat railings to provide a buffer between the boat and the dock. I would have offered to help, but they were almost done by the time I emerged. We were pulling up alongside what must have been the town's main thoroughfare. Scooters and cars whooshed by on the waterfront street about five metres away.

'Why aren't we berthing at the marina?' I asked.

'There's no room for us there,' replied Duncan. 'We're docking here for tonight – maybe tomorrow night too.' I hoped for the former, as not being docked at the marina meant we weren't connected to electricity or water. And that meant the water supply we had on board needed to last, and we wouldn't be able to generate power for hot water. And *that* meant cold rinses for the foreseeable future instead of hot showers. *Bugger*.

I wasn't bummed out for too long, though. As Duncan expertly manoeuvred the boat alongside the dock, I checked out the town. We were docking at Ermoupoli on the island of Syros, the capital of the Cyclades Islands. Unlike other towns and villages we had seen on our journey, this place didn't look typically Greek. It was more like somewhere in Italy, or Spain – perhaps Southern France.

And it was spectacular.

Pops of pastels dotted the densely packed hillside, which overlooked the dock. I could see influences from several different types of architecture: classical, Byzantine, French provincial, and a few I couldn't identify. It was like the European Union of architecture. And we were right in the thick of things. I mean *right there* in the town. There was a bus stop about three metres away, and the dock was filled with evening commuters heading home after a workday. They ignored us; perhaps they saw a yacht full of travellers docked there all the time.

I was in heaven. Juxtaposed against the sleepy village that had greeted us on Ios and the relaxed marina we'd left on Naxos, Ermoupoli was a thriving, bustling metropolis. I couldn't wait to get out into it.

I turned to Hannah, who I'd barely spoken to since she taunted me that morning, and she looked as excited as I was. 'Want to go exploring with me?' I asked.

'Oh yeah,' she said. Without another word, we both slipped below deck. Within minutes, our cabin became a flurry of discarded clothes, as we complimented each other on our choices and competed for the mirror on the back of the door. 'You look hot,' she declared. I looked down at my outfit of skinny jeans and a flouncy top. I had my high-heeled sandals ready to slip on once we left the boat.

'You think?'

'Absolutely. What about me?' I loved how she shamelessly fished for a compliment. It was easy to give, though, because she looked great. She was wearing a floaty summer dress, had fluffed her hair, and was wearing a slick of pretty pink lip gloss.

'Hot, definitely hot.'

'Well, then let's go and explore!' She grabbed her purse and was checking the contents when I got a twinge of guilt.

'Hannah?'

'Mm-hmm?' She was distracted, counting her euros and loading up her bag with a compact and her lip gloss.

'Should we see what the others are doing?' She stopped fussing with her bag.

'You mean, see what *Josh* is doing?'

'I, uh, no, I mean everyone. We usually have dinner together. Shouldn't we wait to see what the others want to do for dinner?' She was wearing a frown. It said, 'Sarah, stop being such a wuss.' And the frown was right.

She slung the purse over her shoulder. Because of the confined space, I was standing in the bathroom, and she was standing in the cabin, but she was still close enough for me to see her nostrils flare in frustration.

'Sarah *Jane!*' *Uh oh*. She was using my middle name. Why did I ever tell her that? 'You mean to tell me, we finally get to a town that looks hip and fun and cool – *all the things* we haven't seen yet on this trip – and you recruit me to be your partner in crime to explore this town – and *then* you go all pussy on me because of some misguided sense of obligation to the others? Is that what is going on here?'

I flinched at the word 'pussy' – I hate that word – but she had a point. Just because we'd had dinner together most nights, didn't mean we needed to spend every moment together. We weren't the Brady Bunch. I also thought it would be good for me to have a night away from Josh – *completely* away from him. If I was going to keep him at arm's length – why shouldn't my plan start immediately?

182

'You're right,' I admitted. And then I felt it again, the twinge of guilt.

'Can we at least invite the girls? Girls' night out?' I tried to sell it with my best smile. I liked Gerry and Marie, and maybe if they came along too, they could help me keep Hannah out of trouble.

She sighed heavily. She certainly was one for the dramatics. '*Fine*. I'll be up on deck.' With that, she left our cabin. I put the finishing touches on my makeup, prepped my own purse with what I needed for the night, and went to find Gerry and Marie.

*

'We're going to need cocktails. Stat,' said Hannah. The four of us – Marie, Gerry, Hannah and I – were seated at a beautiful little bar right off the main drag of Ermoupoli. If we sat up tall on our stools and stretched our necks, we could see the water, but really, after living on a boat for the better part of a week, I was okay with being on solid ground and having a view of the bougainvillaea growing on the wall across from us.

'Why 'stat'?' asked Marie.

'Because, we are four beautiful women out on the town, and we have a lot to talk about, and nights like this start out best with a cocktail – or two,' she replied, as though it was the most logical thing in the world. The three of us shared a look, then burst out laughing.

'What?!' demanded Hannah. She looked annoyed.

'Hey, we're not making fun – we *all* agree with you.' Marie, ever the diplomat.

183

'Oh,' Hannah said, a little contrite. 'That's cool, actually. If you think about it, we didn't even know each other a week ago, and here we are, girlfriends out for the night.' She smiled.

'That's so sweet, Hannah,' said Gerry. 'Now I want a drink so I can cheers to my girlfriends.'

Another endearing mangling of English from Gerry – and I don't mean that condescendingly. Spanish was her native tongue, and she spoke far more English than I spoke Spanish, that's for sure. In fact, I still only know about fourteen words of Spanish, and most of those are menu items. What I admired about Gerry was how she charged into the depths of English, fearlessly embracing the idioms – *that* was the endearing part.

A gorgeous – and I mean Greek-god-gorgeous – waiter came to the table to take our order. Even Marie raised her eyebrows at me and she was married to a Harrison Ford lookalike. Hannah had commandeered the cocktail menu, and she selected four drinks without the three of us having any say. She practically shooed the waiter away to fetch them.

'So, Hannah, what are we having?' asked Marie.

'You'll see.' She smiled to herself. 'Trust me, ladies, this is one of my superpowers – selecting the perfect drink for my girls. It's one of the things I do back home with my girlfriends.'

'Do you go out a lot in Vancouver?' asked Marie.

'I guess – what's 'a lot'?' replied Hannah.

'Well, I don't go out much with my girlfriends – maybe, if we're lucky, four or five times a year – so I guess, anything more than that.'

I couldn't work out if Hannah was shocked or if she pitied Marie. Maybe it was both.

'By those standards, yes, I go out a lot. Usually a couple of times a week. Vancouver has an amazing bar scene. You can choose exactly what kind of night you want – are you going out for a rowdy night drinking beer and eating bar food? Do you want something more sophisticated? Somewhere like this for cocktails? There are some awesome speak-easies – some with live jazz. So, yeah. I mean, I'm single –' an edge crept into her voice '– and I like to enjoy myself. The friends I go out with are super fun, so I guess I do go out a lot.'

Marie smiled, and there was a touch of sadness in it. I think it may have been her who pitied Hannah – or maybe she empathised. Hannah said a lot about being an independent woman, but I was pretty sure she was hoping to find someone special to share her life with.

The drinks arrived.

As the waiter held up each one, Hannah directed him to put it in front of a specific person. When they were all in place, she raised hers and proposed a toast.

'To my new girlfriends. No matter what else happens in this world, no matter who screws us over, we can always count on our girls.' Boy, her ex had done the dirty on her. Talk about a backhanded toast.

'To my new girlfriends,' I said. We all raised our glasses, clinked them against the rims of the others, and took a sip of our drinks. Mine was delicious. I could see from the looks on Marie and Gerry's faces that theirs were too. Hannah looked proud of herself.

'How did you know, Hannah? That I like tangy drinks?' I asked, taking another sip of my citrusy cocktail.

'I pay attention. You like gin and tonic – you like the tang, and the aromatics, but nothing too sweet.' She was right. The girl was good.

'Gerry, you love your sweet treats, so lychee for you.'

'I love it!'

'And, Marie, something tropical for you – you've mentioned how much you've loved your travels to Hawaii and Mexico – I figured you'd like it.'

Marie laughed. 'I'm impressed, Hannah. If only it was the type of skill you could market.'

'Well, it is, isn't it? Attention to detail, empathy, listening skills.'

We all laughed. 'Hannah, you're absolutely right. I'll drink to that.' Marie raised her glass, and we all clinked again.

'So,' said Gerry, turning her full attention to me. *Uh oh.* 'I have waited all day to ask this, and now here we are away from the boat – and the men.' *Double uh oh.* 'What is happening with you and your two suitors?' Seriously, where did she learn that word?

I sighed. I bought some more time by taking another sip of my drink. The eyes looked on, unblinking. 'To be honest, I don't know.' Three pairs of eyes rolled at the same time. 'I don't!' I insisted.

Marie put her hand on mine. 'Maybe it will help to talk it through.' She was probably right. I mean, I had talked it through a little with each of them, but that was before I'd had the evening with the silver fox.

But where to start?

'Okay.' I took a deep breath and blew it out. 'So, I came on this trip – not expecting, not *wanting* to meet anyone. And right off the bat, I meet Josh. And he's far too young for me, and he lives so far away, but he is smart, and he makes me laugh, and I get the sense he really *sees* me, you know?' It was a rhetorical question, and I continued without interruption. 'I mean, today he showed me this photo he took of me,

186

and I didn't know he was taking it at the time – which I promise isn't as creepy as it sounds – and it's a really beautiful shot. It captured something about me I haven't seen in myself for a long time. And it got me thinking that maybe this is a guy who could know the real me – maybe even *love* the real me.

'But, I know he isn't that guy, because this whole time, he keeps telling me how he doesn't want a girlfriend, and I don't mean *now*. I mean *ever*. He is planning a life of bachelorhood, and when he and I were just friends, that was fine – he could tell me that stuff, but now there's something else there. He says one thing and does another. I can tell he likes me – but I know there's no future. And even if there is, *he lives on the other side of the world*, so how *can* there be a future?' Again, a rhetorical question.

'And *then*, as if that wasn't enough confusion, there's the silver fox, who I *never in a million years* thought I would see again after our *very* brief encounter on Santorini.' The eyes looked on, unwavering. 'James is wicked smart, and accomplished, charming, and he really wants to get to know me, and it doesn't matter if he lives on the other side of the world, because he's ridiculously rich, and he can come to Sydney whenever he wants – or fly me to London – or wherever he wants to, for that matter.

'And did I mention I had no intention of meeting anyone on this trip?'

I sat back in my seat and took a proper swig from my cocktail. I dared a glance at my new friends to gauge their reactions. They were all silent as if they were trying to come up with the right thing to say.

Hannah spoke up. 'Well, that sucks.'

187

And she was bang on. Which made me laugh. Loud, long and hard, and then the others joined in. When the laughter died down, I felt calm, and for some reason, reassured that everything would work out well.

'You know,' I began, 'part of me – an ever-increasing part of me – wants to tell them both to bugger off.' That elicited some more laughter until Gerry said something that pinpointed why I hadn't.

'But then you would be left wondering for the rest of your life – about both of them.'

'Ah, yes.' I nodded. 'Therein lies the rub.'

'You know what I think?' said Marie. I looked at her, my eyes encouraging her to go on. 'I think Josh will figure out soon that what he *really* wants is you. And when he does, it will all work out.'

Maybe she was right.

Chapter Twelve

Four women drunk on cocktails cannot sneak onto a boat quietly. Fortunately, the menfolk were waiting up for us. I wondered if they were as drunk as we were.

'Hello, ladies,' slurred Duncan. Well, Duncan definitely was.

'Did you have fun?' asked Gary, as he stood and wrapped his arms around his wife. It looked like Gary was a little more in control of his faculties than Duncan.

'We had soooo much fun!' Marie giggled from the confines of her husband's tall frame. I'd never heard such a girly giggle from her.

'Let's get you to bed, beautiful. Lots of water first, I think,' Gary said, taking her hand and leading her below deck.

She tossed a joyful 'Goodnight' over her shoulder.

Gerry had snuggled up with Duncan under a chunky rug and seemed to have lost consciousness in a matter of moments. 'What about you two?' Duncan asked Hannah and me. 'You have a good night too?'

'We had a great night,' I replied. 'I haven't had a girls' night out for a long time, and it was exactly what I needed.' Hannah went on to describe the bar where we'd spent the evening, and I watched Josh. He looked glum. I may have decided to keep my distance, but it didn't mean I had to be rude.

189

'How about you guys?' I asked him.

He smiled feebly. 'Sure, yes. It was fun. We grabbed a bite at one of the gyros places and then came back here – hung out. Duncan made some cocktails.'

'Sounds fun.' He nodded and then stared at me. I couldn't think of anything else to say. 'Well, goodnight.' Without waiting for a reply – from Josh, or the others – I went below deck. I grabbed a bottle of water from the galley and closed the cabin door behind me. *Well, that was awkward.* Maybe I would need to keep my distance from Josh by *actually* keeping my distance.

*

The next morning, I woke to discover I had escaped another hangover. I was grateful I'd had the foresight to down a vitamin B capsule, some aspirin, and the whole bottle of water before I'd drifted off to sleep. I lay still and listened for any signs of life from the others. Nothing but the gentle, rhythmic lap of water slapping the hull. I wondered what time it was, but I knew it didn't matter. I was awake and ravenously hungry, so it was time to get up.

Still in my pyjamas, I slipped out of the cabin and popped my head out of the hatch. The air was already warm, and the sun was bright in the sky. No signs of life on deck either – a solo breakfast *al fresco*, it would be. Ducking back below, I quietly made myself a bowl of muesli with yoghurt and a mug of tea.

By that stage of the trip, I had perfected scaling the short ladder to the deck with both hands full, and I emerged topside without spilling a single drop of my tea. I carefully made my way down the side of the boat and sat myself down cross-legged on the bow. The sun immediately warmed my back, and I took in our surroundings as I sipped from my mug.

There I was, sitting in my pyjamas on the bow of a boat and not three metres away were people dressed for work and waiting at a bus stop. They were so close, I could hear the music from someone's headphones. It was surreal. 'Good morning, Greece,' I said quietly to myself, enjoying a little giggle.

And of course, the person I immediately thought of – the one person who I thought would find the whole situation as amusing as I did – was also the person I had sworn to steer clear of.

'This seat taken?' He had snuck up on me, and I jumped a little. 'Sorry, I didn't mean to scare you.' He hadn't; what had startled me was that he'd appeared the very moment I'd thought about him. I craned my neck to look at him. He was also in his PJs – well, a T-shirt and sweat pants – and held a bowl, which I knew would contain muesli and yoghurt, like mine. 'You didn't scare me – just startled me a little, that's all.'

'Oh, did you want to be left alone?' It was an excellent question, and the longer I pondered it, the more uncomfortable he seemed to get. 'I can eat downstairs,' he said as he turned away.

My plan to steer clear of him wasn't getting off to a good start, but still, I couldn't be rude to him. He didn't deserve it. I could do polite – distant, but polite. It was just breakfast.

'No, no, stay, please. Sorry – I'm a little out of it this morning.' He looked relieved and sat down.

'How cool is it that we're here in our pyjamas eating

breakfast, and right over there is a whole town heading to work?' he asked, voicing the very thought I'd wanted to share with him – damn him. *Polite, but distant, Sarah.*

I nodded non-committedly, and added, 'Mm-hmm.'

He laughed to himself. 'Kind of surreal, actually. I can't believe this is my life right now.'

I remained silent. It was harder than I thought it would be. I wanted to gush, 'I know, right? How fucking cool is it to be us right now?' I took a bite of muesli and chewed pensively – if that's a way you can chew.

'Sarah?' The tone in Josh's voice had changed, and without thinking, I made eye contact. His eyes looked into mine. He was no longer joking or playing. I swallowed my bite of breakfast.

'Yes?' It came out nearly as a whisper.

He looked away and his brow creased. What? What did the sexy American boy want to say? And – damn it, damn it, damn it – why did I care so much?

Finally, he spoke.

'Is it me, or are things weird between us?'

I couldn't believe it; he had said it out loud. He had given the big thing between us a name – it was 'weird'. The breath rushed from my body in a big, fat sigh of relief and suddenly I was half-laughing, half-talking.

'Yes! They *are*!'

He smiled at me. 'I am pretty sure it's my fault. I haven't been straight with you – mostly because I haven't been straight with myself.'

I found myself hanging on his every word – every mature, self-aware word.

'I told you one thing, and then I pursued you – and I

behaved as though I had some propriety over you – which I don't.' I shook my head in agreement, because he didn't – or, *did* he?

'The thing is, you caught me off-guard. I came on this trip almost on a whim. I booked it at the last minute, and the very most I hoped for was seeing a part of the world I'd never seen before. Stupidly, it never occurred to me that there would be *people* on this trip – people who would come to mean something to me – people who would *affect* me.' And then he said something no one had ever said to me before.

'You *affect* me, Sarah. No matter what happens after this trip – if I never see you again – or if I see you every day for the rest of my life, I will never be the same person I was before meeting you, because meeting you has changed me. Forever.

'And I am super pissed at myself if I have fucked that up. I didn't mean to, but I am stupid in some ways – relationships being one of them – and I just want to *be* with you. I don't even know what that means exactly, but if we could rewind to a couple of days ago and be those people again – and laugh and have a fantastic time and talk about everything – then that's what I want.'

He had worked himself up into a bit of a lather. He took a deep breath, blew it out noisily and took a big bite of his breakfast. While he chewed, I focused on my own breathing – my own breakfast forgotten, sitting on the deck getting warm.

Everything Josh had said – all of it – articulated precisely what I felt. Well, not the part about it being a whim to come on the trip – I had been planning it for months – but everything else. I had gone on the trip thinking it was about me – what *I* would see – what *I* would do. I had no idea there

193

would be people I would come to love in a matter of days. People who would bring out the best in me, parts I had hidden behind defiant independence and a giant 'fuck off' to any guy who came near me.

I realised, while sitting on the bow of a boat in my pyjamas as Greek Island commuters boarded a bus to work a couple of metres away, that I loved Josh. And I don't mean that I was in love with him – although I may have been – I really couldn't have said for sure at that precise moment. But I did know I *loved* him – as a dear and treasured friend, as a person who I would know my whole life. And like he had said, 'no matter what happens'.

I couldn't predict the future any more than he could. All I could do was live the moment I was in. The alternative was inauthentic – it was pretending. And I was done pretending. I was done making nice and keeping my distance. I was done being a giant wuss, too scared to get out of my own way.

I snapped out of my reverie. Josh was watching me. He had this kind of amused-but-not-smug look on his face.

I laughed out loud. And he joined in.

'You're a total dork, you know that?' I asked, rhetorically.

Still, he answered me. 'I *do* know that, yes.'

I nudged him with my elbow as I picked up my bowl and took a bite of my muesli. He nudged me back, and I smiled. Then we finished our breakfast without another word or any awkwardness. I had my friend back.

After breakfast, Josh and I retreated to our respective cabins to dress for a day out. I had just picked up my flip-flops when Hannah stirred in her bunk.

'You going out?' she asked, rubbing her eyes and squinting

at me. We'd reversed our roles from the previous morning. I couldn't resist wiggling *my* eyebrow at her this time.

'How's the head?' I asked, knowing from the look of her it was grim. She groaned dramatically and threw her arm across her eyes.

'We're heading into town – me and Josh,' I added the last bit as an afterthought, probably unnecessarily. Hannah seemed to expect that when I said 'we' I meant 'me and Josh'. It was clear she didn't care, though, which meant her hangover must have been massive.

'How do you look like *that*,' she said pointing to my face, 'and I feel like *this*? You had as much to drink as I did.'

'I learned my lesson. I drank a whole bottle of water and downed a couple of aspirin and some vitamin B before I fell asleep last night.'

'I think I hate you.'

'Well, I adore you, so get some more sleep, and I hope you feel better soon.'

She cracked an eyelid and looked at me suspiciously. 'You're mighty chipper this morning.'

I smiled in reply. 'Not having a hangover will do that.' I picked up my leather bag and checked through the contents.

'Wait,' she said as she forced herself to sit upright. 'Did you say you're spending the day with Josh?'

'Wow, yes. I did. Like *half-an-hour* ago.'

She cocked her head to the side. 'So, what? You guys are all made up now? What's going on?'

'Nothing is going on. He's my *friend* – we sorted things out this morning.' Her squinty eyes got even squintier.

'What happened to keeping your distance so you don't get hurt?'

'I already told you—'

She cut me off with a wave of her hand and plopped her head back onto her pillow.

'You two … do whatever you want. I mean, you will anyway,' she said, which was a little bit nasty. I left the cabin without saying goodbye.

Josh was waiting for me on dry land when I got topside. 'Ready?' he asked.

'Ready,' I replied, a big smile on my face. He reached out a hand and helped me over the railing of the boat and onto the dock. I tossed my flip-flops onto the hot pavement and stepped into them.

'Let's go.'

'So, do you have any thoughts about where to go?' I asked, as we walked away from the boat. I felt a little dumb for failing to consider such an important detail until then. When Josh had asked me to spend the day with him exploring, I had eagerly agreed. Duncan had no firm plans for the group, and I hoped a mini-adventure with Josh would seal our reconciliation.

'Actually, yes. Duncan said there's a town square about halfway up the hill. I thought we'd head there, then see where it leads us. That sound okay?' It sounded great.

'Sure. Lead the way.'

'Oh, and I could take you to the top of the town if you like – up into those hills.' He pointed up, and I followed the line of his arm. It looked far. 'I went up there around sunset last night – right after you went out with the girls. It's a bit of a hike, but the views are amazing. I took some awesome photos too. Here.' He stopped walking and took his camera out of his pocket. I leaned closer and looked down at the small screen, as he cupped his hand around it, shading it from the sun.

Josh was right – the view from the lookout was incredible. He flicked through several pictures and then came to one where he was sitting on what looked like the edge of a cliff. He was looking out at the view, with the camera positioned behind him. 'Hang on. Let me look at that one more closely.'

He handed the camera to me, so I could see the photo better. 'But you're in this one. Did someone take it for you?'

'Timer,' he said. 'I put the camera on a rock, lined up the frame, set the timer, and then sat down.'

'On the edge of a cliff?' It looked dangerous.

'Yeah, it's not really a cliff.' He was smiling at me.

'What does that mean? Was it dangerous or not?' I must have had a horrified expression on my face, because he was quick to reassure me.

'Absolutely, *not* dangerous. I promise you, my feet were *not* dangling over a steep drop to certain death. I am adventurous, yes, but I wouldn't risk my life for a good shot.' He looked down at the camera and smiled. 'And it is a *really* good shot, don't you think?'

I did think that, yes. He was silhouetted against a darkening sky painted with streaks of orange, red and pink. It was a *beautiful* shot. 'It's incredible. I know I've said it before, but you're a good photographer. Good eye, good composition.'

He looked half-embarrassed, half-proud. 'Thanks.'

'But if you think I'm going to sit on some cliff so you can take a picture of me like that, you're delusional.' He laughed. 'It's not funny. I'm terrified of heights.'

'Sorry, I didn't mean anything – it's just that it *wasn't a cliff.*

197

More of a slope. So, did you get vertigo from looking at the photo?' he asked, teasing me.

'No, I did not, you cheeky bugger.' I shook my head at him and walked ahead. 'Come on.'

'"Cheeky bugger"? I'm going to assume it's your new term of endearment for me.'

'You can assume whatever you like.'

'You're cute,' he said, catching up to me.

'Yes, I know.' We were setting a dangerously flirtatious tone for the day, but it was fun.

And it was a lot of what made hanging out with Josh so enjoyable – that he teased me and I teased him back. We jousted. Conversing with Josh felt like I was gliding the sharp edge of my mind along a verbal whetstone.

When we arrived at Miaouli Square, it took my breath away. After a week of travelling to islands peppered with whitewashed buildings and pops of blue – which were gorgeous and I'd never tire of seeing, by the way – the square was more reminiscent of the South of France than anywhere I'd seen in other parts of Greece.

Although the waterfront of Ermoupoli, where we were docked, was atypical of the other towns we'd been to on other islands, the square was an even stronger reminder that we were in *Europe*. There may have been distinct lines on maps between countries, but Southern Europe clearly had common threads that surpassed borders.

'This is so beautiful,' I remarked.

'It really is – not like anything we've seen so far,' Josh replied.

'I was just thinking the same thing.'

An imposing but handsome neoclassical building in a pale

apricot colour dominated the square. I guessed it was probably the town hall or some other official government structure.
Ubiquitous pigeons dotted the square, which was, surprisingly,
bordered by fat palm trees.

'Unlikely that those are native, huh?' I mentioned, pointing
to the palm trees standing guard in front of the town hall.

'Mmm. I'm going to say no. We haven't seen any others
during our trip.'

'No.'

'Did you know that the North Africans ruled in Greece for
hundreds of years until about six hundred years ago?' he
asked.

'Uh, no, I didn't know that. I knew they were in Spain for
a long time.'

'Yeah, they ruled most of what we call the Mediterranean
– they could have brought the palm trees with them then.
Maybe they grow on the island now.'

'Maybe.' I figured it was more likely the Islanders had
bought them especially for the square, but Josh's historical
knowledge impressed me nonetheless.

'Your knowledge of history is a little more credible than
Duncan's,' I said.

'Pigeon houses?' he asked.

'Precisely. Did you know that the Greeks thought pigeons
were nice, so they made houses for them?'

'I did *not* know that until I met Duncan and he told us.'
Josh led us towards a statue in the middle of the square.

'Well, did you know that it was the Moors who brought
citrus to Europe?' I asked.

'Really?'

'I think so,' I admitted. 'It's one of the hundreds of factoids we were trained to spout off when I was touring. It sounds like it's true, but who knows? We told our tour groups a lot of stuff that wasn't true – and on purpose.'

'You mean, you *lied*?' he asked, pretending to be aghast.

'Pretty much. Like the time I convinced a whole tour group that the Swiss are such incredible conservationists, they turn off their waterfalls at night to save water.'

'You did not.'

'I did. I had a whole spiel about the Swiss enlisting the Dutch engineers who had saved Venice by engineering failsafe flooding technology – and how they'd designed a way to redirect and harness the waterfalls to save water and generate energy at the same time. It was compelling stuff, my lies.'

'But how do you know they bought it?'

I stopped walking to tell the rest of the story. 'Because we were staying in Lauterbrunnen that night – it's in this unbelievable valley – sheer cliff faces each side of these gorgeous rolling green hills – anyway, there are all these waterfalls that fall from the top of these super high cliffs to the valley floor, throwing up mist-rainbows everywhere – and it's awesome. I mean, it's probably the most beautiful place I've ever been to. *On the planet*,' I added for emphasis.

His eyes widened, indicating he was duly impressed.

'So, I told the tour group that the waterfalls shut off at sunset – around eight o'clock – and that it was a sight to behold. So, there they all are at ten to eight, cameras and phones at the ready, watching the top of the nearest waterfall, waiting for it to stop flowing down the side of the cliff, and I was playing along – I had my camera ready too.

'And at eight o'clock, when someone called out the time, someone else said, "I can see it! Look! It's stopping!" And there's this moment of frenzy and they are all convinced something's happening, and they're taking photos and video footage. And I ran out in front of them and turned and took a snap of all of them looking through their lenses at the top of the waterfall.

'And, then I fell about laughing. And slowly, one by one, they realised I had tricked them. And some of them thought it was cool and even really funny – and others were pissed off with me and stormed away 'cause they felt dumb.

'Anyway, it was all in good fun. I mean, we were camping through Europe for six weeks together. We were like this oddball family on wheels, and we were always playing pranks. I wasn't the only one, you know.'

'I love that you got them to buy that whole thing.' Josh gestured towards a road leading away from the square, and I nodded. We started walking again. 'Was it a bunch of Americans? 'Cause I feel like most Americans – especially if they're travelling – will believe anything.'

'No – only a couple of Americans. Mostly Aussies and Kiwis – a couple of Canadians and a Korean couple. It did kinda backfire on me though.'

'How's that?'

'Well, from then on, they didn't trust anything I said – even the true stuff.'

'Like what?'

'Well, when we got to the Netherlands, I told them that sixty per cent of the country's land is below sea level and that it's the Dutch engineering – the windmills and the dykes – keeping the land dry.'

'But, that's true.'

'I *know* – that's what I'm saying. I'd lost all credibility.

Apparently, the windmill thing sounded too far-fetched; they thought I was making it up.'

'Did you do it again – the waterfall thing?'

'Nope. Learned my lesson. Besides, I'd already pulled it off successfully. I had my story to dine out on.'

'Or walk around on.'

'Exactly.'

'You enjoyed it then, running tours?'

'I did, mostly. But I think if I was ever going to do it again, it would have to be more like this. A handful of people, a few destinations. Not fifty people and ten countries in fifteen days. That kind of travelling gets old, really fast.'

'I'm loving the pace of this trip,' he added.

'Me too. For one thing, I get to wake up when my body says it's time.'

'Yes – no alarm clock. I can't remember a time when I didn't have to wake up to an alarm clock on a weekday. I was at school, then college, then straight into work. I've never even had a real vacation before – a few trips in the US – short ones, but nothing like this – and you know I've never left the States before now.'

'You're setting a high bar for yourself, first international trip and all this.' I spread my arms wide to indicate our surroundings, which were getting prettier as we walked.

A friendly bark sounded behind us and we turned around. There was a tan-coloured Labrador, regarding us with his (her?) head cocked to the side. I looked for a collar – no collar.

'Hey there,' I approached slowly. He (she?) didn't seem aggressive, but I was careful nonetheless.

'Are you lost?' I had reached the dog and held out the back

of my hand for him (her?) to sniff. The dog obliged and then started licking it.

'Actually, I saw that dog in the square; she was part of a pack. She must have followed us,' said Josh. He walked over and squatted down beside her, patting her head. The dog nuzzled his hand and panted in what seemed like a happy way. I liked dogs, but I'd never had one and wasn't too sure how to read them.

'How do you know she's a she?' I asked.

Josh looked at me with an amused look on his face. 'No balls.'

'Oh.'

I was mildly embarrassed because Josh had said, 'balls'. What was I, in primary school?

'I hope that's not weird, or anything,' he added.

'No. Why should it be?'

'I don't want you to think I spend all my spare time looking at dogs' genitals or anything – it's just that I grew up with dogs, and when I saw the pack in the square, I checked them out, sized them up. You know, are they okay? Are they aggressive?'

'You obviously decided they were okay, then.'

'Yeah. I mean, she's a stray. I'd say they're all strays, but she seems friendly enough. Aren't you, girl?' As if on cue, the dog barked. 'Hah!' Josh laughed. 'That's awesome. She's smart too.'

The dog looked from Josh to me and back again and barked once more. It was starting to play out like a scene from a movie. *'What's that, girl? Jimmy's stuck down a ravine?'* *'Woof!'*

Josh stood up, and the dog wagged her tail vigorously. He petted her on the head, and she licked at his fingers again before turning a full circle and running ahead of us. She stopped about ten metres away and looked back at us.

'Uh, I think she wants us to follow her,' I said. Was this really happening?

'Well, she knows the town better than we do,' Josh responded.

And that was how we ended up on a tour of the town, being led by a scrawny stray dog with a smiley face. She stayed about three metres ahead of us the whole time, stopping regularly to check we were still following her. We meandered down streets and walkways, working our way further up the hill until we came upon the enormous church overlooking the town.

The dog sat down and looked out at the vista; we stood behind her and did the same.

'I'm running out of superlatives,' I said, a little out of breath from the last – and steepest – part of our walk up the hill.

'It's amazing, isn't it?'

'Amazing, incredible, breathtaking, beautiful – just – wow.'

'You seem to have a *lot* of superlatives.'

'True, but none of them does this justice. And look at that church! It doesn't look this big when you see it from the marina.' We walked along the wall of the church, taking it in. Our dog decided to stay where she was, still enjoying the water views.

The church looked like it was carved from butter by a very sharp knife, and then piped with cream-coloured icing to highlight its angles and arches. A giant blue cupola and two bell towers punctuated the roofline. It looked down on the town of Ermoupoli, a giant confectionary protector.

'This town is so different from where we've been,' I said.

'I know I keep saying that, but it's such a hodgepodge of European architecture compared with the typical Greek island structures. It's making me a little nostalgic for France, actually.'

'Oh yeah?'

'There's a lot I'm seeing that reminds me of the South of France in particular. Places in Provence, in Nice, Cannes. And some details remind me of Venice – like parts of this church. The dome reminds me of St Marco's Basilica.'

'You've been to a lot of places,' he said without a trace of envy in his tone.

'I have. I think I might have said this to you before, but if I stand still too long, I feel like I *have* to go. I get antsy. And going somewhere new – like here, Syros – that will scratch the itch. But, I know I'm lucky to have been to a lot of places.'

'It's not really luck, though is it? You work hard, you seek out opportunities, and then you make them happen.'

'I suppose. In a way, yes.'

'When you were a tour guide—'

'Tour *manager*,' I corrected.

'Sorry, tour *manager* – did they knock on your door one night and say, "Hey, do you want to tour Europe? We'll pay you," or did you see the opportunity and then make the whole thing happen?'

He was right. It wasn't some grand reveal or anything. I had worked hard for my successes and to be able to travel as much as I did. But, when he called out the whole 'I'm so lucky' thing, I saw myself through his fresh eyes, and I realised I wasn't lucky as much as I was intrepid.

'That's a good reminder. Thanks.' I needed to get off the topic of me. 'Hey, so is this close to where you were last night?'

Josh scanned the rounded tops of the hills. He squinted a

little and then pointed. 'It was somewhere up there. If you remember from the photo, I was looking down on the church, and it was to my left.'

'Oh yeah – the blue of the dome was almost inky.'

He smiled at me. 'Nicely put.' He turned back towards the hills and asked, 'Do you want to head up?'

I did not. I wanted to sit down, and I wanted a beverage – probably an alcoholic one.

'I take it from your scrunched-up nose that's a no.'

'You take it right. I may never come back here, and I know I *should* climb to the highest point on the island, but I can't be stuffed.'

He threw back his head and laughed. I joined in. 'See? All that stuff about me being adventurous and hardworking, and now you learn the truth – sometimes I'm a lazy bugger.'

'So, you're a bugger too, then?'

I didn't know what he meant. 'Huh?'

'I'm a cheeky bugger, and you're a lazy bugger – those are your words, not mine!'

'Ohhh, yes. Well, that's true then. We're both buggers.'

Our dog was where we left her, but we'd apparently been gone too long, and she was curled up asleep.

'Hey, girl,' I called as we approached. Her head snapped up, and the rest of her followed, suddenly a ball of energy again. I was seriously falling for the mutt. 'Shall we head back to the square and get you a treat?'

She seemed very excited at the prospect. She must have spoken some English as well as Greek because she led us off, just like I'd said. Or, maybe the word 'treat' was universal to all dogs.

'I love this dog,' I said as we followed her.

'Yeah, she's sweet. And smart too – she seems to understand us.'

'I was just thinking how she must speak English as well as Greek.'

He laughed. 'Yeah, she's definitely bilingual.'

Then our incredibly smart dog spied a cat on a wall. They both stood stock still and eyed each other off. The cat was fat with orange stripes, and it looked like it had been around the block many, many times. It had a scar over its left eye, and half of its right ear was missing. Our dog started a low growl and the cat responded in kind. The standoff continued with neither of them moving. And then without warning, the cat took off along the wall in the other direction, leapt off, landed deftly and ran around a corner.

Our dog took off after the cat, and I thought it would be the end of our tour. But no. A few minutes later she rounded the corner at a casual lope with her tongue hanging out of her mouth. She looked like she was smiling. The cat was nowhere to be seen.

'Did you chase away that big, ugly kitty?' I asked her as she accepted my praising pat on her head.

'Good girl.' Josh ruffled her ears, which she took as her cue to continue our journey back to the square – at least, that's where I hoped we were going – she wasn't taking us on the same route we'd come. I wasn't too concerned, though. If we headed downhill, we were going in the right direction.

Not long after the cat episode, we spilt out from a narrow street back into the main square. She looked at us like, 'See? I knew where I was taking you the whole time.' And if it's possible for a dog to express pride, she looked well pleased with herself.

'I think we should get her something,' I said to Josh, as I walked towards a little snack stall at the edge of the square.

He followed me, but when I arrived, I was disappointed to see that we were somewhat limited in our choices of treats. I ended up buying two bottles of water – one for her and one for us – and a packet of chips. I poured water into my cupped hand and she lapped it up greedily. 'I wonder where she usually drinks from.'

We both looked around the square. Other strays were lazing about in the sun and the shade, but I didn't see where they would get water.

'Maybe there's a fountain or something close by,' replied Josh. I hoped he was right. I felt proprietary over our dog, and I couldn't bear the thought of her having to scrounge for water every day, especially in that heat. I saved some of the water for after the chips – I knew they were probably too salty for a dog, but it was either chips or ice cream, and I guessed potatoes would be marginally better for dogs than dairy. She gulped down the chips, and then I let her finish the water. She sat at our feet, grinning at us. What a gorgeous girl she was.

I didn't notice until he said, 'Smile!' that Josh had his camera out. The dog and I both turned to the camera and obliged him.

'Bye, girl,' I said petting her head again. She licked my hand. 'Thank you for being our dog today.'

And as if she understood it was goodbye, she stood and trotted away without looking back. I felt tears sting my eyes. And then I immediately felt stupid and glad I was wearing sunglasses. She was a stray – she probably did the 'cute dog' routine with travellers all the time. I blinked away the tears.

'Water?' Josh asked, handing me the second bottle. He'd already taken a swig. I was super thirsty after our little adventure, but my hands were a grimy mess. I poured some of the water into my left hand, gave him back the bottle, and did my best to wash my hands. I wiped them on my shorts. They still felt gross, but not a dog-has-licked-these-hands-all-over gross. I signalled for the water again and took a drink.

'Hey, I haven't charged my phone in a couple of days, and I was thinking of finding an internet café, maybe checking email. Would you be up for that?' Josh asked.

'Uh, yeah, sure. Did you see one near here?'

'I figure if we head back towards the waterfront and keep an eye out, we'll find one.'

'Sure.'

Twenty minutes later we were each sitting in front of an ancient computer. I loaded my Gmail account and started deleting dozens of emails from stores, blogs and services – all soliciting for my time, my money, or both. It felt freeing to delete them without reading them, to ignore the unnecessary minutiae of life I would typically pore over.

And then I saw it. Towards the bottom of my inbox was an email address I didn't recognise, but a subject line that leapt off the screen. 'I hope to see you in London soon.' It was from him! The silver fox had kept his promise and emailed me. My hand trembled a little as I clicked on the message.

Chapter Thirteen

My heart raced as I skim-read the short email, all the while holding my breath. I exhaled and read back through it again, digesting the words.

> *Dear Sarah,*
>
> *I am back in London, ensconced in my house, and already missing Greece. More to the point, I miss you. You cross my mind dozens of times a day – and I'll admit, it has been a long time since I felt any kind of excitement at the thought of seeing someone again. I truly hope you will make time to see me when you arrive in London. I want to see you properly.*
>
> *Yours,*
> *James*

I couldn't help but read it a third time. This time I lingered on some of the words and phrases – 'miss you', 'excitement', and 'properly' – I wanted to know exactly what he meant by *that*. And then his sign-off, 'yours'. Yours! I let out a long sigh.

My mind wandered far outside the confines of the net café. I immediately pictured James in his home in London – it was likely a penthouse with amazing views and expensive furnishings. He was shirtless for some reason and reading the paper while sipping from a mug of tea. He looked delicious.

And then a voice called me back to the net café.

'Everything okay?' asked the voice. I snapped out of my daydream and realised that Josh was reading my screen. I was too stunned to speak. Why was he doing that? I gawped at him, my mouth a huge O.

I finally found my voice and half-whispered, 'What are you doing?'

He shook his head and looked down. 'Oh, god, I'm so sorry – it was just instinct. You read something and reacted. I thought something bad had happened, and I didn't even think – I'm so sorry ...' Then he put his face in his hands, reprimanding himself under his breath.

I was torn. Should I reassure him he'd done nothing wrong, or that James's email didn't matter? Or, should I completely freak out and run out the door? I wasn't even mad. I probably would have done the same thing if he'd reacted oddly to something on his screen – it was a human thing to do. But, he couldn't have read anything worse.

I took a deep breath and patted him on the back. His self-flagellation continued. 'Josh? Josh, listen, I'm not mad. It's all right.' He shook his head. How did I end up in this situation? Consoling one would-be lover, while a message from another would-be lover glared out from the bright screen in front of me? I clicked out of the email and logged out of Gmail.

'*Josh*,' I said more firmly. 'Look at me.' He did, sheepishly, and started to apologise again. I cut him off. 'Hey, don't worry – it's cool. I probably would have done the same thing. It *is* a little awkward,' I added, trying to make a joke. A wry smile appeared, and he nodded in agreement.

'Should we talk about it?' I asked.

'No. Let's just go.' He logged out of his own email account, stood, pushed back his chair, and led the way out of the café.

'Properly' – the word repeated inside my head as I followed Josh into the sunlight.

It was going to be an interesting end to the trip.

*

When we arrived at the dock where we had left our boat, it wasn't there. Josh and I stood looking at an empty berth. We looked at each other, our mouths agape and our eyes wide, and we both burst out laughing as if it was the funniest thing ever.

'Oh my god!' we both kept saying, over and over, in between bursts of laughter. I had no idea what to do – and neither, it seemed, did Josh. We didn't have our phones with us, so we couldn't call anyone – and we had no idea where the others were, or why they would have left without us. We were boat-less. We were people without a boat.

I thanked my foresight to carry my passport with me whenever I left the boat – and a credit card. If I had to – if we actually *had* been abandoned – I could get myself back to London. I hoped it wouldn't come to that. There must have been a good explanation. Still, when our hysterical laughter died down, we were speechless.

After a while of looking at the water where our boat had been, I shook my head. 'Josh?'

'Yeah?'

'Where the fuck is our fucking boat?' And then *that* was then the funniest thing ever, because we were off again, laughing loudly. Tears filled my eyes, and I doubled over. 'Oh, my god,' I gasped through the tears. I sniffled and tried to get it together.

'Right!' I said, more decisively than I felt. I forced myself to stand upright. 'This is not a huge island, and this is not a huge marina. We need to find our boat.' I grabbed Josh's arms, shook him a little, and said, 'Josh, we need to find our people.' He nodded solemnly in agreement.

'And then we need to kill them for abandoning us.' That brought his smile back again. And he had such a sexy smile.

I looked around us. 'Well, we could sit on this bench and hope someone comes looking for us.' I motioned to the bench, which served as the nearest bus stop.

'Or get on the next bus to the airport,' retorted Josh.

'Does Syros even have an airport?'

'Probably. I mean it's the capital of the Cyclades, so I don't see why not. *Santorini* has an airport.'

'Good point. So, you have your passport with you?'

'Yep. You?'

'Yep,' I replied, patting my leather bag. 'So, let's say we fly out of here. Where to, exactly?'

'You could come back to the states with me.' Well, that escalated quickly. My stomach did a little flip as I contemplated what it would mean.

No. Stomach flips or not, I wasn't ready for his hometown. His home. His people. 'Maybe not.'

'What's wrong with Chicago?' Nothing. Chicago was probably a lovely city, but we certainly weren't at the 'meet the family' stage – too many connotations of something more serious. But, I couldn't say that – we'd only just salvaged out friendship.

I deflected instead. 'If we're running away, we don't want to run *home*. We want to go somewhere cool – somewhere neither of us has been before.'

'Good point. What about Hawaii? Have you been there?'

'No,' I answered. 'Never been to Hawaii. You?'

'Nope.'

'It's kind of far. You want to choose somewhere a little closer? Like Spain?' I'd been to Spain, but I knew Josh hadn't. It would be fun to go somewhere like that – just us. Without five other people traipsing around with us. As much as I had come to love those five people, they *had* recently abandoned us.

He grinned at me. 'That would be incredible. I would totally go to Spain with you.'

And then suddenly all the wordplay and the crazy situation of being people without a boat fell away, and it was only him and me. He stepped towards me, and in one motion he put his hands on the small of my back, pulling me closer, and kissed me.

And it wasn't one of those tentative I-don't-know-what-the-hell-I'm-doing-do-you-or-don't-you-like-me?-I-*think*-I-like-you kisses. It was a kiss from a man who knew exactly what he was doing and what he wanted. I fell into it like I was falling into a giant pot of warm honey. Delicious.

When we finally pulled apart, I was – for the second time in only minutes – completely speechless. I hadn't seen it coming, but it felt so right to be in Josh's arms. And kissing him – wow!

He cocked his head to the side as if to say, 'What do you think of that?' I looked him in the eye and said, 'Very nice, Joshua.'

214

He smiled. Sexy.

Recovering slightly from our broad daylight romantic interlude, I forced my head back to the situation at hand. 'I am going to say that they *do* intend to come back for us at some point, so we probably shouldn't run away together in case they worry.'

'You mean like they've worried us – that we'll never see them again? That kind of worry?'

'We'll see them again, silly. They *love* us! Come with me.' I pointed towards the marina as I started walking. Josh fell into step beside me.

'Or maybe,' he exclaimed, as though he had worked it all out, 'they've kicked us off the trip, and this is how they decided to tell us.'

'You're right. It's most likely that,' I replied, deadpan.

We turned onto the pier and were not far along when we saw a man who looked a lot like Gary running towards us, waving madly. When he got closer, it turned out it *was* Gary. Brilliant. We'd found our people.

'Hey, you guys,' he said, coming to a stop in front to us. I noticed he wasn't even puffing from the running.

'Hey, yourself,' I said. I was intrigued about what the explanation could be. I imagined Josh was too, especially as we'd been so close to running away together.

'I'm glad I found you,' he said.

'Well, we kind of found you,' Josh replied. Yep, I could hear it in his voice – he was waiting for a reasonable explanation.

Gary must have sensed that he needed to get straight to the explaining part, because he did. 'We're *so* sorry if we worried you guys. The harbour master came by and said a berth had opened up at the marina, but if we wanted it, we had to move our boat right then. No waiting for passengers who were elsewhere. Just move the boat or lose the berth.'

'And we needed that berth, right?' asked Josh. 'For water and electricity.'

'Right – exactly. If we hadn't moved, we would have been low on water for the sail to Tinos tomorrow morning. Duncan didn't want to risk it, so I helped him get into the berth, and then he sent me to look for you guys.'

'It was a bit of a shock to come back to a missing boat,' I said. Poor Gary looked like he was going to apologise again. I stopped him with a shake of my head. 'No, look, it's totally cool. We understand. Thanks for coming and looking for us.'

'Yeah, no problem. I've got to go find Marie and Gerry now.'

'Oh! We weren't the only ones?' I said.

'No. Only Hannah and I were on board with Duncan. That's why he needed my help. Anyway, I should get back to where the boat was before Marie and Gerry get there.'

'Yes, of course – sorry. Go!' I said. We sent Gary off with another round of thank yous to his back. He waved over his shoulder as he ran down the pier, but didn't turn around.

'He's a good guy,' I said as we continued down the pier.

'He is. I like Gary. At first, I was worried he was a bit of a know-it-all ...' I looked over at Josh, and he was quick to follow up with, 'He's not. I know that now – he just loves conversation and he knows a lot about a lot of things.'

'I have to be honest, I haven't really spent much time talking with him – I mean in groups, yes, but not just the two of us,' I admitted. 'I've talked a lot with Marie – I *adore* her.'

'Yeah, well Gary – he's a good guy. He's the kind of guy

216

you would want on your side if anything went wrong, you know? He'd have your back *and* he'd know what to do.'

'Like with the disappearing boat thing.'

'Exactly. Anyway, if you get the chance, seek him out. He's really interesting.'

'I will. Hey, did you know they have a big age difference?'

'Really? Like us?' he asked, a teasing tone in his voice.

'Actually, it's more than with us.' I poked my tongue out at him, and he laughed. Maybe he was still riding high from that kiss. It was a pretty great kiss.

'Hey!' I exclaimed. 'There's our boat!' Duncan was jumping back and forth between the boat and the pier, hooking up various cables. Hannah sat with her feet up on a bench, apparently absorbed in a magazine.

'Hey, Skipper,' I called out as I slipped off my flip-flops, picked them up from the pier and stepped carefully up the gangplank.

Josh was right behind me. 'Need a hand?' he asked Duncan as he stepped aboard.

'Yeah, that'd be great. Hand me that cable?' Josh obliged him.

'Hey, Hannah.' She hadn't looked up, and I wanted to gauge the extent of her hangover before engaging with her further.

'Oh, hey,' she said, then flicked the magazine to the next page. I assessed from her rather frosty greeting that the hangover she was nursing was monster-sized. I spied the empty mug beside her.

'Cup of tea?' I offered, retrieving the mug.

She looked up at me, squinting behind her sunnies at the bright sun behind me. Her expression softened a little. 'Oh my god, I would *love* that.'

'Coming right up.' I turned back to Duncan and Josh, who were still working on getting the boat situated. 'You guys want anything from the galley? Tea, coffee, cold drink?'

'Is it beer o'clock yet?' asked Duncan, who was bent over some fixture at the back of the boat.

'Always, Duncan. It's got to be five o'clock somewhere.'

'Then I'll take a beer,' he answered, still inverted.

'Josh?'

'Yeah, a beer'd be great.'

I heard Hannah moan behind me – probably at the thought of drinking again.

'Got it – I won't be a sec,' I said to the menfolk. To Hannah, I said, 'Hot tea coming up, Hannah. Hang in there. Do you want toast too?'

'Mmm, yes please.' She licked her lips. 'With lots of butter.'

I went below deck and assembled the odd array of beverages and snacks. Tea and buttered toast for Hannah. Beer and a bowl of salted peanuts for Josh and Duncan, and a Coke No Sugar for me. Okay, the nuts were for me too.

I made it up the ladder without spilling a drop – hot or cold. Hannah practically lurched at the plate of toast and stuffed some into her mouth – I figured I would probably have to make her more.

Duncan opened his beer, took a swig, and sighed out a satisfied, 'Ahhh,' as though he was in a beer commercial. 'So, did Gary find you, or did you find us?' he asked as he rested against the edge of the boat.

'Gary found us – but only after we'd thought to head down the pier,' Josh replied.

'Yeah, sorry about that. Poor timing with most of us off the boat, but I didn't want to miss this berth. Would have made for a shitty trip to Tinos tomorrow – pun totally intended.'

'It's cool, Duncan. We didn't think you'd deserted us or anything,' I said. Josh raised his eyebrows at me, and I laughed. 'Well, maybe a little at first.'

'Yeah, that's a little closer to reality.' Josh was such a bugger. I poked my tongue out at him. 'That's twice,' he said.

'What's twice?

'You keep poking your tongue out at me. I'm starting to think that either you *like* me – or you're in the second grade.'

My first instinct was to poke my tongue out at him. I curbed it. Instead, I sent mock daggers at him through my eyes.

'Oooh, you're kinda scary when you're mad,' he joked.

Hannah piped in with, 'I'm guessing that if Sarah *really* gets mad, she actually *is* scary.' Duncan thought that was hilarious, as evidenced by a loud guffaw coming from the top deck of the boat where he was doing boat things.

'What's that supposed to mean? Are you turning on me too, roomie?'

Hannah waved me off. 'You know what I mean. I heard all about that dinner with the rude Ossies from Marie. You don't put up with anyone's bullshit. You can own that, you know – it's something I like about you.'

'Whaaat? Liddle ol' mee? Wha, Ima sweet as piah.' I donned my best Southern accent and batted my eyelashes at her.

She rolled her eyes in reply. '*Mostly* you're sweet as piah, but if something goes down, you're the girl I'd want to have my back.'

'Thanks, Hannah. That's lovely of you to say.' We must have

been done with touchy-feely time, because she made a sort of squinty-scrunchy face and went back to her magazine.

'Hey, Duncan!' Josh called to our skipper, who was now at the bow of the boat.

'Yo!' we heard in reply.

'Have we got plans for dinner – you know, all of us?' Josh asked.

A mop of blonde hair appeared above us, and Duncan jumped from the top deck to the back deck. 'I dunno,' he said. 'Lots of good places to go on Syros, for sure. Do you think everyone wants to do something together tonight?'

'*I* do,' said Hannah. That surprised me. She seemed a little hot and cold with spending time with the whole group. But then, the other yacht wasn't in the marina, so it's not like she was going to hook up with their skipper that night.

'Yeah, me too,' Josh said.

'Me three.' I put my hand up like we were in school. Maybe it was my near miss with being a person without a boat, but I suddenly craved being with our people, all of us together. Our floating family.

'Cool. I've got a few ideas. I'll have a think, and we'll talk to the girls and Gary when they get back. Tee something up – sound good?'

'Sounds good, Dunc.' I loved Duncan. He was a good bloke, as we say in Australia. I sat back, sipping my Coke and taking it all in – the briny air, the sun warming my face, the beautiful town of Ermoupoli, my new little family, Josh.

Josh ... And then my bugger of a mind made the leap to ...

James. And that email. 'Properly' indeed.

My mind oscillated between the sexy, quick-witted

220

American, and the worldly, exciting European – also sexy, I might add. I remembered what James had said in the email and felt a twinge in my stomach. He wanted to see me. Did I want to see him?

If I was honest with myself, yes. Yes, I did.

And why wouldn't I? He was the fairy tale. Tall, mysterious, handsome, rich. Did I believe in fairy tales anymore? Was I Aurora waiting for the prince to awaken me with a kiss?

A kiss.

Josh's kiss had been tremendous.

Josh.

Josh saw the world through similar eyes to mine. We weren't exactly alike – and I wouldn't ever want that. It was more that when I explained something to him – how I felt about something or what I thought – he didn't look at me like I'd grown two heads. And more and more, we could share a look and just *know* what the other meant.

Don't get me wrong, I had – have – a wonderful network of close, long-treasured friends, but even *they* look at me sideways sometimes, wondering exactly what I'm getting at. I didn't feel that way when I was with Josh.

And, even though I didn't know James as well, I sensed that anything was possible with him, including the stuff of dreams.

And so my thoughts went round and round.

'You off with the fairies, or something Sez?' It was Duncan, and he was talking to me.

'What? Sorry, I was in another world.'

'I could see that.' His reply was gentle like he was talking to his little sister. 'I asked if you could help with the buoys – tie them off like I showed you before?'

221

'Of course,' I said, jumping up from my position. Right as I was finishing up, I heard the voices of the others approaching.

'Perfect timing!' called Duncan as he leapt from the boat to the dock. 'We're just finishing up.'

'Sorry, baby,' purred Gerry. 'We didn't know you'd be moving the boat this early.'

He gave her a loud smack of a kiss. 'Don't worry 'bout it, love. The others were here to help.'

As I made my way to the stern of the boat to greet the others, I looked at Hannah and wondered if she was going to come clean that she hadn't helped at all. She flicked to another page of her magazine. *I guess not.*

Gary was carrying a few shopping bags, which he handed over to Marie and Gerry after they boarded the boat; he was such a gentleman.

'What did you get?' I asked, gathering close to the gals.

'These!' Marie excitedly held up a cute pair of leather sandals. She dug into another bag, 'And this!' She held up a flowing white kaftan.

'How pretty – almost like a toga.'

'Yeah, I thought that too.'

'Ger – what about you?' Gerry held up a gorgeous bright pink leather bag.

'Nice huh?'

I took it from her and admired the leather work. 'Oh, that's a good find!'

'Oh Gary, what about you? What did you buy?' Duncan was teasing us for being so girly, and Gary didn't miss a beat.

'Well, you know I've been looking everywhere for the right T-shirt to go with these shorts, and you know – I think I may have finally found it.' He pulled his T-shirt away from his body to show it off and batted his eyelashes.

'That is adorable,' Josh chimed in. 'I am so jealous. Now I want one too.'

Gerry pushed Duncan in the chest and pretended to tell him off for teasing us, but Marie looked adoringly at her husband – maybe because he'd just carried her shopping bags. Josh, however, got a whack in the arm.

'Oww,' he whined.

'Oh, stop being such a wuss. That didn't hurt.'

He winked at me in reply. I looked around at the whole gang – all of us together for the first time in several days – even though Hannah was on the fringes, her nose buried in a gossip magazine.

'Hey,' I called to get everyone's attention. I had six pairs of eyes on me, even Hannah's. 'Duncan and I were talking about going out to dinner tonight – all of us. What d'you say?' There was general agreement, which delighted me. I wanted to get my fill of family time before we all went off in different directions. It wasn't lost on me that our group's demise was only three days away.

Three days.

As we dispersed to various places on the boat, it started to sink in that soon I wouldn't get to see these people every day. My family, my friends. Josh. It's incredible how fast complete strangers can become important to you.

I had seen this phenomenon while I was working as a tour manager. People forging lifelong friendships in a matter of days or weeks. It had happened to me with some of the people I trained with and even with people who'd been my clients. It may have been a decade before, but we were connected on

Facebook and sent each other messages. If we were in the same city, we'd meet for a drink and catch up. They were as much my people as the friends I saw all the time, because with them, I had shared something extraordinary.

We had travelled together for weeks on end – twenty-four-seven – and we'd had grand adventures. And some big nights out. And even bigger nights in. These were the people who had seen me at my worst – hungover and cranky and existing on a few hours of sleep – and my best – capable in a crisis, gregarious and charming with border guards and locals, skilfully navigating fifty people around an entire continent. I would always consider the friendships I forged in my touring days as something to be treasured, something exceptional.

That's how I felt about the people on the boat. Gerry. Duncan. Gary. Marie. Hannah. And Josh. We'd shared something I'd never experienced before. We'd laughed – some of us had cried. We'd broken bread and broken camp. As I'd called them many times, we were a floating family.

I was at once excited for what the next few days would hold and deeply saddened it was all coming to an end.

*

A few hours later, we were seated around a large wooden table laden with exquisite Greek food. As we had been before and would likely be again, we were the rowdiest table in the place. Duncan was telling us about when he and Gerry went to Chile to see her family. Apparently, they'd been particularly impressed by his attempts at Spanish, even though he barely knew ten words. But that was Duncan all over – such a charmer.

Gerry took over the story. 'But, you know, I have been warning him ahead of time that he should learn some things to say to my family – especially my mother. And so he learns "hello", "nice to meet you", "thank you", "please" – nothing special ...' Her dig at Duncan's lack of linguistic skills was met with laughter.

'And then towards the end of the first day, all the women are there, making preparations for dinner – my mother, my aunts, my grandmother – and Duncan gets up to leave the room, and my mother, she says in her very best English, "Duncan, where are you going?" Well, Duncan, he says – and I am saying this exactly as he said it – "I'm going to change my *pantalones*." Exactly that. *One word* in Spanish and, oh, didn't the women swoon!

'You should have heard them! On and on in fast Spanish – *so impressed*. "Oh, Geraldine, he is so charming, your man."' Gerry looked over at Duncan and rolled her eyes. The rest of us were laughing – including Duncan. And then Gerry's façade broke into a huge smile and she laughed along with us. '*One word* of Spanish ...' She trailed off, laughing too hard to finish.

'What?' asked Duncan, throwing his arms out wide. 'It's a good word – it's, like, one of ten I can remember – even now.'

Gerry grabbed his face in one hand, and kissed him on the mouth with a loud smack. 'My man. You are *so charming*!' She snuggled in closer.

They were such a sweet couple.

'Duncan, *mate*, you speak more Spanish than me, and I took it for four years in high school.' Josh had attempted to say 'mate' with a broad Aussie accent. Abysmal. Still, he'd tried.

225

Maybe he would come and visit me in Sydney some time – pick up some more Aussie lingo. I could teach him how to say 'mate' properly. Hold on. What was I thinking?

Many, *many* times I had let myself fantasise about a future with James, but with Josh, it was less about a fantasy and more about the reality of our situation. I didn't like letting my mind go to that place. How on earth could it work out between us after this trip? Especially as we lived half a world apart?

Was I just scared?

I mean, James was the fantasy, right? A prince to rescue an extremely single princess. I could dream about a life with him the same way I would fantasise about a film star or the super-hot guy at the gym who I never spoke to, but had caught me watching him work out a few times. It was fun to think about. But every time I thought about Josh outside the confines of the trip, I got in a knot in my stomach.

Josh could be the real thing, and truth be told, that terrified me.

If I fell for him – *properly* fell for him – being apart most of the time would be excruciating.

And, what if it *did* work out? What then? I didn't want to move to America. Not really, and I didn't know that I could anyway. It wasn't like green cards grew on trees. We would have to get married if I wanted to move there. Married! The thought of it made my heart race – and not in a good way.

I supposed if Josh moved to Sydney, it would be easier – probably for both of us. He could work anywhere in the world – he was in the tech industry. And maybe someone would employ him and move him to Sydney. Then we could date properly to see if we really were compatible. And then perhaps, after some time dating, we'd move in together. That was much less dramatic than getting married for a green card.

I shook my head, stopping my thoughts from running away with themselves entirely. Planning the logistics of who would move where was doing my head in, and I really needed to focus on the now. I was with my little family, we were having a great night out, and I *had* to stop thinking about all the grim reasons it might not work out with Josh after the trip.

And I needed to remember that the future – if there *was* one with him – may not be so grim after all. Didn't I have two great examples of things working out, right in front of me? Gerry and Duncan had met overseas and lived a world apart, yet they made it work. And Marie and Gary were ten years apart in age, and they were the most in-love couple I'd ever known.

I was getting all worked up about nothing. I didn't need to dwell on the what-ifs, and I didn't need to make any decisions about my love life. I needed to listen to Hannah, who was telling a story, and chill the hell out!

Hannah had the attention of the group and punctuated her story with dramatic pauses to sip from her cocktail.

'My dad was turning sixty and he wanted us all to go somewhere special together, and he'd always wanted to ski in Europe – because we totally grew up skiing – usually every week of the season – Whistler is, like, ninety minutes away. Anyway, so his lifelong dream is to ski in Europe, and we ended up in the French Alps, right on the border of Italy.

'So, it was me and my brother and his wife, my mum, dad – of course – and even my aunt and my cousin, staying in this gorgeous chalet – it slept sixteen – and the very first night there's this huge dump of powder, and the next morning, there was a *brilliant* blue sky. I mean, *perfect* conditions.

'So, we get up, have this huge breakfast, then hit the slopes. And we're out there *all* day. We're, like, texting each other so we could meet for lunch, and I skied with my brother and sister-in-law for a few hours – we found these awesome trails.

'And it gets towards the end of the day – dusk – and we're texting each other to meet up in a particular bar at the end of the last run. And I get there with my brother and his wife, and my mum's with her sister and my cousin – and she's frantic. She looks at us and says, "It's your father ..."'

It was the most I'd ever heard Hannah share in one go – and we were all on the edge of her seats wanting to know what happened to her dad while she took a sip of her martini.

'What happened?' Josh expressed aloud what I could see in the faces of the others.

'Oh, nothing bad,' she dismissed our concern and in return we let out a collective sigh.

'But he *had* accidentally taken the wrong run when he got off the ski lift, and had skied into *Italy*. *Any* other time of the day – no problem. You take the lift to the top and ski back into France. But it was the last run of the day. The lifts were closed until the next morning at nine. *And* his phone was out of battery.'

When the penny dropped, the rest of us laughed out loud and Hannah joined in.

'That's hysterical,' said Marie. 'What did he *do?*'

'Well, he went into the nearest hotel and asked to use the phone, and then he called the bar where the rest of us were and asked for my mum. And *then*, when we knew he was safe – and just stupid – he headed to the bar.'

That brought more laughter.

'That's what I would do,' Duncan added. Gary nodded in agreement.

'So, he had about thirty euros in cash – not enough for a room, but certainly enough for a couple of drinks – and don't forget, this whole time he has his ski gear on – including his boots – 'cause he didn't have anything else.'

By this stage, I was laughing so hard I had ceased making any noise. I could picture the whole scene and for some reason, in my head, her dad looked like John Cleese.

'And then he struck up a conversation with this Austrian family who took pity on him. Turned out they had a three-room apartment in the hotel, and they ended up feeding him and giving him a place to sleep that night.'

Gary actually applauded. 'I *love* that he did that. That's the kind of sixty-year-old I plan to be – adventurous, gregarious, resourceful.'

'Yep, Aussies are like that too,' said Duncan. 'You're overseas, you're on your own, you strike up a conversation, make friends, then you get invited places, looked after.'

'Ah yes,' agreed Gerry. 'You see?' she asked the rest of us. 'That is how he won me – with his, how do I say? Lack of planning? I had to take pity on him.'

More laughter. More applause.

'No, no, that is not what happened. Why are you telling lies to our friends?' Duncan faked incredulity.

Gerry waved him off and shook her head. 'You are so silly. That is exactly how it happened.' Duncan leaned over and kissed her, and we'd come full circle, basking in their adoration for each other.

'I love that story, Hannah.' I turned my attention back to

my roommate. 'I'm guessing you got your dad back the next morning?'

'Oh, yeah, we got him back, after the Austrians insisted on treating him to a huge breakfast in the hotel's café.' I liked the sound of Hannah's dad. I was also glad to hear she had a lovely man in her life – one that would love her no matter what. Hopefully she could – or would soon – see that not all men were awful users.

I looked around the table at the three men we were travelling with. Josh. Gary. Duncan. Each so different, but they were all good men. Kind, fun, thoughtful, interesting men. *They're out there, Hannah*, I thought.

Or maybe that was me talking to myself. Looking over at Josh, I caught him watching me, and we shared a smile. Yep, these were good men. And I was looking at a good man who gave me tummy twinges and knew how to kiss.

Maybe *he* was Prince Charming.

Chapter Fourteen

We were docked at our second-last island, Tinos, and there were only two days left of our trip – well, two and a half. Really, it was closer to three, but the end was looming, and I was intent on squeezing every moment out of those nearly three days – starting with breakfast on the bow of the boat with Josh.

Like the morning before, we were the first ones up, and we moved about the tiny galley in sync. We made a breakfast feast of tea, yoghurt with muesli, and buttered toast. Sitting up on the bow, enjoying our food in an easy silence, we watched the marina come to life.

Around us, people emerged from below their decks and squinted at the morning sun. There were boat chores to do – taking out the rubbish, clearing the deck of things you can trip over – you know, boat chores. There was probably a lot more to it than that, but even after a week of sailing, I still didn't know my bilge from my poop deck.

As I bit into a piece of toast – Greek bread is amazing, by the way – I wondered if I could ever live on a boat. I loved being on the water. I loved the salty air and being under sail. I didn't even mind the boat chores Duncan had assigned to me, like tying off the buoys.

I came at the idea in a different direction. If I *did* live on a boat, what would I miss about my apartment? The first thing that popped into my head was my shower. At home, I had hot water with awesome pressure for days. I had as many towels as I wanted or needed, and cupboards and drawers filled with toiletries. And, when I took a shower at home, I didn't get the toilet, the floor, the sink, *and* the window wet.

And my bed! My big, beautiful, comfortable bed, and my fluffy doona, and my pillow! I let myself daydream a little about sleeping in a proper bed, rather than on a tiny boat bunk with an eight-centimetre foam mattress, a pillow the size of a magazine, and a roommate who wished she had a cabin to herself.

'Daydreaming?' Josh's voice cut through my thoughts.

'So much.'

'Oh yeah? What about?' He took a sip of tea.

'Being in bed,' I replied.

He spat out the tea – fortunately, not in my direction.

I laughed. 'No, not like that. Like, sleeping in a *real* bed.'

He coughed a few times. 'I get it, I get it.'

'You're silly.'

'Yes.'

'We'll get to sleep in real beds tomorrow, remember?' The sailing part of the trip was finishing in Mykonos the next day. We were all staying at different hotels across the island, but we'd agreed to meet up for dinner to say a proper goodbye.

Actually, Josh wasn't officially staying anywhere. He'd booked a ferry for the following afternoon back to Athens. The rest of us had already convinced him to change his ferry ticket and stay another night with us in Mykonos. He was going to find somewhere to stay when we got in.

'That's right,' he said, nodding. 'Kinda sad, though, isn't it?'

'End of the trip ...' I trailed off, fighting the sadness that overwhelmed me.

'Yeah ...' Josh trailed off too and we finished the rest of our breakfast without another word. There was no longer a comfortable silence.

Our afternoon was filled with warm sunshine and cool breezes, with all of us together at the beach. It was called Lichnaftia in English, but I was not going to attempt it the way the native Greeks said it. It was hard enough in my native tongue. Lick-naf-tee-a, in case you wanted to try it aloud. It was tucked away on the east end of the island and we'd arrived there on scooters, solely on Duncan's word that it was something special.

He was right.

The water was aquamarine; although, it was a little chillier than I would have liked. Still, it was a quiet little cove and we had it to ourselves. We'd brought the makings of a picnic lunch, the same lunch menu we'd had each day we sailed: tzatziki, bread, tomatoes (I was going to turn into a tomato with how many I'd eaten), and the king and queen of each meal: feta and olives.

Simple and delicious food.

Duncan had somehow perched a small cooler on the back of his and Gerry's scooter, so we even had beer. For several hours we lounged, swam, ate, talked and picked up pebbles from the mostly sandy beach. It was pretty much like any other family outing to the shore.

After lunch, I waded into the chilly water up to my knees and let it gently lap around me. I heard someone wade in after me and I wasn't surprised when I turned around and saw it was Josh.

'Nice bathing suit,' he said, obviously eyeing me up and down.

'Thank you. You *have* seen me in a bikini before, you know.' We'd done nothing more than kiss – we'd never even had a proper date – and yet, here he was seeing me in my bathers. Parts of our relationship were progressing faster than others. I typically held off on the whole 'see me in a bikini' thing until well after the sex part had started and the guy was already used to, or even madly in love with, my body – lumps, bumps and all.

I sucked in my stomach, subtly I hoped. I didn't want him thinking I was vain – just that my midsection looked phenomenal. He must have read my mind about the proper date thing, because the next thing he said was, 'So, I was thinking, maybe tonight you and I could go for dinner somewhere – the two of us.'

A smile spread across my face. 'Are you asking me out, Joshua?' He met my smile with a shy one of his own.

'Yes, I'm asking you out.'

'Like, on a *date*?' His smile grew bigger.

'Yes, exactly like that. Sarah, will you have dinner with me tonight?'

'Why, I'd be delighted.'

With his mission accomplished, he left me alone and waded back to shore. In my excitement at going on an actual date that night, I forgot the water was cold and dived in. Holy guacamole, Batman. My chest tightened, and when I planted my feet on the sea floor and emerged from the water, I was fighting for my breath.

In an attempt to look cool, I slicked my wet hair back from my face and arched my back like I was in the *Sports Illustrated* swimsuit edition. I glanced at the shore to discover no one was even watching me. They all had their heads down in conversation or were reading. They had missed my fabulous recovery – I was okay with that. It meant they had also missed my epic fail.

*

That evening, Josh lightly clasped my hand in his as we walked down the pier away from the boat. I thought it was a terrific start to the date. Yes, it had only been a couple of minutes, but I already had a good feeling.

After our day at the beach, we'd all gone back to the boat and took turns showering to wash away the sand and sunscreen, because there wasn't enough pressure for more than one shower at a time. I showered last – and quickly – but afterwards, I took my time with my hair and makeup. I pulled my hair back into a long, lose braid – pretty, elegant, and about as much as I could do with my limited products and no hair dryer. I applied some shimmering eye shadow, my ubiquitous mascara, some blush and a slick of lip gloss.

While I made myself up, I could hear the others' laughter floating through the boat from the deck. As I slipped into a floral sundress, I wondered if Josh had mentioned to the rest of the group that we were going out. On our own. On a date.

I took a cute little fabric handbag out of my luggage and packed it with the essentials. It was the first time I'd used it, as it was far prettier than it was practical, and we hadn't really had any 'cute little handbag' occasions. One last look in the mirror confirmed what I already knew. I was nervous. The good kind of nerves. First-date nerves.

'It's *Josh*,' I said to myself quietly in the mirror. 'You've spent twenty-four-seven with him for the past nine days. Get over yourself.' I really know how to give myself a pep talk, huh?

And then I couldn't put it off any longer. I picked up my sandals and with them dangling from my fingers, climbed up the little ladder onto the deck. I was surprised to see only Gerry, Duncan and Josh sitting there.

'Wow, Sarah. You scrub up nice,' said Duncan.

I looked down at my outfit as if to confirm his compliment.

'Uh, thanks.' Gerry was smiling at me in a knowing way, but whatever she knew, it was something I didn't. 'So, where are the others?' I asked.

Gerry replied, as she stifled a yawn. 'Gary and Marie went for dinner, and Hannah went off to meet the skipper. You know, from the other boat.' I did know, yes.

'Oh, cool.'

'Shall we get going?' Josh was standing on the deck, all six-foot-one of him, looking down at me with a sexy smile. He scrubbed up nice too, but I would wait until we were away from prying ears to tell him that. I silently admired his dark jeans, crisp white linen shirt – the sleeves rolled up a few times. In his hands, he held brown leather shoes, which I knew would look great with the rest of the outfit.

'Yes, definitely.'

Then I looked at Gerry and Duncan. 'What are you two up to tonight?' I really didn't want to invite them on our date, but I also didn't want them to feel unwelcome either.

'Sleep!' declared Gerry as she put her hand up to her mouth, another yawn blooming behind it.

'Yep. Eat something, then sleeping. Lots of sleeping,' Duncan concurred.

I was relieved. 'Okay well, have a nice night.'

We exchanged goodnights, then Josh led the way off the boat, taking my hand to steady me as I crossed between the boat and the land. He knew all about my fear of falling in and being squashed. On the pier, we both stepped into our respective shoes, and as we walked away from the boat, Josh grabbed my hand again. That was the moment I decided the date was going well.

'I asked Duncan about some places we could go, and I've picked somewhere I think you will like.'

'That's super thoughtful.' See?

'Well, it's what the guy does, you know? On a date.'

'Oh, really? It's been so long since I've been on a date, I'd forgotten. And you likely don't know this, but Australian men – they don't really know about dating etiquette.'

'They don't?'

'Well, no that's not fair. I'm, sure there are some who do. I know some Aussie guys who treat women respectfully – they're fun and caring, and genuinely want to be with someone.' Josh was listening, but not saying anything. Somehow, I'd managed in only a matter of minutes to leap right into a taboo date topic – other men. I needed to lighten the conversation.

'But in my experience, those men are either gay, or married to my friends.' It had the desired effect and he chuckled at that. 'So, where are we heading?' Changing the subject like a champion.

Josh stopped at the end of the pier and pulled a piece of paper out of his pocket. He looked from the paper to the streets and buildings in front of us, folded the paper and put it back in his pocket.

'This way,' he said, with confidence. 'Duncan drew me a map.'

We strolled while taking in the atmosphere of the early evening crowd. It was a good mix of locals – who chatted with each other in rapid-fire Greek – tourists, and travellers. I distinguished between the two because those I called 'travellers' were clearly not local, but had a relaxed air about them, moving fluidly through the loud, brightly lit streets. The 'tourists' looked either a little lost or utterly annoyed by the bustle surrounding them; I pitied people who could be in paradise, but not see it.

And then there were the pilgrims.

Like Syros, Tinos had a giant church overlooking the town. *Unlike* in Syros, the church on Tinos was a drawcard for thousands of pilgrims each year. The church was called Our Lady of Tinos, Greece's main shrine to the Virgin Mary. Apparently, a holy relic was discovered on the site, and people came from everywhere to partake of its powers and pay their respects.

Red carpet lined the sides of the steep road, which led directly from the marina to the church. People crawled on their hands and knees all the way to the top of the hill, and then up the stairs of the church to honour Mary. It was quite incredible to see this kind of devotion, and throughout our brief stay we had respectfully stayed off the red carpeting as we moved about the town.

That night there were more pilgrims than we'd seen during the day, and they added to the incredible atmosphere around us. We walked up the hill towards the church, and then about halfway we turned off the main road into a side street. Small tavernas occupied spots either side of the street, and bursts of laughter and chatter filled the air around us as we passed. As we approached each one, I wondered if that was where we were heading, but we kept going.

Eventually, Josh led us down a rather steep set of stairs. At the bottom was a small arched entranceway made of stone, and a smiling middle-aged (that word again) man was there to greet us.

'*Kalispera*,' he said softly, nodding his head slightly.

'*Kalispera*,' Josh and I replied in unison.

'My friend called ahead,' said Josh. 'Duncan Ford?'

A smile broke out across the man's face, and he switched seamlessly to English. 'Of course, sir. Duncan is a good friend of ours and we have expected you and the young lady.' 'Young lady' – how nice.

The man led the way into the restaurant, a stone-paved terrace that was open on two sides to views of the water and the town. There were several couples at small tables with white tablecloths dotted about the terrace, and it was subtly lit with candles and warm-coloured lights.

'Josh, this is beautiful,' I said as we followed the *maître d*□ to our table.

He smiled. 'Duncan said it was a special occasion kind of place. I'm glad you like it.'

We were seated at a table with a wonderful view of the town, and yes, the lights below us were twinkling. I couldn't help thinking that the restaurant, the view – all of it – was like something out of a movie. Josh's words lingered in my thoughts.

'So, this is a special occasion?'

He picked up my hand and held it lightly. 'I think so.'

'Me too,' I whispered. A waiter appeared with menus – thankfully, in English as well as Greek. Josh dropped my hand to take his menu, and I was a little disappointed to lose the contact with him so soon.

Until I saw the menu selection, which was extensive and traditional. My hungry eyes scanned it for my favourite Greek dishes and most of them were there.

'Geez, what an awesome menu. Should we just order one of everything?' I asked Josh, only half-joking.

'Yeah, there's some good stuff here. Duncan says the food is incredible too.'

'Well, we'll want a Greek salad – *horiatiki*.'

'Absolutely. And the lamb – it's slow-roasted – we have to get that.'

'God, yes. I thought we did lamb well in Australia, but every time I have it here it blows me away.'

'Shall we get calamari?' asked Josh. 'Or the spinach and feta pie?'

'Calamari, I think.'

'And *briami*. I love that.'

'Which one is that again?' I asked.

'The vegetable stew.'

'Oh, that's fantastic,' I agreed. 'Tzatziki to start, don't you think?' He nodded as his eyes roamed the menu. 'Josh?' He looked up. 'Do you think it would be easier just to go with my original suggestion?'

'One of everything?' I nodded. 'Well, we're getting close.' We laughed at ourselves as our waiter appeared. He didn't seem fazed by the epic order, and soon returned to the table with a carafe of white wine.

We watched in silence as he poured two glasses, and when he was out of earshot I whispered to Josh, 'I'm sure they do great food, but I bet you a million dollars this is shitty wine.' Josh lifted his glass and inspected it, swirling the contents as though he was in a tasting room. He sniffed it and scrunched his nose up.

'Was that for show, or unintentional?' I asked, lifting my own glass and having a sniff. Josh took a sip and cringed as he swallowed.

'I don't know a whole lot about wine, but I think this was probably bottled in the last few days.' He took a liberal sip of water.

'As in, Tuesday was a great vintage, but Wednesday, not so much?'

'Yeah, something like that.'

I put my wine back on the table, untouched. 'Maybe it needs to open up.'

'A lot.'

'Maybe it will be better with the food.'

'We'll see. In the meantime, I would like to propose a toast.'

'With the crappy wine?' I asked, amused.

'Let's go with the water for now.'

'Okay.' I raised my water glass and looked at him expectantly.

'To friends,' he said, and my heart plummeted. *Friends? Really? He brought me to this romantic restaurant to toast to friendship?* The date had taken an unexpected and unwanted turn. I tried to keep the smile fixed on my face, as I moved my glass towards his.

'Hang on,' he said, eyeing my glass. 'There's more ...' *Well, good! Because so far it sucks.* 'To friends – the kind of friends you go far from home to find, only to find that they make you feel at home.' Then he clinked my glass and took a sip of water.

I went through the motions, forcing a smile and drinking from my water glass. Josh's toast was so sweet, so heartfelt, and yet it left me feeling, well, confused. Were we 'just friends'? Is that what he thought? I mean, we were, yes. But wasn't there more? What about the hand-holding and the kissing? What kind of friends did this guy have back home?

I realised I'd been having a conversation with myself for too long and looked at Josh. He hadn't seemed to notice, though – too busy gazing at the view. I wondered what he was thinking. Probably patting himself on the back for such a great toast. I bet he'd rehearsed it; it sounded rehearsed.

Before I could stir myself into any more of a lather, our waiter placed a basket of steaming hot pita bread and a large bowl of tzatziki on the table between us. Saved by the dip! At least Josh's mouth would be full and he couldn't make any more lame toasts.

See how I had gone from feeling wooed and adored to woeful and annoyed in a matter of seconds?

Was I being ridiculous? He *had* asked me out on a date. He'd even called it that. And there we were actually on the date. I told myself to try and enjoy the moment. I took a generous scoop of tzatziki from the bowl and popped it in my mouth. Then I groaned; that stuff was delicious.

'I know, right?' said Josh, going in for another bite. 'How good is this?' We shared a look that said, 'so good,' and he smiled at me, his eyes crinkling at the corners. He was so cute – so sexy – that I couldn't stay annoyed at him. Even though his toast had made me feel like shit, I was pretty sure he hadn't meant for that to happen.

And if I really thought about it, it *was* a beautiful toast. I loaded up another piece of pita with the creamy dip. Of course, he started to ask me a question right as I put it in my mouth.

'So, I've been meaning to ask you something ...' I nodded encouragingly as I chewed as fast as I could. 'I had a question about your ex ...'

I swallowed – hard – the food forming a lump in my throat, or maybe it was the thought of Neil intruding on my date that was hard to swallow.

'Yes,' I croaked. I stared at him, while he toyed with the question, obviously seeking out the best way to phrase it. I wanted to snipe at him to hurry the hell up.

'I've been wondering if you thought there was any chance of the two of you getting back together?' He phrased it like a question, insecurity steeping his voice.

My immediate reaction was to laugh, which I did – only it was more of a snort of derision. 'Be assured, there's absolutely no way in hell I'm ever going back to that prick,' I said, old Sarah slotting right into my place at the table. Josh looked a little taken aback. Maybe I had said that too loudly. I looked around us, and one of the couples close by was watching me. Yep. Too loudly.

'Sorry, Josh,' I said at a more reasonable volume. 'I had a flash of my former, bitter self then.' I took a deep breath and blew it out slowly. 'Neil was mean. And I was weak and sad when I was with him. It's so over that it couldn't be any more over.' I dared to look at him. 'Is that a better answer?'

He nodded and smiled at me. Was that pity in his eyes? 'I

didn't mean to bring up stuff that makes you feel uncomfortable. I'm sorry.' Yes, there was some pity there. *Wonderful.*

I shook my head, 'No, no, it's fine ...'

'I just wanted to know if I had any competition,' he said, winking. That broke the tension. 'Besides James, that is.' And that brought it right back again. The conversation was definitely keeping me on my toes.

I deflected. 'No, Neil is definitely not anywhere near the realm of competition.' I wondered if Josh would ask me again about James, but he didn't. Instead he nodded and helped himself to more tzatziki.

The rest of our order arrived at the table, but I was focused on the conversation. I needed to steer it to a safer topic – meaning, anything but my love life. I drew on a fall-back conversation opener.

'Josh, money matters aside, what is your ultimate dream job?'

'Switching to date talk, huh?' He followed this with a smile, as he loaded up his plate.

'You caught me.' I raised my hands as though he'd said, 'Stick 'em up.' He seemed to consider my blatant change of topic and I wondered if he'd play along.

'Right, dream job ...' I felt myself relaxing, silently grateful for a reprieve from the hot seat. 'I'd like to get to a point where I can do my job from anywhere – and still basically do what I do, consulting, but be location-agnostic.'

'Location-agnostic? I haven't heard that before, but I think I get what you mean.' I filled my plate from the array of dishes while he explained.

'It would mean paring back my possessions and moving about the world freely. A few months here, a year maybe. Asia,

South America, Europe, parts of the States I've never seen. I'll arrive and find a place to live – short-stay apartments, sub-lets, that sort of thing. I'll live like a local as much as possible – try to learn some of the language if it's different ...' He trailed off and took a bite of lamb.

I was intrigued; it sounded like a fascinating way to live. I wondered if I could live like that.

'How do you get to a point where you can do that, do you think?'

'I keep working on my skills as a developer, I put my hand up for the tricky, niche projects and I learn as much as I can over the next few years. I'll want to get to a point where I can strike out on my own, choose which projects I work on, and as long as I have internet, I'll be able to work from anywhere.

'That's the plan anyway.'

'So, how do you get around work visas and those types of restrictions?' The lamb was incredible, by the way.

'Well, you'd be surprised by how easy it is to get a visa for a lot of places. And then for the rest, you usually get at least three months on a tourist visa and can be paid into a US account. There are a few things to work out – like not getting extradited for avoiding local taxes – but I'll do my research.'

'And you'll have what? Your clothes, a laptop, and that's all?'

'And my phone.'

'Oh yes, the *phone*.' At the start of the trip, Josh had found it difficult to switch off from technology, and he'd brought his phone everywhere we went – even when there was no mobile or data coverage. Duncan had teased him relentlessly about it.

Then about halfway through the trip, we went out for the day and Josh purposefully left the phone on board. He'd done that ever since. Still, I got the sense it was something he couldn't do without for very long.

It was like me wearing a watch again when I got back to the real world. Practically my whole life ran to a schedule, and that wouldn't change because I'd taken my watch off for a week while sailing around the Greek Islands. On some level, I understood Josh's attachment to his phone. Still, I was glad he'd left it behind, especially while we were on a date.

'It must sound far-fetched,' Josh said.

'I don't think so; it actually sounds feasible. As technology improves, and as social networks connect us with all these different threads to the people in our lives, it becomes less and less important to be there in person. I think the type of professional life you're describing will one day be mainstream.'

'I hope not! I'm going for this unique kind of "lone wolf wanderer" lifestyle. Hard to do that if everyone is doing it.'

'Of course, by then, you'll have found some other subversive way to live. I would never expect you to settle for being mainstream.' I tried to ignore that he'd freshly declared his dream of a solitary life.

'Right, exactly. Everyone will be off the beaten track, and by then I will have made my way back to Chicago, where it will just be one other guy and me.'

'And Obama.'

'Maybe he'll be the "one other guy".'

'That would be cool. But what you're saying is that you don't let society define what you are – just what you *aren't*.' He eyed me with mock suspicion. Maybe he knew where I was going with my teasing. 'But isn't that the same thing? You're still letting society choose what you are, aren't you?'

'This is getting way too deep for me.' This time it was his turn to deflect. 'You should try the *briami*, by the way. It's fantastic.' I put a large spoonful on my plate and took a bite. Delicious.

'The *briami is* fantastic.'

'Should I write this down?'

'What?'

'That I'm right.'

'Hilarious. You're so funny. No, really. I mean it.' I hoped my accent didn't mask the intended sarcasm, but he laughed, so I guessed not.

'But getting back to what you were saying, I think your goal is impressive. You want to grow professionally, you want to travel, you want to dig into the places you see. It's more than holidaying, it's even more than travelling, because you're buying groceries, you're learning about the neighbourhood, the language, you're meeting the people. It sounds incredible.'

'Thanks. You know, I've never really told anyone about it before.'

'Oh?'

'Well, my friends, we're close in a lot of ways, but – I've talked about this before – mostly they are married, or getting married, and buying houses, having kids. Talking about all this stuff with them – I don't know. I never really thought they would get it, so I haven't ever brought it up.' He shrugged.

'Well, you've thought it through. You have a semblance of a plan. Maybe it's time to trust them with it – your close friends anyway. If they're really your friends, they won't judge you.'

'It's not that I think they will, but you know how you said that sometimes your friends look at you with the 'head tilt' thing, like they don't really understand what you're talking about?'

'Oh yeah. I do. I get it. You're more worried about that – having to explain the 'why' rather than the 'what'.'

'Exactly. That's one of the things I like about being with you. I can tell you this stuff, and not only do you *not* judge me, you get it as well. It's –' he seemed to struggle for the right word, and then he found it '– refreshing.'

For a moment we regarded each other, smiling. The sweet, but awful toast and the awkward question about Neil faded away. It had turned back into a lovely date.

I refrained from stuffing myself with the incredible food by reminding myself – repeatedly – that I was on a date. Even though I was with Josh, who had seen me devour an entire gyro for lunch, it was still a date. And that meant date-like behaviour, and *that* meant not making a pig of myself.

When the waiter brought over a dessert menu, I politely declined and he graciously took it away.

'Oh, sorry. I should have asked,' I said, realising I had declined for both of us. 'Did you want something?'

'I had something else in mind.' Had his voice dripped with innuendo, I would have assumed he meant that *I* was dessert. Men had used that line on me a few times – once it had actually worked. But Josh seemed to genuinely have something else in mind for dessert.

'Oh?' I prompted.

'It's a surprise. It's also a little bit of a walk from here. Is that okay?'

'Of course.' I was intrigued. I also needed to pee, so I excused myself and went in search of the ladies' room. As I washed my hands, I looked at myself in the mirror above the

248

sink. I looked contented, and it sat well on me. I was also excited about the next part of the date.

When I returned to the table, Josh stood up to greet me. 'You know, I should have told you before, you look really beautiful tonight.'

Suddenly shy at the compliment, I said a quiet 'Thank you.'

'How did Duncan put it? You scrub up nice.'

I grinned, my shyness dissipating. He knew just how to disarm me. 'That is the correct saying, yes.'

'Ready?'

'Ready.' He took my hand and led the way out of the restaurant. I smiled at the *maître d* on the way out and we climbed the stairs back onto the narrow street. 'So, where to now?' I asked, more and more curious about the next part of our date.

'You'll see.'

We walked in silence, traversing the hill and heading closer to the marina. When we were in the thick of the bustling energy of the town and without warning, Josh stopped walking and turned towards me. 'I don't know if I can wait any longer.'

'For what?'

'To kiss you.' He didn't wait for my response – he just gathered, me into his arms and kissed me. I forgot where we were – standing in a busy street – and wrapped my arms around his neck. His mouth was hot against mine, and his lips firm and insistent. The tips of our tongues met, the only tentative part of the kiss. I melted into him, my body pressed to his. I felt desirable and treasured all wrapped up in him like that.

What seemed liked minutes later, we broke the kiss. His

forehead pressed against mine, and I could feel his breath on my face when he spoke through a raspy voice. 'Sarah, you're going to be the undoing of me.' I would unpack those words later, analysing every nuance, but in that moment, I took it for what it was. Because I felt the same. Exposed. Electrified. And completely his.

'We're here,' Josh said as he stepped into a darkened doorway. I followed, my eyes adjusting to the dim light inside. Low-slung couches bordered the room, and tall stools lined up against a curved bar. There was a small, but lively crowd holding court at the bar, and a few couples seated on various couches. Josh spied a free one against the side wall, right in front of a low window which opened onto the street. He led me towards it and we sank into the slightly musty fabric. A pseudo-techno beat pulsed from an unseen speaker nearby, but not so loud that it drowned out conversation.

'It doesn't look like much, but Duncan says the cocktails here are incredible.'

'Sounds great!' After the kiss in the street, he could have taken me anywhere and I would have been enthused.

'And they have a special dessert menu,' he added.

My curiosity about this dessert was piquing. 'You mean like they do in Amsterdam?' I asked, imagining a menu of marijuana.

He laughed. 'I hadn't thought of that – that would be cool – but no. It's something else.' A waitress made her way over to us; it was obvious she wasn't a Greek native. She greeted us with a North American accent, which I immediately picked as Canadian.

'Hi, guys. Here's our cocktail menu. We make a sidecar with Metaxa that is to *die* for. It's totally my favourite,' she enthused.

I loved a good sidecar – second only to a gin and tonic – so I signalled I would have one without bothering to read the rest of the menu.

Josh added to the order. 'Two please, and can you bring over the dessert menu?'

'Sure!'

I watched her walk away. She was blonde, ridiculously pretty, and her body was killer. Without even thinking, I heard myself utter aloud the stupidest words I could ever say on a date. 'She's beautiful.' *What?* I came to my senses immediately. Why on earth had I said that? To Josh!

'She's cute, I guess. *You* are beautiful.' That surprised the hell out of me and for a moment I was speechless, with a sort of open-mouthed smile stuck on my face.

'I wasn't fishing.'

'I know you weren't.'

'But that *was* the correct response.'

He threw back his head and laughed. 'That's awesome.' He pulled me in for a quick kiss, his warm, soft lips pressed against mine for one delightful moment.

Our waitress came back. This time I regarded her with fresh eyes. She *was* pretty. But Josh thought I was beautiful. 'Here you go – our dessert menu.'

Josh took it from her and I leaned in close to him – partly so I could read the menu, but mostly because I liked being pressed against him. The entire menu was different flavours of *Loukoumia* – what I would call Turkish delight. I'd bought a quite few pieces throughout our trip, indulging on an almost daily basis. The variety was incredible – so much more than the rosewater flavour I had come to associate with it.

'Oh my god, I *love* this.' I was practically drooling over the menu.

'I thought you'd like this place. You can select it by the piece.'

My eyes widened at the thought of assembling the ideal tasting plate. 'Okay. Here's what I'm thinking – you can only eat two, maybe three, tops *four* pieces of this stuff in one sitting. I mean sure, we could take some away with us – we should do that – but how about we each choose two – no, make it three flavours, and we get two of each of those, and whatever we don't finish tonight we take with us?'

I could hear the excitement – borderline obsession – in my voice, but Josh loved my enthusiasm, right?

'You know,' he started slowly, and I was immediately impatient with him. 'I knew you would like this place, because I have watched you devour *many* pieces of this stuff, but there was no way I could anticipate this level of excitement over *Loukoumia*. I'm digging your passion.'

'Don't take the piss out of me, because I take my dessert seriously.' I eyeballed him until he knew I was completely unserious.

'That really is a charming expression,' he retorted, nonplussed.

Ignoring him, I read from the menu. 'Lemon, mango, and rose – gotta go traditional on my last pick.'

'You're not biting?'

'Charming expression. I know – we Oss-ees are sooo crass! Now pick.' I wasn't biting, no. I was focusing on dessert.

Josh solemnly scanned the menu.

'Okay, I'm going with pistachio ...'

'Good choice.'

'Thank you. And, orange. Aaand, oooh, cherry.'

'Noice,' I said in my broadest Australian accent. 'I loike your choices.'

On cue, the cute Canadian waitress appeared again with our drinks. Josh rattled off our order of *Loukoumia* and asked her to bring them all in a to-go box so we could take what we didn't eat with us.

I lifted the glasses and handed Josh his drink. 'Now I would like to propose a toast.'

'Go for it.'

'I would like to propose a toast to the best date I've ever had.' My words hung in the air for a moment, but I didn't care. It *was* the best date I'd ever had, because it was with Josh, and he'd been so thoughtful, and he was sexy and fun, and I was having a wonderful time. And most of all, because I was falling for him big time. I held my breath waiting for his response. I know that even though it felt like minutes, it must have only been seconds.

Finally, he clinked his glass against mine. 'I'll drink to that.' We held eye contact over the rims of the glasses as we drank.

The Canadian was right. 'Um, hello? This is delicious,' I said, and then took another sip.

'Not only the best date ever, the best sidecar ever.'

'And, I'll drink to that!' I took another sip. Josh grinned at me.

Our selection of *Loukoumia* arrived in a white box lined with rice paper. We didn't know which flavour was which and in the dim light of the bar, all we could do was guess. I bit into a piece, which turned out to be lemon – the lemon zing was so intense. I wondered how I could source some back home.

'I wonder if when I get home I'm going to keep eating dinner at nine o'clock at night. A week ago it seemed weird, but now it's my new normal,' said Josh.

It was my new normal too, and I was fine with pontificating about our lives in the distant, unnamed future, but did I really want to think about what Josh would be doing when he returned to Chicago? No, I did not. It was another reminder that it was all coming to an end – and soon. And even though the trip wasn't finished yet, it had already been the best trip I'd ever had. If I was going to avoid sinking into the moroseness that threatened to take hold, I would have to be honest with Josh.

'You know what? I don't want to think about that – what we'll do when we're all pulled in different directions, and not spending every day together – when we're not a family anymore. It makes me sad. It makes the goodbyes that are coming feel too close.'

'Sorry, I didn't mean to upset you.' *Well, good, because I don't want to be upset.*

'Look,' I said, 'what if we *do* talk about the future, but we do it in the abstract? You know, "one day I think I might ..." It's just that when separation is nigh, I find it difficult to even think about it. I'm worried it will spoil the time we have left.'

'I didn't think of it like that, but I understand.' He raised his glass. 'To the here and now.'

I tapped my glass against his. 'To the here and now.' I took a sip. 'In the broader sense, though, how fucking weird is it that they eat so late here?'

He laughed. '*So* weird.'

'It's the same throughout Europe. The Spaniards! They eat at, like, ten or eleven o'clock!'

'I don't get it. Are they up in the mornings and heading off to work for nine, like we are, or is the whole schedule skewed?' Josh asked.

'I think that they do get up for work the same as us, but the big difference is the siesta.'

'Ahhh, the siesta. I seem to recall that you have availed yourself of that once or twice in the last week.'

'Yes, but this is my *holiday*. We're talking about people's regular, everyday lives. I don't know if I could live here all the time. I'm usually in bed by ten,' I said.

'Oh really?'

'Yep. Does that make me boring? Or *old*?' Anytime I could get in a little jibe about our age difference I did.

'No, it makes you normal. What time do you get up?'

'Most mornings I'm at the gym by six.'

'Six? Why?'

I laughed. '*Because* I like to start my day that way. It energises me. I take it that you're not a morning person?'

'I like to ease into my day. You know, go through my Twitter feed, read about the latest tech, eat a cooked breakfast, have two cups of coffee, and *then* get ready for work.'

'I'm gonna guess that I am *at* work before you even get in the shower.'

'What time do you get to work?'

'Usually before eight.'

'Jesus! Yes, you are correct. At eight in the morning I am still the great hairy unwashed bachelor.'

I laughed.

'By nine, however, I am suited up, clean-shaven, and looking fine.'

'Oh, really?'

'Yes, really. Except for the suit part. I'm in tech, so unless I have a client meeting, it's pretty much business casual most days.'

'Translate for the schoolteacher.'

'Button-up shirt, untucked, nice jeans or khakis.'

'Got it.'

We had finished our drinks and Josh signalled to the wait-ress to bring us another round. I'd also already had *two* pieces of Loukoumia. I needed to pace myself, or I'd end up sleepless on a sugar high.

Halfway through my second sidecar, I was more than a little tipsy. I was glad I'd said no to the crappy wine at the restaurant or 'tipsy' would have been 'thoroughly drunk'.

'Hey, have you seen the movie *Before Sunrise?*' asked Josh. It was a total non sequitur, which threw me a little, so I didn't respond. Josh must have taken my silence for not knowing it, or not being able to place it, because he continued. 'You know, a boy and girl meet in Vienna, and they end up talking all night …'

I recovered from my mild bafflement. 'I know it – they walk around all night talking and then they fall in love. I *love* that movie. I've seen it about a hundred times. And the sequels.'

'Really? A hundred? Each, or all together?' Why was he teasing me when *he* was the one who'd brought up the movie – the movie about the two people who fall in love while travelling?

I deflected Josh's teasing by turning the conversation back to him. 'Why are you asking if I know *Before Sunrise*? Do you think we're like Jesse and Celine?'

'Well, there are similarities don't you think?'

Where was he going with this? 'I suppose. I mean we were

strangers and now we're not. We're in a foreign place. We do a lot of walking and we do talk all the time ...' I left the part about us falling in love unsaid. Because we weren't. Not really.

'Well, I'm glad you like it. It's in my top ten movies of all time.' Oh, so *that's* where he was going with it. I was looking forward to seeing where else the conversation would go.

'Top ten? You must really like it.'

'You're the one who says you've seen it a hundred times.'

'Yeah, but I don't know many people – or maybe *any* people – who love that movie as much as I do.'

'I guess we can add it to the list of things we have in common.'

'So, that's why you brought it up? For the list?'

'Well, I was also thinking about how in the second one they see each other again ten years later. Maybe we'll meet up again in ten years and have a romantic interlude in Paris.' Oops, spoilers – sorry.

Did Josh really want to meet up again after this trip? And if he did – ten years? Really? A decade was a long time. I thought back to where I had been ten years prior and cringed. Late-twenties Sarah was a bit of a mess. Even more so than late-thirties Sarah. And who knew? Maybe in ten years I would be married. Perhaps even married to James. And I would have forgotten all about the boy from Chicago. I decided it was best not to voice all of that.

Instead I said, 'Did you see the last one?'

'I did, yeah. It was a little, uh, realistic for me.'

'How so?'

'Well, they're married. They have kids. They fight a lot.'

'Oh. Well, that fits in with your picture of marriage perfectly then.' I took a sip of my drink, punctuating my annoyance.

How could one person be an idealistic romantic one moment and such a cynic the next?

'I still liked it. I wanted to know what those characters had been up to. They're almost like old friends to me, or something. I mean I saw the first one when I was around sixteen – right before the second one came out.' God, he was young compared to me. 'So, I saw those pretty much back to back, and then I watched them a few more times over the years.'

'Oh *really?* So, I'm not the only one who's seen them over and over again?'

'Busted.' He laughed at himself. 'Anyway, when the third one came out, I sent out invites to watch the trilogy with my friends.'

'Oh, cool.'

'No, not cool, because literally no one showed up.'

'What? That's horrible. My bestie, Lindsey, and I went to the cinema to watch the trilogy – those movies are practically a rite of passage for – for us.' I nearly said, 'for my generation,' but caught myself in time.

'It's fine. I enjoyed it for the most part – it's just that, like I said, the third one got a little depressing in the middle. That whole "familiarity breeds contempt" thing. It was kind of intense.'

I sat quietly and sipped my drink because I couldn't think of anything to say. If Josh was right and we were like Jessie and Celine, we'd gone from romantic figures to a couple on the brink of divorce in a matter of minutes. What sort of trajectory was that for a first date?

I was going to need a third sidecar.

I am pretty sure Josh picked up on my uneasiness, because he started to back-pedal. 'I mean, they do seem to really love each other – despite all the fighting – and it's a fictitious marriage anyway,' he said. It was an anaemic point, but it seemed that there were no hidden messages in Josh's words. He probably just enjoyed the movies, and he liked that we'd met by accident too. But like a total girl, I looked for hidden meaning that wasn't there. *Idiot*.

I *did* love those movies, though, the first one most of all. I set my empty glass on the table in front of us.

'You know what I love about their story?' I asked. He shook his head. 'I loved the whimsy of how they met. How free the characters were to act on their impulses. And they had such freedom to be themselves. I think that's why the connection was so intense between them. There was no pretence. They would probably never see each other again, so why not be authentic about who they really were? I live that freedom vicariously every time I watch it.'

'But don't you have similar feelings about this trip?' he asked. I stopped rerunning scenes from *Before Sunrise* in my mind and looked at him, waiting for him to continue. 'We've both mentioned it before – it's been so freeing. There are no expectations about who we are to each other, no prescribed roles to play, so we can be ourselves.' He was right.

'Like how you obviously soured when I mentioned that Celine and Jessie don't really have a good marriage.' I started to explain myself, but he silenced me with a gentle fingertip to my lips. 'You were being authentic – and I love that about you.'

You what? Relax, Sarah. He said that he loved something about *you, not that he loved* you. Still, it was nice to hear.

'I think you'd better kiss me now,' I whispered. He kissed me with such tenderness, a wave of joy washed over me.

259

Yes, this man infuriated me with his skewed way of looking at love and relationships, but was it any more skewed than mine? For some time, I had presented this cactus-like façade to any man who approached me, but the irony was, I wanted to fall in love. With someone who saw *me*. With someone I could be my most authentic self with.

God, the kiss was good. I didn't want to know how he'd learned how to do that. And I *really* didn't want to say goodbye in a couple of days. I broke out of the kiss, before it could consume me and I ended up an emotional mess.

'People are going to tell us to get a room,' I joked, blinking away the tears and hoping he hadn't seen them.

'Maybe we should.' He raised his eyebrows at me.

'On the first date?' I was only half-joking. I'd had sex on a few first dates before. Of course, not one of those times had led to a second date. That said, we were not having sex that night – *not* on the boat.

'Well, it may officially be our first date, but we have pretty much been living together for the past week.'

'Along with five other people.'

'So? I've seen you in two different bikinis, in your pyjamas, all dressed up like tonight. I've even seen you without makeup on – still beautiful, by the way. I don't think it would be scandalous for us to actually spend the night together, for real.'

'Are you thinking we'll have sex on the boat?'

'Well, I do have a cabin to myself.'

'Josh, we're not having sex on the boat.'

'Should I be insulted by that?'

'No, I don't mean it like that – I fancy the hell out of you. But there's no privacy on the boat. I can hear Marie and Gary roll over in their sleep from my cabin – *at the other end of the boat*. We can't have *sex* – especially with Hannah next door. People will hear us. And they'll *know*.'

'Sarah, I think people know that we're into each other.'

'Yes, but sex is different. I don't care if they know we *had* sex, but there's no way I want them knowing that we're *having* sex, because they can *hear* us having it.'

'We'll be quiet.'

I rolled my eyes.

'Sarah, seriously? I really want to be with you.'

'Me too. But not on the boat.'

We weren't arguing, not really, but it was more than friendly banter. Yes, I really wanted to have sex with Josh. He was super sexy and if the kissing was any indication, then the sex was probably going to be incredible. But I meant what I said about having sex on that boat. It wasn't going to happen.

'Look,' I said, wanting to come up with a feasible solution. 'How about tomorrow when we get to Mykonos, you stay with me?' He looked like he was seriously considering the offer. Would he decline? 'You need to find a place anyway, and this way we will get to spend the night together – without worrying about the others.'

'So, there's definitely no way?'

'No, Josh.'

'In that case I would love to stay with you on Mykonos, Sarah. And, if you think we're going to wait until after dinner tomorrow night – well, we're not. What time can we check in?'

I laughed. 'Any time after noon.'

'Well, good. We'll have a little afternoon delight.' He raised those eyebrows again and I slapped his shoulder.

'Ewww. That reminds me of seedy old men from the 70s.'

'What? Why?'

'I don't know – that song I guess.' I shook my head, wanting to dislodge the thought of hairy-chested men wearing bell-bottoms.

Josh finished his drink. 'Shall we head back?' I looked at him sideways. 'I will behave myself, I promise.' It was the promise of him *not* behaving himself when we got to Mykonos that was giving me tingles.

I finished the last sip of my drink and stood up. 'Sure. Let's head back. I'll just get the bill.'

'No, I'll get this.'

'You got dinner.'

'Sarah, please. I asked you out. Let me get this.' I acquiesced, and he settled the bill at the bar while I waited outside. Then, hand in hand, we walked in silence until we got to the pier.

I stopped, pulling Josh towards me so we faced each other. 'Josh, thank you. It really was the best date I've had in, well, I don't know how long.'

'I am going to walk you all the way home, you know?'

I smiled. 'I know, but I wanted to tell you that – in case the others are up when we get back, and I don't get the chance.'

'Well, in that case, I know how you feel about PDA and we wouldn't want the rest of the gang to watch us kiss good-night, so I better do it here.'

He placed one finger under my chin and tilted my head. His hand moved to my neck as he pulled me towards him and pressed his lips to mine. His mouth was firm, insistent, as though making his mark on me. My hands pressed into his chest, almost a physical resistance of how much I wanted him.

And I really did want him. But *not on the boat*.

We broke apart, both of us breathless.

'Sarah, are you sure ...'

I placed my forehead on his chest. Yes. No. I didn't know. Maybe we could ...

No. It would be better if the first time was not surrounded by our friends – our family. The anticipation may make the next twelve hours unbearable, but then again, maybe it would also make the sex all the sweeter.

I looked up at him. 'I'm sure, Josh. We can wait.'

He groaned and then sighed. 'Okay. But you're killing me here.' We started walking again.

'Drama queen.'

When we got to the boat, Marie, Gary and Hannah were on deck. Duncan and Gerry had apparently done as they'd said and gone to bed early. We said our hellos, and then our goodnights, and I tried to ignore the odd expression on Hannah's face.

Below deck, we stopped right outside of our two cabin doors.

'Goodnight, Sarah.'

'Goodnight, Josh.'

We didn't touch, we didn't kiss. Somehow without speaking it aloud, we both seemed to know that either would crush our resolve. We went into our respective cabins and closed the doors. I realised I had been holding my breath, and let it out in a long, slow and quiet sigh.

The next day was going to be incredible.

Chapter Fifteen

The next day *was* incredible. We set sail from Tinos early, and the weather was postcard beautiful. Clear, brilliant blue skies watched over us as we sailed towards Mykonos under full sail.

I had been to Mykonos a couple of times when I was touring. I knew it as a party island, the gay capital of Europe, populated by handsome, tanned men with hairless bodies and a penchant for girlie cocktails and dance music. It had some incredibly beautiful beaches, and the beach clubs were the stuff of legends – teeming with Adonis bodies and heady with the sound of electronic music. In the late noughties, it was touristy and exciting, and it was my first taste of the Greek Islands.

There was also a traditional side of the island I had loved when I'd been there last. It was the sort of place where you could sit at a waterfront café and watch fishermen haul their catches to the shore, or see an elderly couple transporting fresh produce home from the market on the back of their donkey. Yes, really.

Like Santorini, it was dappled with whitewashed buildings and those gorgeous windmills – fat white cylinders capped with thatched roofs and ragged cloth sails, which seemed more for show than for function. The main port town of Mykonos was crisscrossed with a labyrinth of walkways and paths – by design, I was once told by a local. Nearly two millennia ago, Mykonos was frequently targeted by pirates, so the town was built like a maze to confuse them. It gave the locals an advantage so they could attack the pirates from hiding places.

I wasn't a pirate, but I had certainly found it easy to get lost in the town of Mykonos. It reminded me of Venice. If you found somewhere that you liked – a store, a café, a bar – you'd best make careful note of where it was, otherwise it was practically impossible to find again. There was a jewellery store there I'd found once – *once*, and never again. That was when I'd learned not to say, 'I'll buy it next time I'm here.' I still wish I'd bought that silver bracelet.

The boat leered at a forty-five-degree angle and we all braced against something, anchored in so we remained upright. I was supposedly reading a novel on my Kindle. Even though it was the latest in a crime thriller series I'd been reading for years, it wasn't really holding my attention. Josh's forearms were, though.

He was wearing a pair of shorts and a light blue button-up shirt with the sleeves rolled up to his elbows. He had tanned over the course of the trip, and the whole effect of the tanned forearms and the shirt – and pretty much the rest of Josh – was drawing my attention far more than a well-reviewed thriller.

His eyes were hidden behind the lenses of his sunglasses, but I saw him turn in my direction a few times. He was also reading – or perhaps pretending to, like I was.

Many times, my mind roamed over the memories of the kisses from the night before. And many more times, I thought about the afternoon to come. Those thoughts, in particular, left me breathless.

Someone once told me about future memories, where you imagine something happening so intensely and with such anticipation that you can 'remember' every detail. A lot of people do that and then they're disappointed when reality doesn't measure up to the future memory. I didn't want to fall into that trap, but I was certainly savouring the build-up of anticipation.

I wanted Josh's hands on me, his mouth on mine, the weight of his body on my body, all of it. I wanted him inside me, and to see the pleasure on his face as he entered me. I wanted to move in rhythm with him, a physical manifestation of our mental in-sync-ness. I wanted to hold him tightly to me, my legs wrapped around him. I wanted to feel him shudder against me, inside me, and to lose all conscious control and just *be* together. *Oh my*.

For some reason, I found it challenging to concentrate on my book.

'Dolphins!' My mind snapped back to the boat. No more future memories of romping with the sexy American. Dolphins were swimming alongside us, cresting the swells, and darting under and around the boat. There were about twelve in the pod, although it was tricky to count them as they were always on the move, playing with the boat and with each other.

Duncan remained at the helm, but the rest of us found vantage points around the deck of the boat, and pointed and exclaimed like children. It was a complete moment, my mind nowhere else. I tipped my head to the sun, savoured the salty spray against my skin and shared grins with my floating family. Josh had manoeuvred himself into a spot next to me.

'Isn't this incredible?' he asked over the sound of the sea and the exclamations of the others.

'Unbelievable.' I laughed. 'It's like, "cue the dolphins," and they magically appear.'

'I know! This is the first time I've ever seen dolphins.'

'That's right, you've never been to the ocean before. Look!' I pointed into the water. 'There's a mother and baby!' The baby dolphin was fast, zipping either side of its mother.

'It must be like some sort of slipstream under there. See, they look like they're riding a current.' Josh pointed at the watery wake they left as a trail.

'Yeah, I think you're right.'

'Land ho!' called out Duncan. Six pairs of eyes left the water and looked ahead. Mykonos loomed, and I suddenly felt an intense wave of sadness. Soon the sailing part would be over. As we counted down to when we'd all say goodbye, there were these little markers, milestones to pave the way.

They made me blue.

Last time on the boat. Last meal with the floating family. Last time I saw Josh. Ever.

Ever?

And just like that, the wave of sadness turned into a crescendo of inner turmoil. Elated to deflated with two words. 'Land ho' indeed. I sat back on the bench, bracing myself against the bulkhead, as Duncan started directing Gary to pull ropes and do other sailing things to get us safely to shore.

'You okay?' Josh leaned against the boat next to me and rested his arm across my shoulder. 'You look, well, not good. Are you sick?'

I shook my head, not trusting my voice. I blinked back the stupid tears – crappy timing – and found my voice, squeaky though it was. 'A little post-trip blues that came earlier than I expected.'

He squeezed my shoulder and I put my head on his. 'Don't get pulled into all of that now,' he said. 'We still have the rest of today, tonight, all of tomorrow on the ferry. There's still lots to come before goodbye.'

I nodded. 'Okay.' I plastered a smile I didn't feel onto my face. As the boat slowed and righted, and our world became horizontal again, Duncan called out orders to the rest of us and we scurried about doing as we were told.

For the last time.

As we neared the port, the sails came down and were tucked away, and we moved under power again. The port was much busier than any of the sleepy marinas we'd docked at over the duration of the trip, and I could tell Duncan was concentrating to ensure we stayed safe amongst the array of large ships and faster boats.

We finally found a place to dock our floating home, not far from an enormous cruise ship and amongst some much larger yachts than ours. It was going to be a long walk to the town centre.

As Duncan and Gary tied us off to the dock, I went through the motions of double-checking and then triple-checking I hadn't left anything in any of the dozen little nooks of my cabin. I already knew I hadn't left anything behind, but I didn't want to leave.

'Got everything?' The unmistakable deep timbre of that sexy American voice.

'Yes.'

I didn't turn around, wanting one last look at the tiny cabin I'd called my home for the previous nine days.

'Should we go then?' he asked.

'I guess.'

'Hey,' he said stepping closer and putting a reassuring hand on my shoulder. 'We've still got lots to look forward to.'

Who was he trying to kid? The very next day we would all part ways and go back to our lives. 'Yep.' I put on my brave smile again and turned around.

I changed the subject. 'So, I was going to tip Duncan. Do you think fifty euros is enough?'

He seemed caught off-guard. Maybe he thought we were having a moment or something, and there I was being all practical. 'Uh, yeah. Sounds good. I'll do the same.' He reached into his pocket and pulled out his wallet, removing a fifty-euro note and handing it to me. 'Make it a hundred from both of us.'

I took the note. 'Okay. It's not weird is it?'

'What? That it's from both of us?'

'No, tipping *Duncan*. I mean, I had always planned to – I put this aside at the start of the trip – but that was when he was 'the skipper'. Now, it's ...'

'Like tipping your friend?'

'Yeah.'

'It does feel a little weird, sure, I guess. But didn't that happen with you on your trips? Getting tips from people you became friends with?'

I sifted quickly through only a handful of memories of being tipped. Twenty-something tourists don't really tip all that much. I remembered a time when a group of people had pooled their leftover foreign money and handed it over rather sheepishly.

'Yeah, I did. Once or twice. It was weird.'

'Well, I can give it to him if you like?' Josh offered. 'I'm sure he'll appreciate it.'

I nodded and handed over my cash. I grabbed my bags and we made our way through the boat.

When we got to the ladder, Josh climbed up on deck first and reached down for my bags.

Gentleman. I handed them up to him, straining a little with the big one, and then joined him on deck.

The others were in the midst of saying goodbye to Duncan and Gerry, and we waited awkwardly for our turn. When it came, I had to remind myself how completely uncool it was to cry, especially as I would see everyone that night for dinner.

I kissed Gerry on both cheeks. She had essentially been our boat's first mate, and I couldn't imagine the trip without her dry wit and calming presence. 'Thank you for everything.'

'It was fun, yes?'

I smiled, that time unforced. 'Fun' was an understatement. As I turned towards Duncan, I saw Josh coolly slip the euros into his hand. Duncan, ever the pro, didn't even glance at the money. 'Thanks, mate,' he said and they shook hands.

I felt like Dorothy saying goodbye to the Tin Man. Josh was the Scarecrow, in case you were wondering – sorry if that's obvious. 'Duncan, thank you so much,' I whispered as I wrapped my arms around his neck. He folded me into a bear hug.

'Of course, mate. It was beaut having you.' He pulled out of the hug and said, 'See you tonight, yeah?'

I didn't trust my voice – I just nodded.

Josh and I disembarked, bags in either hand, and made our way into the town along the dusty track. The sun was hot on my back, and I squinted at the sights around me. Even though I had been to Mykonos before, I'd never been to the port or this part of the island. I hadn't been missing out.

When we got to the actual town, I stopped next to a café and put my bags down. 'I need to check the map for the hotel.' I had printed out a map of the hotel's location from Google maps before the trip, because I knew I wouldn't have data on my phone, but the map was buried deep in my backpack. I kneeled on the hot concrete and rifled through it, my knees burning.

'Got it!' I stood and waved it at Josh. *This is a map to the place where we're going to have sex*, I thought. I didn't say that part out loud for obvious reasons.

Referring to it a few times, I led the way through the labyrinth of streets and walkways of Mykonos with Josh half a step behind me. We didn't speak and I wondered if he was thinking about the sex we were going to have. I was. It was all I was thinking of, and I had to force myself to concentrate on getting us to the place where we would have the sex.

I was nervous too. It's hard to say why. I mean, it was Josh, and we were friends. Friends who fancied the hell out of each other and were really looking forward to having sex.

Did I mention we were going to have sex? Yep, I was really nervous.

Maybe it was because it had been so long since I'd done it. I mean, forever – *months!* I was sure I had forgotten how. I mean, I remembered the fundamentals of course, but I'd learned those in health class when I was twelve, and it's hard to forget that the penis goes in the vagina, even if you're pretty much a born-again virgin.

But what about the rest?

271

I can honestly say I can't even remember checking in, but we must have because there we were standing in my room – our room – with both of us staring at the bed. I literally shook my head to dislodge the stupor I'd slipped into. Headshaking was becoming a habit. I had to get myself together. And I really needed to shave my legs and do lots of other bathroom-related activities.

'Josh?'

'Sarah?'

I threw my backpack onto the bed and dug out my toiletries bag. 'You see this bag?' I held it in front of my face, so he could definitely see it.

'I do, yes.'

'Well, as this is the first time I've been able to shower with a proper shower – hot water and a shower stall and everything, I'm going to go in there –' I pointed to what I presumed was the bathroom door '– to use every one of these products. Then when I'm done, *you* can shower, and then we can have sex.'

By this stage he had a grin on his face. 'Okay. So we're clear, I'm also showering because ...?'

'Because we just got off a boat after nine days of sailing about, and neither of us are truly clean.'

'Of course. That makes perfect sense.' He was still grinning, and I got the feeling he thought I was a bit of a twit.

I didn't care. I took myself and my toiletries into the bathroom – it was the bathroom, by the way. It wasn't fancy, but it was clean and it had clean towels. Even better, when I turned on the shower, there was strong water pressure and the water was *hot* – just as I'd been dreaming of.

A week and a half on a boat with a mere trickle of lukewarm

water to ablute with every morning had got a little old. Even if it *was* a part of sailing around paradise on the best trip of my life. I kept to my word and used every product. It was heavenly.

I emerged some time later, scrubbed, shaved, slathered in every lotion I possessed, and smelling great. I felt great too, replenished.

'Your turn!' I declared leaving the bathroom in a haze of steam.

'All righty then.' He grabbed his toiletry bag and retreated to the bathroom. I suddenly thought that maybe I'd insulted him by telling him to shower. I hadn't meant it like that. I'd figured he would want to take advantage of a proper bathroom, but maybe that was just a girl thing. *Oh well.*

I tucked my toiletries away, then spent the next few minutes trying to work out how to arrange myself on the bed. I wanted to appear sexy, but not overly eager. I didn't want to come across like a rabid nympho. And I certainly didn't want to appear to be desperate. Although, to be clear, I *was* a little desperate for sex. I settled for bottom half under the sheet, top half arranged casually – and nakedly – on a pillow.

Josh emerged not long after I'd found the perfect sexy-but-not-a-rabid-nympho position. I guessed he had fewer products in his toiletry bag than I had. His towel was wrapped tightly around his waist and I saw surprise, then delight register on his face when he saw my careful arrangement on the bed. His eyes skimmed over my breasts, then met mine.

I felt like the most beautiful, most desirable woman on earth. We were off to a good start.

He dropped his towel to the floor, and then it was my turn

to admire him. Let's just say there was a lot to admire. And he was so damned sexy. I only hoped his skills matched his looks. Then with a level of assuredness, which both surprised and thrilled me, he joined me on the bed, pulled me to him and locked his lips to mine.

All those future memories – the weight of him on me, the feel of him inside me, giving him pleasure with my hands, my mouth, my body wrapped around him, letting him explore every inch of me until I couldn't stand it, letting myself fall into a delicious, all-consuming orgasm – it was all of that and more. I had definitely *not* set myself up for disappointment by fantasising on the boat.

I hadn't wanted to ask him where he'd learned to kiss as well as he did, and I certainly didn't want to know why a guy who had chosen to be celibate could shag so brilliantly. But he could, and that's all I cared about – for around two hours – yes, *two hours*.

At least I'm guessing it was somewhere around two hours. It certainly felt that long, but for some reason, clock-watching had been the last thing on my mind, so I had no idea what time we'd started.

Still, there came the point where we stopped shagging and lay side by side staring up at the ceiling, breathing heavily like they do in the movies.

'It's never been like that for me.'

'Me neither,' I said, lying a little. It *had* been incredible, but it wasn't the first time I'd had toe-tingling sex.

'I've never even had sex in the daytime before.'

I tore my eyes away from the interesting water stain on the ceiling. 'What?' I propped myself up on one elbow and stared incredulously at my lover.

He laughed in response. 'It's true. Sex for me has always been fumbling around in the dark deep under the covers. Pleasurable in a way, but also a little awkward.'

'Oh.' What else could I say?

'That was ...' He didn't seem to know what to say either.

'That was *good*, Joshua. I don't usually have an orgasm the first time with someone.'

'Really?' He seemed particularly pleased with himself. I suppose he had a right to be.

'Really. Feel free to pat yourself on the back for that. You're a good lover.'

The grin widened. 'Thank you.'

'You're welcome.' I smiled back and kissed him with a loud smack on the lips. 'Though I can't imagine how "fumbling around in the dark" got you those sorts of skills.'

'I *read*,' he replied with perfect comic timing. I burst out laughing. *Well played, Joshua.* Clearly, he was keeping the truth close to his chest.

'So, shall we head to the pool? Go for a swim?' We'd walked past the pool to get to the room, and after all that sex I couldn't wait to dive into the cool, blue water.

'How about we stay here a while longer and *then* go for a swim.' I regarded my lover, who had a particularly wicked look in his eyes. The swim could wait.

'You've talked me into it.'

We did eventually climb out of bed and go to the pool. We were the only ones there, and when I dived in, I was happy to discover it was the ideal temperature for swimming – refreshing without making me gasp for breath. I swam a few lazy laps, working some kinks out of my body, which had formed while living on a boat.

Josh sat on the edge, legs in the water, and watched me. 'Back to the real world tomorrow.'

'You're not supposed to say stuff like that,' I replied between strokes. 'It's bad travellers' karma.'

'Oh,' he said, simply.

'Besides, we still have tonight and then the six-hour ferry back to Athens, remember?'

'Right.'

I swam over to him and held on to the side of the pool. 'Hey, you were the one saying that a few hours ago. We're living in the moment.'

He smiled weakly.

I admit I sounded far more convinced than I felt. Watching the sadness wash over his face made my stomach churn. Goodbyes between friends were hard enough. Josh was also my lover now. And the sex ... well, bobbing there in the pool I realised it had meant something to me. It wasn't just a shag.

And it scared me.

*

'I have absolutely nothing to wear!' There I was hyperbolising again. I *had* things to wear, but they were either dirty, filthy, or I hated the sight of them and couldn't remember why I'd brought them in the first place. Josh peered over my shoulder into my bag.

'You have lots of things to wear.' He reached for a skirt I had tired of on day three of the trip.

'What about this?'

'Ugh. That? I wore that exploring the islands – *during the day*,' I added for extra emphasis. 'It's hardly what you wear to *dinner*. And, it has a stain!' I pointed to a small smudge near the hemline.

'It's fine. No one's going to care.'

'*I* care.' I pouted. Why did guys not get this type of thing? It was the final dinner. With the people I cared about. And we were in *Greece*! 'Well, what are you wearing?' If I was going to wear something sub-par, it wouldn't matter as much if Josh looked just as well travelled.

He sifted through his bag, seeming to mentally discount everything he laid his hands on. He got to the bottom and looked at me with a somewhat baffled look on his face.

'What?' I asked.

'I guess I have nothing to wear either.'

'Hah!' I pointed at him. 'So there.'

'That's not nice.'

'Maybe not, but now you understand my dilemma.' He nodded, acquiescing. 'So, you know what this means, right?'

'We wear stinky old clothes we're sick of?'

'No! Don't be stupid. We're going shopping!' I declared.

'Uh, no thanks.'

'Uh, yes please.' I picked up my leather handbag and stood at the door expectantly. Seriously, why did guys hate shopping so much? He reluctantly followed me outside, past the pool and into the town, the sook.

My tactic was to get him sorted out first. Once he had a pretty salesgirl fawning all over him, he'd be fine. I looked for a men's clothing shop and made a beeline for the first one I saw.

No luck on the pretty salesgirl, but I'd managed to find the next best thing – a gorgeous gay sales guy. I should have known, considering where we were. The sales guy – in my head, I called him Adonis – wasted no time. As soon as we crossed the shop's threshold, it was all about Josh. While I sifted through racks of clothes, Spiros – disappointingly, the sales guy's name was *not* actually Adonis – couldn't keep his hands off Josh's biceps.

'Oh, this fits so well here,' he said, running his hands down Josh's arms. Josh, bless him, seemed to relish the attention. It was hard to believe that only minutes before I'd had to drag him into town to go shopping.

Josh tried on anything Spiros suggested, and I have to say, the guy looked great in most of it. By the time we left, Josh had three new shirts, and a pair of sexy linen pants. I did not tell him that they reminded me of what the silver fox was wearing when we'd met; he did *not* need to know that.

Shopping bags in hand, we waved goodbye to Spiros. He sent Josh off with a wink and blew me a kiss. And why wouldn't he? He must have made a day's worth of commission from us in under an hour.

'Now it's your turn. I can't wait to see you try on a bunch of stuff. It'll be like in *Pretty Woman*!' I threw him a weird look. In a short time, Josh's attitude toward shopping had apparently done a one-eighty. He missed the look, though. He was too busy scouting for women's boutiques.

'There!' he almost shouted, grabbing my hand and pulling me into a shop.

The salesgirl – very pretty – looked up from her iPhone with a bored expression on her face. 'Hi,' said Josh.

'Hi,' said the girl.

'We need an outfit. Something pretty.'

'For you?' she asked him. Either the girl was a comedian, or she was so used to living on an island predominantly populated by gay men that it was not an unusual request for a guy.

Josh laughed. 'No, no, for my ...' And then he paused mid-thought and looked at me as if to say, 'my what?' Then he recovered with: 'friend.' Wonderful. It wasn't that I thought he should refer to me as his girlfriend or anything, but perhaps 'lover'? 'Friend' would have been fine too if he hadn't got stuck deciding what label to put on us.

I pretended none of it mattered and smiled my best smile at the pretty Greek girl. Josh's charm must have worked on her, because she had put down her iPhone, and had even come around to the other side of the counter!

She looked me up and down, scrutinising me. Had we been in another context – let's say, a nightclub – and she had looked at me with that critical look on her face, I probably would have bitch-slapped her. That is, if I'd had a few drinks and she had called me a 'fat cow' or something. I am not a woman who goes around bitch-slapping willy-nilly.

'You have a great body,' she declared when the scrutiny was over. Ohhh, so *not* about to call me a 'fat cow'. I decided not to bitch-slap her and to take it as a compliment. I noticed Josh nodding in agreement, which I also took as a compliment.

She began pulling stuff off the racks, piling them up across one of her arms. 'This – and this. Oh, and this.' When it looked like her tiny, stick arm couldn't bear to hold another item of clothing, she tipped her head at me as if to say, 'Come.'

I followed her to the back of the shop where there was a small makeshift changing room with a full-length mirror. When I caught sight of myself, I was a little taken aback. I had a glow about me that said, 'sun-kissed and recently shagged.' I looked pretty, if I'm completely honest – and apparently, I also had a great body, as assessed by a fashion professional and my new lover.

'Try these,' she commanded, pulling the curtain across tautly. I barely knew where to begin, but I decided on the dress. It was long and made of the type of cotton that's all crinkly and hugs to you.

There were slits up both sides, it was all the colours of a sunset, and it looked as though the fabric had been hand-dyed. Maybe it had.

I shimmied out of my boat-soiled shorts and top and stepped into the dress. When I pulled it up my body, I realised I would need to go braless, because it only had tiny spaghetti straps to hold it up. I wiggled out of my bra and pulled the thin straps over my shoulders.

'Wow,' I whispered to myself. I could barely stand how beautifully it hugged my curves or how much the colours flattered my skin and hair.

'Well?' called an impatient Josh. 'Have you got something on yet?'

I composed myself and drew back the curtain.

'This,' I said, simply.

Josh's mouth dropped open and he stood in absolute silence taking me in. I smiled at him, then looked at the salesgirl. She nodded, and I think I saw a satisfied smile creep across her face, as though she *knew* it would be the perfect dress for me.

Finally, Josh spoke. 'We'll take it.'

I didn't even try on the other clothes. There was nothing that could have come close to that dress, so I couldn't bring myself to do it. It would have been anticlimactic. When a man is speechless at the sight of you – well, let's just say, *that's* the dress.

He even insisted that he buy it as a gift. I argued – wholeheartedly and for a good twenty seconds – until he handed his credit card to the salesgirl over my shoulder and she ran it before I could snatch it back.

We were going to make quite the splash at dinner.

*

We were late, but we had a good reason. We'd spent the rest of the afternoon shagging. Less than fifteen minutes before we were due at dinner, we dragged ourselves out of bed and donned our new outfits. I twisted my bed-hair up into what I hoped was a sexy up-do, but more likely it said, 'I have been royally had – and many times over.' I slicked on some lip gloss and we were out the door.

We arrived at the restaurant, a ten-minute walk from our hotel on the outskirts of town, to a series of hellos and what I suspected were knowing looks. Duncan had booked the back room and not only was our little group there, but so was the group from the other boat. *Oh joy.*

I made a beeline for Hannah, who was crooking her little finger at me. I figured I might as well get it over with. 'You little minx, you.' She didn't wait for a reply. 'Have you spent the whole day fucking, or what?'

It didn't matter what I said, my immediate blushing said it all. Still, I tried to appease her obnoxiously voracious appetite for gossip with a weak response of, 'No, we also went shopping.' I pointed to my dress as evidence. She rolled her eyes at me and pulled me into a corner.

'Tell me everything.'

'No!' I snatched my hand back. 'I didn't ask you to tell me everything each time *you* stayed out all night.'

She waved away my comment like it was a mosquito. 'So what? This is different.'

'How is this different?'

'Because it's *Josh*.' That made no sense at all.

'That's exactly why I am *not* saying anything. It's Josh. And you should know better than anyone what that means to me. It's not just a bunch of lurid details to share with my roommate.'

'So, now I'm just your 'roommate'?' It was my turn to roll my eyes at her. 'Whatever – I don't care about that. At least tell me if it was good.'

'It was good,' I said plainly.

She reacted with far more glee than, A) I thought possible for Hannah to display, and B) than seemed to be appropriate for *anyone* to display at hearing that Josh and I had hooked up. I shook my head and pushed past her just in time to see Josh standing across the room with Kiersten. *And* she had her stupid little ugly hands wrapped around Josh's biceps. *And(!)* she was whispering to him. Worse yet, he was smiling. My temperature spiked and I could almost hear the steam coming out of my ears.

The sound of my mobile ringing from inside my handbag called me back from the brink. I couldn't even remember the last time I'd used it, and here it was ringing at a particularly inopportune time. I dug around inside my bag, pulled it out, and answered without looking at the screen. I don't know who I expected. My sister, I guess. She was the only one who had cause to call me right then. Maybe she wanted to confirm what time my flight got in.

'Hello?' I said, a slight edge in my voice.

'Sarah. I'm glad I finally get to hear your voice again.'

Shit. It was the silver fox – calling me right when I was in the middle of a jealous rage. I couldn't believe the irony. I walked straight back into the corner which, mercifully, Hannah had already vacated, and somehow I found my voice – my pleasant voice. 'Hello, James. How are you?'

'I'm brilliant. And you?' I looked over at Josh and the pretty little redhead, and felt my stomach tighten again. Then I turned my back on them and mustered as much attention for my caller as I could.

'Just lovely, James. Greek Island life agrees with me I think.' I sounded far breezier and more sophisticated than I was. He chuckled. Of course, he was a man who could pull off a chuckle.

'I can imagine,' he replied. 'By my reckoning, you finish your trip tomorrow and are heading back to London, yes?' *Oh dear*.

'Yes.' I am one hundred per cent sure it came out as a squeak.

'Wonderful. I really hope you'll consider seeing me. I'd love to show you *my* London, if you'll let me.' James's London. No doubt it was splendid and fancy and extravagant – all the things I was not, but had often longed to be.

And then I heard myself say something that surprised the hell out of me. 'I'd love to.'

'Excellent. Well, I shall let you get back to it. It sounds like a bit of a party is going on.'

'Yes. Our farewell dinner.'

'Enjoy then. I'll speak to you when you get back from the continent.'

'Okay.'

'Goodbye, Sarah.'

'Bye, James.'

The call ended while the phone was still pressed against my ear. I dropped it in my handbag and turned back to the room. Josh saw me and headed over, leaving Kiersten mid-sentence and talking to his back. She looked pissed off. *Good*.

'Hey,' he said, approaching me with a gentle smile.

'Hey,' I replied, donning a fake smile. I had just agreed to see James in London – and James was seriously serious about me.

'Everything okay?'

'Sure. Why?' Stalling. I was stalling. I couldn't parse the conversation I'd just had with James, and I was already in the middle of another one.

'Just that you look a little, I don't know ... Did that call upset you?'

I recovered myself and properly joined the conversation I was having with Josh. 'No, no. It was nothing. Just my sister. She can't pick me up from the airport anymore, so I'll take a taxi.' *Good lie, Sarah*.

'Oh, that's a bummer.'

'No, it's fine really. It doesn't cost very much from the airport to her flat.' Okay, now I was rambling on about nothing *and* lying – it was an absolute fortune from Heathrow to my sister's flat, but Josh didn't know that.

I suddenly remembered the redhead.

'What about you?' I signalled over his shoulder to where Kiersten was standing, glaring at me. 'What was that all about?'

He laughed. 'Oh, she wanted us to cut out early and go

back to her hotel.' My eyes must have doubled in size. 'That's what I thought,' he said. 'She was even getting a little touchy-feely.'

'I noticed,' I said, unable to stop a mid-sized pout from settling onto my face. *Sarah Parsons! What right do you have to be jealous after that phone call?*

'I know you noticed, and I want to be clear that I am not interested in Kiersten. I told her no, because I am with you.'

'You did?'

'Yes. Of course I did. What did you think? That we'd spend the day together – *in bed* – and then I'd drop you for the first cute girl who comes along?'

'You think she's cute?' Oh boy, I was pathetic.

He laughed again, but this time I suspected it was at my expense rather than Kiersten's. 'Yes, she is cute. You know she is. But you ...' he lingered on the word '... are beautiful, and sexy and so desirable that I don't even want to stay for dinner anymore.' As he spoke, he stepped closer and took me into his arms, and by the time he'd finished speaking, he was in the perfect position to kiss me. Which he did – in front of everyone.

When he pulled away, there was more confidence in his eyes than I had ever seen – as though it was his hidden superpower, and I had unleashed it and it kept growing stronger. It was wildly attractive. When he winked at me, I was breathless.

The kiss was great, but what I loved most was Josh claiming me as his in front of our floating family and our floating neighbours. *And* Kiersten, the redheaded hussy. I looked her way, and she gave me a look that could dissolve granite. I smiled at her smugly until she looked away.

Josh grabbed my hand and pulled me towards the long table. There were two free seats next to each other between Gary and Marie, and Duncan and Gerry, with Hannah across the table. Marie caught my eye as I sat down, and she smiled at me with raised eyebrows. I shrugged as if to say, 'What are you gonna do?'

Duncan, our host until the end, had pre-ordered a banquet-style dinner and the food started arriving soon after we sat down, quickly filling up the long table. Platters were passed, bad Greek wine was poured, and stories were told, mostly by Duncan who was as good a raconteur as he was a skipper.

An hour or so into the meal, I sat back in my chair. I was stuffed, but the food was so good I kept convincing myself I could handle just one more bite. The only problem was, I'd done that about a dozen times already. I looked down to the end of the table where Kiersten was making moves on the other boat's skipper.

Had Hannah noticed? Across the table, I could see her throwing eye daggers at Kiersten. Good grief! We'd created a soap opera's worth of intrigue amongst our two boats. I whispered to her, 'You know, she was hitting on Josh only an hour ago. If you want, I'll bash her for you?'

She stared glumly at her plate and stabbed a piece of *souvlaki* with her fork. 'He's not worth it. He's a pretty lousy lay, actually.' That's not what she'd said about him when I'd caught her sneaking back onto our boat a couple of days before, but I went along with it.

'Well, then good riddance. And if he's interested in that walking mattress, more fool him.'

'Right,' she agreed, forking the *souvlaki* into her mouth.

I felt a tap on my shoulder. It was Marie. 'Hi.'

286

'Hi.'

'So, I wondered when you're going to Chicago.'

I choked on my retsina, spluttering ungracefully. The crappy Greek wine went up my nose and stung the inside of my head. 'Chicago?' I managed to choke out after coughing a few more times. My neck snapped to the left and I saw Josh deep in conversation with Duncan. Thank Zeus for that.

I turned to Marie and she nodded as though we were having the most normal conversation in the world. 'Well, I mean you and Josh are obviously *together* ...' She looked at me, as if to encourage me to agree. I feared that if the wind changed at that very moment, the deep crease of confusion on my forehead would stay there forever.

'Chicago?' I asked again, incredulously. It had been hours since I'd thought about the real world, and when it came to Josh, I certainly hadn't thought as far ahead as going to Chicago. I'd thought about London, about James, going back to Sydney. But not Chicago. Chicago was Josh in the real world, and I'd spent exactly zero minutes thinking about that – until then.

I shook my head. Another time when my thoughts were fuzzy and I actually shook my head to clear them up. I was becoming a cartoon character.

'Uh, no. I mean, yes, for now, for the trip, we're together. I guess. But *no*.' *Okay, Sarah. That was a little too emphatic.* I could tell it was, because Marie suddenly looked like she'd sucked on a lemon. 'I mean, we hardly know each other.' She looked even more horrified at that. I had to back-pedal. And fast. All while the person I was talking about was sitting on the other side of me.

'I have to go to the ladies' room,' I said, a lot louder than

287

the rest of my conversation with Marie. As I stood up, I gave her a pointed look, which – thank goodness – she figured out. She stood up and retrieved her handbag from under her chair.

'I'll come with you.' It was quite the performance from the two of us, considering that neither her husband, nor my lover – even looked up from their conversations as we left the table.

Marie led the way across the room, through the door and down the hallway to the bathroom. I followed, and as soon as the door closed behind me, I let out a sigh.

And in that grimy toilet of a Greek Island taverna, Marie gave me a look that combined amusement, understanding and more than a handful of pity. Not even knowing what I wanted to say, I started to speak. I would have tried anything to make that look go away, because it was making me feel awful. But she cut me off.

'Sarah, wait. Let me say this.' I sighed again, but I shut my mouth. 'We've only known each other a short time, but you are dear to me and I have watched the two of you together over this past week.

'Sarah, that man loves you.'

'What?' *Love? Who said anything about love? I mean, sex, yes. Friendship? That too. But love? I mean … fuck. What?*

'You don't believe me.' It wasn't a question. She stated it like a fact, and she was right. But still, she was my friend and in this scenario, kind of like my big sister. I should at least hear her out, right?

Suddenly, my head hurt. I rubbed at the spot between my eyebrows. Yep – a crease the size of the Grand Canyon. Confusion was not only bad for wrinkles, it also caused tension headaches.

'Look, Gary would say that this is none of my business.' My look must have told her I agreed with Gary. 'But, you're my friend, and I can't *not* say something. I see something special developing between the two of you. From the outside, it looks like what I have with Gary.

'And you know I just love that man. God, he makes me laugh. Being with him fills me up. And he's sexy and fun, and he takes care of me – even when I'm being a grumpy cow.' She laughed then. 'You're looking at me like I'm a little crazy.' I was? 'I *am* grumpy sometimes. I know you haven't seen that, but it's true. And he's there for me. He can handle me like that,' she added.

'What I see with you and Josh is that intense friendship and passion all rolled together. And, again, I know this is totally not my business ...' I was starting to think that it should be her business – I mean an actual business. Like, she should be a counsellor or something. 'But I thought you should know that being on the outside and seeing you two together, well, it's lovely.'

Lovely? Josh and I are lovely? Holy fuck.

'And all of that led to me asking when you're going to Chicago. I'm sorry – I'm so nosy. I just—'

It was my turn to cut her off, finally finding my voice. 'Marie, you're right.' She immediately misunderstood where I was going, and her face lit up into the smile of a matchmaker who'd made the perfect match. 'No, not about that. I mean about us – you and me – we are friends – dear friends – and I am totally fine with you being nosy. It's sweet and you have given me a lot to think about. But until this conversation, I hadn't even thought beyond tomorrow. I mean, I have, but every time I do, it's that Josh and I say goodbye and it's sad, and I never see him again.'

289

Now it was her turn to look confused. 'I think this will end up being a lovely, *lovely* holiday fling, and that I will always remember this time as one of the best of my life. But I don't think I'll ever see Josh again after tomorrow.'

Her eyes started to get teary, and I realised that mine were stinging too. I looked away, and felt the enormity of what I'd said. I took a deep breath. 'Oh Marie,' I almost whispered. When I looked at her again, her expression was bereft. I hadn't realised she was so invested in the 'Josh and Sarah' thing. She forced a smile and gave me a quick hug.

'Okay, then,' she said when she pulled away. 'I promise I won't bring it up again.' And then she left the bathroom and I just stood there, completely still. Eventually – I have no idea how long after – I walked to the sink and looked at myself in the small smudged mirror. The glow I'd seen earlier in the day was gone, and in its place was something indescribable. It wasn't just sadness or confusion or some sort of mutant of the two. It was something I couldn't quite put my finger on. And no matter what it was, I knew it wasn't good.

Had I let myself fall in love with Josh?

Chapter Sixteen

The next morning when I woke up, the sun was forcing its way into the room with only gauzy curtains to hold it back. They weren't very effective, so it was horrendously bright. My eyes didn't like it very much, and my mouth was as dry as the Sahara. I reached for my water bottle on the bedside table and took a few big mouthfuls. Much better. I assessed the state of my head.

How much did I drink last night? I started counting. There was the bad Greek wine – or is that a tautology? – at dinner. Was that three or four glasses? Oh, and the Ouzo at the end of dinner – two shots – Duncan had insisted. Then the beer at the bar. That must have only been two, or three. Oh crap, maybe it was four. Not to mention, I'd mixed different types of drinks, which was a big no-no.

But even though I had pretty much drunk my way around Mykonos, I was in reasonably good shape. There was a dull little ache at the back of my head. Other than that ...

Then I remembered I wasn't in the bed alone.

I flicked my head to look at Josh. *Oww, my head.* I reminded myself that 'reasonably good shape' meant I was still a little delicate. Thankfully, Josh was sound asleep. I eased my head back onto my pillow and, as carefully as I could so I didn't wake him, rolled onto my side to face him. It was only the second time I had woken up next to Josh, and the first time I'd been in such a hurry to get out of there, there was no time to enjoy it.

My eyes scanned his facial features. You know how some people are ugly sleepers? Their faces get all smushed by the pillow and their mouths hang open, or they drool? Josh was the opposite. There was no drool, his mouth was closed and there was no smushing. He looked rather beautiful.

I am almost positive I am one of the ugly sleepers, by the way. It's why I never really sleep properly when there's a guy in my bed. It's also why I get up – and freshen up – before the guy wakes up.

I've lost count of how many times I'd snuck out of bed and gone to the bathroom to swish some mouthwash, splash water on my face, run my fingers through my hair, and pinch my cheeks, then climbed back into bed just in time to pretend I actually woke up looking like a normal person.

Many times. *Too* many times.

Josh started stirring and, in a panic, I realised I hadn't done the thing where I 'woke up' looking lovely and refreshed. Which wasn't fair, because *he* looked lovely and refreshed. When he opened his eyes, he smiled at me.

'Hello, beautiful.' That was him saying it to me, by the way. Nothing makes a girl feel even more self-conscious than she already does than calling her 'beautiful'. But there didn't seem to be any irony in his voice, so maybe he meant it.

'Hello, beautiful back,' I replied. He shook his head and ran his hands over his face.

'I doubt it.' He laughed. 'Come 'ere.' He grabbed me and wrapped me up in his arms. I rested my cheek against his

292

bare chest and listened to his heartbeat. Oh boy, I was now the type of woman who listened to a guy's heartbeat.

'Last night was fun,' he said, a smile in his voice.

'It was,' I replied. We were both quiet for a while and I guessed he was running through the night in his mind, like I was.

It was only when I remembered the very end of the night, and what he'd said right before he drifted off to sleep, that my stomach tightened into a dark little knot. I remained still, torn between enjoying the warmth of him and the jolting memory that made me want to climb out of bed and get on the next ferry back to Athens – alone.

After dinner, we'd gone dancing. Well, Josh, Hannah, Marie and Gary, and I went dancing. Duncan and Gerry decided to call it a night, so I'd had to say my first teary goodbye on the steps of the restaurant. It sucked, because although I adored them both, I knew I would probably never see them again.

I should have been used to it – it's one of the pains of being a traveller. Thank goodness for Facebook – yes, you read that right. For all its evils, Facebook is my pipeline to the people I love who are scattered across the globe.

The dancing was actually my idea. In my touring days there had been a club called the Scandi – short for the Scandinavian – and I wanted to see A) if I could remember where it was and B) if it was still there.

I did and it was.

However, it was a sickly shadow of its former self. Back in the day, it was so packed that the people and the music spilt onto the walkway out front where the rowdy party continued. It was the sort of club where a trip to the bar took nearly an hour, and my touring mates and I would buy drinks in rounds, taking turns to get into line for the next one.

Our arrival at the Scandi the night before had nearly doubled the number of people inside. I was disappointed and I could sense I wasn't the only one.

We were standing in the doorway peering in when I heard, 'Come with me, handsome,' and I watched as Marie pulled her husband onto the dance floor. They were playing 90s dance music – just like they did in the noughties. Apparently, it was still the best music to get people dancing. Well, it looked like Gary and Marie wanted to stay, but what about Hannah and Josh?

'Drinks?' I asked over-enthusiastically. The other advantage of the club being dead was that a trip to the bar for five drinks would take about as many minutes. Hannah looked like she would rather be anywhere else, but Josh was on board and Hannah followed behind us as we made a beeline for the bar.

Even at the end of the trip I was conscious of including Hannah. And I had to give it to her – on the way to the club, she had only mentioned *once* that she was the only single one in our group. As I read the drinks menu above the bar, I watched Hannah out the corner of my eye. Down the bar from us were two ridiculously handsome men – obviously gay, but completely gorgeous – and as soon as they saw Hannah, they broke into huge smiles. Hannah smiled back, and without a word she was gone. Gay men can be the best flirts.

While Josh and I ordered four Mythos beers, we watched as Hannah sidled up to the men and they signalled to the bartender to bring her a cocktail like theirs. I wasn't insulted by Hannah deserting us for the gorgeous men. As a sometimes chronically single woman, I knew that attention from gay men counted in some weird way as attention from *men*.

Josh and I carried the beers back to a table next to the dance floor. Marie and Gary were dancing to 'Groove is in the Heart', an absolute favourite of mine, but they came over to the table when they saw us with the drinks. 'Oh my god,' said Marie, fanning herself with her hand as she sat down. 'I *love* this 90s stuff! I can't remember the last time we went dancing!' She looked at Gary, as though asking if he could.

He smiled at his glowing wife and laughed, 'Babe, I think it might have actually *been* in the 90s.' I knew he was kidding, because they hadn't been together that long, and they shared the joke with a laugh.

'I love this music too,' I said. 'Although, it *is* weird that they're playing the same stuff as when I was here a decade ago.'

'I hope they play some Madonna,' gushed Marie.

I raised my glass. 'Last toast,' I said, feeling a nervous twinge again – another last. 'And then we can all hit the dance floor.' Was that a groan from Josh? And if so, was it about the dancing or the toast? I wanted more than anything to dance with him – even though my expectations were not particularly high. That probably doesn't sound very nice, but he was a geeky computer guy – albeit a sexy, geeky computer guy – so I wasn't expecting much.

My thoughts of dancing with Josh had distracted me, and three faces looked at me expectantly. 'To new friends, friends who became family.' Marie tilted her head to the side and smiled.

'To family,' she said, clinking her bottle against mine.

Gary and Josh, repeated, 'To family,' and added their bottles to the clinking.

'Hey,' said Marie as she looked around. 'Where's Hannah?'

'She's otherwise occupied,' replied Josh, signalling to the bar.

'Ohhh!' Marie's reply was accompanied by raised eyebrows.

'I'm pretty sure they're gay.' I laughed.

'Ooohhh,' she replied and we both laughed. We all had a sip of beer and almost immediately, I heard, 'Strike a pose.'

Marie and I squealed like schoolgirls. 'Madonna!' we yelled together. We put our beers on the table and she grabbed my hand, pulling me onto the dance floor – well, the giant open space in the centre of the room with no one in it – where we each struck a pose. Gary followed right behind his wife.

And then there was Josh, camping it up like the rest of us. As the music kicked in and we took up as much of the dance floor as we wanted, I was gobsmacked to discover that Josh was a really good dancer. I mean, *scarily* good. Like, 'guy who goes to clubs a lot' or 'professional dancer' good.

I shouted over the music. 'You're a really good dancer.'

'You too!' he replied, then did a little hip manoeuvre that was particularly sexy.

'I'm kind of surprised.' *Good one, Sarah – not insulting at all*. Josh's response was to laugh.

'Oh yeah?'

I shook my head, aware that I'd been rude. Why was I so mystified by his dancing prowess – just because he was a geeky tech guy? Maybe he went to clubs a lot – we hadn't really covered that.

'I used to take lessons.' *What? Did he say that he used to take* dance *lessons?*

'Really?' I was impressed we were having a conversation *and* Vogueing – *well*, I might add – but part of my mind was stuck on the whole 'dance lessons' thing.

'Yes, really. I wanted to be like old-school Michael Jackson – you know, like from 'Thriller' days – so my mom put me in dance lessons.'

'Wow. How old were you?'

'I guess I was about ten when I started.'

'Well, that was, like, nearly twenty years ago.' Now I was sceptical. Was he just taking the piss?

'Yeah, but I studied for eight years.' I stopped dancing.

'You studied dance for eight years?'

He kept dancing. I kept standing. 'Yep. Contemporary, jazz, hip-hop. Gave it up when I went to college. But, I still like to dance.' He wiggled his eyebrows at me.

Then he grabbed my hand and pulled me in close. His hips kept moving, and then mine were moving, and we were pretty much dirty dancing in the middle of an empty dance floor in Greece. Somewhere in the background, Marie woo-hooed and I guessed it was meant for us.

Josh was a *dancer*. Who would have thought?

The vivid memory of the dancing made me smile. 'I still can't believe you're such an amazing dancer.'

He chuckled softly, his chest moving under my cheek. 'Oh, I'm full of surprises.'

'I bet.' Then my thoughts shifted to the others. 'Saying goodbye was sad.' I could feel him nodding, but I didn't trust myself to look at him. Tears prickled my eyes.

Around midnight, I had started to feel fatigue kick in. I walked over to Josh – or more likely, I swayed over to him – and put my arms around his neck. Then like a complete dork I said that Top Gun line about taking me to bed or losing me forever. Thank goodness, he is not *so* much younger than me that he didn't get the reference, but still, how cheesy is that? But instead of laughing at me, he kissed me.

Then we said our goodbyes to Gary and Marie.

'You have to come visit us in Cali,' said Gary. It was the sort of thing people said when it was likely they'd never see each other again. But I really wanted to see them again, and I hoped it wasn't an empty invitation.

'I'd love it,' Josh and I both said at the same time. We looked at each other and smiled. Then I realised we had both said 'I', and not 'we'.

I stepped in and hugged Marie tightly. 'Good luck with the adoption,' I whispered. 'You absolutely *must* keep me posted.'

She pulled away and placed her hands on my shoulders. 'I promise to let you know what happens. And you do the same.' She inclined her head ever so slightly towards Josh. I nodded and smiled, and we hugged again.

I stood on tippy-toes to hug Gary. 'You are a prince amongst men,' I said in his ear.

'And you are a wonderful woman.' He couldn't see me smile at his words. Then his voice got a little quieter. 'Make sure he treats you well.' A hard lump of sadness lodged in my throat. When we pulled apart, I forced a smile.

Lastly, it was Hannah – dear, sad, lovely, angry Hannah. At first, she seemed reluctant to tear herself away from Ray and George, the gay couple who had all but adopted her. But then she was hugging me so tight, I couldn't breathe properly.

'You are a sweet, beautiful girl and I will never forget you,' she said into my ear. I hadn't expected that.

'Me neither, Hannah.' I broke the hug first and when we

stepped back, I held on to one of her hands. 'Be happy.' It was all I could think to say.

'Sure,' she said with a bright smile, but I didn't believe her. Hannah was one of those people who had a difficult life, mostly because of her own doing. I saw in her eyes that she didn't really believe herself either.

And then we got to the awkward part where it was actually time to part ways. I turned away from the three of them and by the time we got outside, tears were streaming down my face. Josh seemed to know exactly what to do – he didn't talk, but he did put a strong arm around my shoulder as we walked back to the hotel in silence.

When we got back to the room, we had sex again. But this time, there was something kind of melancholic about it. And though we clung to each other throughout, our bodies as close as two bodies can be, we didn't speak during sex, either.

Afterwards, we lay next to each other in the dark, a little bit of moonlight peeking through the window, and talked quietly.

'You know, Sarah,' he'd started hesitantly, 'I truly hope I know you for the rest of my life.' Tears stung my eyes at the sweetness of his words.

'I've never known anyone like you. You're brilliant and intrepid and amazing and so *open*.' *Open? Me?* He continued, 'I've never felt this okay about being myself around someone. You should know that I've told you things I've never told anyone before.'

Me too, Josh.

'And you deserve a great guy, a guy who adores you and wants to have grand adventures with you.' I felt hope swell within me. He was going to tell me he felt the same way I did – that the feelings between us were incredibly special and we should do everything we could to be together.

'I just don't think I'm that guy.'

Oh.

My hope vanished in a puff of stabbing disappointment. So, it *wasn't* the part where he declared he couldn't live without me. It was the part where he gave me the 'let's just be friends' spiel.

I was relieved he couldn't see the tears sliding down my face into my hair. I hadn't been able to find my voice, so instead I squeezed his hand and feigned sleepiness with a little yawn. I rolled onto my side with my back to him and soon enough, heard his breath steady. Then I had lain awake for an hour or so, thinking. When sleep did come, it was patchy and full of sadness.

That morning, with my head on his chest, I didn't want to wallow in his words – they were too painful. I plastered what I hoped was a reasonable facsimile of a smile on my face and lifted my head. God, he was beautiful.

'Breakfast?' I asked with more cheer than I felt.

He smoothed my hair with his hand. 'Sure.' Then we got out of bed, got dressed and went to breakfast.

Breakfast was hard to swallow – literally and figuratively. I couldn't shift the gnawing thought that we were no longer counting down to the end of the trip in days. Now it was hours. Nine hours, to be precise. My throat was tight with the anticipation of saying goodbye. Goodbye to Greece, goodbye to Josh, and goodbye to the version of Sarah I'd been over the previous week and a half. Pretty soon I would be back in Sydney, tethered again to a life I wasn't sure I wanted.

Josh-less.

No wonder it was hard to choke down dry sweet cake and a hard-boiled egg. Josh had gone equally quiet and I wondered for the thousandth time what he was thinking. Whatever it was, it was weighing heavily, because there was a crease between his eyebrows. Maybe he sensed my disappointment at all those things he'd said the night before. Maybe? Who was I kidding? I am sure it was all over my face.

I sipped my crappy instant coffee. *Yuk*. 'Ready to go?' I wiped my mouth on the napkin and left it on the plate of barely eaten food. I stood up to leave without waiting for an answer and heard his chair scrape across the floor as I exited the dining room.

Back in our room, we both busied ourselves with packing. Busy, busy, busy! We were both so incredibly busy, as we failed to acknowledge the bloated, fat, purple elephant in the room.

'Josh,' I started.

'Sarah,' he said at the exact same time. Then we did the thing that two people do when there's tension and they both want to speak, but they also both want to be polite. 'Go ahead.' 'No, please, you ...' And then we stared at each other for a moment, both holding our respective breaths, waiting for the other to say something.

Josh broke the silence. 'I said some stuff to you last night, and I think it might have upset you.'

You think? My mind went into sarcastic overdrive. Then I shrugged as though I didn't know what he was talking about. He called me out. 'Sarah, please don't pretend. I shouldn't have voiced those things to you.'

'What, all that stuff about how amazing I am?' Was that anger in my voice? Was I angry? I was. Under the sadness, I was completely pissed off.

'No, no, of course not. You *are* amazing. I meant that – you are the most interesting, incredible person I've ever met.'

Liar. 'But?'

'There is no but. That's the whole point. I should have just left it at that. All my doubts about me and you and what I want, and what this can be. That's ...' He stopped talking and it looked like he was having a pretty intense chat with himself, a chat that continued for a few seconds.

He exhaled heavily and looked right at me with an intensity I hadn't seen from him before. 'You are absolutely all of those things and so much more. I don't know what this is –' he signalled that 'this' meant 'him and me' '– *or* how it can become anything else for two people who live in Chicago and Sydney ...'

I am sure that everything I felt – all the confusion and hope and disappointment – was practically etched onto my face, because he stopped himself again.

'Fuck! I really suck at this. I'm so sorry, Sarah.' He shook his head as if to clear it. 'What I *do* know is that you are someone very important to me, and I want to know you for my whole life. I don't know what that can mean, or how we do it, but it's the one thing I do know.'

And there it was.

The most perfect thing he could have said.

I was crying by then – of course I was – and I nodded my agreement. Then he stepped around the bed and enveloped me in his arms.

'Is that okay?' he asked, his breath soft against my neck. It was a simple question laden with everything we both felt.

I pulled out of the hug and sat on the bed. Fresh tears made their way down my cheeks, and I felt like I was a millisecond from dissolving into a fit of real boo-hoo-ey tears. 'Josh, you're my best friend and I'm really scared that after today I'm never going to see you again.'

Because he really was my best friend. I know that probably sounds weird because we'd only known each other ten days, but I couldn't think of another person, besides my sister, who I was closer to. And, when you're that close to someone, you want to hang out and share stuff with them, *all the time*, which is super hard when they live on the other side of the world.

So, maybe all the romantic stuff wasn't the real reason I was upset. I mean, it could have been, but I wasn't sure about all that – *and* there was James, who I also wasn't sure about – but I *was* sure that this person – this smart, funny, warm, wonderful person – was my bestie.

Josh knelt in front of me and took both of my hands in his. 'Don't go getting all fatalistic on me like this is the end of everything, okay? We mean something to each other – we don't quite know what it is yet, but we will work it out, and we *will* see each other again.'

'Okay.' I nodded, needing the additional affirmation.

'And we still have the rest of today on the ferry. Let's enjoy that – can we do that?'

'It's going to suck saying goodbye.'

'Yes, it is. It's going to suck, and I'm going to miss you like crazy.'

'Me too.' I found a tissue in my pocket and wiped my nose.

'And that means we have to make the most of today. All right?' I nodded again, part of me wishing the day was already over so I could stop *anticipating* saying goodbye, and just get on with missing him. Somehow, that part seemed like it would be easier – maybe because I'd be with my sister. Maybe because in the next few days I'd be seeing James.

The silver fox. I forced him from my head – he just complicated things.

I looked into Josh's eyes and saw all the warmth and honesty that made me adore him. I sniffled loudly, which was kind of gross, but to his credit he didn't flinch. 'You're right. There's no reason to ruin a beautiful day on the Aegean Sea. We should pack, go to the marina, have a decent breakfast, and then enjoy the ferry ride back to Athens.'

There, that sounded very mature and reasonable.

He grabbed the back of my head and planted a less than platonic kiss on my mouth and then grinned at me. 'Excellent. But you should probably freshen up before we go, because you look a mess.'

My mouth dropped open, shocked he would be so mean.

He winked. Oh, so he was teasing me. Or was he? While he went back to packing, I went to the bathroom and checked out the damage in the mirror. Teasing or not, he was right. It was probably best if I washed my face and started again. 'Give me five minutes,' I called.

I hoped he knew that five minutes meant ten minutes – at least. I closed the bathroom door and got to work on looking less like a blubbering mess and more like a woman on holiday with a gorgeous man.

*

'I could look at a view like this for the rest of my life, couldn't you?' We were seated outside at a taverna, enjoying a view of island life.

'Yes,' I replied with a tinge of sadness. I didn't want to go home. And it had nothing to do with the sexy American. Well, maybe it did – a *little* – but mostly I was beginning to feel this ominous dread about going back to my life.

My so-called 'full life'. Was it full? Work, gym, home to my cat, read a book, watch TV, and then do it all over again for five days straight. My weekends used to be better – hanging out with my girlfriends – shopping, movies, lunch, day trips, sometimes weekends away. But when most of your friends get married in the space of two years and start having children, their time is eaten up by husbands and babies. 'Eaten up'. That sounds a little judgey. My married friends were happy in their lives and I shouldn't begrudge them that – *didn't* begrudge them that.

The thing was, I could busy myself during the week. Work was demanding and sometimes I went to the gym twice in one day. As a result, I had a pretty good body for someone in their late thirties, but it also meant my weekends felt empty in contrast.

It's not like I never saw my friends, but getting even *one* of them lined up for an outing required military-precision planning. That meant a typical weekend consisted of two sleep-ins until 7:00am (yes, that was a sleep-in, as I usually got up at 5:30am), chores, a coffee at the beach – solo, a movie – solo, maybe wandering around a mall buying things I didn't really need – solo, and then Sunday lunch at my parents' house.

And *that* I tried to limit to every other week, because my parents led more exciting lives than mine and I didn't want to be an intrusion. I should say, much to my mother's disappointment, I showed up to Sunday lunch solo too.

Sitting seaside in Mykonos and doing a mental audit of my life left me feeling miserable. I was such a cliché. What I'd said to Josh was true. I *was* one floral bedspread away from being a certified spinster! *Mental note: if I feel the urge to buy chintz, seek immediate help.*

Josh broke into my thoughts. 'What's going on in there?' I was pretty sure he was referring to my head. 'You look like you're about to break out in hives or something.' He was probably right, but he wasn't helping.

I said the first thing that came to mind. 'Like I said before, I want *my* life to be bigger too. My life is boring and lonely.' But as soon as I said it out loud, I realised how whiny it sounded. 'Wait, I didn't mean ...'

'Bigger how?' he asked, seeming to ignore the whining.

'Bigger how?' It was a good question. I took a deep breath and slowly exhaled while I calmed my thoughts.

'I'm really just complaining about stuff I have the power to change – and I'm realising this as I say it – I *do* want to change it.' He didn't interrupt, which I appreciated, because I was on a bit of a roll.

'I live in *Sydney* – arguably one of the most beautiful cities in the world – and what do I do with my time? Nothing! Nothing important, nothing cultural, nothing that really takes advantage of where I live. I had to come all this way to realise I don't appreciate the incredible city I live in. I mean, Sydney's amazing! There's Circular Quay, there's The Rocks and Darling Harbour and the Botanical Gardens and the cliff walk from Bondi to Coogee, and the galleries and restaurants and wine bars and pubs. I used to have fun. I used to *be* fun. But now I sit in my little flat with Domino, my cat, wishing my friends would come out and play.

306

'Well, fuck that! So what if they're busy being mums and wives? I should find ways to work in with *their* lives – spend more time with them, with their kids. I *love* kids. I may not want any of my own, but I love all my honorary nieces and nephews.

'I should offer to babysit, so my girlfriends can have a night out with their hubbies. And I should get out of the gym and go back to my old running routes along the coast, and swim in the sea pool, not the chlorinated one. My life is too full of stuff I don't need, and empty of the stuff I do – the stuff that matters.

'And I used to travel – *all the time*. Even on weekends, I'd find somewhere new to go. I haven't done that in ages. Neil was a total homebody and I let myself become one too.

'I'm stuck in my own life, and it's my fault.' I stared at a spot on the tablecloth where someone had spilt olive oil and it had left a stain.

Everything I'd said was true. Even a cloistered nun would consider my life dull and sad – and that was my fault.

But that also meant it was me who could change it back into something joyful, something that resembled the days I'd spent under Greek skies. Maybe I could take that feeling home with me. Could I be joyful at home? Could I just embrace life, just breathe and stop stressing myself out all the time? Could I be happy?

I'd almost forgotten Josh was there. When I met his eyes, I affirmed my momentous self-discovery with a nod and added, 'Just bigger.'

He leaned over and whispered close to my ear, 'That's my girl.' He followed it with a kiss on my cheek. And right then, I *was* his girl. Tingles.

'Come on,' he said, as he stood and shouldered his bag, 'it's time to go the ferry.'

The ferry that would take us back to Athens where we would say goodbye. I took a deep breath.

The ferry was packed – we weren't the only ones vacating island life. Josh and I lugged our bags up the gangway and found a bench seat outside, shaded from the sun, and with a view of the water. We'd hit the mother lode.

But right as our bums hit the seat, we heard an obnoxious cry. 'Josh! Sarah!' *Wonderful*. It was Alisha from the other boat – the girl who'd hung out with the spicy redhead. She had a huge grin on her face and looked relieved to see a friendly face. 'Oh my god, I am so happy to see you two! People I *know*!' Yep, totally called it.

I hoped I had a better poker face than she did, though, because I did not want to spend the next few hours on the ferry with Alisha. I smiled at her weakly, as she plonked her stuff down next to ours and sat next to Josh. 'So, how was that trip, huh?' she asked. I took the question as rhetorical, which was a good thing, because she didn't wait for a response.

'I mean, the scenery alone was worth coming for! And the food!!' She certainly was effusive. I felt slightly bad that I wanted her to fuck off and leave us alone. I reminded myself that she was harmless, really, *and* quite nice. She also had a point about the scenery and the food. I wondered if Josh was as peeved as I was.

'So, where's Kiersten?' he asked. 'She with you?' He wanted her gone too – good.

'I lost her on the way in. *So* many people.'

'So, she *is* on the ferry?' I asked, feigning friendliness.

'Uhm yeah, I think she is. I *hope* so. I mean, we're supposed to share a room at the hostel tonight.' She seemed to consider what would happen if she didn't hook up with Kiersten on the ferry and shrugged. 'Although, I guess we could just meet there. She's a big girl.' She sat back against the bench. Awesome, she was getting comfy – and it was turning me into a bit of a bitch.

'Don't you think she'll be looking for you?' I asked hopefully, trying *not* to sound like a bit of a bitch.

She cocked her head to the side, as though considering it for the first time. 'Mmm. I suppose. Do you think I should go and look for her?' *Hallelujah!* 'Will you guys watch my bag? I'll bring her back when I find her.' Bugger – I'd celebrated prematurely.

'Uh, Alisha?' Josh stopped her from going. He made an exaggerated grimace. 'Don't you think it might be a little awkward – *us* hanging out with Kiersten? I mean, Sarah and I are *together*.'

Finally, the penny dropped and Alisha's mouth formed a silent O. She nodded slowly. 'Right, that's a really good point. She was kind of into you, so, yeah, this whole thing might be a bit, uh, weird. I think this will have to be goodbye. Sorry, guys.' *Hallelujah again!*

She signalled it was time to hug it out, so we both stood and let this virtual stranger hug us as though we were all the best of friends. '*So* great to meet you guys. And don't tell Kiersten, okay, but I think you guys make a really cute couple.' Don't tell Kiersten? What planet was this chick from?

We watched her disappear into the crowd on the deck and sighed simultaneously. We looked at each other and laughed. 'I wanted her gone,' I said without a trace of remorse.

'Me too. I don't care if that's selfish. I just want it to be us.'
Then he bent down gave me one of those Josh kisses, the
kind that made me go all wobbly inside. I kissed back. For a
moment the apprehension about saying goodbye disappeared.
The boy really knew how to kiss.

The ferry pulled away from Mykonos and we watched in
silence as the island became smaller and smaller.

'Can I ask you something?' Josh's voice surprised me. I'd
been transfixed by the undulations of the water and my
thoughts were a million miles away.

I'd been thinking about life back in Sydney, the changes I'd
be making when I got back, the whole 'make my life bigger'
thing. I'd already decided I needed to plan something fun to
do with my girlfriends – and soon. I wasn't ready to come
back to the present, but Josh was waiting for a response.

'Sure.'

'Are you going to see that James guy?'

'What?' He suddenly had my complete attention.

'James. Doesn't he live in London?'

'Uh, yes, he does.'

'Are you going to see him while you're there?' I couldn't
quite read his expression. It was mostly pleading, perhaps a
little self-pitying, and there was something almost proprietary
in there too.

What had I expected? Josh was a smart guy and all he had
to do in this situation was put two and two together and get
four. I decided that honesty was the best policy – at least in
this instance. 'I don't know.'

'But he's asked to see you.' It was a statement.

'Yes.'

I couldn't look at him, suddenly very interested in a hangnail

310

on my left hand. I bit it, which I knew was an obvious tell, but I still didn't know what to say about James.

'Do you want to see him?'

It was the sixty-four-thousand-dollar question. I hesitated for a fraction of a moment, but all I could come up with was: 'I don't know.'

Josh started to say something, stopped, and then said, 'Okay. Hey, do you want something to drink? I'm going to get something to drink.' He was gone before I could even answer.

Right then, I wanted to skip forward two weeks when I would be back in Sydney making changes to my day-to-day life, when I'd be half a world away from both Josh *and* James.

Maybe that was the key. I needed distance. Weren't holiday romances supposed to look completely different under the glaring lights of real life? Perhaps I'd get home and realise I'd had a great time being squired by two handsome men, but that it was all part of the holiday and I needed to get back to reality.

'Here.' A can of Diet Coke appeared in front of me. I took it.

'Thanks.' I figured Josh was probably waiting for me to say more than that, but I still didn't know what to say. I certainly wasn't going to tell him about my time travel fantasy. I opened my drink and sipped it while watching the water.

'I know I don't really have a right to ask this ...' I coughed on some Coke that went down the wrong way. I knew what he was going to say, and I silently begged him not to say the words.

'But, I would really ... I mean ... it would be ...' He ignored my silent plea. 'Please don't see him.'

'Josh, I ...'

'I know. Like I said, I have no right to ask, but I felt I had

311

to say it all the same. I can't expect you to know that *that's* how I feel. So, I've said it and now we can drop it.' He had some of his Coke and looked out at the horizon. 'Hey, we're coming up on another island.'

He stood and walked over to the railing, and I followed tentatively. Did I want to drop the conversation about James? It only took a moment's thought to confirm that I did. Standing next to Josh, I looked at the island we were coming up on. 'That looks like Syros.' The colourful buildings were a bit of a giveaway considering it was the only island we'd been to that didn't have whitewashed, Greek-style buildings.

'Remember our dog?' Josh grinned at me. I grinned back, relieved we'd stopped talking about James.

'That was such an awesome day,' I replied.

As the ferry manoeuvred into place at the dock, Josh pointed to the top of the island. 'We walked up the hill there, along that ridge there, and back down to the marina there.' I followed the line of his finger with my eyes.

'It's so beautiful. I remember when we arrived the first time, I couldn't believe this was a town in Greece. It looks like a totally different part of Europe.' He put his arm around me and I let him. I wrapped my arm around his waist and we stood in companionable silence watching the bustle of passengers disembarking and embarking.

'I also remember sitting on the bow of the boat in our PJs having brekkie while half of the island made their commute to work.'

He laughed. 'Oh yeah, I totally loved that.'

'It was one of those surreal "I'm on holiday" moments.'

'I've been thinking about that. You know what the *real* quest is?'

'Quest?' I asked.

'Yeah, the thing I *really* want.'

I shook my head.

'It's to have that "vacation feeling" when I get home.'

'I hear ya. I've been thinking that myself.'

'To find a way to have that feeling of freedom and adventure ...'

'But every day,' I finished his sentence.

'Exactly.'

I continued with the shared thought. 'And you know, it's not only freedom, or adventure – it's about being *in* my life and appreciating it. Living it, rather than observing it.'

'The bigger life,' he said.

'The bigger life,' I agreed. 'Exactly.' We tapped our cans of Coke together in a toast.

'You know, that's what I took away from your rant earlier?'

'Rant? Are we calling it a rant?'

He looked embarrassed. 'Sorry, no, that's not the right word. I meant ...' He paused while he searched for the elusive word. Eventually, he said, '... pontification.'

'Better.'

'Anyway, that's what I think you meant. Not necessarily making all these big changes or going skydiving every weekend—'

'*Definitely* not that.'

'But, changing how you see things, the perspective – having a sense of awe about the everyday, having gratitude, being open to opportunities, taking the initiative.' He was looking out across the island as he spoke, and I found myself agreeing with him one hundred per cent.

'Does that make sense?' he asked, turning to me.

'So much, so much sense.'

313

'You know, the day I hiked to the top – right up there?' He pointed and I nodded. 'I sat there and watched the tiny world below me, and I had all these cool thoughts zipping round my mind. And it was all this sort of stuff. I'm actually thinking of taking up meditation when I get home.'

'Really? I could see you doing that.'

'What about you?' he asked. 'Do you meditate?'

'I've had limited success with that. Didn't I tell you?' He shook his head. 'Well, I get so caught up in trying to think of nothing that I spend the whole time trying to imagine what nothing looks like, and then it ends up looking like something, which always sets me off on some tangent and then I'm not meditating, I'm thinking.'

'Like in *Ghostbusters*,' he said solemnly.

I cocked my head to the side. 'I'm not following.'

'In *Ghostbusters* they were supposed to clear their minds so that the evil thing couldn't manifest itself, and Ray can't think of nothing, so he tries to think of the most harmless thing there is ...'

'The Stay Puft Marshmallow Man!' I laughed.

'Exactly!' he replied.

'Great, so the next time I try to meditate, I'll just think of the Stay Puft Marshmallow Man.'

'Good plan. That's bound to work.'

We watched the last of the passengers get on board and soon after, the ferry horn sounded and we were on our way again. We sat back in our little spot. Despite the caffeine in the Coke, I was getting sleepy. I hadn't really slept much the previous night, and the lull of the ferry's engines as it cut through the sea was making me drowsy. 'Do you mind if I lie down for a bit and close my eyes?'

'No, of course not.' He slid down the bench and retrieved a jacket from his bag. He bunched it up and put it on his lap. 'Here. You can use me as a pillow.'

I lay down, rested my head in his lap, and closed my eyes. I could hear the drone of the engines and snatches of conversations in different languages. I don't know how long it was before I fell asleep, but I woke with a start. For a millisecond, I didn't know where I was.

'Hey,' said my pillow. 'You fell asleep.'

I made no move to get up. 'How long was I out?'

'It's been around an hour.'

I lifted my head. 'Oh, sorry. Your legs must be numb by now.' I sat up and ran my fingers under my sunglasses to remove any mascara smudges that may have formed.

'It's fine. I'm fine. You know, you were smiling?'

'I was?'

'Yeah. I figured you were probably dreaming about me.' He smiled and I laughed.

'You're so full of yourself.' I playfully pushed him away from me.

His smile turned into a grin. 'That's what you love about me!' What I loved about him was that he made me laugh – and often at his own expense. 'Loved' about him. *Oh dear*, I thought.

'Do you know if we have any more stops before Athens?' I was suddenly hyper-aware that we were now running on minutes rather than days.

'One more, I think – we'll be docking soon.' He pointed towards the horizon and it was filled with a mound of jagged earth. Naxos, was my guess. *I started falling for Josh on Naxos, or was it before?*

315

We watched as the island took shape. My guess of Naxos was right, and not too much time passed before we could make out the marina where we'd docked our little yacht. The time on Naxos had been awesome – the scooters, the beach, that incredible lunch at Martika's.

'Martika,' I said, my thought escaping my lips.

'I was just thinking about her, about that lunch. It's still the best meal I've ever had.'

'Agreed.'

Again, the ferry docked, and again the shuffle of people off and then on, as the memories of the island flooded my mind. I didn't want to leave. I didn't want to go back to my life, a life without *this*, without Greece, and tomatoes so flavourful they touched my soul. Without Josh.

'Do you think you'll ever be able to eat another shitty supermarket tomato after this trip?' I asked.

My non sequitur landed perfectly. 'Nope.'

'Me neither.' Martika and the rest of Greece had ruined me for life. I'd have to start growing my own when I got home. *Mental note: move to a place with a sunny balcony, so I can grow decent tomatoes.*

'I don't think I've ever been that wet and fully clothed,' said Josh.

'You know, it was definitely the best meal of my life – but I think that was also the best *day*.' Although I was a person who was known to exaggerate, I was actually being restrained. I remembered how good it felt to ride on the back of Josh's scooter, my arms wrapped around him, my hands tucked into his pockets as we ascended the island in a downpour. Incredible.

'I'm going to miss you,' he said, reading my thoughts.

316

I wrapped my arms tightly around his waist and buried my head into his shoulder. 'Me too.' It was muffled, but I knew he could hear me, because his arms wrapped tightly around me.

'Hey, Sarah?' The tone of his voice told me he was trying to sound nonchalant, but he was doing a crappy job of it.

I sat back. 'Hey, Josh?'

'I wanted to ask you about something.' Oh no, we were back on James. He really needed to stop bringing him up, because James had been the last person on my mind for quite some time.

My face must have betrayed my thoughts, as always, because he back-pedalled immediately.

'No, no, not that. Not about ... that other thing. Something else.'

I breathed out in relief, 'Okay.'

'I was thinking while you slept ... Have you – do you think you might want to go travelling? With me? Sometime soon? I was thinking about Hawaii. Neither of us have been and it's pretty much halfway between Chicago and Sydney. I thought we could meet there, say, in a few months, and tour around ...'

I realised my mouth was agape and shut it. He looked concerned. 'You haven't said anything. Say something. I'm rambling, and I'll probably keep rambling until you say something. Sarah?'

You know how they say that in the moment before your death, your whole life flashes before your eyes? Well, during that moment, it wasn't my whole life, but it *was* the whole trip – the whole trip where I listened patiently to Josh talking about a life of bachelorhood. The whole trip where I'd suppressed the feelings I'd had, because Josh didn't a want

317

girlfriend. *The whole trip* – every moment when my stomach had done a little flip because he'd kissed me, or flirted with me, or just *looked* at me with that glint in his eye. The whole trip where I'd tried to inoculate myself to his charms and his jealousy over James, his possessiveness.

All that flooded through me, then washed away as I gazed into those steel grey eyes. He wanted me. Josh wanted me. 'Okay.'

'*Really?*' he looked elated.

'Really!' I grinned back at him.

'C'mon, we need to make plans.' He grabbed my hand and led me back to our spot. He pulled his phone out of his bag, and tapped on the calendar app. 'I want to see how the next few months look for me.' He was intensely focused on his phone, while all I had to do was remember when the December school holidays started. Of course, there'd be Christmas with my family, but after that ...

'I could meet you for New Year's Eve,' I said.

'New Year's?'

I nodded. He beamed. 'New Year's in Hawaii. With you. That would be awesome. Let's do it.'

'Okay. So, how much time can you get off work? I'll be on holidays until the end of January, so ...'

'Yeah, probably not that much time. I only get two weeks a year, and I've already taken eight workdays for this trip.'

'Two weeks? Well, that totally sucks!'

'Oh yeah, I forgot – all those vacation days teachers get.'

'You cretin – we've already had that talk. At least in the US it's actually a whole summer. I get, like, *maybe* six weeks off over summer.'

'Six weeks?'

'Yeah, yeah, anyway ...' I wanted to steer the conversation away from how easy it was, or wasn't, to be a teacher. 'How much time do you think you can get by then?'

'I can probably take some unpaid leave. Say, ten days all up, including a weekend in the middle?'

'We can make that work.'

'Sarah, this is going to be awesome.'

I really hoped so. Who knew if Josh and I travelling together would even work? I suppose it was only ten days – the same length of time as the sailing trip had been. If it didn't work out, we could always go our separate ways.

'I'm in,' I said. I could unpack whether or not it was a good idea when I got to London.

We passed the rest of the time using the ferry's patchy Wi-Fi to investigate Hawaii and to look at flights out of Sydney and Chicago. Josh's enthusiasm was infectious, and the time moved far too quickly.

It seemed like only minutes from when we'd decided to go to Hawaii to when the ferry docked at Athens. We packed away our things in silence and, as we made our way to the nearest exit with the other passengers, I had a sick feeling in the pit of my stomach. Dread.

We descended several staircases and then the gangplank. When we reached solid ground, Josh took my free hand and led me away from the milling crowd. He turned to face me and we both put our bags on the ground.

'What time's your flight?' he asked, even though I was sure he already knew.

I looked at my watch – I'd taken it out of my bag that morning and put it on for the first time in over a week. 'Around three hours from now.'

He nodded and looked around us, his face stoic and unreadable. 'I guess this is it, then.'

Tears stung my eyes. I couldn't help it – they just appeared. I didn't want to say goodbye. I didn't want to let go. 'Yep.'

He looked at me with such intensity that my breath caught and the tears spilt onto my face. He took my face in his hands and touched his lips to mine. The kiss was slow and sweet and perfect. I let it wash over me, succumbing to all the promise it held.

We pulled apart and Josh rested his forehead against mine. 'Sarah?' It was almost a whisper.

'Yes.' I dared not move, wanting to stay like that as long as possible.

'Thanks for the sex.'

I threw my head back and laughed, a full-throated, wonderful laugh. Josh joined in. I wiped my tears and sighed. I put one hand on his chest. 'You're funny.'

'I know. Look, this isn't goodbye. Not for good. We're going to Hawaii, okay?'

'Yes. Hawaii. New Year's.' It was time to say goodbye. I needed to get in a taxi and get to the airport. I stood on my tippy-toes and wrapped my arms around his neck. He wrapped his around me and we held the hug for a few moments. I was glad he'd lightened the mood. Goodbyes are the worst and leaving with a smile was far better than leaving in tears.

'So, we'll speak soon, and make plans?' I asked, letting him go.

'Absolutely. I'll call you in a couple of days when I get back to Chicago so we can coordinate our flights.'

'Sounds good.'

'It's going to be so much fun, Sarah. We're going to be travel buds again.'

Travel buds? What? Suddenly the romantic haze lifted. And I was there with a guy who I thought I might be falling in love with, but who had just called me his 'bud'. It was like being slapped.

Josh didn't seem to notice. 'We need to get you a cab.' He picked up our bags, one in each hand, and started walking to where the taxis were lined up to collect disembarking passengers. I followed numbly, and watched as he set the bags down and hailed the next taxi. Before I knew it, my backpack was in the boot, and he was holding the door open for me.

He pressed his mouth against mine. 'I'm going to miss you, Sarah. I'm really going to miss you.'

'Me too.' I didn't know what else to say. 'I think I love you, Josh' didn't seem the appropriate thing to say to a 'travel bud'. My stomach churned, and I felt like I couldn't breathe properly. It was time for the 'being apart' bit.

I kissed him again quickly and said, 'Bye.' I didn't wait for a reply. I got into the back seat of the taxi and pulled the door shut. I looked up as it pulled away and Josh had what I can only describe as a sad smile on his face. He raised one hand and I did the same.

And that was it. The end of the trip.

I wondered if I really would see Josh again – if our trip to Hawaii would even happen. If I *wanted* it to happen. *Travel buds?* I rested my head back on the seat and watched as an ancient city rushed past the windows.

My phone beeped inside my handbag – a text message – and my heart leapt. *He misses me already!* I pulled out the phone and was stunned for half a moment to see that the name on the screen wasn't Josh's.

It was James.

Hello, beautiful. I can't wait to see you. What day should we get together?
J x

Only hours before, Josh had asked me not to see James. But that was before he'd made it clear that ours was nothing more than a friendship – sure, it was a meaningful and lovely friendship, but how many times had Josh told me he didn't want anything more? When was I finally going to get it?

My thumb hovered over the screen, hesitating.

I turned my phone off and put it back in my handbag. The one thing I was sure of was that I was in no state to make plans – with either man.

Less than two weeks earlier I'd embarked on a trip not knowing what would happen, who I'd meet, or how I'd feel when it was over. I'd hoped, at the very least, for some sort of rejuvenating experience like they mention in the brochures. Sun, sea, cocktails – that sort of thing.

How could I possibly have predicted I would return with more yearning than I'd left with? That I'd want to shake up my life so much, that I was considering a future with someone I'd only just met?

I felt raw. I'd have to fix that before I made any decisions about the silver fox and the sexy American boy.

In a few hours, I would be with my sister in her London flat, and for the next week, we'd hang out and talk and drink wine and go shopping. Be *normal*. That's what I needed – to be normal and spend time with someone I was sure about – my closest friend, my sis. Get some clarity and perspective on everything. Surely, if I put James off for a few days he'd understand.

I wondered if Josh really would call like he'd said.

The taxi ride was uneventful. Checking in, flying, landing, immigration and baggage claim – all uneventful. I moved through these activities as if by rote, my mind churning with possibilities, and my heart oscillating between joy, excitement, fear, and sadness – a kaleidoscope of feelings and thoughts.

The sliding doors opened and I walked into a throng of people, all waiting for someone who wasn't me. I could see the disappointment on their respective faces as they looked over my shoulder for the next arriving passenger.

'Sez!' My sister's voice cut through the crowd, and I saw her with her arms outstretched. I dropped my bags as she ran over and enveloped me in a big hug – well, as big a hug as a tiny person can give.

'Hey,' I said, hugging her back. 'I've only been gone ten days.'

'I know, but I missed you. I'm *so* glad it's half-term and we've got the whole week together. We're going to have so much fun!' Her enthusiasm was infectious, and I found myself grinning at her. And just being there with her made everything feel like it was going to be okay. No matter what happened, I would always have my little sis.

Like she had when I'd arrived a couple of weeks before, she took over steering the luggage trolley. I was shattered, so I let her. 'All right. This way,' she said, leading the way through the crowd to the car park. When we got to the car, away from the crowds, she turned to me and asked, 'So? How was it?'

How was it?

It was going to take some time to answer that – and probably a few bottles of wine. I thought I'd start with the biggest thing that had happened.

'Well, I think I might have met someone.'

Her mouth dropped open in a wide-eyed grin. 'Wine,' she declared. 'We're going to need lots and lots of wine.' I laughed. It was exactly what I'd hoped she'd say.

Acknowledgements

This book began as a love letter – to one of my favourite places in the world, Greece, but mostly to my partner, Ben, who I met on a pier in Santorini, just as we were about to embark on a ten-day sailing trip.

Our meet cute inspired this book and I thank you, babe, for letting me borrow snippets from our travel adventures for my writing. Mostly, though, I thank you for championing my dreams with such ferocity and verve; for seeing me through the set-backs with sage advice, side-splitting laughter, bubble baths, tea, and wine; for keeping the home fires burning when I shut myself away to write and edit; for being my partner in crime as we trek about the world, seeing and doing all the things; and for always being the first to celebrate my successes. I could not have done this without you.

Thank you to the most supportive parents, family and dear friends an author could ever ask for. Thank you to my real-life floating family, who witnessed Ben and I falling in love first hand. You have all inspired characters in this book, and hold a special place in my heart, especially you, Skipper.

As an author, I have hit the mother lode and am ecstatic to be collaborating with the incredible Lina Langlee of the Kate Nash Literary Agency. Lina, thank you for your counsel, your support, your good humour and enthusiasm, and for believing in me and my writing. I've learned so much from you already.

A huge thank you to Molly Walker-Sharp of Avon Books for saying yes to my travel romcom with a heart, and for the incredible work you, Hannah, Sabah, and the team have contributed to my debut novel – you have literally made a dream come true.

Thank you to my (earliest) early readers, Jen, Lindsey, and my sister, Vic. As I drip-fed you chapters, your encouragement, support, and honest critiques helped me find my voice and breathe life into Sarah – and her floating family and two suitors – as she found love and ate her way around the Greek Islands.

A massive thank you to my fellow authors, my writing gurus, and my writing community peeps across the world, who I learn from daily, who are supportive, kind, generous and hilarious, and who share their talents and brilliance without reserve.

Thank you, especially, to the authors who have helped me launch my debut book – I have been so inspired by your incredible work and thank you for reading mine: Belinda Missen, Dana L Brown, Ella Hayes, Emma Robinson, Katie Ginger, Lynne Shelby, Samantha Tonge, Karen King, Jenni Fletcher, Lucy Coleman, Aimee Brown, Sarah Louise Smith, Lucy Mitchell, Emily Royal, Eve Corso, Phillipa Ashley, Sue Moorcroft, Kiley Dunbar, Julie Houston, Aimee Brown, Kate Field, and any others who may have read it after I wrote these words.

A huge thank you to the book bloggers and reviewers who have supported *One Summer in Santorini* – you are such an integral part of the writing and reading community and your support is greatly appreciated. Thank you also to the brilliant, talented and hilarious #UKRomChat peeps and #Auswrites authors who keep my Twitter game sharp, and the team at The Pink Heart Society.

Thank you, dear reader, for reading *One Summer in Santorini* – and for reading this far into my acknowledgements. Really, without all the people I've thanked above, you'd be reading a blank page. If you'd like to follow my travel and writing adventures, subscribe to my blog, Off the Beaten Track, at https:// sandybarker.com, or follow me on Twitter, @sandybarker.

Cheers!